Henry Morley

Burlesque Plays and Poems

Henry Morley

Burlesque Plays and Poems

ISBN/EAN: 9783744771238

Printed in Europe, USA, Canada, Australia, Japan

Cover: Foto ©Andreas Hilbeck / pixelio.de

More available books at **www.hansebooks.com**

BURLESQUE
PLAYS AND POEMS

CHAUCER'S
  RIME OF THOPAS

BEAUMONT & FLETCHER'S
  KNIGHT OF THE BURNING PESTLE

GEORGE VILLIERS, DUKE OF BUCKINGHAM'S
  REHEARSAL

JOHN PHILIPS'S
  SPLENDID SHILLING

FIELDING'S
  TOM THUMB THE GREAT

HENRY CAREY'S
  NAMBY PAMBY AND *CHRONONHOTONTHOLOGOS*

CANNING, FRERE & ELLIS'S
  ROVERS

W. B. RHODES'S
  BOMBASTES FURIOSO

HORACE & JAMES SMITH'S
  REJECTED ADDRESSES

AND SOME OF
THOMAS HOOD'S
  ODES AND ADDRESSES TO GREAT PEOPLE

WITH AN INTRODUCTION BY HENRY MORLEY
LL.D., PROFESSOR OF ENGLISH LITERATURE AT THE
UNIVERSITY COLLEGE, LONDON

SECOND EDITION

LONDON
GEORGE ROUTLEDGE AND SONS
BROADWAY, LUDGATE HILL
NEW YORK: 9 LAFAYETTE PLACE
1887

INTRODUCTION.

THE word Burlesque came to us through the French from the Italian "burlesco"; "burla" being mockery or raillery, and implying always an object. Burlesque must, *burlarsi di uno*, mock at somebody or something, and when intended to give pleasure it is nothing if not good-natured. One etymologist associates the word with the old English "bourd," a jest; the Gaelic "burd," he says, means mockery, and "buirleadh," is language of ridicule. Yes, and "burrail" is the loud romping of children, and "burrall" is weeping and wailing in a deep-toned howl. Another etymologist takes the Italian "burla," waggery or banter, as diminutive from the Latin "burra," which means a rough hair, but is used by Ausonius in the sense of a jest. That etymology no doubt fits burlesque to a hair, but, like Launce's sweetheart, it may have more hair than wit.

The first burlesque in this volume—Chaucer's "Rime of Sir Thopas," written towards the close of the fourteenth century—is a jest upon long-winded story-tellers, who expatiate on insignificant detail; for in his day there were many metrical romances written by the ancestors of Mrs. Nickleby. Riding to Canterbury with the other pilgrims, Chaucer good-humouredly takes to himself the part of the companion who jogs along with even flow of words, luxuriating in all trivial detail until he brings Sir Thopas face to face with an adventure, for he meets a giant with three heads. But even then there is the adventure to be waited for. The story-teller finds that he must trot his knight back home to fetch his armour, and when he "is comen again to toune," it takes so many words to get him his supper, get his armour on, and trot him out again, that the inevitable end comes, with rude intrusion of some faint-hearted lording who has not courage to listen until the point of the story can be descried from afar. So the best of the old story-tellers, in a book full of examples of tales told as they should be, burlesqued misuse of his art, and the "Rime of Sir Thopas" became a warning buoy over the shallows. "I cannot," said Sir Thomas Wyatt, in Henry VIII.'s reign,

> "say that Pan
> Passeth Apollo in music manyfold ;
> Praisé Sir Thopas for a noble tale,
> And scorn the story that the Knighté told."

The second burlesque in this volume, Beaumont and Fletcher's "Knight of the Burning Pestle," written in eight days, appeared in 1611, six years after the publication of the First Part, and four years earlier than the Second Part, of Don Quixote. The first English translation of Don Quixote (Shelton's) appeared in 1612. The Knight of the Burning Pestle is, like Don Quixote, a burlesque upon the tasteless affectations of the tales of chivalry. Francis Beaumont and John Fletcher worked together as play-wrights in the reign of James I. All their plays were produced during that reign. Beaumont died in the same year as Shakespeare, having written thirteen plays in fellowship with Fletcher. Forty more were written by Fletcher alone, but the name of Beaumont is, by tradition of a loving fellowship, associated with them all. "The Knight of the Burning Pestle" is all the merrier for being the work of men who were themselves true poets. It should be remembered that this play was written for a theatre without scenery, in which gentlemen were allowed to hire stools on the stage itself for a nearer view of the actors ; and it is among this select part of the audience that the citizen intrudes and the citizen's wife is lifted up, when she cries, "Husband, shall I come up, husband?" "Ay, cony ; Ralph, help your mistress up this way; pray, gentlemen, make her a little room ; I pray you, sir, lend me your hand to help up my wife. . . . . Boy, let my wife and I have a couple of stools, and then begin."

The next burlesque in our collection is "The Rehearsal," which was produced in 1671 to ridicule the extravagance of the "heroic" plays of the Restoration. The founder of this school in England was Sir William Davenant who was living and was Poet Laureate—and wearer of the bays, therefore, was Bayes—when the jest was begun by George Villiers, Duke of Buckingham, and other wits of the day. The jest was so long in hand that, in 1668, when Davenant died, and Dryden succeeded him as Laureate, the character of Bayes passed on to him. The plaster on the nose pointed at Davenant, who had lost great part of his nose. The manner of speaking, and the "hum and buzz," pointed at Dryden, who was also in 1671 the great master of what was called heroic drama. Bold rhodomontade was, on the stage, preferred to good sense at a time when the new French criticism was enforcing above all things "good sense" upon poets, as a reaction against the strained ingenuities that had come in under Italian influence. Let us leave to Italy her paste brilliants, said Boileau, in his *Art Poétique,* produced at the same time as "The Rehearsal," all should tend to good sense. But Dryden in his plays (not in his other poems) boldly translated Horace's *serbit humi tutus,* into,

> "He who servilely creeps after sense
> Is safe, but ne'er will reach an excellence."

The particular excellence attained by flying out of sight of sense is burlesqued in the Duke of Buckingham's "Rehearsal."

John Philips, the delicate and gentle son of a vicar of Bampton, read Milton with delight from his boyhood and knew Virgil almost by heart. At college he wrote, for the edification of a comrade who did not know how to keep a shilling in his pocket, "The Splendid Shilling," a poem first published in 1705—which set forth, in Miltonic style applied to humblest images, the comfort of possessing such a coin. The Miltonic grandeur of tone John Philips happily caught from a long and loving study of the English poet whom he reverenced above others, and "The Splendid Shilling" has a special charm as a burlesque in which nobody is ridiculed.

The burlesque poem called "Namby Pamby," of which the title has been added to the English vocabulary, was written by Henry Carey, in ridicule of the little rhymes inscribed to certain babies of distinguished persons by Ambrose Philips, or, as he is translated into nursery language, "Namby Pamby Pilli-pis." Ambrose Philips was a friend and companion of

Addison's, and a gentleman who prospered fairly in Whig government circles. Pope's annoyance at the praise given to Ambrose Philips's pastorals which appeared in the same Miscellany with his own, and Addison's praise in the *Spectator* of his friend's translation of Racine's Andromache as "The Distrest Mother," have caused Ambrose Philips to be better remembered in the history of literature than might otherwise have been necessary. When he wrote no longer of

> " Mammy
> Andromache and her lammy
> Hanging panging at the breast
> Of a matron most distrest,"

and took to nursery lyrics, he gave Henry Carey an opportunity of putting a last touch to his monument for the instruction of posterity. The two specimens here given of the original poems that suggested "Namby Pamby" are addressed severally to two babes in the nursery of Daniel Pulteney, Esq. Another of the babies who inspired him was an infant Carteret, whose name Carey translated into "Tartaretta Tartaree." Some lines here and there, seven in all, which are not the wittier for being coarse, have been left out of "Namby Pamby." This burlesque was first published in 1725 or 1726; my copy is of the fifth edition, dated 1726, and was appended to "A Learned Dissertation on Dumpling; its Dignity, Antiquity, and Excellence, with a Word upon Pudding, and many other Useful Discoveries of great Benefit to the Publick. To which is added, Namby Pamby, A Panegyric on the new Versification address'd to A—— P——, Esq."

Henry Fielding produced his "Tom Thumb" in 1730, and added the notes of Scriblerus Secundus in 1731, following the example set by the Dunciad as published in April 1729, with the "Prolegomena of Scriblerus and Notes Variorum." Paul Whitehead added notes of a Scriblerus Tertius to his "Gymnasiad" in 1744. Fielding was twenty-four years old when he added to his "Tom Thumb" the notes that transmit to us lively examples of the stilted language of the stage by which, as a gentleman's son left to his own resources, he was then endeavouring to live. This was four years before his marriage, and ten years before he revealed his transcendent powers as a novelist.

Henry Carey's "Chrononhotonthologos," three years later, in 1734, carried on the war against pretentious dulness on the stage. The manner of the great actors was, like the plays of their generation, pompous and rhetorical, full of measured sound and fury signifying nothing. Garrick, who made his first appearance as an actor in 1741, put an end to this. "If the young fellow is right," said Quin, "we are all in the wrong;" little suspecting that they really were all in the wrong. Henry Carey, a musician by profession, played in the orchestra and also supplied the stage with ballad and burlesque farces and operas. But also he wrote "Namby Pamby." It was said of him that "he led a life free from reproach, and hanged himself October 4th, 1743."

"The Rovers, or the Double Arrangement," was a contribution to "The Anti-Jacobin," by George Canning, and his friends George Ellis and John Hookham Frere. Canning had established "The Anti-Jacobin," of which the first number was published on the 20th of November, 1797. Its poetry, generally levelled through witty burlesque at the false sentiment of the day, was collected in 1801 into a handsome quarto. This includes "The Rovers," which is a lively caricature of the sentimental German drama. Goethe's "Stella," as read in the translation used by the caricaturists, is not less comical than the caricature. I have a copy of the "Poetry of the Anti-Jacobin," in which one of the original writers has, for the friend to whom he gave the book, marked with his pen and ink details of authorship. From this it appears that the description of the *dramatis personæ* in "The Rovers" was by Frere, the Prologue by Canning and Ellis, the opening scene by Frere as far as Rogero's famous song, which was by Canning and Ellis. All that follows to the beginning of the fourth act was by Canning, except that Frere wrote the scene in the second act on the delivery of a newspaper to Beefington and Puddingfield. The fourth act and the final stage directions were by Frere, except the Recitative and Chorus of Conspirators. These were by George Ellis.

"Bombastes Furioso," first produced in 1810, was by William Barnes Rhodes, who had published a translation of Juvenal in 1801 and "Epigrams" in 1803. He formed a considerable dramatic library, of which there was a catalogue printed in 1825.

Next comes in this collection the series of burlesques of the styles of poets famous and popular in 1812, published in that year as "Rejected Addresses," by Horace and James Smith. Of these brothers, sons of an attorney, one was an attorney, the other a stockbroker, one aged thirty-seven, the other thirty-three, when the book appeared which made them famous, and of which the first edition is reprinted in this volume. The book went through twenty-four editions. James Smith wrote no more, but Horace to the last amused himself with literature. "Is it not odd," Leigh Hunt wrote of him to Shelley, "that the only truly generous person I ever knew, who had money to be generous with, was a stockbroker! And he writes poetry too; he writes poetry, and pastoral dramas, and yet knows how to make money, and does make it, and is still generous." The Fitzgerald who is subject of the first burlesque used to recite his laudatory poems at the annual dinners of the Literary Fund, and is the same who was referred to in the opening lines of Byron's "English Bards and Scotch Reviewers:"

> "Still must I hear?—shall hoarse Fitzgerald bawl
> His creaking couplets in a tavern hall,
> And I not sing."

This Miscellany closes with some of the "Odes and Addresses to Great People," with which Thomas Hood, at the age of twenty-six, first made his mark as a wit. The little book from which these pieces are taken was the joint work of himself and John Hamilton Reynolds, whose sister he had married. It marks the rise of the pun in burlesque writing through Thomas Hood, who, when dying of consumption, suggested for his epitaph, "Here lies one who spat more blood and made more puns than any other man."

H. M.

June, 1885.

Burlesque Plays and Poems.

———

THE RIME OF SIR THOPAS.

PROLOGUE TO SIR THOPAS.

WHEN said was this mirácle, every man
As sober was, that wonder was to see,
Till that our host to japen he began,
And then at erst he lookéd upon me,
And saidé thus : " What man art thou ?" quod he.
Thou lookest, as thou wouldest find an hare,
For ever upon the ground I see thee stare.

" Approché near, and look up merrily.
Now ware you, sirs, and let this man have place.
He in the waist is shapen as well as I :
This were a popet in an arm to embrace
For any woman, small and fair of face.
He seemeth elvish by his countenance,
For unto no wight doth he dalliance.

" Say now somewhat, sin other folk han said ;
Tell us a tale of mirth, and that anon."
" Hosté," quod I, " ne be not evil apaid,
For other talé certes, can I none,
But of a Rime I learnéd yore agone."
" Yea, that is good," quod he, " we shullen hear
Some dainty thing, me thinketh by thy cheere."

THE RIME OF SIR THOPAS.

LISTENETH, lordings, in good entent,
And I wol tell you *verament*
   Of mirth and of solás,
All of a knight was fair and gent
In battle and in tournamént,
   His name was Sir Thopás.

Yborn he was in far countree,
In Flanders, all beyond the sea,
   At Popering in the place,
His father was a man full free,
And lord he was of that countree,
   As it was Goddés grace.

Sir Thopas was a doughty swain,
White was his face as paindemaine
   His lippés red as rose.
His rudde is like scarlét in grain,
And I you tell in good certain
   He had a seemly nose.

His hair, his beard, was like saffroun,
That to his girdle raught adown,
   His shoon of cordewaine ;
Of Bruges were his hosen brown ;
His robé was of ciclatoun,
   That costé many a jane.

He could hunt at the wildé dere,
And ride on hawking for the rivere
   With grey goshawk on hand :
Thereto he was a good archere,
Of wrestling was there none his peer,
   Where any ram should stand.

Full many a maiden bright in bower
They mournéd for him *par amour*,
   When them were bet to slepe ;
But he was chaste and no lechóur,
And sweet as is the bramble flower,
   That beareth the red hepe.

And so it fell upon a day,
Forsooth, as I you tellen may,
  Sir Thopas would out ride ;
He worth upon his stedé gray,
And in his hand a launcegay,
  A long sword by his side.

He pricketh through a fair forést,
Therein is many a wildé beast,
  Yea bothé buck and hare,
And as he prickéd North and Est,
I tell it you, him had almest
  Betid a sorry care.

There springen herbés great and smale,
The liquorice and the setewale,
  And many a clove gilofre,
And nutémeg to put in ale,
Whether it be moist or stale,
  Or for to lain in cofre.

The birdés singen, it is no nay,
The sparhawk and the popingay,
  That joy it was to hear,
The throstel cock made eke his lay,
The wodé dove upon the spray
  He sang full loud and clear.

Sir Thopas fell in love-longíng
All when he heard the throstel sing,
  And pricked as he were wood ;
His fairé steed in his prickíng
So swatté, that men might him wring,
  His sidés were all blood.

Sir Thopas eke so weary was
For pricking on the softé gras,
  So fierce was his couráge,
That down he laid him in that place
To maken his stedé som solace,
  And gave him good foráge.

Ah, Seinte Mary, *benedicite*,
What aileth this love at me
  To bindé me so sore ?
Me dreaméd all this night pardé,
An elf-queen shal my leman be,
  And sleep under my gore.

An elf-queen will I love ywis,
For in this world no woman is
   Worthy to be my make
     In town,—
All other women I forsake,
And to an elf-queen I me take
   By dale and eke by down.

Into his saddle he clomb anon,
And pricked over stile and stone
   An elf-queen for to espie,
Till he so long had ridden and gone,
That he found in a privee wone
   The contree of Faerié.

Wherein he soughté North and South,
And oft he spiéd with his mouth
   In many a forest wild,
For in that contree n'as ther non,
That to him durst ride or gon,
   Neither wife ne child.

Till that there came a great geaunt,
His namé was Sir Oliphaunt,
   A perilous man of deed,
He saidé, Childe by Termagaunt,
But if thou prick out of mine haunt,
   Anon I slay thy stede
     With mace.
Here is the Queen of Faerie,
With harp, and pipe, and symphonie,
   Dwelling in this place.

The Childe said, All so mote I thee,
To morrow wol I meten thee,
   When I have min armóur,
And yet I hopé *par ma fay,*
That thou shalt with this launcegay
   Abien it full soure ;
     Thy mawe
Shal I perce, if I may,
Or it be fully prime of the day,
   For here thou shalt be slawe.

Sir Thopas drew aback full fast ;
This geaunt at him stonés cast
   Out of a fell staff sling :
But faire escapéd Childe Thopás,
And all it was through Goddes grace,
   And through his fair bearing.

Yet listeneth, lordings, to my tale,
Merrier than the nightingale,
  For now I will you roune,
How Sir Thopás with sidés smale,
Pricking over hill and dale,
  Is comen again to toune.

His merry men commandeth he,
To maken him bothe game and glee,
  For needés must he fight,
With a geaunt with heades three,
For paramour and jolitee
  Of one that shone full bright.

Do come, he said, my minestrales
And gestours for to tellen tales
  Anon in mine armíng,
Of romauncés that ben reáles,
Of popés and of cardináles,
  And eke of love-longíng.

They fet him first the swetè wine,
And mead eke in a maseline,
  And regal spicerie,
Of ginger-bread that was full fine,
And liquorice and eke cummine,
  With sugar that is trie.

He diddé next his whité lere
Of cloth of laké fine and clere
  A breche and eke a sherte,
And next his shert an haketon,
And over that an habergeon,
  For piercing of his herte,

And over that a fine hauberk,
Was all ywrought of Jewes werk,
  Full strong it was of plate,
And over that his cote-armoure,
As white as is the lily floure,
  In which he would debate.

His shield was all of gold so red,
And therein was a boarés hed,
  A carbuncle beside ;
And there he swore on ale and bread
How that the geaunt shuld be dead,
  Betide what so betide.

His jambeux were of cuirbouly,
His swordés sheth of ivory,
   His helm of latoun bright,
His saddle was of rewel bone,
His bridle as the sonné shone,
   Or as the moné light.

His speré was of fin cypréss,
That bodeth war, and nothing peace,
   The head full sharp yground.
His stedé was all dapple gray,
It goeth an amble in the way
   Full softély and round
      In londe—
Lo, Lordes mine, here is a fytte ;
If ye wol ony more of it,
   To tell it wol I fond.

Now hold your mouth *pour charité*,
Bothé knight and lady free,
   And herkeneth to my spell,
Of bataille and of chivalrie,
Of ladies love and druerie,
   Anon I wol you tell.

Men speken of romauncés of pris,
Of Hornchild, and of Ipotis,
   Of Bevis, and Sir Guy,
Of Sir Libeux, and Pleindamour,
But Sir Thopás, he bears the flour
   Of reál chivalrie.

His goodé steed he all bestrode,
And forth upon his way he glode,
   As sparkle out of brond ;
Upon his crest he bare a tower,
And therein sticked a lily flower,
   God shield his corps fro shond.

And for he was a knight auntrous,
He n'olde slepen in none house,
   But liggen in his hood,
His brighté helm was his wangér,
And by him baited his destrér
   Of herbés fine and good.

Himself drank water of the well,
As did the knight Sir Percivell
   So worthy under weede,
Till on a day—— ——

" No more of this for Goddés dignitee,"
Quod ouré hosté, "for thou makest me
So weary of thy veray lewédnesse,
That all so wisly God my soulé blesse,
Min erés aken of thy drafty speche.
Now swiche a rime the devil I beteche ;
This may wel be rime dogérel," quod he.
" Why so ? " quod I, " why wolt thou letten me
More of my talé than an other man,
Sin that it is the besté rime I can ? "
" Thou dost nought ellés but dispendest time.
Sir, at one word, thou shalt no longer rime."

THE

KNIGHT OF THE BURNING PESTLE.

————•◦•————

DRAMATIS PERSONÆ.

THE PROLOGUE.
Then a Citizen.
The Citizen's Wife, and RALPH,
  *her man, sitting below amidst
  the spectators.*
A rich Merchant.
JASPER, *his apprentice.*
MASTER HUMPHREY, *a friend to the
  Merchant.*
LUCE, *the Merchant's daughter.*
MISTRESS MERRY-THOUGHT, JAS-
  PER'S *mother.*

MICHAEL, *a second son of* MISTRESS
  MERRY-THOUGHT.
OLD MR. MERRY-THOUGHT.
A Squire.
A Dwarf.
A Tapster.
A Boy that danceth and singeth.
An Host.
A Barber.
Two Knights.
A Captain.
A Sergeant.
Soldiers.

Enter PROLOGUE.

FROM all that's near the court, from all that's great
Within the compass of the city walls,
We now have brought our scene.

Enter CITIZEN.

Cit. Hold your peace, good-man boy.

Pro. What do you mean, sir?

Cit. That you have no good meaning: these seven years
there hath been plays at this house, I have observed it, you
have still girds at citizens; and now you call your play "The
London Merchant." Down with your title, boy, down with your
title.

Pro. Are you a member of the noble city?

Cit. I am.

Pro. And a freeman?

Cit. Yea, and a grocer.

Pro. So, grocer, then by your sweet favour, we intend no
abuse to the city.

Cit. No, sir, yes, sir, if you were not resolved to play the jacks, what need you study for new subjects, purposely to abuse your betters? Why could not you be contented, as well as others, with the legend of Whittington, or the Life and Death of Sir Thomas Gresham? with the building of the Royal Exchange? or the story of Queen Eleanor, with the rearing of London Bridge upon woolsacks?

Pro. You seem to be an understanding man; what would you have us do, sir?

Cit. Why, present something notably in honour of the commons of the city.

Pro. Why, what do you say to the Life and Death of fat Drake, or the repairing of Fleet privies?

Cit. I do not like that; but I will have a citizen, and he shall be of my own trade.

Pro. Oh, you should have told us your mind a month since, our play is ready to begin now.

Cit. 'Tis all one for that, I will have a grocer, and he shall do admirable things.

Pro. What will you have him do?

Cit. Marry I will have him——

Wife. Husband, husband!   [WIFE *below.*

Ralph. Peace, mistress.   [RALPH *below.*

Wife. Hold thy peace, Ralph, I know what I do, I warrant ye. Husband, husband!

Cit. What sayest thou, cony?

Wife. Let him kill a lion with a pestle, husband; let him kill a lion with a pestle.

Cit. So he shall, I'll have him kill a lion with a pestle.

Wife. Husband, shall I come up, husband?

Cit. Ay, cony. Ralph, help your mistress up this way: pray, gentlemen, make her a little room; I pray you, sir, lend me your hand to help up my wife; I thank you, sir, so.

Wife. By your leave, gentlemen all, I'm something troublesome, I'm a stranger here, I was ne'er at one of these plays, as they say, before; but I should have seen "Jane Shore" once; and my husband hath promised me anytime this twelvemonth, to carry me to the "Bold Beauchamps," but in truth he did not; I pray you bear with me.

Cit. Boy, let my wife and I have a couple of stools, and then begin, and let the grocer do rare things.

Pro. But, sir, we have never a boy to play him, every one hath a part already.

Wife. Husband, husband, for God's sake let Ralph play him; beshrew me if I do not think he will go beyond them all.

Cit. Well remembered wife; come up, Ralph; I'll tell you, gentlemen, let them but lend him a suit of reparrel, and necessaries, and by Gad, if any of them all blow wind in the tail on him, I'll be hanged.

Wife. I pray you, youth, let him have a suit of reparrel : I'll be sworn, gentlemen, my husband tells you true, he will act you sometimes at our house, that all the neighbours cry out on him : he will fetch you up a couraging part so in the garret, that we are all as feared I warrant you, that we quake again. We fear our children with him, if they be never so unruly, do but cry " Ralph comes, Ralph comes " to them, and they'll be as quiet as lambs. Hold up thy head, Ralph, show the gentlemen what thou canst do ; speak a huffing part, I warrant you the gentlemen will accept of it.

Cit. Do, Ralph, do.

Ralph. By heaven (methinks) it were an easy leap
To pluck bright honour from the pale-faced moon,
Or dive into the bottom of the sea,
Where never fathom line touched any ground,
And pluck drowned honour from the lake of hell.

Cit. How say you, gentlemen, is it not as I told you ?

Wife. Nay, gentlemen, he hath played before, my husband says, " Musidorus," before the wardens of our company.

Cit. Ay, and he should have played " Jeronimo " with a shoe-maker for a wager.

Pro. He shall have a suit of apparel, if he will go in.

Cit. In, Ralph, in, Ralph, and set out the grocers in their kind, if thou lovest me.

Wife. I warrant our Ralph will look finely when he's dressed.

Pro. But what will you have it called ?

Cit. "The Grocer's Honour."

Pro. Methinks " The Knight of the Burning Pestle " were better.

Wife. I'll be sworn, husband, that's as good a name as can be.

Cit. Let it be so, begin, begin ; my wife and I will sit down.

Pro. I pray you do.

Cit. What stately music have you ? Have you shawns ?

Pro. Shawns ? No.

Cit. No ? I'm a thief if my mind did not give me so. Ralph plays a stately part, and he must needs have shawns : I'll be at the charge of them myself rather than we'll be without them.

Pro. So you are like to be.

Cit. Why and so I will be, there's two shillings, let's have the waits of Southwark, they are as rare fellows as any are in England ; and that will fetch them all o'er the water with a vengeance, as if they were mad.

Pro. You shall have them ; will you sit down, then ?

Cit. Ay, come, wife.

Wife. Sit you, merry all gentlemen, I'm bold to sit amongst you for my ease.

Pro. From all that's near the Court, from all that's great
Within the compass of the city walls,

We now have brought our scene. Fly far from hence
All private taxes, all immodest phrases,
Whatever may but show like vicious,
For wicked mirth never true pleasure brings,
But honest minds are pleased with honest things.
Thus much for that we do. But for Ralph's part you must
answer for't yourself.

Cit. Take you no care for Ralph, he'll discharge himself, I
warrant you.

Wife. I'faith, gentlemen, I'll give my word for Ralph.

ACT I.—SCENE I.

Enter MERCHANT *and* JASPER *his man.*

Merch. Sirrah, I'll make you know you are my prentice,
And whom my charitable love redeem'd
Even from the fall of fortune ; gave thee heat
And growth, to be what now thou art ; new cast thee,
Adding the trust of all I have at home,
In foreign staples, or upon the sea,
To thy direction ; tied the good opinions
Both of myself and friends to thy endeavours,—
So fair were thy beginnings. But with these,
As I remember, you had never charge
To love your master's daughter, and even then,
When I had found a wealthy husband for her,
I take it, sir, you had not ; but, however,
I'll break the neck of that commission,
And make you know you're but a merchant's factor.

Jasp. Sir, I do lib'rally confess I'm yours,
Bound both by love and duty to your service :
In which my labour hath been all my profit.
I have not lost in bargain, nor delighted
To wear your honest gains upon my back,
Nor have I giv'n a pension to my blood,
Or lavishly in play consum'd your stock.
These, and the miseries that do attend them,
I dare with innocence proclaim are strangers
To all my temperate actions ; for your daughter,
If there be any love to my deservings
Borne by her virtuous self, I cannot stop it :
Nor am I able to refrain her wishes.
She's private to herself, and best of knowledge
Whom she will make so happy as to sigh for.
Besides, I cannot think you mean to match her
Unto a fellow of so lame a presence,
One that hath little left of nature in him.

Merch. 'Tis very well, sir, I can tell your wisdom
How all this shall be cured.
Jasp.   Your care becomes you.
Merch. And thus it shall be, sir ; I here discharge you
My house and service.   Take your liberty,
And when I want a son I'll send for you.   [*Exit.*
Jasp. These be the fair rewards of them that love,
Oh you that live in freedom never prove
The travail of a mind led by desire.

Enter LUCE.

Luce. Why how now, friend, struck with my father's thunder ?
Jasp. Struck, and struck dead, unless the remedy
Be full of speed and virtue ; I am now,
What I expected long, no more your father's.
Luce. But mine.
Jasp. But yours, and only yours I am,
That's all I have to keep me from the statute ;
You dare be constant still ?
Luce.   O fear me not.
In this I dare be better than a woman.
Nor shall his anger nor his offers move me,
Were they both equal to a prince's power.
Jasp. You know my rival ?
Luce.   Yes, and love him dearly,
E'en as I love an ague, or foul weather ;
I prithee, Jasper, fear him not.
Jasp.   Oh no,
I do not mean to do him so much kindness.
But to our own desires : you know the plot
We both agreed on.
Luce.   ·   Yes, and will perform
My part exactly.
Jasp.   I desire no more,
Farewell, and keep my heart, 'tis yours.
Luce.   I take it,
He must do miracles, makes me forsake it.   [*Exeunt.*
Cit. Fie upon 'em, little infidels, what a matter's here now ?
Well, I'll be hang'd for a half-penny, if there be not some
abomination knavery in this play ; well, let 'em look to it, Ralph
must come, and if there be any tricks a brewing——
Wife. Let 'em brew and bake too, husband, a God's name.
Ralph will find all out I warrant you, and they were older than
they are.   I pray, my pretty youth, is Ralph ready ?
Boy. He will be presently.
Wife. Now I pray you make my commendations unto him,
and withal, carry him this stick of liquorice ; tell him his

mistress sent it him, and bid him bite a piece, 'twill open his
pipes the better, say.

Enter MERCHANT *and* MASTER HUMPHREY.

Merch. Come, sir, she's yours, upon my faith she's yours,
You have my hand ; for other idle lets,
Between your hopes and her, thus with a wind
They're scattered, and no more. My wanton prentice,
That like a bladder blew himself with love,
I have let out, and sent him to discover
New masters yet unknown.

Hum.   I thank you, sir,
Indeed I thank you, sir ; and ere I stir,
It shall be known, however you do deem,
I am of gentle blood, and gentle seem.

Merch. Oh, sir, I know it certain.

Hum.   Sir, my friend,
Although, as writers say, all things have end,
And that we call a pudding, hath his two,
Oh let it not seem strange, I pray to you,
If in this bloody simile, I put
My love, more endless than frail things or gut.

Wife. Husband, I prithee, sweet lamb, tell me one thing, but
tell me truly. Stay, youths, I beseech you, till I question my
husband.

Cit. What is it, mouse ?

Wife. Sirrah, didst thou ever see a prettier child ? how it
behaves itself, I warrant you : and speaks and looks, and perts
up the head ? I pray you brother, with your favour, were you
never one of Mr. Muncaster's scholars ?

Cit. Chicken, I prithee heartily contain thyself, the childer
are pretty childer, but when Ralph comes, lamb !

Wife. Ay, when Ralph comes, cony !   Well, my youth, you
may proceed.

Merch. Well, sir, you know my love, and rest, I hope,
Assured of my consent ; get but my daughter's,
And wed her when you please ; you must be bold,
And clap in close unto her ; come, I know
You've language good enough to win a wench.

Wife. A toity tyrant, hath been an old stringer in his days,
I warrant him.

Hum. I take your gentle offer, and withal
Yield love again for love reciprocal.

Mar. What, Luce, within there ?

Enter LUCE.

Luce.   Called you, sir ?

Merch. I did ;
Give entertainment to this gentleman ;
And see you be not froward : to her, sir, [*Exit.*
My presence will but be an eyesore to you.
  Hum. Fair mistress Luce, how do you, are you well?
Give me your hand, and then I pray you tell,
How doth your little sister, and your brother,
And whether you love me or any other ?
  Luce. Sir, these are quickly answered.
  Hum. So they are,
Where women are not cruel ; but how far
Is it now distant from the place we are in,
Unto that blessed place, your father's warren.
  Luce. What makes you think of that, sir?
  Hum. E'en that face,
For stealing rabbits whilome in that place,
God Cupid, or the keeper, I know not whether,
Unto my cost and charges brought you thither,
And there began——
  Luce. Your game, sir.
  Hum. Let no game,
Or anything that tendeth to the same,
Be evermore remembered, thou fair killer,
For whom I sate me down and brake my tiller.
  Wife. There's a kind gentleman, I warrant you. When will
you do as much for me, George?
  Luce. Beshrew me, sir, I'm sorry for your losses,
But as the proverb says, I cannot cry ;
I would you had not seen me.
  Hum. So would I,
Unless you had more maw to do me good.
  Luce. Why, cannot this strange passion be withstood?
Send for a constable, and raise the town.
  Hum. Oh no, my valiant love will batter down
Millions of constables, and put to flight
E'en that great watch of Midsummer Day at night.
  Luce. Beshrew me, sir, 'twere good I yielded then,
Weak women cannot hope, where valiant men
Have no resistance.
  Hum. Yield then, I am full
Of pity, though I say it, and can pull
Out of my pocket thus a pair of gloves.
Look, Luce, look, the dog's tooth, nor the doves
Are not so white as these ; and sweet they be,
And whipt about with silk, as you may see.
If you desire the price, shoot from your eye
A beam to this place, and you shall espy
F. S., which is to say, my sweetest honey,
They cost me three-and-twopence, and no money.

Luce. Well, sir, I take them kindly, and I thank you; what
What would you more?
    Hum.   Nothing.
    Luce.   Why then, farewell.
    Hum. Nor so, nor so, for, lady, I must tell,
Before we part, for what we met together,
God grant me time, and patience, and fair weather.
    Luce. Speak and declare your mind in terms so brief.
    Hum. I shall; then first and foremost, for relief
I call to you, if that you can afford it,
I care not at what price, for on my word it
Shall be repaid again, although it cost me
More than I'll speak of now, for love hath tost me
In furious blanket like a tennis-ball,
And now I rise aloft, and now I fall.
    Luce. Alas, good gentleman, alas the day.
    Hum. I thank you heartily, and as I say,
Thus do I still continue without rest,
I' th' morning like a man, at night a beast,
Roaring and bellowing mine own disquiet,
That much I fear, forsaking of my diet,
Will bring me presently to that quandary,
I shall bid all adieu.
    Luce.   Now, by St. Mary
That were great pity,
    Hum.   So it were, beshrew me,
Then ease me, lusty Luce, and pity shew me.
    Luce. Why, sir, you know my will is nothing worth
Without my father's grant; get his consent,
And then you may with full assurance try me.
    Hum. The worshipful your sire will not deny me,
For I have ask'd him, and he hath replied,
Sweet Master Humphrey, Luce shall be thy bride.
    Luce. Sweet Master Humphrey, then I am content.
    Hum. And so am I, in truth.
    Luce.   Yet take me with you.
There is another clause must be annext,
And this it is I swore, and will perform it,
No man shall ever joy me as his wife,
But he that stole me hence. If you dare venture,
I'm yours; you need not fear, my father loves you,
If not, farewell, for ever.
    Hum.   Stay, nymph, stay,
I have a double gelding, colour'd bay,
Sprung by his father from Barbarian kind,
Another for myself, though somewhat blind,
Yet true as trusty tree.

Luce.   I'm satisfied,
And so I give my hand ; our course must lie
Through Waltham Forest, where I have a friend
Will entertain us ; so farewell, Sir Humphrey,
And think upon your business.   [*Exit* LUCE.
   Hum.   Though I die,
I am resolv'd to venture life and limb,
For one so young, so fair, so kind, so trim.   [*Exit* HUM.

   Wife. By my faith and troth, George, and as I am virtuous,
it is e'en the kindest young man that ever trod on shoe-leather ;
well, go thy ways, if thou hast her not, 'tis not thy fault
i'faith.
   Cit. I prithee, mouse, be patient, a shall have her, or I'll make
some of 'em smoke for't.
   Wife. That's my good lamb, George ; fie, this stinking
tobacco kills me, would there were none in England. Now I
pray, gentlemen, what good does this stinking tobacco do you ?
nothing ; I warrant you make chimnies o' your faces. Oh, husband, husband, now, now there's Ralph, there's Ralph !

Enter RALPH, *like a grocer in his shop, with two prentices,*
reading " Palmerin of England."

   Cit. Peace, fool, let Ralph alone ; hark you, Ralph, do not
strain yourself too much at the first. Peace, begin, Ralph.
   Ralph. Then Palmerin and Trineus, snatching their lances
from their dwarfs, and clasping their helmets, galloped amain
after the giant, and Palmerin having gotten a sight of him,
came posting amain, saying, " Stay, traitorous thief, for thou
mayst not so carry away her that is worth the greatest lord in
the world;" and, with these words, gave him a blow on the
shoulder, that he struck him beside his elephant ; and Trineus
coming to the knight that had Agricola behind him, set him soon
beside his horse, with his neck broken in the fall, so that the
princess, getting out of the throng, between joy and grief said,
" All happy knight, the mirror of all such as follow arms, now
may I be well assured of the love thou bearest me." I wonder
why the kings do not raise an army of fourteen or fifteen hundred
thousand men, as big as the army that the Prince of Portigo
brought against Rosicler, and destroy these giants ; they do
much hurt to wandering damsels that go in quest of their
knights.
   Wife. Faith, husband, and Ralph says true, for they say the
King of Portugal cannot sit at his meat but the giants and the
ettins will come and snatch it from him.
   Cit. Hold thy tongue ; on, Ralph.
   Ralph. And certainly those knights are much to be com-

mended who, neglecting their possessions, wander with a squire
and a dwarf through the deserts to relieve poor ladies.

Wife. Ay, by my faith are they, Ralph, let 'em say what they
will, they are indeed ; our knights neglect their possessions well
enough, but they do not the rest.

Ralph. There are no such courteous and fair well-spoken
knights in this age ; they will call one the son of a sea-cook that
Palmerin of England would have called fair sir ; and one that
Rosicler would have called right beautiful damsel they will call
old witch.

Wife. I'll be sworn will they, Ralph ; they have called me so
an hundred times about a scurvy pipe of tobacco.

. Ralph. But what brave spirit could be content to sit in his
shop, with a flapet of wood, and a blue apron before him, selling
Methridatam and Dragons' Water to visited houses, that might
pursue feats of arms, and through his noble achievements
procure such a famous history to be written of his heroic
prowess ?

Cit. Well said, Ralph ; some more of those words, Ralph.

Wife. They go finely, by my troth.

Ralph. Why should I not then pursue this course, both for
the credit of myself and our company ? for amongst all the
worthy books of achievements, I do not call to mind that I yet
read of a grocer errant : I will be the said knight. Have you
heard of any that hath wandered unfurnished of his squire and
dwarf? My elder prentice Tim shall be my trusty squire, and
little George my dwarf. Hence, my blue apron ! Yet, in remem-
brance of my former trade, upon my shield shall be portrayed a
burning pestle, and I will be called the Knight of the Burning
Pestle.

Wife. Nay, I dare swear thou wilt not forget thy old trade,
thou wert ever meek. Ralph ! Tim !

Tim. Anon.

Ralph. My beloved squire, and George my dwarf, I charge
you that from henceforth you never call me by any other name
but the Right courteous and valiant Knight of the Burning
Pestle ; and that you never call any female by the name of a
woman or wench, but fair lady, if she have her desires ; if not,
distressed damsel ; that you call all forests and heaths, deserts;
and all horses, palfreys.

Wife. This is very fine : faith, do the gentlemen like Ralph,
think you, husband ?

Cit. Ay, I warrant thee, the players would give all the shoes
in their shop for him.

Ralph. My beloved Squire Tim, stand out. Admit this were a
desert, and over it a knight errant pricking, and I should bid
you inquire of his intents, what would you say ?

Tim. Sir, my master sent me to know whither you are riding ?

Ralph. No, thus : Fair sir, the Right courteous and valiant Knight of the Burning Pestle, commanded me to inquire upon what adventure you are bound, whether to relieve some distressed damsel or otherwise.

Cit. Dunder blockhead cannot remember.

Wife. I'faith, and Ralph told him on't before ; all the gentlemen heard him ; did he not, gentlemen, did not Ralph tell him on't ?

George. Right courteous and valiant Knight of the Burning Pestle, here is a distressed damsel to have a halfpenny-worth of pepper.

Wife. That's a good boy, see, the little boy can hit it ; by my troth it's a fine child.

Ralph. Relieve her with all courteous language ; now shut up shop : no more my prentice, but my trusty squire and dwarf, I must bespeak my shield, and arming pestle.

Cit. Go thy ways, Ralph, as I am a true man, thou art the best on 'em all.

Wife. Ralph ! Ralph ! .

Ralph. What say you, mistress ?

Wife. I prithee come again quickly, sweet Ralph.

Ralph. By-and-by.   [*Exit* RALPH.

Enter JASPER *and his mother* MISTRESS MERRY-THOUGHT.

Mist. Mer. Give thee my blessing ? No, I'll never give thee my blessing, I'll see thee hang'd first ; it shall ne'er be said I gave thee my blessing. Thou art thy father's own son, of the blood of the Merry-thoughts ; I may curse the time that e'er I knew thy father, he hath spent all his own, and mine too, and when I tell him of it, he laughs and dances and sings, and cries " A merry heart lives long-a." And thou art a wast-thrift, and art run away from thy master, that lov'd thee well, and art come to me, and I have laid up a little for my younger son Michael, and thou thinkest to bezle that, but thou shalt never be able to do it. Come hither, Michael, come Michael, down on thy knees, thou shalt have my blessing.

Enter MICHAEL.

Mich. I pray you, mother, pray to God to bless me.

Mist. Mer. God bless thee ; but Jasper shall never have my blessing, he shall be hang'd first, shall he not, Michael ? how sayest thou ?

Mich. Yes forsooth, mother, and grace of God.

Mist. Mer. That's a good boy.

Wife. I'faith, it's a fine spoken child.

Jasp. Mother, though you forget a parent's love,

I must preserve the duty of a child.
I ran not from my master, nor return
To have your stock maintain my idleness.

Wife. Ungracious child I warrant him, hark how he chops logic with his mother; thou hadst best tell her she lies, do, tell her she lies.

Cit. If he were my son, I would hang him up by the heels, and flea him, and salt him, humpty halter-sack.

Jasp. My coming only is to beg your love,
Which I must ever, though I never gain it;
And howsoever you esteem of me,
There is no drop of blood hid in these veins,
But I remember well belongs to you,
That brought me forth, and would be glad for you
To rip them all again, and let it out.

Mist. Mer. I'faith I had sorrow enough for thee, God knows; but I'll hamper thee well enough : get thee in, thou vagabond, get thee in, and learn of thy brother Michael.

Old Mer. [within]. " Nose, nose, jolly red nose,
    And who gave thee this jolly red nose?"

Mist. Mer. Hark, my husband he's singing and hoiting,
And I'm fain to cark and care, and all little enough.
Husband, Charles, Charles Merry-thought!

Enter OLD-MERRY-THOUGHT.

Old Mer. "Nutmegs and ginger, cinnamon and cloves,
    And they gave me this jolly red nose."

Mist. Mer. If you would consider your estate, you would have little list to sing, I wis.

Old Mer. It should never be considered, while it were an estate, if I thought it would spoil my singing.

Mist. Mer. But how wilt thou do, Charles? Thou art an old man, and thou canst not work, and thou hast not forty shillings left, and thou eatest good meat, and drinkest good drink, and laughest?

Old Mer. And will do.

Mist. Mer. But how wilt thou come by it, Charles?

Old Mer. How? Why how have I done hitherto these forty years? I never came into my dining-room, but at eleven and six o'clock I found excellent meat and drink o' th' table. My clothes were never worn out, but next morning a tailor brought me a new suit, and without question it will be so ever! Use makes perfectness; if all should fail, it is but a little straining myself extraordinary, and laugh myself to death.

Wife. It's a foolish old man this : is not he, George?

Cit. Yes, honey.

Wife. Give me a penny i' th' purse while I live, George.

Cit. Ay, by'r lady, honey hold thee there.

Mist. Mer. Well, Charles, you promised to provide for Jasper, and I have laid up for Michael. I pray you pay Jasper his portion, he's come home, and he shall not consume Michael's stock ; he says his master turned him away, but I promise you truly, I think he ran away.

Wife. No indeed, Mistress Merry-thought, though he be a notable gallows, yet I'll assure you his master did turn him away, even in this place; 'twas i'faith within this half-hour, about his daughter ; my husband was by.

Cit. Hang him, rogue, he served him well enough : love his master's daughter ! By my troth, honey, if there were a thousand boys, thou wouldst spoil them all, with taking their parts ; let his mother alone with him.

Wife. Ay, George, but yet truth is truth.

Old Mer. Where is Jasper ? He's welcome, however, call him in, he shall have his portion ; is he merry ?

Mist. Mer. Ay, foul chive him, he is too merry. Jasper ! Michael !

Enter JASPER *and* MICHAEL.

Old Mer. Welcome, Jasper, though thou runn'st away, welcome! God bless thee ! It is thy mother's mind thou should'st receive thy portion ; thou hast been abroad, and I hope hast learnt experience enough to govern it. Thou art of sufficient years. Hold thy hand : one, two, three, four, five, six, seven, eight, nine, there is ten shillings for thee ; thrust thyself into the world with that, and take some settled course. If fortune cross thee, thou hast a retiring place ; come home to me, I have twenty shillings left. Be a good husband, that is, wear ordinary clothes, eat the best meat, and drink the best drink ; be merry, and give to the poor, and believe me, thou hast no end of thy goods.

Jasp. Long may you live free from all thought of ill,
And long have cause to be thus merry still.
But, father ?

Old Mer. No more words, Jasper, get thee gone, thou hast my blessing, thy father's spirit upon thee. Farewell, Jasper.

> " But yet, or e'er you part (oh cruel),
> Kiss me, kiss me, sweeting,
> Mine own dear jewel."

So, now begone, no words.   [*Exit* JASPER.

Mist. Mer. So, Michael, now get thee gone too.

Mich. Yes forsooth, mother, but I'll have my father's blessing first.

Mist. Mer. No, Michael, 'tis no matter for his blessing ; thou hast my blessing. Begone ; I'll fetch my money and jewels and follow thee : I'll stay no longer with him I warrant thee. Truly, Charles, I'll be gone too.

Old Mer. What ? You will not.

Mist. Mer. Yes indeed will I.

Old Mer. " Heyho, farewell, Nan,
      I'll never trust wench more again, if I can."

Mist. Mer. You shall not think (when all your own is gone)
to spend that I have been scraping up for Michael.

Old Mer. Farewell, good wife, I expect it not, all I have to do
in this world is to be merry ; which I shall, if the ground be not
taken from me ; and if it be,
      "When earth and seas from me are reft,
      The skies aloft for me are left."   [*Exeunt.*
                        [*Boy dances. Music.*

Finis Actus Primi.

Wife. I'll be sworn he's a merry old gentleman for all that.
Hark, hark, husband, hark, fiddles, fiddles ; now surely they go
finely. They say 'tis present death for these fiddlers to tune
their rebecks before the great Turk's grace, is't not, George ?
But look, look, here's a youth dances ; now, good youth, do a turn
o' the toe. Sweetheart, i'faith I'll have Ralph come and do
some of his gambols: he'll ride the wild mare, gentlemen,
'twould do your hearts good to see him : I thank you, kind youth,
pray bid Ralph come.

Cit. Peace, conie. Sirrah, you scurvy boy, bid the players
send Ralph, or an' they do not I'll tear some of their periwigs
beside their heads ; this is all riff-raff.

ACT II.—SCENE I.

Enter MERCHANT *and* HUMPHREY.

Merch. And how faith ? how goes it now, son Humphrey ?

Hum. Right worshipful and my beloved friend,
And father dear, this matter's at an end.

Merch. 'Tis well, it should be so, I'm glad the girl
Is found so tractable.

Hum.   Nay, she must whirl
From hence (and you must wink : for so I say,
The story tells), to-morrow before day.

Wife. George, dost thou think in thy conscience now 'twill be
a match ? tell me but what thou thinkest, sweet rogue. thou seest
the poor gentleman (dear heart) how it labours and throbs I
warrant you, to be at rest : I'll go move the father for't.

Cit. No, no, I prithee sit still, honeysuckle, thou't spoil all ;
if he deny him, I'll bring half a dozen good fellows myself, and
in the shutting of an evening knock it up, and there's an end.

Wife. I'll buss thee for that i'faith, boy ; well, George, well, you have been a wag in your days I warrant you ; but God forgive you, and I do with all my heart.

Merch. How was it, son? you told me that to-morrow before daybreak, you must convey her hence.

Hum. I must, I must, and thus it is agreed,
Your daughter rides upon a brown bay steed,
I on a sorrel, which I bought of Brian,
The honest host of the Red Roaring Lion,
In Waltham situate : then if you may,
Consent in seemly sort, lest by delay,
The fatal sisters come, and do the office,
And then you'll sing another song.
   Merch.   Alas,
Why should you be thus full of grief to me,
That do as willing as yourself agree
To anything, so it be good and fair ?
Then steal her when you will, if such a pleasure
Content you both, I'll sleep and never see it,
To make your joys more full : but tell me why
You may not here perform your marriage?

Wife. God's blessing o' thy soul, old man, i'faith thou art loath to part true hearts : I see a has her, George, and I'm glad on't ; well, go thy ways, Humphrey, for a fair-spoken man. I believe thou hast not a fellow within the walls of London ; an' I should say the suburbs too, I should not lie. Why dost not thou rejoice with me, George?

Cit. If I could but see Ralph again, I were as merry as mine host i'faith.

Hum. The cause you seem to ask, I thus declare ;
Help me, O Muses nine : your daughter sware
A foolish oath, the more it was the pity :
Yet no one but myself within this city
Shall dare to say so, but a bold defiance
Shall meet him, were he of the noble science.
And yet she sware, and yet why did she swear?
Truly I cannot tell, unless it were
For her own ease ; for sure sometimes an oath,
Being sworn thereafter, is like cordial broth :
And this it was she swore, never to marry,
But such a one whose mighty arm could carry
(As meaning me, for I am such a one)
Her bodily away through stick and stone,
Till both of us arrive, at her request,
Some ten miles off in the wide Waltham Forest.

Merch. If this be all, you shall not need to fear
Any denial in your love ; proceed,
I'll neither follow nor repent the deed.

Hum. Good night, twenty good nights, and twenty more,
And twenty more good nights : that makes threescore. [*Exeunt.*

Enter MISTRESS MERRY-THOUGHT *and her son* MICHAEL.

Mist. Mer. Come, Michael, art thou not weary, boy ?
Mich. No, forsooth, mother, not I.
Mist. Mer. Where be we now, child ?
Mich. Indeed forsooth, mother, I cannot tell, unless we be at
Mile End. Is not all the world Mile End, mother ?
Mist. Mer. No, Michael, not all the world, boy; but I can
assure thee, Michael, Mile End is a goodly matter. There has
been a pitched field, my child, between the naughty Spaniels
and the Englishmen ; and the Spaniels ran away, Michael, and
the Englishmen followed. My neighbour Coxstone was there,
boy, and killed them all with a birding-piece.
Mich. Mother, forsooth.
Mist. Mer. What says my white boy ?
Mich. Shall not my father go with us too ?
Mist. Mer. No, Michael, let thy father go snick-up, he shall
never come between a pair of sheets with me again while he
lives : let him stay at home and sing for his supper, boy. Come,
child, sit down, and I'll show my boy fine knacks indeed ; look
here, Michael, here's a ring, and here's a brooch, and here's a
bracelet, and here's two rings more, and here's money, and gold
by th' eye, my boy.
Mich. Shall I have all this, mother ?
Mist. Mer. Ay, Michael, thou shalt have all, Michael.
Cit. How lik'st thou this, wench ?
Wife. I cannot tell, I would have Ralph, George ; I'll see no
more else indeed la : and I pray you let the youths understand
so much by word of mouth, for I will tell you truly, I'm afraid o'
my boy. Come, come, George, let's be merry and wise, the
child's a fatherless child, and say they should put him into a
strait pair of gaskins, 'twere worse than knot-grass, he would
never grow after it.

Enter RALPH, SQUIRE, *and* DWARF.

Cit. Here's Ralph, here's Ralph.
Wife. How do you, Ralph ? You are welcome, Ralph, as I
may say, it's a good boy, hold up thy head, and be not afraid,
we are thy friends, Ralph. The gentlemen will praise thee,
Ralph, if thou play'st thy part with audacity ; begin, Ralph a
God's name.
Ralph. My trusty squire, unlace my helm, give me my hat ;
where are we, or what desert might this be ?

Dwarf. Mirror of knighthood, this is, as I take it, the perilous
Waltham down, in whose bottom stands the enchanted valley.

Mist. Mer. Oh, Michael, we are betrayed, we are betrayed,
here be giants ; fly, boy ; fly, boy ; fly!
                                    [*Exeunt* MOTHER *and* MICHAEL.

Ralph. Lace on my helm again ; what noise is this ?
A gentle lady flying the embrace
Of some uncourteous knight : I will relieve her.
Go, squire, and say, the knight that wears this pestle
In honour of all ladies, swears revenge
Upon that recreant coward that pursues her ;
Go, comfort her, and that same gentle squire
That bears her company.

Squire.   I go, brave knight.

Ralph. My trusty dwarf and friend, reach me my shield,
And hold it while I swear, first by my knighthood,
Then by the soul of Amadis de Gaul,
My famous ancestor, then by my sword,
The beauteous Brionella girt about me,
By this bright burning pestle, of mine honour
The living trophy, and by all respect
Due to distressed damsels, here I vow
Never to end the quest of this fair lady,
And that forsaken squire, till by my valour
I gain their liberty.

Dwarf.   Heaven bless the knight
That thus relieves poor errant gentlewomen.   [*Exit.*

Wife. Ay marry, Ralph, this has some savour in it, I would
see the proudest of them all offer to carry his books after him.
But, George, I will not have him go away so soon, I shall be sick
if he go away, that I shall ; call Ralph again, George, call
Ralph again : I prithee, sweetheart, let him come fight before me,
and let's have some drums and trumpets, and let him kill all
that comes near him, an' thou lov'st me, George.

Cit. Peace a little, bird, he shall kill them all, an' they were
twenty more on 'em than there are.

Enter JASPER.

Jasp. Now, Fortune (if thou be'st not only ill),
Show me thy better face, and bring about
Thy desperate wheel, that I may climb at length
And stand ; this is our place of meeting,
If love have any constancy. Oh age
Where only wealthy men are counted happy :
How shall I please thee ? how deserve thy smiles,
When I am only rich in misery ?
My father's blessing, and this little coin

Is my inheritance. A strong revenue !
From earth thou art, and unto earth I give thee.
There grow and multiply, whilst fresher air
Breeds me a fresher fortune. How, illusion ! [*Spies the casket.*
What, hath the devil coined himself before me ?
'Tis metal good, it rings well, I am waking,
And taking too I hope ; now God's dear blessing
Upon his heart that left it here, 'tis mine ;
These pearls, I take it, were not left for swine.   [*Exit.*

Wife. I do not like this unthrifty youth should embezzle away
the money ; the poor gentlewoman his mother will have a heavy
heart for it, God knows.

Cit. And reason good, sweetheart.

Wife. But let him go, I'll tell Ralph a tale in's ear, shall
fetch him again with a wanion, I warrant him, if he be above
ground ; and besides, George, here be a number of sufficient
gentlemen can witness, and myself, and yourself, and the
musicians, if we be called in question ; but here comes Ralph,
George ; thou shalt hear him speak, as he were an Emperal.

Enter RALPH *and* DWARF.

Ralph. Comes not Sir Squire again ?

Dwarf. Right courteous knight,
Your squire doth come, and with him comes the lady
Fair, and the squire of damsels, as I take it.

Enter MISTRESS MERRY-THOUGHT, MICHAEL, *and* SQUIRE.

Ralph. Madam, if any service or devoir
Of a poor errant knight may right your wrongs,
Command it. I am prest to give you succour,
For to that holy end I bear my armour.

Mist. Mer. Alas, sir, I am a poor gentlewoman, and I have
lost my money in this forest.

Ralph. Desert, you would say, lady, and not lost
Whilst I have sword and lance ; dry up your tears,
Which ill befit the beauty of that face,
And tell the story, if I may request it,
Of your disastrous fortune.

Mist. Mer. Out alas, I left a thousand pound, a thousand
pound, e'en all the money I had laid up for this youth, upon the
sight of your mastership. You looked so grim, and as I may say
it, saving your presence, more like a giant than a mortal man.

Ralph. I am as you are, lady, so are they
All mortal ; but why weeps this gentle squire ?

Mist. Mer. Has he not cause to weep do you think, when he
has lost his inheritance ?

Ralph. Young hope of valour, weep not, I am here

That will confound thy foe, and pay it dear
Upon his coward head, that dare deny
Distresséd squires and ladies equity.
I have but one horse, upon which shall ride
This lady fair behind me, and before
This courteous squire, fortune will give us more
Upon our next adventure ; fairly speed
Beside us squire and dwarf, to do us need.   [*Exeunt.*

Cit. Did not I tell you, Nell; what your man would do? by
the faith of my body, wench, for clean action and good delivery,
they may all cast their caps at him.

Wife. And so they may i'faith, for I dare speak it boldly, the
twelve companies of London cannot match him, timber for
timber. Well, George, an' he be not inveigled by some of these
paltry players, I ha' much marvel : but, George, we ha' done our
parts, if the boy have any grace to be thankful.

Cit. Yes, I warrant you, duckling.

Enter HUMPHREY *and* LUCE.

Hum. Good Mistress Luce, however I in fault am
For your lame horse, you're welcome unto Waltham !
But which way now to go, or what to say
I know not truly, till it be broad day.

Luce. O fear not, Master Humphrey, I am guide
For this place good enough.

Hum.   Then up and ride,
Or if it please you, walk for your repose,
Or sit, or if you will, go pluck a rose :
Either of which shall be indifferent
To your good friend and Humphrey, whose consent
Is so entangled ever to your will,
As the poor harmless horse is to the mill.

Luce. Faith and you say the word, we'll e'en sit down,
And take a nap.

Hum.   'Tis better in the town,
Where we may nap together; for believe me,
To sleep without a match would mickle grieve me.

Luce. You're merry, Master Humphrey.

Hum.   So I am,
And have been ever merry from my dam.

Luce. Your nurse had the less labour.

Hum.   Faith it may be,
Unless it were by chance I did bewray me.

Enter JASPER.

Jasp. Luce, dear friend Luce.

Luce.   Here, Jasper.

D 2

Jasp.   You are mine.
Hum. If it be so, my friend, you use me fine :
What do you think I am?
    Jasp.   An arrant noddy.
Hum. A word of obloquy ; now by my body,
I'll tell thy master, for I know thee well.
    Jasp. Nay, an' you be so forward for to tell,
Take that, and that, and tell him, sir, I gave it :   [*Beats him.*
And say I paid you well.
    Hum.   O, sir, I have it,
And do confess the payment, pray be quiet.
    Jasp. Go, get you to your night-cap and the diet,
To cure your beaten bones.
    Luce.   Alas, poor Humphrey,
Get thee some wholesome broth with sage and cumfry :
A little oil of roses, and a feather
To 'noint thy back withal.
    Hum.   When I came hither,
Would I had gone to Paris with John Dory.
    Luce. Farewell, my pretty numps, I'm very sorry
I cannot bear thee company.
    Hum.   Farewell,
The devil's dam was ne'er so bang'd in hell.   [*Exeunt.*

Manet HUMPHREY.

Wife. This young Jasper will prove me another things, a my
conscience, and he may be suffered ; George, dost not see,
George, how a swaggers, and flies at the very heads a folks as
he were a dragon ; well, if I do not do his lesson for wronging
the poor gentleman, I am no true woman ; his friends that
brought him up might have been better occupied, I wis, than
have taught him these fegaries : he's e'en in the highway to the
gallows, God bless him.
    Cit. You're too bitter, cony, the young man may do well
enough for all this.
    Wife. Come hither, Master Humphrey, has he hurt you ?
Now beshrew his fingers for't ; here, sweetheart, here's some
green ginger for thee, now beshrew my heart, but a has pepper-
nel in's head, as big as a pullet's egg ; alas, sweet lamb, how
thy temples beat ; take the peace on him, sweetheart, take the
peace on him.

Enter a BOY.

    Cit. No, no, you talk like a foolish woman ; I'll ha' Ralph
fight with him, and swinge him up well-favour'dly. Sirrah boy,
come hither, let Ralph come in and fight with Jasper.

Wife. Ay, and beat him well, he's an unhappy boy.

Boy. Sir, you must pardon us, the plot of our play lies contrary, and 'twill hazard the spoiling of our play.

Cit. Plot me no plots, I'll ha' Ralph come out; I'll make your house too hot for you else.

Boy. Why, sir, he shall; but if anything fall out of order, the gentlemen must pardon us.

Cit. Go your ways, goodman boy, I'll hold him a penny he shall have his belly full of fighting now. Ho, here comes Ralph; no more.

Enter RALPH, MISTRESS MERRY-THOUGHT, MICHAEL, SQUIRE, *and* DWARF.

Ralph. What knight is that, squire? Ask him if he keep
The passage bound by love of lady fair,
Or else but prickant.

Hum.   Sir, I am no knight,
But a poor gentleman, that this same night,
Had stolen from me, upon yonder green,
My lovely wife, and suffered (to be seen
Yet extant on my shoulders) such a greeting,
That whilst I live, I shall think of that meeting.

Wife. Ay, Ralph, he beat him unmercifully, Ralph, an' thou spar'st him, Ralph, I would thou wert hang'd.

Cit. No more, wife, no more.

Ralph. Where is the caitiff wretch hath done this deed?
Lady, your pardon, that I may proceed
Upon the quest of this injurious knight.
And thou, fair squire, repute me not the worse,
In leaving the great 'venture of the purse
And the rich casket, till some better leisure.

Enter JASPER *and* LUCE.

Hum. Here comes the broker hath purloined my treasure.

Ralph. Go, squire, and tell him I am here,
An errant knight at arms, to crave delivery
Of that fair lady to her own knight's arms.
If he deny, bid him take choice of ground,
And so defy him.

Squire.   From the knight that bears
The golden pestle, I defy thee, knight,
Unless thou make fair restitution
Of that bright lady.

Jasp.   Tell the knight that sent thee
He is an ass, and I will keep the wench,
And knock his head-piece.

Ralph. Knight, thou art but dead,
If thou recall not thy uncourteous terms.

Wife. Break his pate, Ralph ; break his pate, Ralph, soundly.

Jasp. Come, knight, I'm ready for you, now your pestle
                    [*Snatches away his pestle.*
Shall try what temper, sir, your mortar's of ;
With that he stood upright in his stirrups,
And gave the knight of the calves-skin such a knock,
That he forsook his horse, and down he fell,
And then he leaped upon him, and plucking off his helmet——

Hum. Nay, an' my noble knight be down so soon,
Though I can scarcely go, I needs must run——
                    [*Exit* HUMPHREY *and* RALPH.

Wife. Run, Ralph ; run, Ralph ; run for thy life, boy ; Jasper
comes, Jasper comes !

Jasp. Come, Luce, we must have other arms for you.
Humphrey and Golden Pestle, both adieu.   [*Exeunt.*

Wife. Sure the devil, God bless us, is in this springald ; why,
George, didst ever see such a fire-drake ?   I am afraid my boy's
miscarried ; if he be, though he were Master Merry-thought's
son a thousand times, if there be any law in England, I'll make
some of them smart for't.

Cit. No, no, I have found out the matter, sweetheart.   Jasper
is enchanted as sure as we are here, he is enchanted ; he could
no more have stood in Ralph's hands than I can stand in my
Lord Mayor's ; I'll have a ring to discover all enchantments,
and Ralph shall beat him yet.   Be no more vexed, for it shall
be so.

Enter RALPH, SQUIRE, DWARF, MISTRESS MERRY-THOUGHT,
        and MICHAEL.

Wife. Oh, husband, here's Ralph again ; stay, Ralph, let me
speak with thee ; how dost thou, Ralph ? Art thou not shrewdly
hurt ? The foul great lunges laid unmercifully on thee ! There's
some sugar-candy for thee ; proceed, thou shalt have another
bout with him.

Cit. If Ralph had him at the fencing-school, if he did not
make a puppy of him, and drive him up and down the school,
he should ne'er come in my shop more.

Mist. Mer. Truly, Master Knight of the Burning Pestle, I am
weary.

Mich. Indeed la mother, and I'm very hungry.

Ralph. Take comfort, gentle dame, and your fair squire.
For in this desert there must needs be placed
Many strong castles, held by courteous knights,
And till I bring you safe to one of those
I swear by this my order ne'er to leave you.

Wife. Well said, Ralph : George, Ralph was ever comfortable, was he not?

Cit. Yes, duck.

Wife. I shall ne'er forget him. When we had lost our child, you know it was strayed almost alone to Puddle Wharf, and the criers were abroad for it, and there it had drowned itself but for a sculler, Ralph was the most comfortablest to me : "Peace mistress," says he, "let it go, I'll get you another as good." Did he not, George ? Did he not say so?

Cit. Yes indeed did he, mouse.

Dwarf. I would we had a mess of pottage and a pot of drink, squire, and were going to bed.

Squire. Why, we are at Waltham town's end, and that's the Bell Inn.

Dwarf. Take courage, valiant knight, damsel, and squire,
I have discovered, not a stone's cast off,
An ancient castle held by the old knight
Of the most holy order of the Bell,
Who gives to all knights errant entertain ;
There plenty is of food, and all prepar'd
By the white hands of his own lady dear.
He hath three squires that welcome all his guests :
The first, high Chamberlino, who will see
Our beds prepared, and bring us snowy sheets ;
The second hight Tapstero, who will see
Our pots full filléd, and no froth therein ;
The third, a gentle squire Ostlero hight,
Who will our palfries slick with wisps of straw,
And in the manger put them oats enough,
And never grease their teeth with candle-snuff.

Wife. That same dwarf's a pretty boy, but the squire's a grout-nold.

Ralph. Knock at the gates, my squire, with stately lance.

Enter TAPSTER.

Tap. Who's there, you're welcome, gentlemen ; will you see a room ?

Dwarf. Right courteous and valiant Knight of the Burning Pestle, this is the squire Tapstero.

Ralph. Fair squire Tapstero, I a wandering knight,
Hight of the Burning Pestle, in the quest
Of this fair lady's casket and wrought purse,
Losing myself in this vast wilderness,
Am to this castle well by fortune brought,
Where hearing of the goodly entertain
Your knight of holy order of the Bell,

Gives to all damsels, and all errant knights,
I thought to knock, and now am bold to enter.

Tapst. An't please you see a chamber, you are very welcome.
[*Exeunt.*

Wife. George, I would have something done, and I cannot
tell what it is.

Cit. What is it, Nell?

Wife. Why, George, shall Ralph beat nobody again? Prithee,
sweetheart, let him.

Cit. So he shall, Nell, and if I join with him, we'll knock them
all.

Enter HUMPHREY *and* MERCHANT.

Wife. O George, here's Master Humphrey again now, that
lost Mistress Luce, and Mistress Luce's father. Master
Humphrey will do somebody's errand I warrant him.

Hum. Father, it's true in arms I ne'er shall clasp her,
For she is stol'n away by your man Jasper.

Wife. I thought he would tell him.

Mer. Unhappy that I am to lose my child:
Now I begin to think on Jasper's words,
Who oft hath urg'd to me thy foolishness;
Why didst thou let her go? thou lov'st her not,
That wouldst bring home thy life, and not bring her.

Hum. Father, forgive me, I shall tell you true,
Look on my shoulders, they are black and blue,
Whilst to and fro fair Luce and I were winding,
He came and basted me with a hedge binding.

Mer. Get men and horses straight, we will be there
Within this hour; you know the place again?

Hum. I know the place where he my loins did swaddle,
I'll get six horses, and to each a saddle.

Mer. Mean time I will go talk with Jasper's father. [*Exeunt.*

Wife. George, what wilt thou lay with me now, that Master
Humphrey has not Mistress Luce yet; speak, George, what wilt
thou lay with me?

Cit. No, Nell, I warrant thee, Jasper is at Puckeridge with
her by this.

Wife. Nay, George, you must consider Mistress Luce's feet
are tender, and besides, 'tis dark, and I promise you truly, I do
not see how he should get out of Waltham Forest with her
yet.

Cit. Nay, honey, what wilt thou lay with me that Ralph has
her not yet?

Wife. I will not lay against Ralph, honny, because I have
not spoken with him: but look, George, peace, here comes the
merry old gentleman again.

Enter OLD MERRY-THOUGHT.

Old Mer. "When it was grown to dark midnight,
    And all were fast asleep,
    In came Margaret's grimly ghost,
    And stood at William's feet."
I have money, and meat, and drink beforehand, till to-morrow at noon, why should I be sad? Methinks I have half a
dozen jovial spirits within me, "I am three merry men, and three
merry men." To what end should any man be sad in this world?
Give me a man that when he goes to hanging cries "Troul the
black bowl to me;" and a woman that will sing a catch in her
travail. I have seen a man come by my door with a serious
face, in a black cloak, without a hatband, carrying his head as
if he look'd for pins in the street. I have look'd out of my
window half a year after, and have spied that man's head upon
London Bridge. 'Tis vile! Never trust a tailor that does not
sing at his work, his mind is of nothing but filching.

Wife. Mark this, George, 'tis worth noting: Godfrey, my
tailor, you know, never sings, and he had fourteen yards to make
this gown: and I'll be sworn, Mistress Penistone, the draper's
wife, had one made with twelve.

Old Mer. "'Tis mirth that fills the veins with blood,
    More than wine; or sleep, or food,
    Let each man keep his heart at ease,
    No man dies of that disease!
    He that would his body keep
    From diseases, must not weep,
    But whoever laughs and sings,
    Never he his body brings
    Into fevers, gouts, or rhumes,
    Or lingringly his lungs consumes;
    Or meets with aches in the bone,
    Or catarrhs, or griping stone:
    But contented lives by aye,
    The more he laughs, the more he may."

Wife. Look, George. How say'st thou by this, George? Is't
not a fine old man? Now God's blessing a thy sweet lips.
When wilt thou be so merry, George? Faith, thou art the
frowningst little thing, when thou art angry, in a country.

Enter MERCHANT.

Cit. Peace, coney; thou shalt see him took down too, I
warrant thee. Here's Luce's father come now.

Old Mer. "As you came from Walsingham,
    From the Holy Land,

There met you not with my true love
By the way as you came?"

Merch. Oh, Master Merry-thought! my daughter's gone!
This mirth becomes you not, my daughter's gone!

Old Mer. "Why an' if she be, what care-I?
Or let her come, or go, or tarry."

Merch. Mock not my misery, it is your son
(Whom I have made my own, when all forsook him),
Has stol'n my only joy, my child, away.

Old Mer. "He set her on a milk-white steed,
And himself upon a gray,
He never turned his face again,
But he bore her quite away."

Merch. Unworthy of the kindness I have shown
To thee and thine; too late, I well perceive
Thou art consenting to my daughter's loss.

Old Mer. Your daughter? what a stir's here wi' y'r daughter?
Let her go, think no more on her, but sing loud. If both my
sons were on the gallows I would sing,

"Down, down, down: they fall
Down, and arise they never shall."

Merch. Oh, might but I behold her once again,
And she once more embrace her aged sire.

Old Mer. Fie, how scurvily this goes:
"And she once more embrace her aged sire?"
You'll make a dog on her, will ye; she cares much for her aged
sire, I warrant you.

"She cares not for her daddy, nor
She cares not for her mammy,
For she is, she is, she is my
Lord of Low-gaves lassie."

Merch. For this thy scorn I will pursue
That son of thine to death.

Old Merch. Do, and when you ha' killed him,
"Give him flowers enow, Palmer, give him flowers enow,
Give him red and white, blue, green, and yellow."

Merch. I'll fetch my daughter.

Old Mer. I'll hear no more o' your daughter, it spoils my
mirth.

Merch. I say I'll fetch my daughter.

Old Mer. "Was never man for lady's sake, down, down,
Tormented as I, Sir Guy? de derry down,
For Lucy's sake, that lady bright, down, down,
As ever man beheld with eye? de derry down."

Merch. I'll be revenged, by heaven!   [*Exeunt.*

Finis Actus Secundi. [*Music.*

Wife. How dost thou like this, George?

Cit. Why this is well, dovey; but if Ralph were hot once, thou shouldst see more.

Wife. The fiddlers go again, husband.

Cit. Ay, Nell, but this is scurvy music; I gave the young gallows money, and I think he has not got me the waits of Southwark. If I hear 'em not anon, I'll twing him by the ears. You musicians, play Baloo.

Wife. No, good George, let's have Lachrymæ.

Cit. Why this is it, bird.

Wife. Is't? All the better, George; now, sweet lamb, what story is that painted upon the cloth? the Confutation of Saint Paul?

Cit. No, lamb, that's Ralph and Lucrece.

Wife. Ralph and Lucrece? Which Ralph? our Ralph?

Cit. No, mouse, that was a Tartarian.

Wife. A Tartarian? well, I would the fiddlers had done, that we might see our Ralph again.

ACT III.—SCENE I.

Enter JASPER *and* LUCE.

Jasp. Come, my dear dear, though we have lost our way
We have not lost ourselves. Are you not weary
With this night's wand'ring, broken from your rest?
And frighted with the terror that attends
The darkness of this wild unpeopled place?

Luce. No, my best friend, I cannot either fear
Or entertain a weary thought, whilst you
(The end of all my full desires) stand by me.
Let them that lose their hopes, and live to languish
Amongst the number of forsaken lovers,
Tell the long weary steps and number Time,
Start at a shadow, and shrink up their blood,
Whilst I (possessed with all content and quiet)
Thus take my pretty love, and thus embrace him.

Jasp. You've caught me, Luce, so fast, that whilst I live
I shall become your faithful prisoner,
And wear these chains for ever. Come, sit down,
And rest your body, too too delicate
For these disturbances; so, will you sleep?
Come, do not be more able than you are,
I know you are not skilful in these watches,
For women are no soldiers; be not nice,
But take it, sleep, I say.

Luce.   I cannot sleep,
Indeed I cannot, friend.
  Jasp.   .Why then we'll sing,
And try how that will work upon our senses.
  Luce. I'll sing, or say, or anything but sleep.
  Jasp. Come, little mermaid, rob me of my heart
With that enchanting voice.
  Luce. You mock me, Jasper.

SONG.

Jasp. Tell me, dearest, what is love?
Luce. 'Tis a lightning from above,
          'Tis an arrow, 'tis a fire,
          'Tis a boy they call Desire.
            'Tis a smile
            Doth beguile
Jasp. The poor hearts of men that prove.
          Tell me more, are women true?
Luce. Some love change, and so do you.
Jasp.   Are they fair, and never kind?
Luce.   Yes, when men turn with the wind.
Jasp. Are they froward?
Luce. Ever toward
          Those that love, to love anew.

  Jasp. Dissemble it no more, I see the god
Of heavy sleep, lays on his heavy mace
Upon your eyelids.
  Luce.   I am very heavy.
  Jasp. Sleep, sleep, and quiet rest crown thy sweet thoughts :
Keep from her fair blood all distempers, startings,
Horrors and fearful shapes : let all her dreams
Be joys and chaste delights, embraces, wishes,
And such new pleasures as the ravish'd soul
Gives to the senses. So, my charms have took.
Keep her, ye Powers Divine, whilst I contemplate
Upon the wealth and beauty of her mind.
She's only fair, and constant, only kind,
And only to thee, Jasper. O my joys !
Whither will you transport me ? let not fulness
Of my poor buried hopes come up together,
And over-charge my spirits ; I am weak.
Some say (however ill) the sea and women
Are govern'd by the moon, both ebb and flow,
Both full of changes : yet to them that know,
And truly judge, these but opinions are,
And heresies to bring on pleasing war
Between our tempers, that without these were
Both void of after-love, and present fear ;

Which are the best of Cupid.   O thou child !
Bred from despair, I dare not entertain thee,
Having a love without the faults of women,
And greater in her perfect goods than men ;
Which to make good, and please myself the stronger,
Though certainly I'm certain of her love,
I'll try her, that the world and memory
May sing to after-times her constancy.
Luce, Luce, awake !
    Luce.   Why do you fright me, friend,
With those distempered looks ? what makes your sword
Drawn in your hand ? who hath offended you ?
I prithee, Jasper, sleep, thou'rt wild with watching.
    Jasp. Come, make your way to Heav'n, and bid the world,
With all the villanies that stick upon it,
Farewell ; you're for another life.
    Luce.   Oh, Jasper,
How have my tender years committed evil,
Especially against the man I love,
Thus to be cropt untimely ?
    Jasp.   Foolish girl,
Canst thou imagine I could love his daughter
That flung me from my fortune into nothing ?
Dischargéd me his service, shut the doors
Upon my poverty, and scorn'd my prayers,
Sending me, like a boat without a mast,
To sink or swim ? Come, by this hand you die,
I must have life and blood, to satisfy
Your father's wrongs.
    Wife. Away, George, away, raise the watch at Ludgate, and
bring a mittimus from the justice for this desperate villain.
Now, I charge you, gentlemen, see the King's peace kept. O
my heart, what a varlet's this, to offer manslaughter upon the
harmless gentlewoman ?
    Cit. I warrant thee, sweetheart, we'll have him hampered.
    Luce. Oh, Jasper ! be not cruel,
If thou wilt kill me, smile, and do it quickly,
And let not many deaths appear before me.
I am a woman made of fear and love,
A weak, weak woman, kill not with thy eyes,
They shoot me through and through.   Strike, I am ready,
And dying, still I love thee.

    Enter MERCHANT, HUMPHREY, *and his* MEN.

Merch. Where abouts ?
Jasp. No more of this, now to myself again.
Hum. There, there he stands with sword, like martial knight,

Drawn in his hand, therefore beware the fight
You that are wise; for were I good Sir Bevis,
I would not stay his coming, by your leaves.

Merch. Sirrah, restore my daughter.

Jasp. Sirrah, no.

Merch. Upon him then.

Wife. So, down with him, down with him, down with him!
Cut him i'the leg, boys, cut him i'the leg!

Merch. Come your ways, minion, I'll provide a cage for you,
you're grown so tame. Horse her away.

Hum. Truly I am glad your forces have the day. [*Exeunt.*

Manet JASPER.

Jasp. They're gone, and I am hurt; my love is lost,
Never to get again. Oh, me unhappy!
Bleed, bleed and die—— I cannot; oh, my folly!
Thou hast betrayed me; hope, where art thou fled?
Tell me, if thou be'st anywhere remaining.
Shall I but see my love again? Oh, no!
She will not deign to look upon her butcher,
Nor is it fit she should; yet I must venture.
Oh chance, or fortune, or whate'er thou art
That men adore for powerful, hear my cry,
And let me loving live, or losing die. [*Exit.*

Wife. Is he gone, George?

Cit. Ay, coney.

Wife. Marry, and let him go, sweetheart, by the faith a my
body, a has put me into such a fright, that I tremble (as they
say) as 'twere an aspin leaf. Look a my little finger, George,
how it shakes: now, in truth, every member of my body is the
worse for't.

Cit. Come, hug in mine arms, sweet mouse, he shall not
fright thee any more; alas, mine own dear heart, how it quivers.

Enter MISTRESS MERRY-THOUGHT, RALPH, MICHAEL, SQUIRE,
DWARF, HOST, *and a* TAPSTER.

Wife. O Ralph, how dost thou, Ralph? How hast thou slept
to-night? Has the knight used thee well?

Cit. Peace, Nell, let Ralph alone.

Tap. Master, the reckoning is not paid.

Ralph. Right courteous Knight, who for the orders' sake
Which thou hast ta'en, hang'st out the holy Bell,
As I this flaming pestle bear about,
We render thanks to your puissant self,
Your beauteous lady, and your gentle squires,
For thus refreshing of our wearied limbs,
Stiffened with hard achievements in wild desert,

Tap. Sir, there is twelve shillings to pay.

Ralph. Thou merry squire Tapstero, thanks to thee
For comforting our souls with double jug,
And if adventurous fortune prick thee forth,
Thou jovial squire, to follow feats of arms,
Take heed thou tender ev'ry lady's cause,
Ev'ry true knight, and ev'ry damsel fair,
But spill the blood of treacherous Saracens,
And false enchanters, that with magic spells
Have done to death full many a noble knight.

Host. Thou valiant Knight of the Burning Pestle, give ear to
me : there is twelve shillings to pay, and as I am a true knight,
I will not bate a penny.

Wife. George, I prithee tell me, must Ralph pay twelve
shillings now?

Cit. No, Nell, no, nothing ; but the old knight is merry with
Ralph.

Wife. O, is't nothing else? Ralph will be as merry as he.

Ralph. Sir Knight, this mirth of yours becomes you well,
But to requite this liberal courtesy,
If any of your squires will follow arms,
He shall receive from my heroic hand
A knighthood, by the virtue of this pestle.

Host. Fair knight, I thank you for your noble offer ; therefore, gentle knight, twelve shillings you must pay, or I must
cap you.

Wife. Look, George, did not I tell thee as much? The
knight of the Bell is in earnest. Ralph shall not be beholding
to him ; give him his money, George, and let him go snick-up.

Cit. Cap Ralph? No ; hold your hand, Sir Knight of the Bell,
there's your money. Have you anything to say to Ralph now?
Cap Ralph?

Wife. I would you should know it, Ralph has friends that
will not suffer him to be capt for ten times so much, and ten
times to the end of that. Now take thy course, Ralph.

Mist. Mer. Come, Michael, thou and I will go home to thy
father, he hath enough left to keep us a day or two, and we'll set
fellows abroad to cry our purse and casket. Shall we, Michael?

Mich. Ay, I pray mother, in truth my feet are full of chilblains with travelling.

Wife. Faith and those chilblains are a foul trouble. Mistress
Merry-thought, when your youth comes home let him rub all the
soles of his feet and his heels and his ankles with a mouse-skin ;
or if none of you can catch a mouse, when he goes to bed let
him roll his feet in the warm embers, and I warrant you he shall
be well, and you may make him put his fingers between his toes
and smell to them, it's very sovereign for his head if he be
costive.

Mist. Mer. Master Knight of the Burning Pestle, my son
Michael and I bid you farewell; I thank your worship heartily
for your kindness.

Ralph. Farewell, fair lady, and your tender squire.
If pricking through these deserts, I do hear
Of any trait'rous knight, who, through his guile
Hath light upon your casket and your purse,
I will despoil him of them and restore them.

Mist. Mer. I thank your worship.   [*Exit with* MICHAEL.

Ralph. Dwarf, bear my shield; squire, elevate my lance,
And now farewell, you knight of holy Bell.

Cit. Ay, ay, Ralph, all is paid.

Ralph. But yet before I go, speak, worthy knight,
If aught you do of sad adventures know,
Where errant knight may through his prowess win
Eternal fame, and free some gentle souls
From endless bonds of steel and lingring pain.

Host. Sirrah, go to Nick the Barber, and bid him prepare
himself, as I told you before, quickly.

Tap. I am gone, sir.   [*Exit* TAPSTER.

Host. Sir Knight, this wilderness affordeth none
But the great venture, where full many a knight
Hath tried his prowess, and come off with shame,
And where I would not have you lose your life,
Against no man, but furious fiend of hell.

Ralph. Speak on, Sir Knight, tell what he is, and where:
For here I vow upon my blazing badge,
Never to lose a day in quietness;
But bread and water will I only eat,
And the green herb and rock shall be my couch,
Till I have quell'd that man, or beast, or fiend,
That works such damage to all errant knights.

Host. Not far from hence, near to a craggy cliff
At the north end of this distressèd town,
There doth stand a lowly house
Ruggedly builded, and in it a cave,
In which an ugly giant now doth dwell,
Yclepèd Barbaroso: in his hand
He shakes a naked lance of purest steel,
With sleeves turned up, and he before him wears
A motley garment, to preserve his clothes
From blood of those knights which he massacres,
And ladies gent: without his door doth hang
A copper bason, on a prickant spear;
At which, no sooner gentle knights can knock,
But the shrill sound fierce Barbaroso hears,
And rushing forth, brings in the errant knight,
And sets him down in an enchanted chair:

Then with an engine, which he hath prepar'd
With forty teeth, he claws his courtly crown,
Next makes him wink, and underneath his chin
He plants a brazen piece of mighty bore,
And knocks his bullets round about his cheeks,
Whilst with his fingers, and an instrument
With which he snaps his hair off, he doth fill
The wretch's ears with a most hideous noise.
Thus every knight adventurer he doth trim,
And now no creature dares encounter him.

Ralph. In God's name, I will fight with him, kind sir.
Go but before me to this dismal cave
Where this huge giant Barbaroso dwells, ,
And by that virtue that brave Rosiclere,
That wicked brood of ugly giants slew,
And Palmerin Frannarco overthrew :
I doubt not but to curb this traitor foul,
And to the devil send his guilty soul.

Host. Brave sprighted knight, thus far I will perform
This your request, I'll bring you within sight
Of this most loathsome place, inhabited
By a more loathsome man : but dare not stay,
For his main force swoops all he sees away.   - .

Ralph. Saint George ! set on, before march squire and page.
                                               [*Exeunt.*

Wife. George, dost think Ralph will confound the giant ?

Cit. I hold my cap to a farthing he does. Why, Nell, I saw
him wrestle with the great Dutchman, and hurl him.

Wife. Faith and that Dutchman was a goodly man, if all things
were answerable to his bigness. And yet they say there was a
Scottishman higher than he, and that they two on a night met,
and saw one another for nothing.

Cit. Nay, by your leave, Nell, Ninivie was better.

Wife. Ninivie, O that was the story of Joan and the
Wall, was it not, George ?

Cit. Yes, lamb.

Enter MISTRESS MERRY-THOUGHT.

Wife. Look, George, here comes Mistress Merry-thought
again, and I would have Ralph come and fight with the giant.
I tell you true, I long to see't.

Cit. Good Mistress Merry-thought, be gone, I pray you for
my sake ; I pray you forbear a little, you shall have audience
presently : I have a little business.

Wife. Mistress Merry-thought, if it please you to refrain your passion a little, till Ralph have dispatched the giant out of the way, we shall think ourselves much bound to thank you. I thank you, good Mistress Merry-thought.

                [*Exit* MISTRESS MERRY-THOUGHT.

Enter a BOY.

Cit. Boy, come hither, send away Ralph and this master giant quickly.

Boy. In good faith, sir, we cannot; you'll utterly spoil our play, and make it to be hissed, and it cost money; you will not suffer us to go on with our plots. I pray, gentlemen, rule him.

Cit. Let him come now and dispatch this, and I'll trouble you no more.

Boy. Will you give me your hand of that?

Wife. Give him thy hand, George, do, and I'll kiss him; I warrant thee the youth means plainly.

Boy. I'll send him to you presentiy.   [*Exit* BOY.

Wife. I thank you, little youth; faith the child hath a sweet breath, George, but I think it be troubled with the worms; Carduus Benedictus and mare's milk were the only thing in the world for it. Oh, Ralph's here, George! God send thee good luck, Ralph!

Enter RALPH, HOST, SQUIRE *and* DWARF.

Host. Puissant knight, yonder his mansion is,
Lo, where the spear and copper bason are,
Behold the string on which hangs many a tooth,
Drawn from the gentle jaw of wandering knights;
I dare not stay to sound, he will appear.   [*Exit* HOST.

Ralph. O faint not, heart: Susan, my lady dear,
The cobbler's maid in Milk Street, for whose sake
I take these arms, O let the thought of thee
Carry thy knight through all adventurous deed,
And in the honour of thy beauteous self,
May I destroy this monster Barbaroso.
Knock, squire, upon the bason till it break
With the shrill strokes, or till the giant speak.

Enter BARBAROSO.

Wife. O George, the giant, the giant! Now, Ralph, for thy life!

Bar. What fond unknowing wight is this, that dares
So rudely knock at Barbaroso's cell,
Where no man comes, but leaves his fleece behind?

Ralph. I, traitorous caitiff, who am sent by fate
To punish all the sad enormities
Thou hast committed against ladies gent,
And errant knights, traitor to God and men.
Prepare thyself, this is the dismal hour
Appointed for thee to give strict account
Of all thy beastly treacherous villanies.

Bar. Foolhardy knight, full soon thou shalt aby
This fond reproach, thy body will I bang,

        [*He takes down his pole.*
And lo, upon that string thy teeth shall hang ;
Prepare thyself, for dead soon shalt thou be.

Ralph. Saint George for me !   [*They fight.*

Bar. Gargantua for me !

Wife. To him, Ralph, to him : hold up the giant, set out thy leg before, Ralph !

Cit. Falsify a blow, Ralph, falsify a blow ; the giant lies open on the left side.

Wife. Bear't off, bear't off still ; there, boy. Oh, Ralph's almost down, Ralph's almost down !

Ralph. Susan, inspire me, now have up again.

Wife. Up, up, up, up, up, so, Ralph ; down with him, down with him, Ralph !

Cit. Fetch him over the hip, boy.

Wife. There, boy ; kill, kill, kill, kill, kill, Ralph !

Cit. No, Ralph, get all out of him first.

Ralph. Presumptuous man, see to what desperate end
Thy treachery hath brought thee ; the just gods,
Who never prosper those that do despise them,
For all the villanies which thou hast done
To knights and ladies, now have paid thee home
By my stiff arm, a knight adventurous.
But say, vile wretch, before I send thy soul
To sad Avernus, whither it must go,
What captives hold'st thou in thy sable cave ?

Bar. Go in and free them all, thou hast the day.

Ralph. Go, squire and dwarf, search in this dreadful cave,
And free the wretched prisoners from their bonds.

       [*Exeunt* SQUIRE *and* DWARF.

Bar. I crave for mercy as thou art a knight,
And scorn'st to spill the blood of those that beg.

Ralph. Thou showest no mercy, nor shalt thou have any ;
Prepare thyself, for thou shalt surely die.

  Enter SQUIRE, *leading one winking, with a bason
     under his chin.*

Squire. Behold, brave knight, here is one prisoner,
Whom this wild man hath used as you see

Wife. This is the wisest word I hear the squire speak.

Ralph. Speak what thou art, and how thou hast been us'd,
That I may give him condign punishment.

1st Knight. I am a knight that took my journey post
Northward from London, and in courteous wise,
This giant train'd me to his loathsome den,
Under pretence of killing of the itch,
And all my body with a powder strew'd,
That smarts and stings ; and cut away my beard,
And my curl'd locks wherein were ribands ty'd,
And with a water washt my tender eyes
(Whilst up and down about me still he skipt),
Whose virtue is, that till my eyes be wip'd
With a dry cloth, for this my foul disgrace,
I shall not dare to look a dog i' th' face.

Wife. Alas, poor knight. Relieve him, Ralph ; relieve poor
knights whilst you live.

Ralph. My trusty squire, convey him to the town,
Where he may find relief ; adieu, fair knight.   [*Exit* KNIGHT.

Enter DWARF, *leading one with a patch over his nose.*

Dwarf. Puissant Knight of the Burning Pestle hight,
See here another wretch, whom this foul beast
Hath scotch'd and scor'd in this inhuman wise.

Ralph. Speak me thy name, and eke thy place of birth,
And what hath been thy usage in this cave.

2nd Knight. I am a knight, Sir Partle is my name,
And by my birth I am a Londoner,
Free by my copy, but my ancestors
Were Frenchmen all ; and riding hard this way,
Upon a trotting horse, my bones did ache,
And I, faint knight, to ease my weary limbs,
Light at this cave, when straight this furious fiend,
With sharpest instrument of purest steel,
Did cut the gristle of my nose away,
And in the place this velvet plaster stands.
Relieve me, gentle knight, out of his hands.

Wife. Good Ralph, relieve Sir Partle, and send him away,
for in truth his breath stinks.

Ralph. Convey him straight after the other knight. Sir
Partle, fare you well.

3rd Knight. Kind sir, good night.   [*Exit.*
                                      [*Cries within.*

Man. Deliver us !

Wom. Deliver us !

Wife. Hark, George, what a woful cry there is. I think some
one is ill there.

Man. Deliver us !
Wom. Deliver us !
Ralph. What ghastly noise is this ? Speak, Barbaroso,
Or by this blazing steel thy head goes off.
Bar. Prisoners of mine, whom I in diet keep.
Send lower down into the cave,
And in a tub that's heated smoking hot,
There may they find them, and deliver them.
Ralph. Run, squire and dwarf, deliver them with speed.
[*Exeunt* SQUIRE *and* DWARF.
Wife. But will not Ralph kill this giant ? Surely I am afraid if
he let him go he will do as much hurt as ever he did.
Cit. Not so, mouse, neither, if he could convert him.
Wife. Ay, George, if he could convert him; but a giant is not
so soon converted as one of us ordinary people. There's a
pretty tale of a witch, that had the devil's mark about her, God
bless us, that had a giant to her son, that was call'd Lob-lie-by-
the-fire. Didst never hear it, George ?

Enter SQUIRE *leading a man with a glass of lotion in his hand,
and the* DWARF *leading a woman, with diet bread and drink.*

Cit. Peace, Nell, here come the prisoners.
Dwarf. Here be these pined wretches, manful knight,
That for these six weeks have not seen a wight.
Ralph. Deliver what you are, and how you came
To this sad cave, and what your usage was ?
Man. I am an errant knight that followed arms,
With spear and shield, and in my tender years
I strucken was with Cupid's fiery shaft,
And fell in love with this my lady dear,
And stole her from her friends in Turnball Street,
And bore her up and down from town to town,
Where we did eat and drink, and music hear ;
Till at the length at this unhappy town
We did arrive, and coming to this cave,
This beast us caught, and put us in a tub,
Where we this two months sweat, and should have done
Another month if you had not relieved us.
Wom. This bread and water hath our diet been,
Together with a rib cut from a neck
Of burned mutton ; hard hath been our fare.
Release us from this ugly giant's snare.
Man. This hath been all the food we have receiv'd ;
But only twice a day, for novelty,
He gave a spoonful of this hearty broth   [*Pulls out a syringe.*
To each of us, through this same slender quill.
Ralph. From this infernal monster you shall go,

That useth knights and gentle ladies so.
Convey them hence.   [*Exeunt Man and Woman.*
   Cit. Mouse, I can tell thee, the gentlemen like Ralph.
   Wife. Ay, George, I see it well enough. Gentlemen, I thank
you all heartily for gracing my man Ralph, and I promise you,
you shall see him oftener.
   Bar. Mercy, great knight, I do recant my ill,
And henceforth never gentle blood will spill.
   Ralph. I give thee mercy, but yet thou shalt swear
Upon my burning pestle to perform
Thy promise utter'd.
   Bar. I swear and kiss.
   Ralph. Depart then, and amend.
Come, squire and dwarf, the sun grows towards his set,
And we have many more adventures yet.   [*Exeunt.*
   Cit. Now Ralph is in this humour, I know he would ha' beaten
all the boys in the house, if they had been set on him.
   Wife. Ay, George, but it is well as it is. I warrant you the
gentlemen do consider what it is to overthrow a giant. But look,
George, here comes Mistress Merry-thought, and her son
Michael. Now you are welcome, Mistress Merry-thought; now
Ralph has done, you may go on.

Enter MISTRESS MERRY-THOUGHT *and* MICHAEL.

   Mist. Mer. Mick, my boy.
   Mick. Ay forsooth, mother.
   Mist. Mer. Be merry, Mick, we are at home now, where I
warrant you, you shall find the house flung out of the windows.
Hark! hey dogs, hey, this is the old world i'faith with my
husband. I'll get in among them, I'll play them such lesson,
that they shall have little list to come scraping hither again.
Why, Master Merry-thought, husband, Charles Merry-thought!
   Old Mer. [within]. " If you will sing and dance and laugh,
          And holloa, and laugh again ;
          And then cry, there boys, there ; why then,
          One, two, three, and four,
          We shall be merry within this hour."
   Mist. Mer. Why, Charles, do you not know your own natural
wife ? I say, open the door, and turn me out those mangy companions ; 'tis more than time that they were fellow like with
you. You are a gentleman, Charles, and an old man, and father
of two children ; and I myself, though I say it, by my mother's
side, niece to a worshipful gentleman, and a conductor ; he has
been three times in his Majesty's service at Chester, and is
now the fourth time, God bless him, and his charge upon his
journey,

Old Mer. " Go from my window, love, go ;
  Go from my window, my dear,
 The wind and the rain will drive you back again,
  You cannot be lodgéd here."
Hark you, Mistress Merry-thought, you that walk upon ad-
ventures, and forsake your husband because he sings with never
a penny in his purse; what, shall I think myself the worse?
Faith no, I'll be merry. You come not here, here's none but
lads of mettle, lives of a hundred years and upwards ; care never
drunk their bloods, nor want made them warble,
  " Heigh-ho, my heart is heavy."
 Mist. Mer. Why, Master Merry-thought, what am I that you
should laugh me to scorn thus abruptly ? Am I not your fellow-
feeler, as we may say, in all our miseries? your comforter in
health and sickness? Have I not brought you children? Are
they not like you, Charles ? Look upon thine own image, hard-
hearted man ; and yet for all this——
 Old Mer. [within]. " Begone, begone, my juggy, my puggy,
  Begone, my love, my dear ;
  The weather is warm,
  'Twill do thee no harm,
  Thou canst not be lodged here."
Be merry, boys, some light music, and more wine.
 Wife. He's not in earnest, I hope, George, is he ?
 Cit. What if he be, sweetheart ?
 Wife. Marry if he be, George, I'll make bold to tell him he's
an ingrant old man to use his wife so scurvily.
 Cit. What, how does he use her, honey ?
 Wife. Marry come up, Sir Sauce-box ; I think you'll take his
part, will you not ? Lord, how hot are you grown ; you are a
fine man, an' you had a fine dog, it becomes you sweetly.
 Cit. Nay, prithee Nell, chide not ; for as I am an honest
man, and a true Christian grocer, I do not like his doings.
 Wife. I cry you mercy then, George ; you know we are all
frail, and full of infirmities. D'ye hear, Master Merry-thought,
may I crave a word with you ?
 Old Mer. [within]. Strike up lively, lads.
 Wife. I had not thought in truth, Master Merry-thought,
that a man of your age and discretion, as I may say, being a
gentleman, and therefore known by your gentle conditions, could
have used so little respect to the weakness of his wife ; for your
wife is your own flesh, the staff of your age, your yoke-fellow,
with whose help you draw through the mire of this transitory
world. Nay, she is your own rib. And again——
 Old Mer. " I come not hither for thee to teach,
  I have no pulpit for thee to preach,
  As thou art a lady gay."
 Wife. Marry with a vengeance ! I am heartily sorry for the

poor gentlewoman; but if I were thy wife, i'faith, gray beard, i'faith——

Cit. I prithee, sweet honeysuckle, be content.

Wife. Give me such words that am a gentlewoman born, hang him, hoary rascal! Get me some drink, George, I am almost molten with fretting. Now beshrew his knave's heart for it.

Old Mer. Play me a light lavalto. Come, be frolic, fill the good fellows wine.

Mist. Mer. Why, Master Merry-thought, are you disposed to make me wait here. You'll open, I hope; I'll fetch them that shall open else.

Old Mer. Good woman, if you will sing, I'll give you something, if not——

SONG.

You are no love for me, Marget,
I am no love for you.
Come aloft, boys, aloft.

Mist. Mer. Now a churl's fist in your teeth, sir. Come, Mick, we'll not trouble him, a shall not ding us i' th' teeth with his bread and his broth, that he shall not. Come, boy, I'll provide for thee, I warrant thee. We'll go to Master Venterwels the merchant; I'll get his letter to mine host of the Bell in Waltham, there I'll place thee with the tapster; will not that do well for thee, Mick? And let me alone for that old rascally knave, your father; I'll use him in his kind, I warrant ye.

Wife. Come, George, where's the beer?

Cit. Here, love.

Wife. This old fumigating fellow will not out of my mind yet. Gentlemen, I'll begin to you all, I desire more of your acquaintance, with all my heart. Fill the gentlemen some beer, George.

ACT IV.—SCENE I.

Boy danceth.

Wife. Look, George, the little boy's come again; methinks he looks something like the Prince of Orange, in his long stocking, if he had a little harness about his neck. George, I will have him dance Fading; Fading is a fine jig, I'll assure you, gentlemen. Begin, brother; now a capers, sweetheart; now a turn a th' toe, and then tumble. Cannot you tumble, youth?

Boy. No, indeed, forsooth.
Wife. Nor eat fire ?
Boy. Neither.
Wife. Why, then I thank you heartily ; there's two pence to buy you points withal.

Enter JASPER *and* BOY.

Jasp. There, boy, deliver this.   But do it well.
Hast thou provided me four lusty fellows,
Able to carry me ?   And art thou perfect
In all thy business?
   Boy. Sir, you need not fear,
I have my lesson here, and cannot miss it :
The men are ready for you, and what else
Pertains to this employment.
   Jasp. There, my boy,
Take it, but buy no land.
   Boy. Faith, sir, 'twere rare
To see so young a purchaser.   I fly,
And on my wings carry your destiny.   [*Exit.*
   Jasp. Go, and be happy.   Now my latest hope
Forsake me not, but fling thy anchor out,
And let it hold.   Stand fixt, thou rolling stone,
Till I possess my dearest.   Hear me, all
You Powers, that rule in men, celestial.   [*Exit.*
   Wife. Go thy ways, thou art as crooked a sprig as ever grew in London.   I warrant him he'll come to some naughty end or other ; for his looks say no less.   Besides, his father (you know, George) is none of the best ; you heard him take me up like a gill flirt, and sing bad songs upon me.   But i'faith, if I live, George——
   Cit. Let me alone, sweetheart, I have a trick in my head shall lodge him in the Arches for one year, and make him sing Peccavi, ere I leave him, and yet he shall never know who hurt him neither.
   Wife. Do, my good George, do.
   Cit. What shall we have Ralph do now, boy?
   Boy. You shall have what you will, sir.
   Cit. Why so, sir, go and fetch me him then, and let the Sophy of Persia come and christen him a child.
   Boy. Believe me, sir, that will not do so well ; 'tis stale, it has been had before at the Red Bull.
   Wife. George, let Ralph travel over great hills, and let him be weary, and come to the King of Cracovia's house, covered with black velvet, and there let the king's daughter stand in her window all in beaten gold, combing her golden locks with a comb of ivory, and let her spy Ralph, and fall in love with him,

and come down to him, and carry him into her father's house, and then let Ralph talk with her.

Cit. Well said, Nell, it shall be so. Boy, let's ha't done quickly.

Boy. Sir, if you will imagine all this to be done already, you shall hear them talk together. But we cannot present a house covered with black velvet, and a lady in beaten gold.

Cit. Sir Boy, let's ha't as you can then.

Boy. Besides, it will show ill-favouredly to have a grocer's prentice to court a king's daughter.

Cit. Will it so, sir? You are well read in histories : I pray you what was Sir Dagonet? Was not he prentice to a grocer in London? Read the play of the "Four Prentices of London," where they toss their pikes so. I pray you fetch him in, sir ; fetch him in.

Boy. It shall be done, it is not our fault, gentlemen.   [*Exit.*

Wife. Now we shall see fine doings, I warrant thee, George. Oh, here they come ; how prettily the King of Cracovia's daughter is drest.

Enter RALPH *and the* LADY, SQUIRE *and* DWARF.

Cit. Ay, Nell, it is the fashion of that country, I warrant thee.

Lady. Welcome, Sir Knight, unto my father's court,
King of Moldavia, unto me Pompiona,
His daughter dear. But sure you do not like
Your entertainment, that will stay with us
No longer but a night.

Ralph.   Damsel right fair,
I am on many sad adventures bound,
That call me forth into the wilderness.
Besides, my horse's back is something gall'd,
Which will enforce me ride a sober pace.
But many thanks, fair lady, be to you,
For using errant knight with courtesy.

Lady. But say, brave knight, what is your name and birth?

Ralph. My name is Ralph. I am an Englishman,
As true as steel, a hearty Englishman,
And prentice to a grocer in the Strand,
By deed indent, of which I have one part :
But fortune calling me to follow arms,
On me this holy order I did take,
Of Burning Pestle, which in all men's eyes
I bear, confounding ladies' enemies.

Lady. Oft have I heard of your brave countrymen,
And fertile soil, and store of wholesome food ;
My father oft will tell me of a drink
In England found, and Nipitato call'd,
Which driveth all the sorrow from your hearts.

Ralph. Lady, 'tis true, you need not lay your lips
To better Nipitato than there is.

Lady. And of a wildfowl he will often speak,
Which powdered beef and mustard called is :
For there have been great wars 'twixt us and you ;
But truly, Ralph, it was not long of me.
Tell me then, Ralph, could you contented be
To wear a lady's favour in your shield?

Ralph. I am a knight of a religious order,
And will not wear a favour of a lady
That trusts in Antichrist, and false traditions.

Cit. Well said, Ralph, convert her if thou canst.

Ralph. Besides, I have a lady of my own
In merry England ; for whose virtuous sake
I took these arms, and Susan is her name,
A cobbler's maid in Milk Street, whom I vow
Ne'er to forsake, whilst life and pestle last.

Lady. Happy that cobbling dame, whoe'er she be,
That for her own (dear Ralph) hath gotten thee.
Unhappy I, that ne'er shall see the day
To see thee more, that bear'st my heart away.

Ralph. Lady, farewell ; I must needs take my leave.

Lady. Hard-hearted Ralph, that ladies dost deceive.

Cit. Hark thee, Ralph, there's money for thee ; give something in the King of Cracovia's house ; be not beholding to him.

Ralph. Lady, before I go, I must remember
Your father's officers, who, truth to tell,
Have been about me very diligent :
Hold up thy snowy hand, thou princely maid.
There's twelve pence for your father's chamberlain,
And there's another shilling for his cook,
For, by my troth, the goose was roasted well.
And twelve pence for your father's horse-keeper,
For 'nointing my horse back ; and for his butter,
There is another shilling; to the maid
That wash'd my boot-hose, there's an English groat,
And two pence to the boy that wip'd my boots.
And last, fair lady, there is for your self
Three pence to buy you pins at Bumbo Fair.

Lady. Full many thanks, and I will keep them safe
Till all the heads be off, for thy sake, Ralph.

Ralph. Advance, my squire and dwarf, I cannot stay.

Lady. Thou kill'st my heart in parting thus away.   [*Exeunt.*

Wife. I commend Ralph yet, that he will not stoop to a Cracovian ; there's properer women in London than any are there, I wis. But here comes Master Humphrey and his love again ; now, George.

Cit. Ay, bird, peace.

Enter MERCHANT, HUMPHREY, LUCE, *and* BOY.

Merch. Go, get you up, I will not be entreated.
And, gossip mine, I'll keep you sure hereafter
From gadding out again with boys and unthrifts ;
Come, they are women's tears, I know your fashion.
Go, sirrah, lock her in, and keep the key [*Exeunt* LUCE *and* BOY.
Safe as your life.   Now, my son Humphrey,
You may both rest assuréd of my love
In this, and reap your own desire.
    Humph. I see this love you speak of, through your daughter,
Although the hole be little, and hereafter
Will yield the like in all I may or can,
Fitting a Christian and a gentleman.
    Merch. I do believe you, my good son, and thank you,
For 'twere an impudence to think you flattered.
    Humph. It were indeed, but shall I tell you why,
I have been beaten twice about the lie.
    Merch. Well, son, no more of compliment ; my daughter
Is yours again : appoint the time and take her.
We'll have no stealing for it, I myself
And some few of our friends will see you married.
    Humph. I would you would i'faith, for be it known
I ever was afraid to lie alone.
    Merch. Some three days hence, then.
    Humph. Three days, let me see,
'Tis somewhat of the most, yet I agree,
Because I mean against the 'pointed day,
To visit all my friends in new array.

Enter SERVANT.

Serv. Sir, there's a gentlewoman without would speak with
your worship.
    Merch. What is she ?
    Serv. Sir, I asked her not.
    Merch. Bid her come in.

Enter MISTRESS MERRY-THOUGHT *and* MICHAEL.

Mist. Mer Peace be to your worship, I come as a poor suitor
to you, sir, in the behalf of this child.
    Merch. Are you not wife to Merry-thought ?
    Mist. Mer. Yes truly, would I had ne'er seen his eyes, he has
undone me and himself, and his children, and there he lives at
home and sings and hoits, and revels among his drunken com-

panions ; but I warrant you, where to get a penny to put bread
in his mouth, he knows not.   And therefore if it like your
worship, I would entreat your letter to the honest host of the
Bell in Waltham, that I may place my child under the protection
of his tapster, in some settled course of life.

Merch. I'm glad the Heav'ns have heard my prayers.   Thy
        husband,
When I was ripe in sorrows, laughed at me ;
Thy son, like an unthankful wretch, I having
Redeem'd him from his fall, and made him mine,
To show his love again, first stole my daughter :
Then wrong'd this gentleman, and last of all
Gave me that grief, had almost brought me down
Unto my grave, had not a stronger hand
Reliev'd my sorrows.   Go, and weep as I did,
And be unpitied, for here I profess
An everlasting hate to all thy name.

Mist. Mer. Will you so, sir, how say you by that ?   Come,
Mick, let him keep his wind to cool his pottage ; we'll go to thy
nurse's, Mick, she knits silk stockings, boy ; and we'll knit too,
boy, and be beholding to none of them all.
                              [*Exeunt* MICHAEL *and* MOTHER.

Enter a BOY *with a letter.*

Boy. Sir, I take it you are the master of this house.
Merch. How then, boy ?
Boy. Then to yourself, sir, comes this letter.
Merch. From whom, my pretty boy ? .
Boy. From him that was your servant, but no more
Shall that name ever be, for he is dead.
Grief of your purchas'd anger broke his heart ;
I saw him die, and from his hand receiv'd
This paper, with a charge to bring it hither ;
Read it, and satisfy yourself in all.

LETTER.

*Merch. Sir, that I have wronged your love I must confess, in
which I have purchas'd to myself, besides mine own undoing, the
ill opinion of my friends ; let not your anger, good sir, outlive
me, but suffer me to rest in peace with your forgiveness ; let my
body (if a dying man may so much prevail with you) be brought
to your daughter, that she may know my hot flames are now
buried, and withal receive a testimony of the zeal I bore her
virtue.   Farewell for ever, and be ever happy.*—JASPER.

God's hand is great in this, I do forgive him,
Yet am I glad he's quiet, where I hope

He will not bite again.   Boy, bring the body,
And let him have his will, if that be all.
  Boy. 'Tis here without, sir.
  Merch. So, sir, if you please
You may conduct it in, I do not fear it.
  Humph. I'll be your usher, boy, for though I say it,
He ow'd me something once, and well did pay it.   [*Exeunt.*

Enter LUCE *alone.*

  Luce. If there be any punishment inflicted
Upon the miserable, more than yet I feel,
Let it together seize me, and at once
Press down my soul ; I cannot bear the pain
·Of these delaying tortures.   Thou that art
The end of all, and the sweet rest of all,
Come, come, O Death, and bring me to thy peace,
And blot out all the memory I nourish
Both of my father and my cruel friend.
O wretched maid, still living to be wretched,
To be a say to Fortune in her changes,
And grow to number times and woes together.
How happy had I been, if being born
My grave had been my cradle ?

Enter SERVANT.

  Serv. By your leave,
Young mistress, here's a boy hath brought a coffin,
What a would say I know not ; but your father
Charg'd me to give you notice.   Here they come.

Enter two bearing a coffin, JASPER *in it.*

  Luce. For me I hope 'tis come, and 'tis most welcome.
  Boy. Fair mistress, let me not add greater grief
To that great store you have already ; Jasper
(That whilst he liv'd was yours, now's dead,
And here inclos'd) commanded me to bring
His body hither, and to crave a tear
From those fair eyes, though he deserv'd not pity,
To deck his funeral, for so he bid me
Tell her for whom he died.
  Luce. He shall have many.
              [*Exeunt* COFFIN-CARRIER *and* BOY.
Good friends, depart a little, whilst I take
My leave of this dead man, that once I lov'd :
Hold, yet a little, life, and then I give thee

To thy first Heav'nly Being. O my friend !
Hast thou deceiv'd me thus, and got before me ?
I shall not long be after, but believe me,
Thou wert too cruel, Jasper, 'gainst thyself,
In punishing the fault I could have pardon'd,
With so untimely death ; thou didst not wrong me,
But ever wert most kind, most true, most loving :
And I the most unkind, most false, most cruel.
Didst thou but ask a tear ? I'll give thee all,
Even all my eyes can pour down, all my sighs,
And all myself, before thou goest from me.
These are but sparing rites ; but if thy soul
Be yet about this place, and can behold
And see what I prepare to deck thee with,
It shall go up, borne on the wings of peace,
And satisfied. First will I sing thy dirge,
Then kiss thy pale lips, and then die, myself,
And fill one coffin, and one grave together.

SONG.

Come you whose loves are dead,
  And whilst I sing,
  Weep and wring
Every hand, and every head
Bind with cypress and sad yew ;
Ribbons black and candles blue,
For him that was of men most true.

Come with heavy moaning,
  And on his grave
  Let him have
Sacrifice of sighs and groaning ;
Let him have fair flowers enow,
White and purple, green and yellow,
For him that was of men most true.

Thou sable cloth, sad cover of my joys,
I lift thee up, and thus I meet with death.
  Jasp. And thus you meet the living.
  Luce. Save me, Heav'n !
  Jasp. Nay, do not fly me, fair, I am no spirit ;
Look better on me, do you know me yet ?
  Luce. O thou dear shadow of my friend !
  Jasp. Dear substance,
I swear I am no shadow ; feel my hand,
It is the same it was : I am your Jasper,
Your Jasper that's yet living, and yet loving ;
Pardon my rash attempt, my foolish proof
I put in practice of your constancy.

For sooner should my sword have drunk my blood,
And set my soul at liberty, than drawn
The least drop from that body, for which boldness
Doom me to anything ; if death, I take it
And willingly.

  Luce.   This death I'll give you for it :
So, now I'm satisfied ; you are no spirit,
But my own truest, truest, truest friend,
Why do you come thus to me ?

  Jasp.   First, to see you,
Then to convey you hence.

  Luce.   It cannot be,
For I am lock'd up here, and watch'd at all hours,
That 'tis impossible for me to 'scape.

  Jasp. Nothing more possible : within this coffin
Do you convey yourself ; let me alone,
I have the wits of twenty men about me,
Only I crave the shelter of your closet
A little, and then fear me not ; creep in
That they may presently convey you hence.
Fear nothing, dearest love, I'll be your second ;
Lie close, so, all goes well yet. Boy !

  Boy. At hand, sir.

  Jasp. Convey away the coffin, and be wary.

  Boy. 'Tis done already.

  Jasp. Now must I go conjure.   [*Exit.*

Enter MERCHANT.

  Merch. Boy, boy !

  Boy. Your servant, sir.

  Merch. Do me this kindness, boy ; hold, here's a crown :
before thou bury the body of this fellow, carry it to his old
merry father, and salute him from me, and bid him sing : he
hath cause.

  Boy. I will, sir.

  Merch. And then bring me word what tune he is in,
And have another crown ; but do it truly.
I've fitted him a bargain, now, will vex him.

  Boy. God bless your worship's health, sir.

  Merch. Farewell, boy.   [*Exeunt.*

Enter MASTER MERRY-THOUGHT.

  Wife. Ah, Old Merry-thought, art thou there again ? Let's
hear some of thy songs.

  Old Mer. " Who can sing a merrier note
     Than he that cannot change a groat ? "

Not a denier left, and yet my heart leaps; I do wonder yet, as old as I am, that any man will follow a trade, or serve, that may sing and laugh, and walk the streets. My wife and both my sons are I know not where; I have nothing left, nor know I how to come by meat to supper, yet am I merry still; for I know I shall find it upon the table at six o'clock; therefore, hang thought.

> " I would not be a serving-man
> To carry the cloak-bag still,
> Nor would I be a falconer
> The greedy hawks to fill ;
> But I would be in a good house,
> And have a good master too ;
> But I would eat and drink of the best,
> And no work would I do."

This is it that keeps life and soul together, mirth.   This is the philosopher's stone that they write so much on, that keeps a man ever young.

Enter a BOY.

Boy. Sir, they say they know all your money is gone, and they will trust you for no more drink.

Old Mer. Will they not? Let 'em choose. The best is, I have mirth at home, and need not send abroad for that. Let them keep their drink to themselves.

> " For Jillian of Berry, she dwells on a hill,
> And she hath good beer and ale to sell,
> And of good fellows she thinks no ill,
> And thither will we go now, now, now, and
> thither will we go now.
> And when you have made a little stay,
> You need not know what is to pay,
> But kiss your hostess and go your way.
> And thither, &c."

Enter another BOY.

2nd Boy. Sir, I can get no bread for supper.

Old Mer. Hang bread and supper, let's preserve our mirth, and we shall never feel hunger, I'll warrant you ; let's have a catch. Boy, follow me ; come sing this catch :

> " Ho, ho, nobody at home,
> Meat, nor drink, nor money ha' we none ;
> Fill the pot, Eedy,
> Never more need I."

So, boys, enough, follow me ; let's change our place, and we shall laugh afresh.   [*Exeunt.*

Wife. Let him go, George, a shall not have any countenance

c

from us, not a good word from any i' th' company, if I may
strike stroke in't.

Cit. No more a sha'not, love; but, Nell, I will have Ralph
do a very notable matter now, to the eternal honour and glory
of all grocers. Sirrah, you there, boy, can none of you hear?

Boy. Sir, your pleasure.

Cit. Let Ralph come out on May-day in the morning, and
speak upon a conduit with all his scarfs about him, and his
feathers, and his rings, and his knacks.

Boy. Why, sir, you do not think of our plot, what will become
of that, then?

Cit. Why, sir, I care not what become on't. I'll have him
come out, or I'll fetch him out myself, I'll have something done
in honour of the city; besides, he hath been long enough upon
adventures. Bring him out quickly, for I come amongst you——

Boy. Well, sir, he shall come out; but if our play miscarry,
sir, you are like to pay for't. [*Exit.*

Cit. Bring him away, then.

Wife. This will be brave, i'faith. George, shall not he dance
the morrice, too, for the credit of the Strand?

Cit. No, sweetheart, it will be too much for the boy. Oh,
there he is, Nell; he's reasonable well in reparel, but he has not
rings enough.

Enter RALPH.

Ralph. "London, to thee I do present the merry month of
    May,
Let each true subject be content to hear me what I say:
For from the top of conduit head, as plainly may appear,
I will both tell my name to you, and wherefore I came here.
My name is Ralph, by due descent, though not ignoble I,
Yet far inferior to the flock of gracious grocery.
And by the common counsel of my fellows in the Strand,
With gilded staff, and crossed scarf, the May lord here I stand.
Rejoice, O English hearts, rejoice; rejoice, O lovers dear;
Rejoice, O city, town, and country; rejoice eke every shire;
For now the fragrant flowers do spring and sprout in seemly
    sort,
The little birds do sit and sing, the lambs do make fine sport;
And now the birchin tree doth bud that makes the schoolboy
    cry,
The morrice rings while hobby-horse doth foot it featuously:
The lords and ladies now abroad, for their disport and play,
Do kiss sometimes upon the grass, and sometimes in the hay.
Now butter with a leaf of sage is good to purge the blood,
Fly Venus and Phlebotomy, for they are neither good.
Now little fish on tender stone begin to cast their bellies,

And sluggish snail, that erst were mew'd, do creep out of their shellies.
The rumbling rivers now do warm, for little boys to paddle,
The sturdy steed now goes to grass, and up they hang his saddle.
The heavy hart, the blowing buck, the rascal and the pricket,
Are now among the yeoman's pease, and leave the fearful thicket.
And be like them, O you, I say, of this same noble town,
And lift aloft your velvet heads, and slipping of your gown,
With bells on legs, and napkins clean unto your shoulders ty'd,
With scarfs and garters as you please, and Hey for our town ! cry'd.
March out and show your willing minds, by twenty and by twenty,
To Hogsdon, or to Newington, where ale and cakes are plenty.
And let it ne'er be said for shame, that we the youths of London,
Lay thrumming of our caps at home, and left our custom undone.
Up then I say, both young and old, both man and maid a-maying,
With drums and guns that bounce aloud, and merry tabor playing.
Which to prolong, God save our king, and send his country peace,
And root out treason from the land ; and so, my friends, I cease.

ACT V.—Scene I.

Enter Merchant, *solus.*

Merch. I will have no great store of company at the wedding: a couple of neighbours and their wives ; and we will have a capon in stewed broth, with marrow, and a good piece of beef, stuck with rosemary.

Enter Jasper, *with his face mealed.*

Jasp. Forbear thy pains, fond man, it is too late.
Merch. Heav'n bless me ! Jasper !
Jasp. Ay, I am his ghost,
Whom thou hast injur'd for his constant love :
Fond worldly wretch, who dost not understand
In death that true hearts cannot parted be.
First know, thy daughter is quite borne away
On wings of angels, through the liquid air
Too far out of thy reach, and never more
Shalt thou behold her face : but she and I
Will in another world enjoy our loves,

C 2

Where neither father's anger, poverty,
Nor any cross that troubles earthly men,
Shall make us sever our united hearts.
And never shalt thou sit, or be alone
In any place, but I will visit thee
With ghastly looks, and put into thy mind
The great offences which thou didst to me.
When thou art at thy table with thy friends,
Merry in heart, and fill'd with swelling wine,
I'll come in midst of all thy pride and mirth,
Invisible to all men but thyself,
And whisper such a sad tale in thine ear,
Shall make thee let the cup fall from thy hand,
And stand as mute and pale as death itself.

Merch. Forgive me, Jasper! Oh! what might I do,
Tell me, to satisfy thy troubled ghost?

Jasp. There is no means, too late thou think'st on this.

Merch. But tell me what were best for me to do?

Jasp. Repent thy deed, and satisfy my father,
And beat fond Humphrey out of thy doors.   [*Exit* JASPER.

Enter HUMPHREY.

Wife. Look, George, his very ghost would have folks beaten.

Humph. Father, my bride is gone, fair Mistress Luce.
My soul's the font of vengeance, mischief's sluice.

Merch. Hence, fool, out of my sight, with thy fond passion
Thou hast undone me.

Humph.   Hold, my father dear,
For Luce thy daughter's sake, that had no peer.

Merch. Thy father, fool? There's some blows more, begone.
                                        [*Beats him.*

Jasper, I hope thy ghost be well appeased
To see thy will perform'd; now will I go
To satisfy thy father for thy wrongs.   [*Exit.*

Humph. What shall I do? I have been beaten twice,
And Mistress Luce is gone. Help me, device:
Since my true love is gone, I never more,
Whilst I do live, upon the sky will pore;
But in the dark will wear out my shoe-soles
In passion, in Saint Faith's Church under Paul's.   [*Exit.*

Wife. George, call Ralph hither; if you love me, call Ralph
hither. I have the bravest thing for him to do, George; prithee
call him quickly.

Cit. Ralph, why Ralph, boy!

Enter RALPH.

Ralph. Here, sir.

Cit. Come hither, Ralph, come to thy mistress, boy.

Wife. Ralph, I would have thee call all the youths together in battle-ray, with drums, and guns, and flags, and march to Mile End in pompous fashion, and there exhort your soldiers to be merry and wise, and to keep their beards from burning, Ralph; and then skirmish, and let your flags fly, and cry, Kill, kill, kill! My husband shall lend you his jerkin, Ralph, and there's a scarf; for the rest, the house shall furnish you, and we'll pay for't : do it bravely, Ralph, and think before whom you perform, and what person you represent.

Ralph. I warrant you, mistress, if I do it not, for the honour of the city, and the credit of my master, let me never hope for freedom.

Wife. 'Tis well spoken i'faith ; go thy ways, thou art a spark indeed.

Cit. Ralph, double your files bravely, Ralph.

Ralph. I warrant you, sir.   [*Exit* RALPH.

Cit. Let him look narrowly to his service, I shall take him else ; I was there myself a pike-man once, in the hottest of the day, wench ; had my feather shot sheer away, the fringe of my pike burnt off with powder, my pate broken with a scouring-stick, and yet I thank God I am here.   [*Drum within.*

Wife. Hark, George, the drums !

Cit. Ran, tan, tan, tan, ran tan. Oh, wench, an' thou hadst but seen little Ned of Aldgate, drum Ned, how he made it roar again, and laid on like a tyrant, and then struck softly till the Ward came up, and then thundered again, and together we go : " Sa, sa, sa," bounce quoth the guns ; " Courage, my hearts," quoth the captains : " Saint George," quoth the pike-men ; and withal here they lay, and there they lay ; and yet for all this I am here, wench.

Wife. Be thankful for it, George, for indeed 'tis wonderful.

Enter RALPH *and his Company, with drums and colours.*

Ralph. March fair, my hearts ; lieutenant, beat the rear up : ancient, let your colours fly ; but have a great care of the butchers' hooks at Whitechapel, they have been the death of many a fair ancient.   Open your files, that I may take a view both of your persons and munition.   Sergeant, call a muster.

Serg. A stand. William Hamerton, pewterer.

Ham. Here, Captain.

Ralph. A croslet and a Spanish pike ; 'tis well, can you shake it with a terror?

Ham. I hope so, captain.

Ralph. Charge upon me—'tis with the weakest. Put more strength, William Hamerton, more strength. As you were again ; proceed, sergeant.

Serg. George Green-goose, poulterer.

Green. Here.

Ralph. Let me see your piece, neighbour Green-goose. When was she shot in ?

Green. An' like you, master captain, I made a shot even now, partly to scour her, and partly for audacity.

Ralph. It should seem so, certainly, for her breath is yet inflamed ; besides, there is a main fault in the touch-hole, it stinketh.   And I tell you, moreover, and believe it, ten such touch-holes would poison the army ; get you a feather, neighbour, get you a feather, sweet oil and paper, and your piece may do well enough yet.   Where's your powder ?

Green. Here.

Ralph. What, in a paper ?   As I am a soldier and a gentleman, it craves a martial court : you ought to die for't.   Where's your horn ?   Answer me to that.

Green. An't like you, sir, I was oblivious.

Ralph. It likes me not it should be so ; 'tis a shame for you, and a scandal to all our neighbours, being a man of worth and estimation, to leave your horn behind you : I am afraid 'twill breed example.   But let me tell you no more on't ; stand till I view you all.   What's become o' th' nose of your flask ?

1st Sold. Indeed, la' captain, 'twas blown away with powder.

Ralph. Put on a new one at the city's charge.   Where's the flint of this piece ?

2nd Sold. The drummer took it out to light tobacco.

Ralph. 'Tis a fault, my friend ; put it in again.   You want a nose, and you a flint : sergeant, take a note on't, for I mean to stop it in their pay.   Remove and march ; soft and fair, gentlemen, soft and fair : double your files ; as you were ; faces about. Now you with the sodden face, keep in there : look to your match, sirrah, it will be in your fellow's flask anon.   So make a crescent now, advance your pikes, stand and give ear.   Gentlemen, countrymen, friends, and my fellow-soldiers, I have brought you this day from the shop of security and the counters of content, to measure out in these furious fields honour by the ell and prowess by the pound.   Let it not, O let it not, I say, be told hereafter, the noble issue of this city fainted ; but bear yourselves in this fair action like men, valiant men, and free men. Fear not the face of the enemy, nor the noise of the guns ; for believe me, brethren, the rude rumbling of a brewer's car is more terrible, of which you have a daily experience : neither let the stink of powder offend you, since a more valiant stink is always with you.   To a resolved mind his home is everywhere. I speak not this to take away the hope of your return ; for you shall see (I do not doubt it), and that very shortly, your loving wives again, and your sweet children, whose care doth bear you company in baskets.   Remember, then, whose cause you have in hand, and like a sort of true-born scavengers, scour me this famous realm of enemies.   I have no more to say but this :

Stand to your tacklings, lads, and show to the world you can as well brandish a sword as shake an apron. Saint George, and on, my hearts !

Omnes. Saint George, Saint George !　　　　　　　　[*Exeunt.*

Wife. 'Twas well done, Ralph ; I'll send thee a cold capon a field, and a bottle of March beer ; and, it may be, come myself to see thee.

Cit. Nell, the boy hath deceived me much ; I did not think it had been in him. He has perform'd such a matter, wench, that, if I live, next year I'll have him Captain of the Gallifoist, or I'll want my will.

Enter OLD MERRY-THOUGHT.

Old Mer. Yet, I thank God, I break not a wrinkle more than I had ; not a stoop, boys. Care, live with cats, I defy thee ! My heart is as sound as an oak ; and tho' I want drink to wet my whistle, I can sing,

　" Come no more there, boys ; come no more there :
　　For we shall never, whilst we live, come any more there."

Enter a BOY with a coffin.

Boy. God save you, sir.

Old Mer. It's a brave boy. Canst thou sing ?

Boy. Yes, sir, I can sing, but 'tis not so necessary at this time.

Old Mer. " Sing we, and chaunt it,
　　　　　Whilst love doth grant it."

Boy. Sir, sir, if you knew what I have brought you, you would have little list to sing.

Old Mer. " Oh, the Mimon round,
　　　　　Full long I have thee sought,
　　　　　And now I have thee found,
　　　　　And what hast thou here brought ?"

Boy. A coffin, sir, and your dead son Jasper in it.

Old Mer. Dead !
　　　　" Why farewell he :
　　　　　Thou wast a bonny boy,
　　　　　And I did love thee."

Enter JASPER.

Jasp. Then I pray you, sir, do so still.

Old Mer. Jasper's ghost !
　　　　" Thou art welcome from Stygian-lake so soon,
　　　　　Declare to me what wondrous things
　　　　　In Pluto's Court are done."

Jasp. By my troth, sir, I ne'er came there, 'tis too hot for me, sir.

Old Mer. A merry ghost, a very merry ghost.
　　　　" And where is your true love ? Oh, where is yours ?"

Jasp. Marry look you, sir.　　　　　　[*Heaves up the coffin.*
Old Mer. Ah ha! Art thou good at that i'faith?
　　　　"With hey trixie terleric-whiskin,
　　　　　The world it runs on wheels;
　　　　　When the young man's frisking
　　　　　Up goes the maiden's heels."

MISTRESS MERRY-THOUGHT *and* MICHAEL *within.*

Mist. Mer. What, Mr. Merry-thought, will you not let's in?
What do you think shall become of us?
Old Mer. What voice is that that calleth at our door?
Mist. Mer. You know me well enough, I am sure I have not
been such a stranger to you.
Old Mer. "And some they whistled, and some they sung,
　　　　　Hey down, down:
　　　　And some did loudly say,
　　　　Ever as the Lord Barnet's horn blew,
　　　　Away, Musgrave, away."
Mist. Mer. You will not have us starve here, will you, Master
Merry-thought?
Jasp. Nay, good sir, be persuaded, she is my mother. If
her offences have been great against you, let your own love
remember she is yours, and so forgive her.
Luce. Good Master Merry-thought, let me entreat you, I will
not be denied.
Mist. Mer. Why, Master Merry-thought, will you be a vext
thing still?
Old Mer. Woman, I take you to my love again, but you shall
sing before you enter; therefore despatch your song, and so
come in.
Mist. Mer. Well, you must have your will when all's done.
Michael, what song canst thou sing, boy?
Mich. I can sing none forsooth but "A Lady's Daughter of
Paris," properly.
Mist. Mer. [song.] "It was a lady's daughter," &c.
Old Mer. Come, you're welcome home again.
　　　　"If such danger be in playing,
　　　　　And jest must to earnest turn,
　　　　　You shall go no more a-maying"——
Merch. [within.] Are you within, Sir Master Merry-thought?
Jasp. It is my master's voice, good sir; go hold him in talk
whilst we convey ourselves into some inward room.
Old Mer. What are you? Are you merry? You must be very
merry if you enter.
Merch. I am, sir.
Old Mer. Sing, then.
Merch. Nay, good sir, open to me.

Old Mer. Sing, I say, or by the merry heart you come not in.

Merch. Well, sir, I'll sing.

"Fortune my foe," &c.

Old Mer. You are welcome, sir, you are welcome: you see
your entertainment, pray you be merry.

Merch. Oh, Master Merry-thought, I'm come to ask you   .
Forgiveness for the wrongs I offered you,
And your most virtuous son ; they're infinite,
Yet my contrition shall be more than they.
I do confess my hardness broke his heart,
For which just Heav'n hath given me punishment
More than my age can carry; his wand'ring sprite,
Not yet at rest, pursues me everywhere,
Crying, I'll haunt thee for thy cruelty.
My daughter she is gone, I know not how,
Taken invisible, and whether living,
Or in grave, 'tis yet uncertain to me.
Oh, Master Merry-thought, these are the weights
Will sink me to my grave.   Forgive me, sir.

Old Mer. Why, sir, I do forgive you, and be merry.
And if the wag in's lifetime play'd the knave,
Can you forgive him too?

Merch.   With all my heart, sir.

Old Mer. Speak it again, and heartily.

Merch.   I do, sir.
Now by my soul I do.

Old Mer. "With that came out his paramour,
        She was as white as the lily flower,
            Hey troul, troly loly.
        With that came out her own dear knight,
        He was as true as ever did fight," &c.

Enter LUCE *and* JASPER.

Sir, if you will forgive 'em, clap their hands together, there's no
more to be said i' th' matter.

Merch. I do, I do!

Cit. I do not like this.   Peace, boys, hear me one of you,
everybody's part is come to an end but Ralph's, and he's left
out.

Boy. 'Tis long of yourself, sir, we have nothing to do with
his part.

Cit. Ralph, come away, make on him as you have done of
the rest, boys, come.

Wife. Now, good husband, let him come out and die.

Cit. He shall, Nell ; Ralph, come away quickly and die, boy.

Boy. 'Twill be very unfit he should die, sir, upon no occasion,
and in a comedy too.

Cit. Take you no care for that, Sir Boy; is not his part at an end, think you, when he's dead? Come away, Ralph.

Enter RALPH *with a forked arrow through his head.*

Ralph. When I was mortal, this my costive corps
Did lap up figs and raisins in the Strand,
Where sitting, I espy'd a lovely dame,
Whose master wrought with lingel and with awl,
And underground he vampéd many a boot.
Straight did her love prick forth me, tender sprig,
To follow feats of arms in warlike wise,
Through Waltham Desert; where I did perform
Many achievements, and did lay on ground
Huge Barbaroso, that insulting giant,
And all his captives soon set at liberty.
Then honour prick'd me from my native soil
Into Moldavia, where I gain'd the love
Of Pompiana, his beloved daughter;
But yet prov'd constant to the black-thumbed maid
Susan, and scornéd Pompiana's love.
Yet liberal I was, and gave her pins,
And money for her father's officers.
I then returnéd home, and thrust myself
In action, and by all men chosen was
The Lord of May, where I did flourish it,
With scarfs and rings, and posie in my hand.
After this action I preferréd was,
And chosen City Captain at Mile End,
With hat and feather, and with leading staff,
And train'd my men, and brought them all off clean,
Save one man that berayed him with the noise.
But all these things I, Ralph, did undertake,
Only for my belovéd Susan's sake.
Then coming home, and sitting in my shop
With apron blue, Death came unto my stall
To cheapen aquavitæ, but ere I
Could take the bottle down, and fill a taste,
Death caught a pound of pepper in his hand,
And sprinkled all my face and body o'er,
And in an instant vanishéd away.
 Cit. 'Tis a pretty fiction, i'faith.
 Ralph. Then took I up my bow and shaft in hand,
And walkéd in Moorfields to cool myself,
But there grim cruel Death met me again,
And shot his forkéd arrow through my head,
And now I faint; therefore be warn'd by me,
My fellows every one, of forkéd heads.

Farewell, all you good boys in merry London,
Ne'er shall we more upon Shrove Tuesday meet,
And pluck down houses of iniquity.
My pain increaseth : I shall never more
When clubs are cried be brisk upon my legs,
Nor daub a satin gown with rotten eggs.
Set up a stake, oh never more I shall ;
I die !   Fly, fly, my soul, to Grocers Hall !   Oh, oh, oh, &c.

 Wife. Well said, Ralph, do your obeisance to the gentlemen,
and go your ways.   Well said, Ralph.   [*Exit* RALPH.

 Old Mer. Methinks all we, thus kindly and unexpectedly,
reconciled, should not part without a song.

 Merch. A good motion.

 Old Mer. Strike up, then.

SONG.

Better music ne'er was known,
Than a quire of hearts in one.
Let each other, that hath been
Troubled with the gall or spleen,
Learn of us to keep his brow
Smooth and plain, as yours are now.
Sing though before the hour of dying,
He shall rise, and then be crying
Heyho, 'tis nought but mirth
That keeps the body from the earth.   [*Exeunt omnes.*

EPILOGUS.

 Cit. Come, Nell, shall we go ?   The play's done.

 Wife. Nay, by my faith, George, I have more manners than
so, I'll speak to these gentlemen first. I thank you all, gentlemen, for your patience and countenance to Ralph, a poor fatherless child, and if I may see you at my house, it should go hard
but I would have a pottle of wine, and a pipe of tobacco for you ;
for truly I hope you like the youth, but I would be glad to know
the truth. I refer it to your own discretions, whether you will
applaud him or no, for I will wink, and whilst, you shall do what
you will.—I thank you with all my heart : God give you good
night.   Come, George.

The Rehearsal.

—◦◦◦—

DRAMATIS PERSONÆ.

Bayes.	Players.
Johnson.	Soldiers.
Smith.	Two Heralds.
Two Kings of Brentford.	Four Cardinals.
Prince Pretty-man.	Mayor.
Prince Volscius.	Judges.
Gentleman-Usher.	Serjeant-at-Arms.
Physician.	Amaryllis.
Drawcansir.	Cloris.
General.	Parthenope.
Lieutenant-General.	Pallas.
Cordelio.	Lightning.
Tom Thimble.	Moon.
Fisherman.	Earth.
Sun.	Attendants of Men and Women.
Thunder.	

Four Cardinals, Mayor, Judges, Serjeant-at-Arms. } Mutes.

SCENE.—Brentford.

PROLOGUE.

We might well call this short mock-play of ours,
A posy made of weeds instead of flowers;
Yet such have been presented to your noses,
And there are such, I fear, who thought 'em roses.
Would some of 'em were here, to see, this night,
What stuff it is in which they took delight.
Here brisk insipid rogues, for wit, let fall
Sometimes dull sense; but oft'ner none at all.
There, strutting heroes, with a grim-fac'd train,
Shall brave the gods, in King Cambyses' vein.
For (changing rules, of late, as if man writ
In spite of reason, nature, art and wit)
Our poets make us laugh at tragedy,

And with their comedies they make us cry.
Now critics, do your worst, that here are met ;
For, like a rook, I have hedg'd in my bet.
If you approve, I shall assume the state
Of those high-flyers whom I imitate :
And justly too, for I will teach you more
Than ever they would let you know before.
I will not only show the feats they do,
But give you all their reasons for 'em too.
Some honour may to me from hence arise ;
But if, by my endeavours you grow wise,
And what you once so prais'd, shall now despise ;
Then I'll cry out, swell'd with poetic rage,
'Tis I, John Lacy, have reform'd your stage.

ACT I.—SCENE I.

JOHNSON *and* SMITH.

Johns. Honest Frank ! I am glad to see thee with all my heart : how long hast thou been in town?

Smith. Faith, not above an hour : and, if I had not met you here, I had gone to look you out ; for I long to talk with you freely of all the strange new things we have heard in the country.

Johns. And, by my troth, I have long'd as much to laugh with you at all the impertinent, dull, fantastical things, we are tired out with here.

Smith. Dull and fantastical ! that's an excellent composition. Pray, what are our men of business doing ?

Johns I ne'er inquire after 'em. Thou knowest my humour lies another way. I love to please myself as much, and to trouble others as little as I can ; and therefore do naturally avoid the company of those solemn fops, who, being incapable of reason, and insensible of wit and pleasure, are always looking grave, and troubling one another, in hopes to be thought men of business.

Smith. Indeed, I have ever observed, that your grave lookers are the dullest of men.

Johns. Ay, and of birds and beasts too : your gravest bird is an owl, and your gravest beast is an ass.

Smith. Well : but how dost thou pass thy time ?

Johns. Why, as I used to do ; eat, drink as well as I can, have a friend to chat with in the afternoon, and some-times see a play ; where there are such things, Frank, such hideous, monstrous things, that it has almost made me forswear the stage, and resolve to apply myself to the solid nonsense of your men of business, as the more ingenious pastime.

Smith. I have heard, indeed, you have had lately many new plays ; and our country wits commend 'em.

Johns. Ay, so do some of our city wits too ; but they are of the new kind of wits.

Smith. New kind ! what kind is that ?

Johns. Why, your virtuosi ; your civil persons, your drolls ; fellows that scorn to imitate nature ; but are given altogether to elevate and surprise.

Smith. Elevate and surprise ! prithee, make me understand the meaning of that.

Johns. Nay, by my troth, that's a hard matter : I don't understand that myself. 'Tis a phrase they have got among them, to express their no-meaning by. I'll tell you, as near as I can, what it is. Let me see ; 'tis fighting, loving, sleeping, rhyming, dying, dancing, singing, crying ; and everything, but thinking and sense.

MR. BAYES *passes over the stage.*

Bayes. Your most obsequious, and most observant, very servant, sir.

Johns. Odso, this is an author. I'll go fetch him to you.

Smith. No, prithee let him alone.

Johns. Nay, by the Lord, I'll have him.   [*Goes after him.* Here he is ; I have caught him. Pray, sir, now for my sake, will you do a favour to this friend of mine ?

Bayes. Sir, it is not within my small capacity to do favours, but receive 'em ; especially from a person that does wear the honourable title you are pleased to impose, sir, upon this— sweet sir, your servant.

Smith. Your humble servant, sir.

Johns. But wilt thou do me a favour, now ?

Bayes. Ay, sir, what is't ?

Johns. Why, to tell him the meaning of thy last play.

Bayes. How, sir, the meaning ? Do you mean the plot ?

Johns. Ay, ay ; anything.

Bayes. Faith, sir, the intrigo's now quite out of my head ; but I have a new one in my pocket that I may say is a virgin ; it has never yet been blown upon. I must tell you one thing : 'tis all new wit, and, though I say it, a better than my last ; and you know well enough how that took. In fine, it shall read, and write, and act, and plot, and show, ay, and pit, box, and gallery, egad, with any play in Europe.* This morning is its last rehearsal, in their habits, and all that, as it is to be acted ; and if you and your friend will do it but the honour to see it in its virgin attire ; though, perhaps, it may blush, I shall not be

* The usual language of the Honourable Edward Howard, Esq., at the rehearsal of his plays,

ashamed to discover its nakedness unto you. I think it is in
this pocket.   [*Puts his hand in his pocket.*

Johns. Sir, I confess I am not able to answer you in this new
way ; but if you please to lead, I shall be glad to follow you, and
I hope my friend will do so too.

Smith. Sir, I have no business so considerable as should keep
me from your company.

Bayes. Yes, here it is. No, cry you mercy : this is my book of
Drama Commonplaces, the mother of many other plays.

Johns. Drama Commonplaces ! .pray what's that ?

Bayes. Why, sir, some certain helps that we men of art have
found it convenient to make use of.

Smith. How, sir, helps for wit ?

Bayes. Ay, sir, that's my position. And I do here aver that
no man yet the sun e'er shone upon has parts sufficient to
furnish out a stage, except it were by the help of these my rules.*

Johns. What are those rules, I pray ?

Bayes. Why, sir, my first rule is the rule of transversion, or
Regula Duplex ; changing verse into prose, or prose into verse,
alternativè as you please.

Smith. Well ; but how is this done by a rule, sir ?

Bayes. Why thus, sir ; nothing so easy when understood. I
take a book in my hand, either at home or elsewhere, for that's
all one ; if there be any wit in't, as there is no book but has
some, I transverse it ; that is, if it be prose, put it into verse
(but that takes up some time), and if it be verse, put it into
prose.

Johns. Methinks, Mr. Bayes, that putting verse into prose
should be called transprosing.

Bayes. By my troth, sir, 'tis a very good notion ; and hereafter it shall be so.

Smith. Well, sir, and what d'ye do with it then ?

Bayes. Make it my own. 'Tis so changed that no man can
know it. My next rule is the rule of record, by way of table-
book. Pray observe.

Johns. We hear you, sir ; go on.

Bayes. As thus. I come into a coffee-house, or some other
place where witty men resort, I make as if I minded nothing ;
do you mark ? but as soon as any one speaks, pop I slap it down,
and make that too my own.

Johns. But, Mr. Bayes, are you not sometimes in danger of

* He who writ this, not without pain and thought,
  From French and English theatres has brought
  Th' exactest rules, by which a play is wrought.
  The unity of action, place, and time ;
  The scenes unbroken ; and a mingled chime,
  Of Johnson's humour, with Corneille's rhyme.
                    Prologue to the Maiden Queen.

their making you restore, by force, what you have gotten thus by art?

Bayes. No, sir; the world's unmindful : they never take notice of these things.

Smith. But pray, Mr. Bayes, among all your other rules, have you no one rule for invention?

Bayes. Yes, sir, that's my third rule that I have here in my pocket.

Smith. What rule can that be, I wonder?

Bayes. Why, sir, when I have anything to invent, I never trouble my head about it, as other men do ; but presently turn over this book, and there I have, at one view, all that Persius, Montaigne, Seneca's Tragedies, Horace, Juvenal, Claudian, Pliny, Plutarch's Lives, and the rest, have ever thought upon this subject : and so, in a trice, by leaving out a few words, or putting in others of my own, the business is done.

Johns. Indeed, Mr. Bayes, this is as sure and compendious a way of wit as ever I heard of.

Bayes. Sir, if you make the least scruples of the efficacy of these my rules, do but come to the playhouse, and you shall judge of 'em by the effects.

Smith. We'll follow you, sir. [*Exeunt.*

Enter three PLAYERS *on the stage.*

1st Play. Have you your part perfect?

2nd Play. Yes, I have it without book ; but I don't understand how it is to be spoken.

3rd Play. And mine is such a one, as I can't guess for my life what humour I'm to be in ; whether angry, melancholy, merry, or in love. I don't know what to make on't.

1st Play. Phoo! the author will be here presently, and he'll tell us all. You must know, this is the new way of writing, and these hard things please forty times better than the old plain way. For, look you, sir, the grand design upon the stage is to keep the auditors in suspense ; for to guess presently at the plot, and the sense, tires them before the end of the first act : now here, every line surprises you, and brings in new matter. And then, for scenes, clothes, and dances, we put quite down all that ever went before us ; and those are the things, you know, that are essential to a play.

2nd Play. Well, I am not of thy mind ; but, so it gets us money, 'tis no great matter.

Enter BAYES, JOHNSON, *and* SMITH.

Bayes. Come, come in, gentlemen. You're very welcome, Mr. —a—. Ha' you your part ready?

1st Play. Yes, sir.

Bayes. But do you understand the true humour of it?

1st Play. Ay, sir, pretty well.

Bayes. And Amaryllis, how does she do? does not her armour become her?

3rd Play. Oh, admirably!

Bayes. I'll tell you now a pretty conceit. What do you think I'll make 'em call her anon, in this play?

Smith. What, I pray?

Bayes. Why, I make 'em call her Armaryllis, because of her armour: ha, ha, ha!

Johns. That will be very well indeed.

Bayes. Ay, 'tis a pretty little rogue; but—a—come, let's sit down. Look you, sirs, the chief hinge of this play, upon which the whole plot moves and turns, and that causes the variety of all the several accidents, which, you know, are the things in nature that make up the grand refinement of a play, is, that I suppose two kings of the same place; as for example, at Brentford, for I love to write familiarly. Now the people having the same relations to 'em both, the same affections, the same duty, the same obedience, and all that, are divided among themselves in point of devoir and interest, how to behave themselves equally between 'em : these kings differing sometimes in particular; though, in the main, they agree. (I know not whether I make myself well understood.)

Johns. I did not observe you, sir : pray say that again.

Bayes. Why, look you, sir (nay, I beseech you be a little curious in taking notice of this, or else you'll never understand my notion of the thing), the people being embarrass'd by their equal ties to both, and the sovereigns concern'd in a reciprocal regard, as well to their own interest, as the good of the people, make a certain kind of a—you understand me—upon which, there do arise several disputes, turmoils, heart-burnings, and all that—in fine, you'll apprehend it better when you see it.

[Exit, to call the Players.

Smith. I find the author will be very much obliged to the players, if they can make any sense out of this.

Enter BAYES.

Bayes. Now, gentlemen, I would fain ask your opinion of one thing. I have made a prologue and an epilogue, which may both serve for either; that is, the prologue for the epilogue, or the epilogue for the prologue;* (do you mark?) nay, they may both serve too, egad, for any other play as well as this.

Smith. Very well; that's indeed artificial.

* . . two prologues to the " Maiden Queen."

Bayes. And I would fain ask your judgments, now, which of them would do best for the prologue? for, you must know there is, in nature, but two ways of making very good prologues : the one is by civility, by insinuation, good language, and all that, to —a—in a manner, steal your plaudit from the courtesy of the auditors : the other, by making use of some certain personal things, which may keep a hank upon such censuring persons, as cannot otherways, egad, in nature, be hindered from being too free with their tongues. To which end, my first prologue is, that I come out in a long black veil, and a great huge hangman behind me, with a furr'd cap, and his sword drawn ; and there tell 'em plainly, that if out of good-nature, they will not like my play, egad, I'll e'en kneel down, and he shall cut my head off. Whereupon they all clapping—a—

Smith. Ay, but suppose they don't.

Bayes. Suppose ! sir, you may suppose what you please ; I have nothing to do with your suppose, sir ; nor am at all mortified at it ; not at all, sir ; egad, not one jot, sir. Suppose, quoth-a !—ha, ha, ha !   [*Walks away.*

Johns. Phoo ! prithee, Bayes, don't mind what he says ; he is a fellow newly come out of the country, he knows nothing of what's the relish, here, of the town.

Bayes. If I writ, sir, to please the country, I should have follow'd the old plain way ; but I write for some persons of quality, and peculiar friends of mine, that understand what flame and power in writing is ; and they do me the right, sir, to approve of what I do.

Johns. Ay, ay, they will clap, I warrant you ; never fear it.

Bayes. I'm sure the design's good ; that cannot be denied. And then, for language, egad, I defy 'em all, in nature, to mend it. Besides, sir, I have printed above a hundred sheets of paper to insinuate the plot into the boxes ; * and, withal, have appointed two or three dozen of my friends to be ready in the pit, who, I'm sure, will clap, and so the rest, you know, must follow ; and then, pray, sir, what becomes of your suppose? Ha, ha, ha !

Johns. Nay, if the business be so well laid, it cannot miss.

Bayes. I think so, sir ; and therefore would choose this to be the prologue. For, if I could engage 'em to clap, before they see the play, you know it would be so much the better ; because then they were engag'd ; for let a man write ever so well, there are, now-a-days, a sort of persons they call critics, that, egad, have no more wit in them than so many hobby-horses ; but they'll laugh at you, sir, and find fault, and censure things that,

---

* There were printed papers given the audience before the acting the "Indian Emperor;" telling them that it was the sequel of the "Indian Queen," part of which play was written by Mr. Bayes, &c.

egad, I'm sure, they are not able to do themselves. A sort of
envious persons that emulate the glories of persons of parts,
and think to build their fame by calumniating of persons * that,
egad, to my knowledge, of all persons in the world, are, in
nature, the persons that do as much despise all that as—a·— In
fine, I'll say no more of 'em.   .

Johns. Nay, you have said enough of 'em, in all conscience;
I'm sure more than they'll e'er be able to answer.

Bayes. Why, I'll tell you, sir, sincerely and *bonâ fide*, were it
not for the sake of some ingenious persons and choice female
spirits, that have a value for me, I would see 'em all hang'd,
egad, before I would e'er more set pen to paper, but let 'em
live in ignorance like ingrates.

Johns. Ay, marry! that were a way to be reveng'd of 'em
indeed; and, if I were in your place, now, I would do so.

Bayes. No, sir; there are certain ties upon me that I cannot
be disengag'd from;† otherwise, I would.   But pray, sir, how do
you like my hangman?

Smith. By my troth, sir, I should like him very well.

Bayes. By how do you like it, sir? (for, I see, you can judge)
would you have it for a prologue, or the epilogue?

Johns. Faith, sir, 'tis so good, let it e'en serve for both.

Bayes. No, no; that won't do. Besides, I have made another.

Johns. What other, sir?

Bayes. Why, sir, my other is Thunder and Lightning.

Johns. That's greater; I'd rather stick to that.

Bayes. Do you think so? I'll tell you then; tho' there have
been many witty prologues written of late, yet, I think, you'll
say this is a *non pareillo:* I'm sure nobody has hit upon it yet.
For here, sir, I make my prologue to be a dialogue; and as, in
my first, you see, I strive to oblige the auditors by civility, by
good-nature, good language, and all that; so, in this, by the
other way, *in terrorem,* I choose for the persons Thunder and
Lightning.   Do you apprehend the conceit?

Johns. Phoo, phoo! then you have it cock-sure. They'll be
hang'd before they'll dare affront an author that has 'em at that
lock.

Bayes. I have made, too, one of the most delicate dainty
similes in the whole world, egad, if I knew but how to apply it.

---

* " Persons, egad, I vow to Gad, and all that," is the constant style of
Failer in the " Wild Gallant:" for which, take this short speech, instead of
many :
"*Failer.* Really, madam, I look upon you, as a person of such worth, and
all that, that I vow to Gad, I honour you of all persons in the world; and
tho' I am a person that am inconsiderable in the world, and all that, madam,
yet for a person of your worth and excellency I would," &c.—" Wild
Gallant," p. 8.

† He contracted with the King's company of actors, in the year 1668, for
a whole share, to write them four plays a year.

Smith. Let's hear it, I pray you.

Bayes. 'Tis an allusion to love.

   * "So boar and sow, when any storm is nigh,
      Snuff up, and smell it gath'ring in the sky ;
      Boar beckons sow to trot in chestnut-groves,
      And there consummate their unfinish'd loves :
      Pensive in mud they wallow all alone,
      And snore and gruntle to each other's moan."

How do you like it now, ha?

Johns. Faith, 'tis extraordinary fine ; and very applicable to Thunder and Lightning, methinks, because it speaks of a storm.

Bayes. Egad, and so it does, now I think on't : Mr. Johnson, I thank you ; and I'll put it in *profecto.* Come out, Thunder and Lightning.

Enter THUNDER *and* LIGHTNING.

Thun. I am the bold Thunder.

Bayes. Mr. Cartwright, prithee speak that a little louder, and with a hoarse voice. I am the bold *Thunder :* pshaw! speak it me in a voice that thunders it out indeed: I am the bold *Thunder.*

Thun. I am the bold *Thunder.*†

Light. The brisk Lightning, I.

Bayes. Nay, you must be quick and nimble.
The brisk *Lightning*, I.   That's my meaning.

Thun. I am the bravest Hector of the sky.

Light. And I fair Helen, that made Hector die.

Thun. I strike men down.

Light. I fire the town.

Thun. Let critics take heed how they grumble,
      For then begin I for to rumble.

Light. Let the ladies allow us their graces,
      Or I'll blast all the paint on their faces,
      And dry up their petre to soot.

Thun. Let the critics look to't.

Light. Let the ladies look to't.‡

---

* In ridicule of this :
    "So two kind turtles, when a storm is nigh,
     Look up, and see it gathering in the sky ;
     Each calls his mate to shelter in the groves,
     Leaving, in murmurs, their unfinish'd loves ;
     Perch'd on some dropping branch, they sit alone,
     And coo, and hearken to each other's moan."
              "Conquest of Granada," Part ii. p. 48.
† " I am the evening dark as night."—"Slighted Maid," p. 49.
‡ " Let the men 'ware the ditches.
    Maids look to their breeches,
    We'll scratch them with briars and thistles."—"Slighted Maid," p. 49.

Thun. For Thunder will do't.
Light. For Lightning will shoot.
Thun. I'll give you dash for dash.
Light. I'll give you flash for flash.
　　　Gallants, I'll singe your feather
Thun. I'll thunder you together.
Both. Look to't, look to't ; we'll do't, we'll do't. Look to't,
we'll do't. 　　　　　　　　　　　[*Twice or thrice repeated.*
　　　　　　　　　　　　　　　　　　[*Exeunt ambo.*
Bayes. There's no more. 'Tis but a flash of a prologue : a droll.
Smith. Yes, 'tis short indeed ; but very terrible.
Bayes. Ay, when the simile's in, it will do to a miracle, egad. Come, come, begin the play.

Enter FIRST PLAYER.

1st *Play.* Sir, Mr. Ivory is not come yet ; but he'll be here presently, he's but two doors off.*
Bayes. Come then, gentlemen, let's go out and take a pipe of tobacco. 　　　　　　　　　　　　　　　　　[*Exeunt.*

ACT II.—SCENE I.

BAYES, JOHNSON, *and* SMITH.

Bayes. Now, sir, because I'll do nothing here that ever was done before, instead of beginning with a scene that discovers something of the plot, I begin this play with a whisper.†
Smith. Umph ! very new indeed.
Bayes. Come, take your seats. Begin, sirs.

Enter GENTLEMAN-USHER *and* PHYSICIAN.

Phys. Sir, by your habit, I should guess you to be the Gentleman-usher of this sumptuous place.
Ush. And by your gait and fashion, I should almost suspect

---

* Abraham Ivory had formerly been a considerable actor of women's parts ; but afterwards stupefied himself so far, with drinking strong waters, that, before the first acting of this farce, he was fit for nothing but to go of errands ; for which, and mere charity, the company allowed him a weekly salary.
† *Drake, Sen.* " Draw up our men ;
　　　　And in low whispers give our orders out."
　　　　　　　　　　　　　" Play House to be Let," p. 100.
See the " Amorous Prince," pp. 20, 22, 39, 69, where all the chief commands, and directions, are given in whispers.

you rule the healths of both our noble kings, under the notion of
Physician.

Phys. You hit my function right.

Ush. And you mine.

Phys. Then let's embrace.

Ush. Come.

Phys. Come.

Johns. Pray, sir, who are those so very civil persons?

Bayes. Why, sir, the gentleman-usher and physician of the
two kings of Brentford.

Johns. But, pray then, how comes it to pass, that they know
one another no better?

Bayes. Phoo! that's for the better carrying on of the plot.

Johns. Very well.

Phys. Sir, to conclude.

Smith. What, before he begins?

Bayes. No, sir, you must know they had been talking of this
a pretty while without.

Smith. Where? in the tyring-room?

Bayes. Why, ay, sir. He's so dull! come, speak again.

Phys. Sir, to conclude, the place you fill has more than
amply exacted the talents of a wary pilot; and all these
threat'ning storms, which, like impregnate clouds, hover o'er
our heads, will (when they once are grasped but by the eye of
reason) melt into fruitful showers of blessings on the people.

Bayes. Pray mark that allegory. Is not that good?

Johns. Yes, that grasping of a storm with the eye is admirable.

Phys. But yet some rumours great are stirring; and if Lorenzo
should prove false (which none but the great gods can tell), you
then perhaps would find that——   [*Whispers.*

Bayes. Now he whispers.

Ush. Alone do you say?

Phys. No, attended with the noble——   [*Whispers.*

Bayes. Again.

Ush. Who, he in grey?

Phys. Yes, and at the head of——   [*Whispers.*

Bayes. Pray mark.

Ush. Then, sir, most certain 'twill in time appear,
These are the reasons that have mov'd him to't;
First, he——   [*Whispers.*

Bayes. Now the other whispers.

Ush. Secondly, they——   [*Whispers.*

Bayes. At it still.

Ush. Thirdly, and lastly, both he and they——   [*Whispers.*

Bayes. Now they both whisper.   .[*Exeunt whispering.*
Now, gentlemen, pray tell me true, and without flattery, is not
this a very odd beginning of a play?

Johns. In troth, I think it is, sir. But why two kings of the same place?

Bayes. Why, because it's new, and that's it I aim at. I despise your Jonson and Beaumont, that borrowed all they writ from nature : I am for fetching it purely out of my own fancy, I.

Smith. But what think you of Sir John Suckling?

Bayes. By gad, I am a better poet than he.

Smith. Well, sir, but pray why all this whispering?

Bayes. Why, sir (besides that it is new, as I told you before), because they are supposed to be politicians, and matters of state ought not to be divulg'd.

Smith. But then, sir, why——

Bayes. Sir, if you'll but respite your curiosity till the end of the fifth act, you'll find it a piece of patience not ill recompensed.

[*Goes to the door.*

Johns. How dost thou like this, Frank? Is it not just as I told thee?

Smith. Why, I never did before this see anything in nature, and all that (as Mr. Bayes says) so foolish, but I could give some guess at what moved the fop to do it; but this, I confess, does go beyond my reach.

Johns. It is all alike : Mr. Wintershull* has informed me of this play already. And I'll tell thee, Frank, thou shalt not see one scene here worth one farthing, or like anything thou canst imagine has ever been the practice of the world. And then, when he comes to what he calls good language, it is, as I told thee, very fantastical, most abominably dull, and not one word to the purpose.

Smith. It does surprise me, I'm sure, very much.

Johns. Ay, but it won't do so long : by that time thou hast seen a play or two, that I'll show thee, thou wilt be pretty well acquainted with this new kind of foppery.

Smith. Plague on't, but there's no pleasure in him : he's too gross a fool to be laugh'd at.

Enter BAYES.

Johns. I'll swear, Mr. Bayes, you have done this scene most admirably; tho' I must tell you, sir, it is a very difficult matter to pen a whisper well.

Bayes. Ay, gentlemen, when you come to write yourselves, on my word, you'll find it so.

Johns. Have a care of what you say, Mr. Bayes; for Mr. Smith there, I assure you, has written a great many fine things already.

---

* Mr. William Wintershull was a most excellent, judicious actor; and the best instructor of others; he died in July, 1679.

Bayes. Has he, i'fackins? why then pray, sir, how do you do when you write?

Smith. Faith, sir, for the most part, I am in pretty good health.

Bayes. Ay, but I mean, what do you do when you write? -

Smith. I take pen, ink, and paper, and sit down.

Bayes. Now I write standing; that's one thing; and then another thing is, with what do you prepare yourself?

Smith. Prepare myself! what the devil does the fool mean?

Bayes. Why, I'll tell you, now, what I do. If I am to write familiar things, as sonnets to Armida, and the like, I make use of stew'd prunes only : but, when I have a grand design in hand, I ever take physic, and let blood; for, when you would have pure swiftness of thought, and fiery flights of fancy, you must have a care of the pensive part. In fine, you must purge the stomach.

Smith. By my troth, sir, this is a most admirable receipt for writing.

Bayes. Ay, 'tis my secret; and, in good earnest, I think one of the best I have.

Smith. In good faith, sir, and that may very well be.

Bayes. May be, sir? Egad, I'm sure on't : *Experto crede Roberto.* But I must give you this caution by the way, be sure you never take snuff,* when you write.

Smith. Why so, sir?

Bayes. Why, it spoil'd me once, egad, one of the sparkishest plays in all England. But a friend of mine, at Gresham College, has promised to help me to some spirit of brains, and, egad, that shall do my business.

SCENE II.

Enter the two KINGS, *hand in hand.*

Bayes. Oh, these are now the two kings of Brentford; take notice of their style, 'twas never yet upon the stage : but if you like it, I could make a shift perhaps to show you a whole play, writ all just so.

1st King. Did you observe their whispers, brother king?

2nd King. I did, and heard, besides, a grave bird sing,
That they intend, sweetheart, to play us pranks.

Bayes. This is now familiar, because they are both persons of the same quality.

Smith. S'death, this would make a man sick.

1st King. If that design appears,
      I'll lug them by the ears,
      Until I make 'em crack.

---

* He was a great taker of snuff; and made most of it himself.

2nd King. And so will I, i'fack.

1st King. You must begin, *Ma foy.*

2nd King. Sweet sir, *Pardonnez moy.*

Bayes. Mark that ; I make 'em both speak French, to show their breeding.

Johns. Oh, 'tis extraordinary fine!

2nd King. Then spite of fate, we'll thus combined stand,
        And, like two brothers, walk still hand in hand.

> [*Exeunt Reges.*

Johns. This is a majestic scene indeed.

Bayes. Ay, 'tis a crust, a lasting crust for your rogue-critics, egad : I would fain see the proudest of 'em all but dare to nibble at this ; egad, if they do, this shall rub their gums for 'em, I promise you.   It was I, you must know, that have written a whole play just in this very same style ; it was never acted yet.

Johns. How so?

Bayes. Egad, I can hardly tell you for laughing : ha, ha, ha ! it is so pleasant a story : ha, ha, ha !

Smith. What is't ?

Bayes. Egad, the players refuse to act it.   Ha, ha, ha !

Smith. That's impossible !

Bayes. Egad, they did it, sir; point-blank refus'd it, egad, ha, ha, ha !

Johns. Fie, that was rude.

Bayes. Rude ! ay, egad, they are the rudest, uncivillest persons, and all that, in the whole world, egad.   Egad, there's no living with 'em.   I have written, Mr. Johnson, I do verily believe, a whole cartload of things, every whit as good as this ; and yet, I vow to gad, these insolent rascals have turn'd 'em all back upon my hands again.

Johns. Strange fellows indeed!

Smith. But pray, Mr. Bayes, how came these two kings to know of this whisper ? for, as I remember, they were not present at it.

Bayes. No, but that's the actors' fault, and not mine ; for the two kings should (a plague take 'em) have popp'd both their heads in at the door, just as the other went off.

Smith. That indeed would have done it.

Bayes. Done it ! ay, egad, these fellows are able to spoil the best things in Christendom.   I'll tell you, Mr. Johnson, I vow to gad, I have been so highly disoblig'd by the peremptoriness of these fellows, that I'm resolved hereafter to bend my thoughts wholly for the service of the nursery, and mump your proud players, egad.   So, now Prince Prettyman comes in, and falls asleep, making love to his mistress; which you know was a grand intrigue in a late play, written by a very honest gentleman, a knight.*

* "The Lost Lady," by Sir Robert Stapleton.

Enter PRINCE PRETTYMAN.

Pret. How strange a captive am I grown of late !
　　　Shall I accuse my love, or blame my fate !
　　　My love, I cannot ; that is too divine :
　　　And against fate what mortal dares repine ? *

Enter CHLORIS.

But here she comes.
Sure 'tis some blazing comet ! is it not !　　　　　　[*Lies down.*
　　Bayes. Blazing comet ! mark that, egad, very fine !
　　Pret. But I am so surpris'd with sleep, I cannot speak the
rest.　　　　　　　　　　　　　　　　　　　　　[*Sleeps.*
　　Bayes. Does not that, now, surprise you, to fall asleep in the
nick ? his spirits exhale with the heat of his passion, and all
that, and swop he falls asleep, as you see. Now here she must
make a simile.
　　Smith. Where's the necessity of that, Mr. Bayes ?
　　Bayes. Because she's surpris'd. That's a general rule ; you
must ever make a simile when you are surpris'd ; 'tis the new
way of writing.
　　*Cloris.** As some tall pine, which we on Ætna find
　　　　T' have stood the rage of many a boist'rous wind,
　　　　Feeling without that flames within do play,
　　　　Which would consume his root and sap away ;
　　　　He spreads his worsted arms unto the skies,
　　　　Silently grieves, all pale, repines and dies :
　　　　So shrouded up, your bright eye disappears.
　　　　Break forth, bright scorching sun, and dry my tears.
　　　　　　　　　　　　　　　　　　　　　　　[*Exit.*
　　Johns. Mr. Bayes, methinks this simile wants a little
application too.
　　Bayes. No, faith ; for it alludes to passion, to consuming, to
dying, and all that ; which, you know, are the natural effects of

---

　* Compare this with Prince Leonidas in "Marriage A-la-mode."
　† In imitation of this passage :—
　　　" As some fair tulip, by a storm opprest,
　　　Shrinks up, and folds its silken arms to rest ;
　　　And, bending to the blast, all pale, and dead,
　　　Hears from within the wind sing round its head :
　　　So shrouded up your beauty disappears ;
　　　Unveil, my love, and lay aside your fears :
　　　The storm, that caus'd your fright, is past and gone."
　　　　　　　　　　　　　　"Conquest of Granada," Part I. p. 54.

an amour. But I'm afraid this scene has made you sad ; for, I
must confess, when I writ it, I wept myself.

Smith. No truly, sir, my spirits are almost exhal'd too, and
I am likelier to fall asleep.

PRINCE PRETTYMAN *starts up, and says—*

Pret. It is resolved ! [*Exit.*
Bayes. That's all.
Smith. Mr. Bayes, may one be so bold as to ask you one
question, now, and you not be angry?
Bayes. O Lord, sir, you may ask me anything; what you
please ; I vow to gad, you do me a great deal of honour : you
do not know me, if you say that, sir.
Smith. Then pray, sir, what is it that this prince here has
resolved in his sleep?
Bayes. Why, I must confess, that question is well enough
asked, for one that is not acquainted with this new way of
writing. But you must know, sir, that to outdo all my fellow-
writers, whereas they keep their intrigo secret, till the very last
scene before the dance ; I now, sir (do you mark me?)--a—
Smith. Begin the play, and end it, without ever opening the
plot at all?
Bayes. I do so, that's the very plain truth on't : ha, ha, ha !
I do, egad. If they cannot find it out themselves, e'en let 'em
alone for Bayes, I warrant you. But here, now, is a scene of
business : pray observe it ; for I dare say you'll think it no un-
wise discourse this, nor ill argued. To tell you true, 'tis a discourse I overheard once betwixt two grand, sober, governing
persons.

SCENE IV.

Enter GENTLEMAN-USHER *and* PHYSICIAN.

Ush. Come, sir; let's state the matter of fact, and lay our
heads together.
Phys. Right ; lay our heads together. I love to be merry
sometimes ; but when a knotty point comes, I lay my head close
to it, with a snuff-box in my hand ; and then I fegue it away,
i'faith.
Bayes. I do just so, egad, always.
Ush. The grand question is, whether they heard us whisper?
which I divide thus.
Phys. Yes, it must be divided so indeed.
Smith. That's very complaisant, I swear, Mr. Bayes, to be of
another man's opinion, before he knows what it is.
Bayes. Nay, I bring in none here but well-bred persons, I
assure you.

Ush. I divide the question into when they heard, what they heard, and whether they heard or no.

Johns. Most admirably divided, I swear !

Ush. As to the when ; you say, just now : so that is answer'd. Then, as for what ; why, that answers itself ; for what could they hear, but what we talk'd of? so that, naturally, and of necessity, we come to the last question, *videlicet*, whether they heard or no.

Smith. This is a very wise scene, Mr. Bayes.

Bayes. Ay, you have it right ; they are both politicians.

Ush. Pray, then, to proceed in method, let me ask you that question.

Phys. No, you'll answer better ; pray let me ask it you.

Ush. Your will must be a law.

Phys. Come, then, what is't I must ask ?

Smith. This politician, I perceive, Mr. Bayes, has somewhat a short memory.

Bayes. Why, sir, you must know, that t'other is the main politician, and this is but his pupil.

Ush. You must ask me whether they heard us whisper.

Phys. Well, I do so.

Ush. Say it then.

Smith. Heyday ! here's the bravest work that ever I saw.

Johns. This is mighty methodical.

Bayes. Ay, sir ; that's the way ; 'tis the way of art ; there is no other way, egad, in business.

Phys. Did they hear us whisper?

Ush. Why, truly, I can't tell ; there's much to be said upon the word whisper : to whisper in Latin is *susurrare*, which is as much as to say, to speak softly ; now, if they heard us speak softly, they heard us whisper ; but then comes in the *quomodo*, the *how ;* how did they hear us whisper? why as to that, there are two ways : the one, by chance or accident ; the other, on purpose ; that is, with design to hear us whisper.

Phys. Nay, if they heard us that way, I'll never give them physic more.

Ush. Nor I e'er more will walk abroad before 'em.

Bayes. Pray mark this, for a great deal depends upon it, towards the latter end of the play.

Smith. I suppose that's the reason why you brought in this scene, Mr. Bayes.

Bayes. Partly, it was, sir ; but I confess I was not unwilling, besides, to show the world a pattern, here, how men should talk of business.

Johns. You have done it exceeding well indeed.

Bayes. Yes, I think this will do.

Phys. Well, if they heard us whisper, they will turn us out, and nobody else will take us.

Smith. Not for politicians, I dare answer for it.
Phys. Let's then no more ourselves in vain bemoan :
    We are not safe until we them unthrone.
Ush. 'Tis right :
    And, since occasion now seems debonair,
    I'll seize on this, and you shall take that chair.
        [*They draw their swords, and sit in the two great
                                chairs upon the stage.*

Bayes. There's now an odd surprise ; the whole state's turned
quite topsy-turvy, without any pother or stir in the whole world,
egad.*

Johns. A very silent change of government, truly, as ever I
heard of.

Bayes. It is so. And yet you shall see me bring 'em in again,
by-and-by, in as odd a way every jot.
        [*The Usurpers march out, flourishing their swords.*

Enter SHIRLY.

Shir. Heyho ! heyho ! what a change is here ! heyday, heyday !
    I know not what to do, nor what to say.†   [*Exit.*

---

* Such easy turns of state are frequent in our modern plays ; where we
see princes dethroned, and governments changed, by very feeble means, and
on slight occasions : particularly in " Marriage A-la-mode ;" a play writ
since the first publication of this farce. Where (to pass by the dulness of
the state-part, the obscurity of the comic, the near resemblance Leonidas
bears to our Prince Prettyman, being sometimes a king's son, sometimes a
shepherd's ; and not to question how Amalthea comes to be a princess, her
brother, the king's great favourite, being but a lord) it is worth our while to
observe, how easily the fierce and jealous usurper is deposed, and the right
heir placed on the throne ; and it is thus related by the said imaginary
princess :—
    " *Amalth.* Oh, gentlemen ! if you have loyalty,
        Or courage, show it now. Leonidas,
        Broke on a sudden from his guards, and snatching
        A sword from one, his back against the scaffold,
        Bravely defends himself ; and owns aloud
        He is our long lost king, found for this moment ;
        But, if your valours help not, lost for ever.
        Two of his guards mov'd by the sense of virtue,
        Are turn'd for him ; and there they stand at bay,
        Against a host of foes."—" Marriage A-la-mode," p. 6r.
This shows Mr. Bayes to be a man of constancy, and firm to his resolution,
and not to be laughed out of his own method ; agreeable to what he says in
the next act : "As long as I know my things are good, what care I what
they say?"
    † " I know not what to say, or what to think !
        I know not when I sleep, or when I wake !"—
                                " Love and Friendship," p. 46.
        " My doubts and fears my reason do dismay :
        I know not what to do, or what to say."—" Pandora," p. 46.

Johns. Mr. Bayes, in my opinion, now, that gentleman might have said a little more upon this occasion.

Bayes. No, sir, not at all ; for I underwrit his part on purpose to set off the rest.

Johns. Cry you mercy, sir.

Smith. But pray, sir, how came they to depose the kings so easily ?

Bayes. Why, sir, you must know, they long had a design to do it before ; but never could put it in practice till now : and to tell you true, that's one reason why I made 'em whisper so at first.

Smith. Oh, very well ; now I'm fully satisfied.

Bayes. And then to show you, sir, it was not done so very easily neither, in the next scene you shall see some fighting.

Smith. Oh, oh ; so then you make the struggle to be after the business is done ?

Bayes. Ay.

Smith. Oh, I conceive you : that, I swear, is very natural.

SCENE V.

Enter four Men at one door, and four at another, with their swords drawn.

1st Sold. Stand. Who goes there ?
2nd Sold. A friend.
1st Sold. What friend ?
2nd Sold. A friend to the house.
1st Sold. Fall on !   [*They all kill one another.*
                                          [*Music strikes.*
Bayes. Hold, hold.   [*To the music. It ceases.*
Now, here's an odd surprise : all these dead men you shall see rise up presently, at a certain note that I have, in *effaut flat*, and fall a-dancing. Do you hear, dead men ? remember your note in *effaut flat*.
Play on.   [*To the music.*
Now, now, now ! [*The music plays his note, and the dead men rise ; but cannot get in order.*
O Lord ! O Lord ! Out, out, out ! did ever men spoil a good thing so ! no figure, no ear, no time, nothing. Udzookers, you dance worse than the angels in " Harry the Eighth," or the fat spirits in the " Tempest," egad.

1st Sold. Why, sir, 'tis impossible to do anything in time, to this tune.

Bayes. O Lord, O Lord ! impossible ! Why, gentlemen, if there be any faith in a person that's a Christian, I sat up two whole nights in composing this air, and apting it for the business ; for, if you observe, there are two several designs in this tune : it begins swift, and ends slow. You talk of time, and time ; you shall see me do it. Look you, now : here I am dead.

[Lies down flat upon his face.

Now mark my note *effaut flat.* Strike up, music.

Now. *[As he rises up hastily, he falls down again.* Ah, gadzookers ! I have broke my nose.

Johns. By my troth, Mr. Bayes, this is a very unfortunate note of yours, in *effaut.*

Bayes. A plague on this old stage, with your nails, and your tenter-hooks, that a gentleman can't come to teach you to act, but he must break his nose, and his face, and the devil and all. Pray, sir, can you help me to a wet piece of brown paper ?

Smith. No, indeed, sir, I don't usually carry any about me.

2nd Sold. Sir, I'll go get you some within presently.

Bayes. Go, go, then ; I follow you. Pray dance out the dance, and I'll be with you in a moment. Remember you dance like horse-men. *[Exit* BAYES.

Smith. Like horse-men ! what a plague can that be ?

They dance the dance, but can make nothing of it.

1st Sold. A devil ! let's try this no longer. Play my dance that Mr. Bayes found fault with so. *[Dance, and Exeunt.*

Smith. What can this fool be doing all this while about his nose ?

Johns. Prithee let's go see. *[Exeunt.*

ACT III.—SCENE I.

BAYES *with a paper on his nose, and the two Gentlemen.*

Bayes. Now, sirs, this I do, because my fancy, in this play, is, to end every act with a dance.

Smith. Faith, that fancy is very good ; but I should hardly have broke my nose for it, tho'.

Johns. That fancy I suppose is new too.

Bayes. Sir, all my fancies are so. I tread upon no man's heels ; but make my flight upon my own wings, I assure you. Now, here comes in a scene of sheer wit, without any mixture in the whole world, egad ! between Prince Prettyman and his tailor : it might properly enough be call'd a prize of wit ; for you shall see them come in one upon another snip-snap, hit for hit, as fast as can be. First, one speaks, then presently t'other's upon him, slap, with a repartee ; then he at him again, dash with a new conceit ; and so eternally, eternally, egad, till they go quite off the stage. *[Goes to call the Players.*

Smith. What a plague does this fop mean, by his snip-snap, hit for hit, and dash !

Johns. Mean ! why, he never meant anything in's life; what dost talk of meaning for ?

Enter BAYES.

Bayes. Why don't you come in ?

Enter PRINCE PRETTYMAN *and* TOM THIMBLE.*

This scene will make you die with laughing, if it be well acted, for 'tis as full of drollery as ever it can hold. 'Tis like an orange stuff'd with cloves, as for conceit.

Pret. But prithee, Tom Thimble, why wilt thou needs marry ? if nine tailors make but one man, what work art thou cutting out here for thyself, trow ?

Bayes. Good.

Thim. Why, an't please your highness, if I can't make up all the work I cut out, I shan't want journeymen enow to help me, I warrant you.

Bayes. Good again.

Pret. I am afraid thy journeymen, tho', Tom, won't work by the day.

Bayes. Good still.

Thim. However, if my wife sits but as I do, there will be no great danger : not half so much as when I trusted you, sir, for your coronation-suit.

Bayes. Very good, i'faith.

Pret. Why the times then liv'd upon trust ; it was the fashion. You would not be out of time, at such a time as that, sure : a tailor, you know, must never be out of fashion.

Bayes. Right.

Thim. I'm sure, sir, I made your clothes in the court-fashion, for you never paid me yet.

Bayes. There's a bob for the court.†

Pret. Why, Tom, thou art a sharp rogue when thou art angry, I see : thou pay'st me now, methinks.

Bayes. There's pay upon pay ! as good as ever was written, egad !

---

* Prince Prettyman and Tom Thimble ; Failer, and Bibber his tailor, in the "Wild Gallant," pp. 5. 6.

† "Nay, if that be all, there's no such haste. The courtiers are not so forward to pay their debts."—"Wild Gallant," p. 9.

D

Thim. Ay, sir, in your own coin ; you give me nothing but words.*

Bayes. Admirable !

Pret. Well, Tom, I hope shortly I shall have another coin for thee; for now the wars are coming on, I shall grow to be a man of metal.

Bayes. Oh, you did not do that half enough.

Johns. Methinks he does it admirably.

Bayes. Ay, pretty well ; but he does not hit me in't : he does not top his part.†

Thim. That's the way to be stamp'd yourself, sir. I shall see you come home, like an angel for the king's evil, with a hole bor'd thro' you. [*Exeunt.*

Bayes. Ha, there he has hit it up to the hilts, egad ! How do you like it now, gentlemen ? is not this pure wit ?

Smith. 'Tis snip-snap, sir, as you say ; but methinks not pleasant, nor to the purpose ; for the play does not go on.

Bayes. Play does not go on ! I don't know what you mean : why, is not this part of the play ?

Smith. Yes ; but the plot stands still.

Bayes. Plot stand still ! why, what a devil is the plot good for, but to bring in fine things ?

Smith. Oh, I did not know that before.

Bayes. No, I think you did not, nor many things more, that I am master of. Now, sir, egad, this is the bane of all us writers ; let us soar but never so little above the common pitch, egad, all's spoil'd, for the vulgar never understand it ; they can never conceive you, sir, the excellency of these things.

Johns. 'Tis a sad fate, I must confess ; but you write on still for all that !

Bayes. Write on ? Ay, egad, I warrant you. 'Tis not their talk shall stop me ; if they catch me at that lock, I'll give them leave to hang me. As long as I know my things are good, - what care I what they say ? What, are they gone without singing my last new song ? 'sbud would it were in their bellies. I'll tell you, Mr. Johnson, if I have any skill in these matters, I vow to gad this song is peremptorily the very best that ever yet was

---

* " Take a little Bibber,
  And throw him in the river ;
  And if he will trust never,
  Then there let him lie ever.
    Bibber. Then say I,
  Take a little Failer,
  And throw him to the jailer,
  And there let him lie
  Till he has paid his tailor."—" Wild Gallant," p. 12.

† A great word with Mr. Edward Howard.

written : you must know it was made by Tom Thimble's first wife after she was dead.

Smith. How, sir, after she was dead ?

Bayes. Ay, sir, after she was dead. Why, what have you to say to that ?

Johns. Say ? why nothing, He were a devil that had anything to say to that.

Bayes. Right.

Smith. How did she come to die, pray, sir ?

Bayes. Phoo ! that's no matter ; by a fall : but here's the conceit, that upon his knowing she was kill'd by an accident, he supposes, with a sigh, that she died for love of him.

Johns. Ay, ay, that's well enough ; let's hear it, Mr. Bayes.

Bayes. 'Tis to the tune of " Farewell, fair Armida ;" on seas, and in battles, in bullets, and all that.

SONG.*

> In swords, pikes, and bullets, 'tis safer to be,
> Than in a strong castle, remoted from thee :
> My death's bruise pray think you gave me, tho' a fall
> Did give it me more from the top of a wall :
> For then if the moat on her mud would first lay,
> And after before you my body convey :
> The blue on my breast when you happen to see,
> You'll say with a sigh, there's a true blue for me.

Ha, rogues ! when I am merry, I write these things as fast as hops, egad ; for, you must know, I am as pleasant a cavalier as ever you saw ; I am, i'faith.

Smith. But, Mr. Bayes, how comes this song in here ? for methinks there is no great occasion for it.

Bayes. Alack, sir, you know nothing ; you must ever interlard your plays with songs, ghosts, and dances, if you mean to—a—

Johns. Pit, box, and gallery,† Mr. Bayes.

---

* In imitation of this :—

> "On seas, and in battles, through bullets and fire,
> The danger is less, than in hopeless desire ;
> My death's wound you gave me, tho' far off I bear
> My fall from your sight, not to cost you a tear :
> But if the kind flood on a wave would convey,
> And under your window my body would lay ;
> When the wound on my breast you happen to see,
> You'll say with a sigh, it was given by me."

This is the latter part of a song, made by Mr. Bayes on the death of Captain Digby, son of George, Earl of Bristol, who was a passionate admirer of the Duchess Dowager of Richmond, called by the author Armida. He lost his life in a sea-fight against the Dutch, the 28th of May, 1672.

† Mr. Edward Howard's words.

Bayes. Egad, and you have nick'd it.   Hark you, Mr. Johnson, you know I don't flatter ; egad, you have a great deal of wit.

Johns. O Lord, sir, you do me too much honour.

Bayes. Nay, nay, come, come, Mr. Johnson, i'faith this must not be said amongst us that have it.   I know you have wit, by the judgment you make of this play ; for that's the measure we go by : my play is my touchstone.   When a man tells me such a one is a person of parts : is he so? say I ; what do I do, but bring him presently to see this play : if he likes it, I know what to think of him ; if not, your most humble servant, sir ; I'll no more of him, upon my word, I thank you.   I am *Clara voyant,* egad.   Now here we go on to our business.

SCENE II.

Enter the two USURPERS,* *hand in hand.*

Ush. But what's become of Volscius the Great ;
          His presence has not grac'd our court of late.
Phys. I fear some ill, from emulation sprung,
          Has from us that illustrious hero wrung.
Bayes. Is not that majestical ?
Smith. Yes, but who the devil is that Volscius ?
Bayes. Why, that's a prince I make in love with Parthenope.
Smith. I thank you, sir.

Enter CORDELIO.

Cor. My lieges, news from Volscius the prince.
Ush. His news is welcome, whatsoe'er it be.†
Smith. How, sir, do you mean whether it be good or bad ?
Bayes. Nay, pray, sir, have a little patience : gadzookers, you'll spoil all my play.   Why, sir, 'tis impossible to answer every impertinent question you ask.
Smith. Cry you mercy, sir.
Cor. His highness, sirs, commanded me to tell you,
That the fair person whom you both do know,
Despairing of forgiveness for her fault,
In a deep sorrow, twice she did attempt
Upon her precious life ; but, by the care
Of standers-by, prevented was.
Smith. Why, what stuff's here ?
Cor. At last,
Volscius the Great this dire resolve embrac'd :
His servants he into the country sent,

---

* See the two kings in " The Conquest of Granada."
† " *Albert.* Curtius, I've something to deliver to your ear.
     Cur. Anything from Alberto is welcome."—"Amorous Prince," p. 39.

And he himself to Piccadilly went ;
Where he's inform'd by letters that she's dead.

Ush. Dead ! is that possible ? dead !

Phys. O ye gods !   [*Exeunt.*

Bayes. There's a smart expression of a passion : O ye gods !
that's one of my bold strokes, egad.

Smith. Yes ; but who's the fair person that's dead ?

Bayes. That you shall know anon, sir.

Smith. Nay, if we know at all, 'tis well enough.

Bayes. Perhaps you may find, too, by-and-by, for all this, that
she's not dead neither.

Smith. Marry, that's good news indeed. I am glad of that
with all my heart.

Bayes. Now here's the man brought in that is supposed to
have kill'd her.   [*A great shout within.*

SCENE III.

Enter AMARYLLIS, *with a book in her hand, and attendants.*

Ama. What shout triumphant's that ?

Enter a SOLDIER.

Sold. Shy maid, upon the river brink, near Twic'nam town,
the false assassinate is ta'en.

Ama. Thanks to the powers above for this deliverance. I
hope,
    Its slow beginning will portend
    A forward exit to all future end.

Bayes. Pish ! there you are out ; to all future end ! no, no ; to
all future END ! You must lay the accent upon " end," or else
you lose the conceit.

Smith. I see you are very perfect in these matters.

Bayes. Ay, sir, I have been long enough at it, one would
think, to know something.

Enter SOLDIERS, *dragging in an old* FISHERMAN.

Ama. Villain, what monster did corrupt thy mind
    T' attack the noblest soul of human kind ?
Tell me who set thee on.

Fish. Prince Prettyman.

Ama. To kill whom ?

Fish. Prince Prettyman.

Ama. What ! did Prince Prettyman hire you to kill Prince
Prettyman ?

Fish. No ; Prince Volscius.

Ama. To kill whom ?

Fish. Prince Volscius.

Ama. What! did Prince Volscius hire you to kill Prince Volscius?

Fish. No, Prince Prettyman.

Ama. So drag him hence,
  Till torture of the rack produce his sense.   [*Exeunt.*

Bayes. Mark how I make the horror of his guilt confound his intellects; for he's out at one and t'other: and that's the design of this scene.

Smith. I see, sir, you have a several design for every scene.

Bayes. Ay, that's my way of writing; and so, sir, I can dispatch you a whole play, before another man, egad, can make an end of his plot.

SCENE IV.

So now enter Prince Prettyman in a rage. Where the devil is he? why, Prettyman? why, where I say? O fie, fie, fie, fie! all's marr'd, I vow to gad, quite marr'd.

Enter PRETTYMAN.

Phoo, phoo! you are come too late, sir; now you may go out again, if you please. I vow to gad, Mr. —a— I would not give a button for my play, now you have done this.

Pret. What, sir?

Bayes. What, sir! why, sir, you should have come out in choler, rouse upon the stage, just as the other went off. Must a man be eternally telling you of these things?

Johns. Sure this must be some very notable matter that he's so angry at.

Smith. I am not of your opinion.

Bayes. Pish! come let's hear your part, sir.

Pret. * Bring in my father: why d'ye keep him from me?
  Altho' a fisherman, he is my father:
  Was ever son yet brought to this distress,
  To be, for being a son, made fatherless!
  Ah! you just gods, rob me not of a father:
  The being of a son take from me rather.   [*Exit.*

Smith. Well, Ned, what think you now?

Johns. A devil, this is worst of all: Mr. Bayes, pray what's the meaning of this scene?

Bayes. O cry you mercy, sir: I protest I had forgot to tell you. Why, sir, you must know, that long before the beginning of this play, this prince was taken by a fisherman.

Smith. How, sir, taken prisoner?

Bayes. Taken prisoner! O Lord, what a question's there!

---

* See the Prince in "Marriage A-la-mode."

did ever any man ask such a quetions? Plague on him, he has put the plot quite out of my head with this—this—question! what was I going to say?

Johns. Nay, Heaven knows: I cannot imagine.

Bayes. Stay, let me see: taken! O 'tis true. Why, sir, as I was going to say, his highness here, the prince, was taken in a cradle by a fisherman, and brought up as his child!

Smith. Indeed!

Bayes. Nay, prithee, hold thy peace. And so, sir, this murder being committed by the river-side, the fisherman, upon suspicion, was seiz'd, and thereupon the prince grew angry.

Smith. So, so; now 'tis very plain.

Johns. But, Mr. Bayes, is not this some disparagement to a prince, to pass for a fisherman's son? Have a care of that, I pray.

Bayes. No, no, not at all;-for 'tis but for a while: I shall fetch him off again presently, you shall see.

Enter PRETTYMAN and THIMBLE.

Pret. By all the gods, I'll set the world on fire,
    Rather than let 'em ravish hence my sire.

Thim. Brave Prettyman, it is at length reveal'd,
    That he is not thy sire who thee conceal'd.

Bayes. Lo, you now; there, he's off again.

Johns. Admirably done, i'faith!

Bayes. Ay, now the plot thickens very much upon us.

Pret. What oracle this darkness can evince!
    Sometimes a fisher's son, sometimes a prince.
    It is a secret, great as is the world;
    In which I, like the soul, am toss'd and hurl'd,
    The blackest ink of Fate sure was my lot,
    And when she writ my name, she made a blot.   [*Exit.*

Bayes. There's a blustering verse for you now.

Smith. Yes, sir; but why is he so mightily troubled to find he is not a fisherman's son?

Bayes. Phoo! that is not because he has a mind to be his son, but for fear he should be thought to be nobody's son at all.

Smith. Nay, that would trouble a man, indeed.

Bayes. So, let me see.

SCENE V.

Enter PRINCE VOLSCIUS, going out of town.

Smith. I thought he had been gone to Piccadilly.

Bayes. Yes, he gave it out so; but that was only to cover his design.

Johns. What design?

Bayes. Why, to head the army that lies conceal'd for him at Knightsbridge.

Johns. I see here's a great deal of plot, Mr. Bayes.

Bayes. Yes, now it begins to break : but we shall have a world of more business anon,

Enter PRINCE VOLSCIUS, CLORIS, AMARYLLIS, *and* HARRY, *with a riding-cloak and boots.*

Ama. Sir, you are cruel thus to leave the town,
     And to retire to country solitude.

Clo. We hop'd this summer that we should at least
     Have held the honour of your company.

Bayes. Held the honour of your company ; prettily express'd : held the honour of your company ! gadzookers, these fellows will never take notice of anything.

Johns. I assure you, sir,.I admire it extremely ; I don't know what he does.

Bayes. Ay, ay, he's a little envious ; but 'tis no great matter. Come.

Ama. Pray let us two this single boon obtain !
     That you will here, with poor us, still remain !
     Before your horses come, pronounce our fate,
     For then, alas, I fear 'twill be too late.

Bayes. Sad !
     Harry, my boots ; for I'll go range among

Vols. My blades encamp'd, and quit this urban throng.*

Smith. But pray, Mr. Bayes, is not this a little difficult, that you were saying e'en now, to keep an army thus conceal'd in Knightsbridge ?

Bayes. In Knightsbridge ? stay.

Johns. No, not if the inn-keepers be his friends.

Bayes. His friends ! ay, sir, his intimate acquaintance ; or else indeed I grant it could not be.

Smith. Yes, faith, so it might be very easy.

Bayes. Nay, if I do not make all things easy, egad, I'll give you leave to hang me. Now you would think that he's going out of town ; but you shall see how prettily I have contriv'd to stop him presently.

Smith. By my troth, sir, you have so amaz'd me, that I know not what to think.

---

  * '' Let my horses be brought ready to the door, for I'll go out of town this evening.
          Into the country I'll with speed,
          With hounds and hawks my fancy feed, &c.
          Now I'll away, a country life
          Shall be my mistress, and my wife.''
                       '' English Monsieur,'' pp. 36, 38, 39.

Enter PARTHENOPE.

Vols. Bless me ! how frail are all my best resolves !
  How, in a moment, is my purpose chang'd !
  Too soon I thought myself secure from love.
  Fair madam, give me leave to ask her name,*
  Who does so gently rob me of my fame :
  For I should meet the army out of town,
  And if I fail, must hazard my renown.
Par. My mother, sir, sells ale by the town-walls ;
  And me her dear Parthenope she calls.
Bayes. Now that's the Parthenope I told you of.
Johns. Ay, ay, egad, you are very right.
Vols. Can vulgar vestments high-born beauty shroud ?
  Thou bring'st the morning pictur'd in a cloud.†
Bayes. The morning pictur'd in a cloud ! ah, gadzookers, what
a conceit is there !
Par. Give you good even, sir.   [*Exit.*
Vols. O inauspicious stars ! that I was born
  To sudden love, and to more sudden scorn !
Ama. ⎱ How ! Prince Volscius in love ? ha, ha, ha ! ‡
Clo. ⎰   [*Exeunt laughing.*
Smith. Sure, Mr. Bayes, we have lost some jest here, that they
laugh at so.
Bayes. Why, did you not observe ? he first resolves to go out
of town, and then as he's pulling on his boots, falls in love with
her ; ha, ha, ha !
Smith. Well, and where lies the jest of that ?
Bayes. Ha ?   [*Turns to* JOHNS.
Johns. Why, in the boots : where should the jest lie ?
Bayes. Egad, you are in the right : it does lie in the boots——
        [*Turns to* SMITH.
Your friend and I know where a good jest lies, though you don't,
sir.
Smith. Much good do't you, sir.
Bayes. Here now, Mr. Johnson, you shall see a combat
betwixt love and honour. An ancient author has made a whole
play on't ;§ but I have dispatch'd it all in this scene.

VOLSCIUS *sits down to pull on his boots :* BAYES *stands by, and
over-acts the part as he speaks it.*

Vols. How has my passion made me Cupid's scoff !
  This hasty boot is on, the other off,

---

 * "And what's this maid's name ?"—" English Monsieur," p. 40
 † " I bring the morning pictur'd in a cloud."—"Siege of Rhodes," part I.
p. 10.
 ‡ " Mr. Comely in love."—" English Monsieur," p. 49.
 § Sir William D'Avenant's play of " Love and Honour."

And sullen lies, with amorous design,
To quit loud fame, and make that beauty mine.

Smith. Prithee, mark what pains Mr. Bayes takes to act this speech himself!

Johns. Yes, the fool, I see, is mightily transported with it.

Vols. My legs the emblem of my various thought
Show to what sad distraction I am brought.
Sometimes with stubborn honour, like this boot,
My mind is guarded, and resolv'd to do't :
Sometimes again, that very mind, by love
Disarméd, like this other leg does prove.
Shall I to honour or to love give way?
Go on, cries honour ;* tender love says, nay ;
Honour aloud commands, pluck both boots on ;
But softer love does whisper, put on none.
What shall I do ! what conduct shall I find,
To lead me thro' this twilight of my mind?
For as bright day, with black approach of night
Contending, makes a doubtful puzzling light ;
So does my honour and my love together
Puzzle me so; I can resolve for neither.

[*Goes out hopping, with one boot on, and t'other off.*

Johns. By my troth, sir, this is as difficult a combat as ever I saw, and as equal ; for 'tis determin'd on neither side.

Bayes. Ay, is't not now egad, ha ? for to go off hip-hop, hip-hop, upon this occasion, is a thousand times better than any conclusion in the world, egad.

Johns. Indeed, Mr. Bayes, that hip-hop, in this place, as you say, does a very great deal.

Bayes. Oh, all in all, sir ! they are these little things that mar, or set you off a play ; as I remember once in a play of mine, I set off a scene, egad, beyond expectation, only with a petticoat, and the gripes.†

Smith. Pray how was that, sir ?

Bayes. Why, sir, I contriv'd a petticoat to be brought in upon a chair (nobody knew how) into a prince's chamber, whose father was not to see it, that came in by chance.

Johns. By-my-life, that was a notable contrivance indeed.

Smith. Ay, but Mr. Bayes, how could you contrive the stomach-ache ?

Bayes. The easiest i' th' world, egad : I'll tell you how. I made the prince sit down upon the petticoat, no more than so, and pretended to his father that he had just then got the gripes : whereupon his father went out to call a physician, and his man ran away with the petticoat.

* " But honours says not so."—" Siege of Rhodes," part i. p. 19.
† " Love in a Nunnery," p. 34.

Smith. Well, and what follow'd upon that?

Bayes. Nothing, no earthly thing, I vow to gad,

Johns. On my word, Mr. Bayes, there you hit it.

Bayes. Yes, it gave a world of content.   And then I paid 'em away besides; for it made them all talk beastly : ha, ha, ha, beastly ! downright beastly upon the stage, egad, ha, ha, ha ! but with an infinite deal of wit, that I must say.

Johns. That, ay, that, we know well enough, can never fail you.

Bayes. No, egad, can't it.   Come, bring in the dance.

                [*Exit to call the Players.*

Smith. Now, the plague take thee for a silly, confident, unnatural, fulsome rogue.

Enter BAYES *and* PLAYERS.

Bayes. Pray dance well before these gentlemen; you are commonly so lazy, but you should be light and easy, tah, tah, tah.   [*All the while they dance,* BAYES *puts them out with teaching them.*

Well, gentlemen, you'll see this dance, if I am not deceiv'd, take very well upon the stage, when they are perfect in their motions, and all that.

Smith. I don't know how 'twill take, sir ; but I am sure you sweat hard for't.

Bayes. Ay, sir, it costs me more pains and trouble to do these things than almost the things are worth.

Smith. By my troth, I think so, sir.

Bayes. Not for the things themselves ; for I could write you, sir, forty of 'em in a day : but, egad, these players are such dull persons, that if a man be not by 'em upon every point, and at every turn, egad, they'll mistake you, sir, and spoil all.

Enter a PLAYER.

What, is the funeral ready?

Play. Yes, sir.

Bayes. And is the lance fill'd with wine?

Play. Sir, 'tis just now a-doing.

Bayes. Stay, then, I'll do it myself.

Smith. Come, let's go with him.

Bayes. A match.   But, Mr. Johnson, egad, I am not like other persons ; they care not what becomes of their things, so they can but get money for 'em : now, egad, when I write, if it be not just as it should be in every circumstance, to every particular, egad, I am no more able to endure it, I am not myself, I'm out of my wits, and all that ; I'm the strangest person in the whole world : for what care I for money ?   I write for reputation.

                [*Exeunt.*

ACT IV.—SCENE I.

BAYES, *and the two Gentlemen.*

Bayes. Gentlemen, because I would not have any two things alike in this play, the last act beginning with a witty scene of mirth, I make this to begin with a funeral.

Smith. And is that all your reason for it, Mr. Bayes?

Bayes. No, sir, I have a precedent for it besides. A person of honour, and a scholar, brought in his funeral just so; * and he was one, let me tell you, that knew as well what belong'd to a funeral as any man in England, egad.

Johns. Nay, if that be so, you are safe.

Bayes. Egad, but I have another device, a frolic, which I think yet better than all this; not for the plot or characters (for, in my heroic plays, I make no difference as to those matters), but for another contrivance.

Smith. What is that, I pray?

Bayes. Why, I have design'd a conquest that cannot possibly, egad, be acted in less than a whole week; and I'll speak a bold word, it shall drum, trumpet, shout, and battle, egad, with any the most warlike tragedy we have, either ancient or modern.†

Johns. Ay, marry, sir, there you say something.

Smith. And pray, sir, how have you order'd this same frolic of yours?

Bayes. Faith, sir, by the rule of romance; for example, they divide their things into three, four, five, six, seven, eight, or as many tomes as they please. Now I would very fain know what should hinder me from doing the same with my things, if I please?

Johns. Nay, if you should not be master of your own works, 'tis very hard.

Bayes. That is my sense. And then, sir, this contrivance of mine has something of the reason of a play in it too; for as every one makes you five acts to one play, what do I, but make five plays to one plot: by which means the auditors have every day a new thing.

---

* Col. Henry Howard, son of Thomas, Earl of Berkshire, made a play called the "United Kingdoms," which began with a funeral; and had also two kings in it. This gave the duke a just occasion to set up two kings in Brentford, as it is generally believed; tho' others are of opinion, that his grace had our two brothers, King Charles and the Duke of York, in his thoughts. It was acted at the Cockpit, in Drury Lane, soon after the Restoration; but miscarrying on the stage, the author had the modesty not to print it; and therefore, the reader cannot reasonably expect any particular passages of it. Others say, that they are Boabdelin and Abdalla, the two contending kings of Granada; and Mr. Dryden has, in most of his serious plays, two contending kings of the same place.

† "Conquest of Granada," in two parts.

Johns. Most admirably good, i'faith ! and must certainly take, because it is not tedious.

Bayes. Ay, sir, I know that ; there's the main point. And then upon Saturday to make a close of all (for I ever begin upon a Monday), I make you, sir, a sixth play that sums up the whole matter to 'em, and all that, for fear they should have forgot it. -

Johns. That consideration, Mr. Bayes, indeed I think will be very necessary.

Smith. And when comes in your share, pray, sir ?

Bayes. The third week.

Johns. I vow you'll get a world of money.

Bayes. Why, faith, a man must live ; and if you don't thus pitch upon some new device, egad, you'll never do't ; for this age (take it o' my word) is somewhat hard to please. But there is one pretty odd passage in the last of these plays, which may be executed two several ways, wherein I'd have your opinion, gentlemen.

Johns. What is't, sir.

Bayes. Why, sir, I make a male person to be in love with a female.

Smith. Do you mean that, Mr. Bayes, for a new thing ?

Bayes. Yes, sir, as I have order'd it. You shall hear : he having passionately lov'd her through my five whole plays, finding at last that she consents to his love, just after that his mother had appear'd to him like a ghost, he kills himself : that's one way. The other is, that she coming at last to love him, with as violent a passion as he lov'd her, she kills herself. Now my question is, which of these two persons should suffer upon this occasion ?

Johns. By my troth, it is a very hard case to decide.

Bayes. The hardest in the world, egad, and has puzzled this pate very much. What say you, Mr. Smith ?

Smith. Why truly, Mr. Bayes, if it might stand with your justice now, I would spare 'em both.

Bayes. Egad, and I think—ha—why then, I'll make him hinder her from killing herself. Ay, it shall be so. Come, come, bring in the funeral.

Enter a Funeral, with the two USURPERS *and Attendants.*

Lay it down there ; no, no, here, sir. So now speak.

K. Ush. Set down the funeral pile, and let our grief
　　　　Receive from its embraces some relief.

K. Phys. Was't not unjust to ravish hence her breath,
　　　　And in life's stead, to leave us nought but death ?
　　　　The world discovers now its emptiness,
　　　　And by her loss demonstrates we have less.

Bayes. Is not this good language now ? is not that elevate ?

'tis my *non ultra*, egad ; you must know they were both in love with her.

Smith. With her ! with whom ?

Bayes. Why, this is Lardella's funeral.

Smith. Lardella ! ay, who is she?

Bayes. Why, sir, the sister of Drawcansir; a lady that was drown'd at sea, and had a wave for her winding-sheet.*

K. Ush. Lardella, O Lardella, from above
    Behold the tragic issues of our love :
    Pity us, sinking under grief and pain,
    For thy being cast away upon the main.

Bayes. Look you now, you see I told you true.

Smith. Ay, sir, and I thank you for it very kindly.

Bayes. Ay, egad, but you will not have patience ; honest Mr. —a— you will not have patience.

Johns. Pray, Mr. Bayes, who is that Drawcansir ?

Bayes. Why, sir, a fierce hero, that frights his mistress, snubs up kings, baffles armies, and does what he will, without regard to numbers, good manners, or justice.†

Johns. A very pretty character !

Smith. But, Mr. Bayes, I thought your heroes had ever been men of great humanity and justice.

Bayes. Yes, they have been so ; but for my part, I prefer that one quality of singly beating of whole armies, above all your moral virtues put together, egad. You shall see him come in presently. Zookers, why don't you read the paper ?

        [*To the Players.*

K. Phys. O, cry you mercy.   [*Goes to take the paper.*

Bayes. Pish ! nay you are such a fumbler. Come, I'll read it myself.   [*Takes the paper from off the coffin.*
Stay, it's an ill hand, I must use my spectacles. This now is a copy of verses, which I make Lardella compose just as she is dying, with design to have it pinn'd upon her coffin, and so read by one of the usurpers, who is her cousin.

Smith. A very shrewd design that, upon my word, Mr. Bayes.

Bayes. And what do you think now, I fancy her to make love like, here, in this paper ?

Smith. Like a woman : what should she make love like ?

Bayes. O' my word you are out tho', sir ; egad you are.

Smith. What then, like a man ?

Bayes. No, sir ; like a humble-bee.

Smith. I confess, that I should not have fancy'd.

---

* "On seas I bore thee, and on seas I died,
    I died : and for a winding-sheet, a wave
    I had ; and all the ocean for my grave."
                "Conquest of Granada," part ii. p. 113.
† Almanzor in the "Conquest of Granada,"

Bayes. It may be so, sir; but it is tho', in order to the opinion of some of our ancient philosophers, who held the transmigration of the soul.

Smith. Very fine.

Bayes. I'll read the title : " To my dear Couz, King Physician."

Smith. That's a little too familiar with a king, tho', sir, by your favour, for a humble-bee.

Bayes. Mr. Smith, in other things, I grant your knowledge may be above me ; but as for poetry, give me leave to say I understand that better : it has been longer my practice; it has indeed, sir.

Smith. Your servant, sir.

Bayes. Pray mark it.   [*Reads.*

" Since death my earthly part will thus remove,
    I'll come a humble-bee to your chaste love :
    With silent wings I'll follow you, dear couz ;
    Or else, before you, in the sunbeams, buz.
    And when to melancholy groves you come,
    An airy ghost, you'll know me by my hum ;
    For sound, being air, a ghost does well become." *

Smith (after a pause). Admirable!

Bayes. "At night, into your bosom I will creep,
    And buz but softly if you chance to sleep :
    Yet in your dreams, I will pass sweeping by,
    And then both hum and buz before your eye."

Johns. By my troth, that's a very great promise.

Smith. Yes, and a most extraordinary comfort to boot.

Bayes. " Your bed of love from dangers I will free ;
    But most from love of any future bee.
    And when with pity your heart-strings shall crack,
    With empty arms I'll bear you on my back."

* In ridicule of this :—

                                    " My earthly part,
    Which is my tyrant's right, death will remove ;
    I'll come all soul and spirit to your love.
    With silent steps I'll follow you all day ;
    Or else before you in the sunbeams play.
    I'll lead you hence to melancholy groves,
    And there repeat the scenes of our past loves ;
    At night, I will within your curtains peep,
    With empty arms embrace you, while you sleep.
    In gentle dreams I often will be by,
    And sweep along before your closing eye.
    All dangers from your bed I will remove ;
    But guard it most from any future love.
    And when at last in pity you will die,
    I'll watch your birth of immortality :
    Then, turtle like, I'll to my mate repair,
    And teach you your first flight in open air."—

                        " Tyrannic Love," p. 25.

Smith. A pick-a-pack, a pick-a-pack.

Bayes. Ay, egad, but is not that *tuant* now, ha? is it not *tuant?* Here's the end.

"Then at your birth of immortality,
　Like any wingéd archer hence I'll fly,
　And teach you your first fluttering in the sky."

Johns. Oh, rare! this is the most natural, refined fancy that ever I heard, I'll swear.

Bayes. Yes, I think, for a dead person, it is a good way enough of making love ; for, being divested of her terrestrial part, and all that, she is only capable of these little, pretty, amorous designs that are innocent, and yet passionate. Come, draw your swords.

K. Phys. Come, sword, come sheath thyself within this breast;
　　　Which only in Lardella's tomb can rest.

K. Ush. Come, dagger, come and penetrate this heart,
　　　Which cannot from Lardella's love depart.

Enter PALLAS.

Pal. Hold, stop your murd'ring hands
　　At Pallas's commands :
　　For the supposéd dead, O kings,
　　Forbear to act such deadly things.
　　Lardella lives ; I did but try
　　If princes for their loves could die.
　　Such celestial constancy
　　Shall, by the gods, rewarded be :
　　And from these funeral obsequies,
　　A nuptial banquet shall arise.
　　　　[*The coffin opens, and a banquet is discovered.*

Bayes. So, take away the coffin. Now 'tis out. This is the very funeral of the fair person which Volscius sent word was dead ; and Pallas, you see, has turned it into a banquet.

Smith. Well, but where is this banquet?

Bayes. Nay, look you, sir ; we must first have a dance, for joy that Lardella is not dead. Pray, sir, give me leave to bring in my things properly at least.

Smith. That, indeed, I had forgot ; I ask your pardon.

Bayes. Oh, d'ye so, sir? I am glad you will confess yourself once in an error, Mr. Smith.

[*Dance.*]

K. Ush. Resplendent Pallas, we in thee do find
　　　The fiercest beauty, and a fiercer mind :
　　　And since to thee Lardella's life we owe,
　　　We'll supple statues in thy temple grow.

K. Phys. Well, since alive Lardella's found,
　　　　Let in full bowls her health go round.
　　　　　　[*The two Usurpers take each of them*
　　　　　　　　a bowl in their hands.

K. Ush. But where's the wine ?
Pal. That shall be mine.
　　　　Lo, from this conquering lance
　　　　Does flow the purest wine of France :
　　　　　　[*Fills the bowls out of her lance.*
　　　　And to appease your hunger, I
　　　　Have in my helmet brought a pie :
　　　　Lastly, to bear a part with these,
　　　　Behold a buckler made of cheese.*　　[*Vanish* PALLAS.
Bayes. That's the banquet.　Are you satisfied now, sir ?
Johns. By my troth now, that is new, and more than I expected.
Bayes. Yes, I knew this would please you ; for the chief art in poetry is to elevate your expectation, and then bring you off some extraordinary way.

Enter DRAWCANSIR.

K. Phys. What man is this that dares disturb our feast ?
Draw. He that dares drink, and for that drink dares die ;
　　　　And knowing this, dares yet drink on, am I.†
Johns. That is, Mr. Bayes, as much as to say, that though he would rather die than not drink, yet he would fain drink for all that too.
Bayes. Right ; that's the conceit on't.
Johns. 'Tis a marvellous good one, I swear.
Bayes. Now, there are some critics that have advis'd me to put out the second *dare*, and print *must* in the place on't ;‡ but, egad, I think 'tis better thus a great deal.
Johns. Whoo ! a thousand times.
Bayes. Go on then.
K. Ush. Sir, if you please, we should be glad to know,
　　　　How long you here will stay, how soon you'll go?
Bayes. Is not that now like a well-bred person, egad? so modest, so gent !
Smith. O very like.

---

* See the scene in the "Villain." Where the host furnishes his guests with a collation out of his clothes ; a capon from his helmet, a tansey out of the lining of his cap, cream out of his scabbard, &c.
† In ridicule of this :—
　　"*Almah.* Who dares to interrupt my private walk ?
　　Alman. He who dares love, and for that love must die ;
　　　　And, knowing this, dares yet love on, am I."
　　　　　　　　　　　　"Granada," part ii. pp. 114, 115.
‡ It was at first, "dares die."—*Ibid.*

Draw. You shall not know how long I here will stay ;
But you shall know I'll take your bowls away.*
[*Snatches the bowls out of the kings' hands and drinks them off.*

Smith. But, Mr. Bayes, is that, too, modest and gent ?

Bayes. No, egad, sir, but 'tis great.

K. Ush. Tho', brother, this grum stranger be a clown,
He'll leave us sure a little to gulp down.

Draw. Whoe'er to gulp one drop of this dare think,
I'll stare away his very power to drink,†
[*The two Kings sneak off the stage with their attendants.*

I drink, I huff, I strut, look big and stare ;
And all this I can do because I dare.‡   [*Exit.*

Smith. I suppose, Mr. Bayes, this is the fierce hero you spoke of ?

Bayes. Yes ; but this is nothing. You shall see him in the last act win above a dozen battles, one after another, egad, as fast as they can possibly come upon the stage.

Johns. That will be a fight worth the seeing, indeed.

Smith. But pray, Mr. Bayes, why do you make the kings let him use them so scurvily ?

Bayes. Phoo ! that's to raise the character of Drawcansir.

Johns. O' my word, that was well thought on.

Bayes. Now, sirs, I'll show you a scene indeed ; or rather, indeed, the scene of scenes. 'Tis an heroic scene.

Smith. And pray, what's your design in this scene ?

Bayes. Why, sir, my design is gilded truncheons, forc'd conceit, smooth verse and a rant ; in fine, if this scene don't take, egad, I'll write no more. Come, come in, Mr. —a— nay, come in as many as you can. Gentlemen, I must desire you to remove a little, for I must fill the stage.

Smith. Why fill the stage ?

Bayes. Oh, sir, because your heroic verse never sounds well but when the stage is full.

● " *Alman.* I would not now, if thou wouldst beg me, stay ;
But I will take my Almahide away."—
                    "Conquest of Granada," p. 32.

† In ridicule of this :—
" *Alman.* Thou dar'st not marry her, while I'm in sight ;
    With a bent brow, thy priest and thee I'll fright :
    And, in that scene, which all thy hopes and wishes should content,
    The thoughts of me shall make thee impotent."—*Ibid.* p. 5.

‡ " Spite of myself, I'll stay, fight, love, despair ;
    And all this I can do, because I dare."—"Tyrannic Love," part ii. p. 89.

Enter PRINCE PRETTYMAN *and* PRINCE VOLSCIUS.

Nay, hold, hold ; pray by your leave a little.   Look you, sir, the drift of this scene is somewhat more than ordinary ; for I make 'em both fall out because they are not in love with the same woman.

Smith. Not in love?   You mean, I suppose, because they are in love, Mr. Bayes?

Bayes. No, sir ; I say not in love ; there's a new conceit for you.   Now speak.

Pret. Since fate, Prince Volscius, now has found the way
  For our so long'd-for meeting here this day,
  Lend thy attention to my grand concern.

Vols. I gladly would that story from thee learn ;
  But thou to love dost, Prettyman, incline ;
  Yet love in thy breast is not love in mine.

Bayes. Antithesis ! thine and mine.

Pret. Since love itself's the same, why should it **be**
  Diff'ring in you from what it is in me ?

Bayes. Reasoning ! egad, I love reasoning in verse.

Vols. Love takes, caméleon-like, a various dye
  From every plant on which itself doth lie.

Bayes. Simile !

Pret. Let not thy love the course of nature fright :
  Nature does most in harmony delight.

Vols. How weak a deity would nature prove,
  Contending with the powerful god of love !

Bayes. There's a great verse !

Vols. If incense thou wilt offer at the shrine
  Of mighty Love, burn it to none but mine.
  Her rosy lips eternal sweets exhale ;
  'And her bright flames make all flames else look pale.

Bayes. Egad, that is right.

Pret. Perhaps dull incense may thy love suffice ;
  But mine must be ador'd with sacrifice.
  All hearts turn ashes, which her eyes control :
  The body they consume, as well as soul.

Vols. My love has yet a power more divine ;
  Victims her altars burn not, but refine ;
  Amidst the flames they ne'er give up the ghost,
  But, with her looks, revive still as they roast.
  In spite of pain and death they're kept alive ;
  Her fiery eyes make 'em in fire survive.

Bayes. That is as well, egad, as I can do.

Vols. Let my Parthenope at length prevail.

Bayes. Civil, egad.

Pret. I'll sooner have a passion for a whale ;
    In whose vast bulk, tho' store of oil doth lie,
    We find more shape, more beauty in a fly.

Smith. That's uncivil, egad.

Bayes. Yes ; but as far-fetched a fancy, tho', egad, as e'er you saw.

Vols. Soft, Prettyman, let not thy vain pretence
    Of perfect love defame love's excellence :
    Parthenope is, sure, as far above
    All other loves, as above all is Love.

Bayes. Ah ! egad, that strikes me.

Pret. To blame my Cloris, gods would not pretend—

Bayes. Now mark—

Vols. Were all gods join'd, they could not hope to mend
    My better choice : for fair Parthenope
    Gods would themselves un-god themselves to see. *

Bayes. Now the rant's a-coming.

Pret. Durst any of the gods be so uncivil,
    I'd make that god subscribe himself a devil.†

Bayes. Ay, gadzookers, that's well writ !

              [*Scratching his head, his peruke falls off.*

Vols. Could'st thou that god from heaven to earth translate,
    He could not fear to want a heav'nly state ;
    Parthenope, on earth, can heav'n create.

Pret. Cloris does heav'n itself so far excel,
    She can transcend the joys of heav'n in hell.

Bayes. There's a bold flight for you now ! 'sdeath, I have lost my peruke. Well, gentlemen, this is what I never yet saw any one could write, but myself. Here's true spirit and flame all through, egad. So, so, pray clear the stage.

              [*He puts 'em off the stage.*

Johns. I wonder how the coxcomb has got the knack of writing smooth verse thus.

Smith. Why, there's no need of brain for this : 'tis but scanning the labours on the finger ; but where's the sense of it ?

Johns. Oh ! for that he desires to be excus'd : he is too proud

---

* In ridicule of this :—
    "*Max.* Thou liest. There's not a god inhabits there,
      But, for this Christian, would all heaven forswear :
      Even Jove would try new shapes her love to win,
      And in new birds, and unknown beasts would sin ;
      At least, if Jove could love like Maximin."—
                        "Tyrannic Love," p. 17.

† "Some god now, if he dare relate what pass'd ;
    Say, but he's dead, that god shall mortal be."—*Ibid.* p. 7.
  "Provoke my rage no farther, lest I be
    Reveng'd at once upon the gods, and thee."—*Ibid.* p. 8.
  "What had the gods to do with me, or mine."—*Ibid.* p. 57.

a man to creep servilely after sense, I assure you.* But pray, Mr. Bayes, why is this scene all in verse?

Bayes. Oh, sir, the subject is too great for prose.

Smith. Well said, i'faith; I'll give thee a pot of ale for that answer; 'tis well worth it.

Bayes. Come, with all my heart.

I'll make that god subscribe himself a devil;
That single line, egad, is worth all that my brother poets·ever
   writ.
Let down the curtain.   [*Exeunt.*

ACT. V.—SCENE I.

BAYES, *and the two Gentlemen.*

Bayes. Now, gentlemen, I will be bold to say, I'll show you the greatest scene that ever England saw : I mean not for words, for those I don't value; but for state, show and magnificence. In fine, I'll justify it to be as grand to the eye every whit, egad, as that great scene in "Harry the Eighth," and grander too, egad ; for instead of two bishops, I bring in here four cardinals.

> [*The curtain is drawn up, the two usurping Kings appear in state with the four Cardinals,* PRINCE PRETTY-MAN, PRINCE VOLSCIUS, AMARYLLIS, CLORIS, PAR-THENOPE, &c., *before them, Heralds and Sergeants-at-arms, with maces.*

Smith. Mr. Bayes, pray what is the reason that two of the cardinals are in hats, and the other in caps?

Bayes. Why, sir, because—— By gad I won't tell you. Your country friend, sir, grows so troublesome—

K. Ush. Now, sir, to the business of the day.

K. Phys. Speak, Volscius.

Vols. Dread sovereign lords, my zeal to you must not invade my duty to your son ; let me entreat that great Prince Pretty-man first to speak; whose high pre-eminence in all things, that do bear the name of good, may justly claim that privilege.

Bayes. Here it begins to unfold ; you may perceive, now, that he is his son.

Johns. Yes, sir, and we are very much beholden to you for that discovery.

---

    * " Poets, like lovers, should be bold, and dare ;
        They spoil their business with an over-care :
        And he, who servilely creeps after sense,
        Is safe ; but ne'er can reach to excellence."—
                         " Prologue to Tyrannic Love. '

Pret. Royal father, upon my knees I beg,
      That the illustrious Volscius first be heard.
Vols. That preference is only due to Amaryllis, sir.
Bayes. I'll make her speak very well, by-and-by, you shall see.
Ama. Invincible sovereigns——   [*Soft music.*
K. Ush. But stay, what sound is this invades our ears?*
K. Phys. Sure 'tis the music of the moving spheres.
Pret. Behold, with wonder, yonder comes from far
      A god-like cloud, and a triumphant car;
      In which our two right kings sit one by one,
      With virgins' vests, and laurel garlands on.
K. Ush. Then, brother Phys., 'tis time we should be gone.
      [*The two Usurpers steal out of the throne, and go away.*
Bayes. Look you now, did not I tell you, that this would be as
easy a change as the other?
Smith. Yes, faith, you did so; tho' I confess I could not
believe you: but you have brought it about, I see.
           [*The two right kings of Brentford descend in the
                clouds, singing, in white garments; and three
                fiddlers sitting before them, in green.*
Bayes. Now, because the two right kings descend from above,
I make 'em sing to the tune and style of our modern spirits.
  1st King. Haste, brother king, we are sent from above.
  2nd King. Let us move, let us move;
      Move to remove the fate
      Of Brentford's long united state.†

"What various noises do my ears invade;
   And have a concert of confusion made?"—"Siege of Rhodes," p. 4.
† In ridicule of this:—
 "*Naker.* Hark, my Damilcar, we are call'd below.
     Dam. Let us go, let us go:
        Go to relieve the care,
        Of longing lovers in despair.
   Naker. Merry, merry, merry, we sail from the east,
        Half tippled at a rainbow feast.
     Dam. In the bright moonshine, while winds whistle loud,
        Tivy, tivy, tivy, we mount and we fly,
        All racking along in a downy white cloud;
        And lest our leap from the sky should prove too far,
        We slide on the back of a new-falling star.
   Naker. And drop from above,
        In a jelly of love.
     Dam. But now the sun's down, and the element's red,
        The spirits of fire against us make head.
   Naker. They muster, they muster, like gnats in the air:
        Alas! I must leave thee, my fair;
        And to my light-horsemen repair.
     Dam. O stay! for you need not to fear 'em to-night;
        The wind is for us, and blows full in their sight:
        And o'er the wide ocean we fight,

1st King. Tarra, ran, tarra, full east and by south.
2nd King. We sail with thunder in our mouth,
   In scorching noon-day, whilst the traveller stays ;
   Busy, busy, busy, busy, we bustle along,
   Mounted upon warm Phœbus's rays,
   Through the heavenly throng,
      Hasting to those
Who will feast us at night with a pig's petty-toes.
1st King.   And we'll fall with our plate
      In an *ollio* of hate. ·
2nd King. But now supper's done, the servitors try,
   Like soldiers, to storm a whole half-moon pie.
1st King. They gather, they gather hot custards in spoons :
   But alas, I must leave these half-moons,
   And repair to my trusty dragoons.
2nd King. Oh, stay, for you need not as yet go astray :
   The tide, like a friend, has brought ships in our way,
   And on their high ropes we will play
   Like maggots in filberts we'll snug in our shell,
     We'll frisk in our shell,
     We'll frisk in our shell,
     And farewell.
1st King. But the ladies have all inclination to dance,
   And the green frogs croak out a coranto of France.
Bayes. Is not that pretty, now ? The fiddlers are all in green.
Smith. Ay, but they play no coranto.
Johns. No, but they play a tune that's a great deal better.
Bayes. No coranto, quoth-a ! that's a good one, with all my
heart. Come, sing on.
2nd King.   Now mortals that hear
     How we tilt and career,
     With wonder will fear
The event of such things as shall never appear.

    Like leaves in the autumn, our foes will fall down,
    And hiss in the water . . . .
Both. And hiss in the water, and drown.
Naker. But their men lie securely intrench'd in a cloud,
    And a trumpeter-hornet to battle sounds loud.
Dam. Now mortals that spy
    How we tilt in the sky,
    With wonder will gaze ;
    And fear such events as will ne'er come to pass.
Naker. Stay you to perform what the man will have done.
Dam. Then call me again when the battle is won.
Both. So ready and quick is a spirit of air,
    To pity the lover, and succour the fair,
    That silent and swift, that little soft god,
    Is here with a wish, and is gone with a nod."—
          "Tyrannic Love," pp. 24, 25.

1st King. Stay you to fulfil what the gods have decreed.
2nd King. Then call me to help you, if there shall be need.
1st King. So firmly resolv'd is a true Brentford king,
     To save the distress'd, and help to 'em to bring,
     That ere a full pot of good ale you can swallow,
     He's here with a whoop, and gone with a holla.
          [BAYES *fillips his finger, and sings after them.*
Bayes. "He's here with a whoop, and gone with a holla."
This, sir, you must know, I thought once to have brought in
with a conjuror.*

Johns. Ay, that would have been better.
Bayes. No, faith, not when you consider it ; for thus it is more
compendious, and does the thing every whit as well.
Smith. Thing ! what thing ?
Bayes. Why, bring 'em down again into the throne, sir. What
thing would you have ?
Smith. Well, but methinks the sense of this song is not very
plain !
Bayes. Plain ! why, did you ever hear any people in clouds
speak plain ? They must be all for flight of fancy at its full
range, without the least check or control upon it. When once
you tie up spirits and people in clouds, to speak plain, you
spoil all.
Smith. Bless me, what a monster's this !
          [*The two Kings light out of the clouds, and
                              step into the throne.*
1st King. Come, now to serious counsel we'll advance.
2nd King. I do agree ; but first, let's have a dance.
Bayes. Right. You did that very well, Mr. Cartwright. But
first, let's have a dance. Pray remember that ; be sure you do
it always just so : for it must be done as if it were the effect of
thought and premeditation. But first, let's have a dance ; pray
remember that.
Smith. Well, I can hold no longer, I must gag this rogue,
there's no enduring of him.
Johns. No, prithee make use of thy patience a little longer,
let's see the end of him now. _   [*Dance a grand dance.*
Bayes. This, now, is an ancient dance, of right belonging to
the Kings of Brentford ; but since derived, with a little alteration,
to the Inns of Court.

          An Alarm.   Enter two Heralds.

1st King. What saucy groom molests our privacies ?
1st Her. The army's at the door, and in disguise,
     Desires a word with both your majesties.

          * See "Tyrannic Love," act iv. sc. 1.

2nd Her. Having from Knightsbridge hither marched by
stealth.

2nd King. Bid 'em attend awhile, and drink our health.

Smith. How, Mr. Bayes, the army in disguise !

Bayes. Ay, sir, for fear the usurpers might discover them, that
went out but just now.

Smith. Why, what if they had discover'd them ?

Bayes. Why, then they had broke the design.

1st King. Here take five guineas for those warlike men.

2nd King. And here's five more, that makes the sum just ten.

1st Her. We have not seen so much, the Lord knows when.
[*Exeunt Heralds.*

1st King. Speak on, brave Amaryllis.

Ama. Invincible sovereigns, blame not my modesty, if at this
grand conjuncture——   [*Drum beats behind the stage.*

1st King. What dreadful noise is this that comes and goes ?

Enter a Soldier with his sword drawn.

Sold. Haste hence, great sirs, your royal persons save,
        For the event of war no mortal knows :*
        The army, wrangling for the gold you gave,
        First fell to words, and then to handy-blows.   [*Exit.*

Bayes. Is not that now a pretty kind of a stanza, and a handsome come-off ?

2nd King. O dangerous estate of sovereign power !.
        Obnoxious to the change of every hour.

1st King. Let us for shelter in our cabinet stay ;
        Perhaps these threatning storms may pass away.
        [*Exeunt.*

Johns. But, Mr. Bayes, did not you promise us just now, to
make Amaryllis speak very well ?

Bayes. Ay, and so she would have done, but that they hinder'd
her.

Smith. How, sir, whether you would or no ?

Bayes. Ay, sir, the plot lay so, that I vow to gad, it was not
to be avoided.

Smith. Marry, that was hard.

Johns. But, pray, who hinder'd her ?

---

* In ridicule of this :—
            "What new misfortunes do these cries presage?
    1st Mess. Haste all you can, their fury to assuage :
            You are not safe from their rebellious rage.
    2nd Mess. This minute, if you grant not their desire,
            They'll seize your person, and your palace fire."—
                                    "Granada," part ii. p. 71.

Bayes. Why, the battle, sir, that's just coming in at the door : and I'll tell you now a strange thing; tho' I don't pretend to do more than other men, egad, I'll give you both a whole week to guess how I'll represent this battle.

Smith. I had rather be bound to fight your battle, I assure you, sir.

Bayes. Whoo! there's it now : fight a battle! there's the common error. I knew presently where I should have you. Why, pray, sir, do but tell me this one thing : can you think it a decent thing, in a battle before ladies, to have men run their swords thro' one another, and all that?

Johns. No, faith, 'tis not civil.

Bayes. Right ; on the other side, to have a long relation of squadrons here, and squadrons there : what is it, but dull prolixity?

Johns. Excellently reason'd, by my troth !

Bayes. Wherefore, sir, to avoid both those indecorums, I sum up the whole battle in the representation of two persons only, no more : and yet so lively, that, I vow to gad, you would swear ten thousand men were at it really engag'd. Do you mark me?

Smith. Yes, sir : but I think I should hardly swear tho', for all that.

Bayes. By my troth, sir, but you would tho', when you see it : for I make 'em both come out in armour *cap-a-pie*, with their swords drawn, and hung with a scarlet ribbon at their wrist ; which, you know, represents fighting enough.

Johns. Ay, ay ; so much, that if I were in your place, I would make 'em go out again, without ever speaking one word.

Bayes. No, there you are out ; for I make each of 'em hold a lute in his hand.

Smith. How, sir, instead of a buckler?

Bayes. O Lord, O Lord! instead of a buckler? pray, sir, do you ask no more questions. I make 'em, sirs, play the battle *in recitativo*. And here's the conceit just at the very same instant that one sings, the other, sir, recovers you his sword, and puts himself into a warlike posture : so that you have at once your ear entertain'd with music and good language, and your eye satisfied with the garb and accoutrements of war.

Smith. I confess, sir, you stupefy me.

Bayes. You shall see.

Johns. But, Mr. Bayes, might not we have a little fighting ? for I love those plays where they cut and slash one another upon the stage for a whole hour together.

Bayes. Why, then, to tell you true, I have contriv'd it both ways : but you shall have my *recitativo* first.

Johns. Ay, now you are right : there is nothing that can be objected against it.

Bayes. True : and so, egad, I'll make it too a tragedy in a trice.*

Enter at several doors the GENERAL *and* LIEUTENANT-GENERAL, *arm'd cap a-pie, with each of them a lute in his hand, and a sword drawn, and hung with a scarlet ribbon at his wrist.*†

Lieut.-Gen. Villain, thou liest !
Gen. Arm, arm, Gonsalvo,‡ arm, what, ho !
    The lie no flesh can brook, I trow.
Lieut.-Gen. Advance from Acton with the musqueteers.
Gen. Draw down the Chelsea cuirassiers.§
Lieut.-Gen. The band you boast of Chelsea cuirassiers,
    Shall, in my Putney pikes, now meet their peers.‖
Gen.: Chiswickians, aged and renown'd in fight,
    Join with the Hammersmith brigade.
Lieut.-Gen. You'll find my Mortlake boys will do them right,
    Unless by Fulham numbers over-laid.
Gen. Let the left wing of Twick'nam foot advance,
    And line that eastern hedge.
Lieut.-Gen. The horse I rais'd in Petty-France
    Shall try their chance,
    And scour the meadows, overgrown with sedge.
Gen. Stand : give the word,
Lieut.-Gen. Bright sword.
Gen. That may be thine.
    But 'tis not mine.

---

  * "Aglaura," and the "Vestal Virgin," are so contrived by a little alteration towards the latter end of them, that they have been acted both ways, either as tragedies or comedies.

  † There needs nothing more to explain the meaning of this battle, than the perusal of the first part of the "Siege of Rhodes," which was performed in recitative music, by seven persons only : and the passage out of the "Playhouse to be Let."

  ‡ The "Siege of Rhodes" begins thus :—
      "*Admiral.* Arm, arm, Valerius, arm."

  § The third entry thus :—
      "*Solym.* Pyrrhus, draw down our army wide ;
        Then, from the gross, two strong reserves divide,
        And spread the wings,
        As if we were to fight,
        In the lost Rhodians' sight,
        With all the western kings.
        Each with Janizaries line ;
        The right and left to Haly's sons assign ;
        The gross, to Zangiban ;
        The main artillery
        To Mustapha shall be :
        Bring thou the rear, we lead the van."

  ‖ "More pikes ! more pikes ! to reinforce
    That squadron, and repulse the horse."—"Playhouse to be Let," p. 72.

Lieut.-Gen. Give fire, give fire, at once give fire,
    And let those recreant troops perceive mine ire.*
Gen. Pursue, pursue ; they fly
    That first did give the lie.   . [*Exeunt.*
Bayes. This now is not improper, I think ; because the
spectators know all these towns, and may easily conceive them
to be within the dominions of the two Kings of Brentford.
Johns. Most exceeding well design'd !
Bayes. How do you think I have contriv'd to give a stop to
this battle ?
Smith. How ?
Bayes. By an eclipse ; which, let me tell you, is a kind of
fancy that was yet never so much as thought of, but by myself,
and one person more, that shall be nameless.

Enter LIEUTENANT-GENERAL.

Lieut.-Gen. What midnight darkness does invade the day,
    And snatch the victor from his conquer'd prey ?
    Is the sun weary of this bloody fight,
    And winks upon us with the eye of light !
    'Tis an eclipse ! this was unkind, O moon,
    To clap between me and the sun so soon.
    Foolish eclipse ! thou this in vain hast done ;
    My brighter honour had eclips'd the sun :
    But now behold eclipses two in one.   [*Exit.*
Johns. This is an admirable representation of a battle as ever
I saw.
Bayes. Ay, sir ; but how would you fancy now to represent an
eclipse ?
Smith. Why, that's to be suppos'd.
Bayes. Suppos'd ! ay, you are ever at your suppose : ha, ha,
ha ! why, you may as well suppose the whole play. No, it
must come in upon the stage, that's certain ; but in some odd
way, that may delight, amuse, and all that. I have a conceit
for't, that I am sure is new, and I believe to the purpose.
Johns. How's that ?
Bayes. Why, the truth is, I took the first hint of this out of a

---

* " Point all the cannon, and play fast ;
        Their fury is too hot to last.   -
        That rampire shakes ; they fly into the town.
Pyr. March up with those reserves to that redoubt ;
        Faint slaves, the Janizaries reel !
        They bend ! they bend ! and seem to feel
        The terrors of a rout.
Must. Old Zanger halts, and reinforcement lacks.
Pyr. March on !
Must. Advance those pikes, and charge their backs."—
                                    " Siege of Rhodes."

dialogue between Phœbus and Aurora, in the "Slighted Maid," which, by my troth, was very pretty ; but I think you'd confess this is a little better.

Johns. No doubt on't, Mr. Bayes, a great deal better.

[BAYES *hugs* JOHNSON, *then turns to* SMITH.

Bayes. Ah, dear rogue ! But —a— sir, you have heard, I suppose, that your eclipse of the moon is nothing else but an interposition of the earth between the sun and moon ; as likewise your eclipse of the sun is caus'd by an interlocation of the moon betwixt the earth and the sun.

Smith. I have heard some such thing indeed.

Bayes. Well, sir, then what do I but make the earth, sun, and moon come out upon the stage, and dance the hey. Hum ! and of necessity, by the very nature of this dance, the earth must be sometimes between the sun and the moon, and the moon between the earth and sun : and there you have both eclipses by demonstration.

Johns. That must needs be very fine, truly.

Bayes. Yes, it has fancy in't. And then, sir, that there may be something in't, too, of a joke, I bring 'em in all singing ; and make the moon sell the earth a bargain. Come, come out, eclipse, to the tune of "Tom Tyler."

Enter LUNA.

Luna. Orbis, O Orbis !
    Come to me, thou little rogue, Orbis.

Enter the EARTH.

Orb. Who calls Terra-firma, pray ? *
Luna. Luna, that ne'er shines by day.
Orb. What means Luna in a veil ?
Luna. Luna means to show her tail.
Bayes. There's the bargain.

Enter SOL, *to the tune of* "Robin Hood."

Sol. Fie, sister, fie ; thou makest me muse,
                Derry down, derry down,
        To see thee Orb abuse.

---

* In ridicule of this :—
        "*Phœb.* Who calls the world's great light !
        Aur. Aurora, that abhors the night.
        Phœb. Why does Aurora, from her cloud,
                To drowsy Phœbus cry so loud ?"—
                                "Slighted Maid," p. 8.

Luna. I hope his anger 'twill not move ;
    Since I show'd it out of love.
                    Hey down, derry down.
Orb. Where shall I thy true love know,
    Thou pretty, pretty moon ?
Luna. To-morrow soon, ere it be noon,
    On Mount Vesuvio.*
Sol. Then I will shine   [*To the tune of* " Trenchmore." *Bis.*
Orb. And I will be fine.
Luna. And I will drink nothing but Lippara wine.†
Omnes. And we, &c.   [*As they dance the hey,* BAYES *speaks.*
Bayes. Now the earth's before the moon : now the moon's
before the sun : there's the eclipse again.
Smith. He's mightily taken with this, I see.
Johns. Ay, 'tis so extraordinary, how can he choose ?
Bayes. So, now, vanish eclipse, and enter t'other battle, and
fight. Here now, if I am not mistaken, you will see fighting
enough.

[*A battle is fought between foot and great hobby-horses. At
last,* DRAWCANSIR *comes in and kills them all on both
sides. All the while the battle is fighting,* BAYES *is telling
them when to shout, and shouts with 'em.*

Draw. Others may boast a single man to kill ;
    But I the blood of thousands daily spill.
    Let petty kings the names of parties know :
    Where'er I come, I slay both friend and foe.
    The swiftest horsemen my swift rage controls,
    And from their bodies drives their trembling souls.
    If they had wings, and to the gods could fly,
    I would pursue and beat 'em through the sky ;
    And make proud Jove, with all his thunder, see
    This single arm more dreadful is than he.   [*Exit.*
Bayes. There's a brave fellow for you now, sirs. You may
talk of your Hectors, and Achilles's, and I know not who ; but I
defy all your histories, and your romances too, to show me one
such conqueror, as this Drawcansir.
Johns. I swear, I think you may.
Smith. But, Mr. Bayes, how shall all these dead men go off ?
for I see none alive to help 'em.
Bayes. Go off ! why, as they came on, upon their legs : how
should they go off ? Why, do you think the people here don't
know they are not dead ? he is mighty ignorant, poor man : your

        * " The burning mount Vesuvio."—" Slighted Maid," p. 81,
          † " Drink, drink wine, Lippara wine."—*Ibid.*

friend here is very silly, Mr. Johnson ; egad, he is. Ha, ha, ha !
Come, sir, I'll show you how they shall go off. Rise, rise, sirs,
and go about your business.* There's go off for you now ; ha,
ha, ha ! Mr. Ivory, a word. Gentlemen, I'll be with you
presently.   [*Exit,*

Johns. Will you so ? Then we'll be gone.

Smith. Ay, prithee let's go, that we may preserve our hearing.
One battle more will take mine quite away.   [*Exeunt,*

Enter BAYES *and* PLAYERS.

Bayes. Where are the gentlemen ?

1st Play. They are gone, sir.

Bayes. Gone ! 'sdeath, this act is best of all. I'll go fetch
'em again.   [*Exit.*

1st Play. What shall we do, now he is gone away ?

2nd Play. Why, so much the better ; then let's go to dinner.

3rd Play. Stay, here's a foul piece of paper. Let's see what
'tis.

3rd or 4th Play. Ay, ay, come, let's hear it.
                       [*Reads.   The argument of the fifth act.*

3rd Play. " Cloris, at length, being sensible of Prince Prettyman's passion, consents to marry him ; but just as they are
going to church, Prince Prettyman meeting, by chance, with old
Joan, the chandler's widow, and remembering it was she that
first brought him acquainted with Cloris ; out of a high point
of honour, breaks off his match with Cloris, and marries old
Joan. Upon which, Cloris, in despair, drowns herself ; and
Prince Prettyman, discontentedly, walks by the river-side."——
This will never do : 'tis just like the rest. Come, let's be gone.

Most of the Players. Ay, plague on't, let's go away. [*Exeunt.*

Enter BAYES.

Bayes. A plague on 'em both for me ! they have made me
sweat, to run after 'em. A couple of senseless rascals, that had
rather go to dinner, than see this play out, with a plague to 'em.
What comfort has a man to write for such dull rogues ! Come,
Mr. —a— where are you, sir ? Come away, quick, quick.

Enter STAGE-KEEPER.

Stage-keep. Sir : they are gone to dinner.

---

* Valeria, daughter to Maximin, having killed herself for the love of
Porphyrius ; when she was to be carried off by the bearers, strikes one of
them a box on the ear, and speaks to him thus :—
        " Hold, are you mad, confounded dog?
        I am to rise, and speak the epilogue."—" Tyrannic Love."

Bayes. Yes, I know the gentlemen are gone; but I ask for the players.

Stage-keep. Why, an't please your worship, sir, the players are gone to dinner too.

Bayes. How! are the players gone to dinner? 'tis impossible: the players gone to dinner! egad, if they are, I'll make 'em know what it is to injure a person that does them the honour to write for 'em, and all that. A company of proud, conceited, humorous, cross-grain'd persons, and all that. Egad, I'll make 'em the most contemptible, despicable, inconsiderable persons, and all that, in the whole world, for this trick. Egad, I'll be revenged on 'em; I'll sell this play to the other house.

Stage-keep. Nay, good sir, don't take away the book; you'll disappoint the company that comes to see it acted here this afternoon.

Bayes. That's all one, I must reserve this comfort to myself, my play and I shall go together; we will not part, indeed, sir.

Stage-keep. But what will the town say, sir?

Bayes. The town! why, what care I for the town? Egad, the town has us'd me as scurvily as the players have done: but I'll be reveng'd on them too; for I'll lampoon 'em all. And since they will not admit of my plays, they shall know what a satirist I am. And so farewell to this stage, egad, for ever.

[Exit BAYES.

Enter PLAYERS.

1st Play. Come, then, let's set up bills for another play.

2nd Play. Ay, ay; we shall lose nothing by this, I warrant you.

1st Play. I am of your opinion. But before we go, let's see Haynes and Shirley practise the last dance; for that may serve us another time.

2nd Play. I'll call 'em in: I think they are but in the tyring-room.

[The dance done.]

1st Play. Come, come; let's go away to dinner.

[Exeunt omnes.

EPILOGUE.

THE play is at an end, but where's the plot?
That circumstance our poet Bayes forgot.
And we can boast, tho' 'tis a plotting age,
No place is freer from it than the stage.

The ancients plotted, tho', and strove to please
With sense that might be understood with ease ;
They every scene with so much wit did store,
That who brought any in, went out with more.
But this new way of wit does so surprise,
Men lose their wits in wond'ring where it lies.
If it be true, that monstrous births presage
The following mischiefs that afflict the age,
And sad disasters to the state proclaim ;
Plays without head or tail may do the same.
Wherefore for ours, and for the kingdom's peace,
May this prodigious way of writing cease.
Let's have at least, once in our lives, a time
When we may hear some reason, not all rhyme.
We have this ten years felt its influence ;
Pray let this prove a year of prose and sense.

THE SPLENDID SHILLING.

"Sing, heavenly Muse,
Things unattempted yet, in prose or rhyme,
A shilling, breeches, and chimeras dire."

HAPPY the man, who void of cares and strife,
In silken, or in leathern purse retains
A Splendid Shilling.   He nor hears with pain
New oysters cry'd, nor sighs for cheerful ale ;
But with his friends when nightly mists arise,
To Juniper's Magpye, or Town Hall* repairs :
Where, mindful of the nymph, whose wanton eye
Transfix'd his soul, and kindled amorous flames,
Cloe, or Philips, he each circling glass
Wisheth her health, and joy, and equal love.
Meanwhile, he smokes, and laughs at merry tale,
Or pun ambiguous, or conundrum quaint.
But I, whom griping penury surrounds,
And hunger, sure attendant upon want,
With scanty offals, and small acid tiff,
Wretched repast ! my meagre corps sustain :
Then solitary walk, or doze at home
In garret vile, and with a warming puff
Regale chill'd fingers ; or from tube as black
As winter-chimney, or well polish'd jet,
Exhale Mundungus, ill-perfuming scent :
Not blacker tube, nor of a shorter size
Smokes Cambro-Briton, vers'd in pedigree,
Sprung from Cadwalador and Arthur, kings
Full famous in romantic tale, when he
O'er many a craggy hill and barren cliff,
Upon a cargo of fam'd Cestrian cheese,
High over-shadowing rides, with a design
To vend his wares, or at th' Arvonian mart,
Or Maridunum, or the ancient town

* Two noted alehouses in Oxford, 1700.

Ycleped Brechinia, or where Vaga's stream
Encircles Ariconium, fruitful soil !
Whence flows nectareous wine, that well may vie
With Massic, Setin, or renown'd Falern.
     Thus, while my joyless minutes tedious flow
With looks demure, and silent pace, a Dun,
Horrible monster ! hated by gods and men,
To my aërial citadel ascends.
With vocal heel thrice thund'ring at my gate,
With hideous accent thrice he calls ; I know
The voice ill-boding, and the solemn sound.
What should I do ? or whither turn ? Amaz'd,
Confounded to the dark recess I fly
Of woodhole; straight my bristling hairs erect
Thro' sudden fear ; a chilly sweat bedews
My shudd'ring limbs, and, wonderful to tell !
My tongue forgets her faculty of speech ;
So horrible he seems ! his faded brow
Entrench'd with many a frown, and conic beard,
And spreading band, admir'd by modern saints,
Disastrous acts forebode.   In his right hand
Long scrolls of paper solemnly he waves,
With characters and figures dire inscrib'd,
Grievous to mortal eyes ; ye gods avert
Such plagues from righteous men !   Behind him stalks
Another monster not unlike himself,
Sullen of aspect, by the vulgar call'd
A Catchpole, whose polluted hands the gods
With force incredible and magic charms
First have endu'd : if he his ample palm
Should haply on ill-fated shoulder lay
Of debtor, straight his body, to the touch
Obsequious as whilom knights were wont,
To some enchanted castle is convey'd,
Where gates impregnable, and coercive chains
In durance strict detain him till, in form
Of money, Pallas sets the captive free.
     Beware, ye debtors, when ye walk, beware !
Be circumspect ; oft with insidious ken
This caitiff eyes your steps aloof, and oft
Lies perdue in a nook or gloomy cave,
Prompt to enchant some inadvertent wretch
With his unhallow'd touch.   So, poets sing,
Grimalkin to domestic vermin sworn
An everlasting foe, with watchful eye
Lies nightly brooding o'er a chinky gap,
Protending her fell claws, to thoughtless mice
Sure ruin.   So her disembowell'd web

Arachne in a hall, or kitchen, spreads,
Obvious to vagrant flies : she secret stands
Within her woven cell ; the humming prey,
Regardless of their fate, rush on the toils
Inextricable, nor will aught avail
Their arts, or arms, or shapes of lovely hue ;
The wasp insidious, and the buzzing drone,
And butterfly proud of expanded wings
Distinct with gold, entangled in her snares,
Useless resistance make : with eager strides,
She tow'ring flies to her expected spoils ;
Then, with envenom'd jaws the vital blood
Drinks of reluctant foes, and to her cave
Their bulky carcasses triumphant drags.
So pass my days.   But when nocturnal shades
This world envelop, and th' inclement air
Persuades men to repel benumbing frosts
With pleasant wines, and crackling blaze of wood ;
Me, lonely sitting, nor the glimmering light
Of make-weight candle, nor the joyous talk
Of loving friend delights ; distress'd, forlorn,
Amidst the horrors of the tedious night,
Darkling I sigh, and feed with dismal thoughts
My anxious mind, or sometimes mournful verse
Indite, and sing of groves and myrtle shades,
Or desp'rate lady near a purling stream,
Or lover pendant on a willow-tree.
Meanwhile I labour with eternal drought,
And restless wish, and rave, my parchéd throat
Finds no relief, nor heavy eyes repose :
But if a slumber haply does invade
My weary limbs, my fancy's still awake,
Thoughtful of drink, and eager, in a dream,
Tipples imaginary pots of ale,
In vain ; awake I find the settled thirst
Still gnawing, and the pleasant phantom curse.
Thus do I live, from pleasure quite debarr'd,
Nor taste the fruits that the sun's genial rays
Mature, John Apple, nor the downy Peach,
Nor Walnut in rough-furrow'd coat secure,
Nor Medlar fruit delicious in decay :
Afflictions great ! yet greater still remains.
My Galligaskins that have long withstood
The winter's fury, and encroaching frosts
By time subdu'd, what will not time subdue !
An horrid chasm disclos'd with orifice
Wide, discontinuous ; at which the winds
Eurus and Auster, and the dreadful force

Of Boreas, that congeals the Cronian waves,
Tumultuous enter with dire chilling blasts,
Portending agues.   Thus a well-fraught ship,
Long sail'd secure, or thro' th' Ægean deep,
Or the Ionian, till cruising near
The Lilybean shore, with hideous crush
On Scylla, or Charybdis, dang'rous rocks !
She strikes rebounding, whence the shatter'd oak,
So fierce a shock unable to withstand,
Admits the sea ; in at the gaping side
The crowding waves gush with impetuous rage,
Resistless, overwhelming ; horrors seize
The mariners, death in their eyes appears,
They stare, they lave, they pump, they swear, they pray :
Vain efforts ! still the batt'ring waves rush in,
Implacable, till delug'd by the foam,
The ship sinks found'ring in the vast abyss.

Two "Odes."

By AMBROSE PHILIPS, Esq.,

From among those which suggested the next following Burlesque.

———•◦•——

To Miss Margaret Pulteney, Daughter of Daniel Pulteney, Esq., in the Nursery.

April 27, 1727.

DIMPLY damsel, sweetly smiling,
All caressing, none beguiling,
Bud of beauty, fairly blowing,
Every charm to nature owing,
This and that new thing admiring,
Much of this and that enquiring,
Knowledge by degrees attaining,
Day by day some virtue gaining,
Ten years hence, when I leave chiming,
Beardless poets, fondly rhyming
(Fescu'd now, perhaps, in spelling),
On thy riper beauties dwelling,
Shall accuse each killing feature
Of the cruel, charming creature,
Whom I knew complying, willing,
Tender, and averse to killing.

To Miss Charlotte Pulteney, in her Mother's Arms.

May 1, 1724.

TIMELY blossom, infant fair,
Fondling of a happy pair,
Every morn, and every night,
Their solicitous delight,
Sleeping, waking, still at ease,
Pleasing, without skill to please,
Little gossip, blithe and hale,
Tatling many a broken tale,

Singing many a tuneless song,
Lavish of a heedless tongue,
Simple maiden, void of art,
Babbling out the very heart,
Yet abandon'd to thy will,
Yet imagining no ill,
Yet too innocent to blush,
Like the linlet in the bush,
To the mother-linnet's note
Moduling her slender throat,
Chirping forth thy petty joys,
Wanton in the change of toys,
Like the linnet green, in May,
Flitting to each bloomy spray,
Wearied then, and glad of rest,
Like the linlet in the nest.
This thy present happy lot,
This, in time, will be forgot.
Other pleasures, other cares,
Ever-busy time prepares ;
And thou shalt in thy daughter see,
This picture, once, resembled thee.

NAMBY PAMBY :

OR, A PANEGYRIC ON THE NEW VERSIFICATION
ADDRESSED TO A——— P———, ESQ.

> "Nauty Pauty Jack-a-dandy
> Stole a piece of sugar-candy
> From the Grocer's shoppy-shop,
> And away did hoppy-hop."

ALL ye poets of the age,
All ye witlings of the stage,
Learn your jingles to reform :
Crop your numbers, and conform :
Let your little verses flow
Gently, sweetly, row by row.
Let the verse the subject fit,
Little subject, little wit.
Namby Pamby is your guide,
Albion's joy, Hibernia's pride.
Namby Pamby Pilli-pis,
Rhimy pim'd on missy-mis ;
Tartaretta Tartaree
From the navel to the knee ;

That her father's gracy-grace
Might give him a placy-place.
He no longer writes of mammy
Andromache and her lammy,
Hanging panging at the breast
Of a matron most distrest.
Now the venal poet sings
Baby clouts, and baby things,
Baby dolls and baby houses,
Little misses, little spouses ;
Little playthings, little toys,
Little girls, and little boys.
As an actor does his part,
So the nurses get by heart
Namby Pamby's little rhymes,
Little jingle, little chimes.
Namby Pamby ne'er will die
While the nurse sings lullaby.
Namby Pamby's doubly mild,
Once a man, and twice a child ;
To his hanging-sleeves restor'd,
Now he foots it like a lord ;
Now he pumps his little wits,
All by little tiny bits.
Now methinks I hear him say,
Boys and girls, come out to play,
Moon does shine as bright as day.
Now my Namby Pamby's found
Sitting on the Friar's ground,
Picking silver, picking gold,
Namby Pamby's never old.
Bally-cally they begin,
Namby Pamby still keeps in.
Namby Pamby is no clown,
London Bridge is broken down :
Now he courts the gay ladee,
Dancing o'er the Lady-lee :
Now he sings of lick-spit liar
Burning in the brimstone fire ;
Liar, liar, lick-spit, lick,
Turn about the candle-stick.
Now he sings of Jacky Horner
Sitting in the chimney corner,
Eating of a Christmas pie,
Putting in his thumb, oh, fie !
Putting in, oh, fie ! his thumb,
Pulling out, oh, strange ! a plum.

Now he acts the Grenadier,
Calling for a pot of beer.
Where's his money? he's forgot,
Get him gone, a drunken sot.
Now on cock-horse does he ride;
And anon on timber stride,
See--and-saw and Sacch'ry down,
London is a gallant town.
Now he gathers riches in
Thicker, faster, pin by pin.
Pins apiece to see his show,
Boys and girls flock row by row;
From their clothes the pins they take,
Risk a whipping for his sake;
From their frocks the pins they pull,
To fill Namby's cushion full.
So much wit at such an age,
Does a genius great presage.
Second childhood gone and past,
Should he prove a man at last,
What must second manhood be,
In a child so bright as he!
   Guard him, ye poetic powers,
Watch his minutes, watch his hours:
Let your tuneful Nine inspire him,
Let poetic fury fire him:
Let the poets one and all
To his genius victims fall.

A WORD UPON PUDDING.

From "A Learned Dissertation upon Dumpling,"
to which the preceding Poem was appended.

WHAT is a tart, a pie, or a pasty, but meat or fruit enclos'd in a wall or covering of pudding? What is a cake, but a bak'd pudding; or a Christmas pie, but a minc'd-meat pudding? As for cheese-cakes, custards, tansies, &c., they are manifest puddings, and all of Sir John's own contrivance; custard being as old, if not older, than Magna Charta. In short, pudding is of the greatest dignity and antiquity; bread itself, which is the very staff of life, being, properly speaking, a bak'd wheat pudding.

To the satchel, which is the pudding-bag of ingenuity, we are indebted for the greatest men in church and state. All arts and sciences owe their original to pudding or dumpling. What is a bagpipe, the mother of all music, but a pudding of harmony?

Or what is music itself, but a palatable cookery of sounds? To little puddings or bladders of colours we owe all the choice originals of the greatest painters. And indeed, what is painting, but a well-spread pudding, or cookery of colours?

The head of man is like a pudding. And whence have all rhymes, poems, plots, and inventions sprang, but from that same pudding? What is poetry, but a pudding of words? The physicians, tho' they cry out so much against cooks and cookery, yet are but cooks themselves; with this difference only, the cooks' pudding lengthens life, the physicians' shortens it. So that we live and die by pudding. For what is a clyster, but a bag-pudding? a pill, but a dumpling? or a bolus, but a tansy, tho' not altogether so toothsome? In a word: physic is only a puddingizing or cookery of drugs. The law is but a cookery of quibbles and contentions. (*a*) * * *
  * * * * * * * * *
  * * * * is but a pudding of * * *
  * * * * * * * * *
  * * * Some swallow everything whole and un-mix'd; so that it may rather be call'd a heap than a pudding. Others are so squeamish, the greatest mastership in cookery is requir'd to make the pudding palatable. The suet which others gape and swallow by gobs, must for these puny stomachs be minced to atoms; the plums must be pick'd with the utmost care, and every ingredient proportion'd to the greatest nicety, or it will never go down.

The universe itself is but a pudding of elements. Empires, kingdoms, states and republics, are but puddings of people differently made up. The celestial and terrestrial orbs are decipher'd to us by a pair of globes or mathematical puddings.

The success of war and fate of monarchies are entirely dependent on puddings and dumplings. For what else are cannon-balls but military puddings? or bullets, but dumplings; with this difference only, they do not sit so well on the stomach as a good marrow pudding or bread pudding.

In short, there is nothing valuable in art or nature, but what, more or less, has an allusion to pudding or dumpling. Why, then, should they be held in disesteem? Why should dumpling-eating be ridiculed, or dumpling-eaters derided? Is it not pleasant and profitable? Is it not ancient and honourable? Kings, princes, and potentates have in all ages been lovers of pudding. Is it not, therefore, of royal authority? Popes, cardinals, bishops, priests and deacons, have, time out of mind, been great pudding-eaters. Is it not, therefore, a holy and religious institution? Philosophers, poets, and learned men in

---

(*a*) The cat ran away with this part of the copy, on which the Author had unfortunately laid some of Mother Crump's sausages.

all faculties, judges, privy councillors, and members of both houses, have, by their great regard to pudding, given a sanction to it that nothing can efface. Is it not, therefore, ancient, honourable, and commendable ?

Quare itaque fremuerunt Auctores?

Why do, therefore, the enemies of good eating, the starveling authors of Grub Street, employ their impotent pens against pudding and pudding-headed, *alias* honest men ? Why do they inveigh against dumpling-eating, which is the life and soul of good-fellowship ; and dumpling-eaters, who are the ornaments of civil society ?

But, alas ! their malice is their own punishment. The hireling author of a late scandalous libel, intituled, "The Dumpling-Eaters Downfall," may, if he has any eyes, now see his error, in attacking so numerous, so august, a body of people. His books remain unsold, unread, unregarded ; while this treatise of mine shall be bought by all who love pudding or dumpling ; to my bookseller's great joy, and my no small consolation. How shall I triumph, and how will that mercenary scribbler be mortified, when I have sold more editions of my books than he has copies of his ? I, therefore, exhort all people, gentle and simple, men, women, and children, to buy, to read, to extol these labours of mine, for the honour of dumpling-eating. Let them not fear to defend every article ; for I will bear them harmless. I have arguments good store, and can easily confute, either logically, theologically, or metaphysically, all those who dare oppose me.

Let not Englishmen, therefore, be ashamed of the name of Pudding-eaters ; but, on the contrary, let it be their glory. For let foreigners cry out ne'er so much against good eating, they come easily into it when they have been a little while in our land of Canaan ; and there are very few foreigners among us who have not learn'd to make as great a hole in a good pudding or sirloin of beef, as the best Englishman of us all.

Why should we then be laughed out of pudding and dumpling ? or why ridicul'd out of good living ? Plots and politics may hurt us, but pudding cannot. Let us, therefore, adhere to pudding, and keep ourselves out of harm's way ; according to the golden rule laid down by a celebrated dumpling-eater now defunct :

" Be of your patron's mind, whate'er he says :
Sleep very much ; think little, and talk less :
Mind neither good nor bad, nor right nor wrong ;
But eat your pudding, fool, and hold your tongue."—PRIOR.

THE TRAGEDY OF TRAGEDIES: OR, THE LIFE AND DEATH OF

TOM THUMB THE GREAT.

WITH THE ANNOTATIONS OF H. SCRIBLERUS SECUNDUS.

FIRST ACTED IN 1730, AND ALTERED IN 1731.

———◦—◦———

H. SCRIBLERUS SECUNDUS, HIS PREFACE.

THE town hath seldom been more divided in its opinion than concerning the merit of the following scenes. Whilst some publicly affirm that no author could produce so fine a piece but Mr. P——, others have with as much vehemence insisted that no one could write anything so bad but Mr. F——.

Nor can we wonder at this dissension about its merit, when the learned world have not unanimously decided even the very nature of this tragedy. For though most of the universities in Europe have honoured it with the name of "Egregium et maximi pretii opus, tragœdiis tam antiquis quàm novis longè anteponendum;" nay, Dr. B—— hath pronounced, "Citiùs Mævii Æneadem quàm Scribleri istius tragœdiam hanc crediderim, cujus autorem Senecam ipsum tradidisse haud dubitârim :" and the great Professor Burman hath styled Tom Thumb " Heroum omnium tragicorum facilè principem;" nay, though it hath, among other languages, been translated into Dutch, and celebrated with great applause at Amsterdam (where burlesque never came) by the title of Mynheer Vander Thumb, the burgomasters received it with that reverent and silent attention which becometh an audience at a deep tragedy. Notwithstanding all this, there have not been wanting some who have represented these scenes in a ludicrous light ; and Mr. D—— hath been heard to say, with some concern, that he wondered a tragical and Christian nation would permit a representation on its theatre so visibly designed to ridicule and extirpate everything that is great and solemn among us.

This learned critic and his followers were led into so great an error by that surreptitious and piratical copy which stole last year into the world ; with what injustice and prejudice to our author will be acknowledged, I hope, by every one who shall happily peruse this genuine and original copy. Nor can I help remarking, to the great praise of our author, that, however imperfect the former was, even that faint resemblance of the true Tom Thumb contained sufficient beauties to give it a run of upwards of forty nights to the politest audiences. But, notwithstanding that applause which it received from all the best judges, it was as severely censured by some few bad ones, and, I believe rather maliciously than ignorantly, reported to have been intended a burlesque on the loftiest parts of tragedy, and designed to banish what we generally call fine things from the stage.

Now, if I can set my country right in an affair of this importance, I shall lightly esteem any labour which it may cost. And this I the rather undertake, first, as it is indeed in some measure incumbent on me to vindicate myself from that surreptitious copy before mentioned, published by some ill-meaning people under my name ; secondly, as knowing myself more capable of doing justice to our author than any other man, as I have given myself more pains to arrive at a thorough understanding of this little piece, having for ten years together read nothing else ; in which time, I think, I may modestly presume, with the help of my English dictionary, to comprehend all the meanings of every word in it.

But should any error of my pen awaken Clariss. Bentleium to enlighten the world with his annotations on our author, I shall not think that the least reward or happiness arising to me from these my endeavours.

I shall waive at present what hath caused such feuds in the learned world, whether this piece was originally written by Shakespeare, though certainly that, were it true, must add a considerable share to its merit, especially with such who are so generous as to buy and commend what they never read, from an implicit faith in the author only : a faith which our age abounds in as much as it can be called deficient in any other.

Let it suffice, that " The Tragedy of Tragedies ; or, The Life and Death of Tom Thumb," was written in the reign of Queen Elizabeth. Nor can the objection made by Mr. D——, that the tragedy must then have been antecedent to the history, have any weight, when we consider that, though " The History of Tom Thumb," printed by and for Edward M—r, at the Looking-glass on London Bridge, be of a later date, still must we suppose this history to have been transcribed from some other, unless we suppose the writer thereof to be inspired : a gift very faintly contended for by the writers of our age. As to this history's not bearing the stamp of second, third, or fourth edition, I see but little in that objection; editions being very uncertain lights to judge of books by: and perhaps Mr. M—r may have joined twenty editions in one, as Mr. C—l hath ere now divided one into twenty.

Nor doth the other argument, drawn from the little care our author hath taken to keep up to the letter of this history, carry any greater force. Are there not instances of plays wherein the history is so perverted, that we can know the heroes whom they celebrate by no other marks than their names? nay, do we not find the same character placed by different poets in such different lights, that we can discover not the least sameness, or even likeness, in the features? The Sophonisba of Mairet and of Lee is a tender, passionate, amorous mistress of Massinissa: Corneille and Mr. Thomson give her no other passion but the love of her country, and make her as cool in her affection to Massinissa as to Syphax. In the two latter she resembles the character of Queen Elizabeth; in the two former she is the picture of Mary Queen of Scotland. In short, the one Sophonisba is as different from the other as the Brutus of Voltaire is from the Marius, jun., of Otway, or as the Minerva is from the Venus of the ancients.

Let us now proceed to a regular examination of the tragedy before us, in which I shall treat separately of the Fable, the Moral, the Characters, the Sentiments, and the Diction. And first of the

Fable; which I take to be the most simple imaginable; and, to use the words of an eminent author, "one, regular, and uniform, not charged with a multiplicity of incidents, and yet affording several revolutions of fortune, by which the passions may be excited, varied, and driven to their full tumult of emotion." Nor is the action of this tragedy less great than uniform. The spring of all is the love of Tom Thumb for Huncamunca; which caused the quarrel between their majesties in the first act; the passion of Lord Grizzle in the second; the rebellion, fall of Lord Grizzle and Glumdalca, devouring of Tom Thumb by the cow, and that bloody catastrophe, in the third.

Nor is the Moral of this excellent tragedy less noble than the Fable; it teaches these two instructive lessons, viz., that human happiness is exceeding transient, and that death is the certain end of all men: the former whereof is inculcated by the fatal end of Tom Thumb; the latter, by that of all the other personages.

The Characters are, I think, sufficiently described in the *dramatis personæ*; and I believe we shall find few plays where greater care is taken to maintain them throughout, and to preserve in every speech that characteristical mark which distinguishes them from each other. "But," says Mr. D——, "how well doth the character of Tom Thumb (whom we must call the hero of this tragedy, if it hath any hero) agree with the precepts of Aristotle, who defineth, 'tragedy to be the imitation of a short but perfect action, containing a just greatness in itself?' &c. What greatness can be in a fellow whom history related to have been no higher than a span?" This gentleman seemeth to think, with Serjeant Kite, that the greatness of a man's soul is in proportion to that of his body, the contrary of which is affirmed by our English physiognominical writers. Besides, if I understand Aristotle right, he speaketh only of the greatness of the action, and not of the person.

As for the Sentiments and the Diction, which now only remain to be spoken to, I thought I could afford them no stronger justification than by producing parallel passages out of the best of our English writers. Whether this sameness of thought and expression which I have quoted from them proceeded from an agreement in their way of thinking, or whether they have borrowed from our author, I leave the reader to determine. I shall adventure to affirm this of the Sentiments of our author, that they are generally the most familiar which I have ever met with, and at the same time delivered with the highest dignity of phrase; which brings me to speak of his diction. Here I shall only beg one postulatum, viz., that the greatest perfection of the language of a tragedy is, that it is not to be understood; which granted (as I think it must be), it will necessarily follow that the only way to avoid this is by being too high or too low for the understanding, which will comprehend everything within its reach. Those two extremities of style Mr. Dryden illustrates by the familiar image of two inns, which I shall term the aërial and the subterrestrial.

Horace goes further, and showeth when it is proper to call at one of these inns, and when at the other :—

> Telephus et Peleus, cùm pauper et exul uterque,
> Projicit ampullas et sesquipedalia verba.

That he approveth of the *sesquipedalia verba* is plain ; for, had not Telephus and Peleus used this sort of diction in prosperity, they could not have dropped it in adversity. The aërial inn, therefore (says Horace), is proper only to be frequented by princes and other great men in the highest affluence of fortune ; the subterrestrial is appointed for the entertainment of the poorer sort of people only, whom Horace advises,

> —dolere sermone pedestri.

The true meaning of both which citations is, that bombast is the proper language for joy, and doggrel for grief ; the latter of which is literally implied in the *sermo pedestris*, as the former is in the *sesquipedalia verba*.

Cicero recommendeth the former of these: "Quid est tam furiosum vel tragicum quàm verborum sonitus inanis, nullâ subjectâ sententiâ neque scientiâ." What can be so proper for tragedy as a set of big sounding words, so contrived together as to convey no meaning? which I shall one day or other prove to be the sublime of Longinus. Ovid declareth absolutely for the latter inn:

Omne genus scripti gravitate trngœdia vincit.

Tragedy hath, of all writings, the greatest share in the bathos; which is the profound of Scriblerus.

I shall not presume to determine which of these two styles be properer for tragedy. It sufficeth that our author excelleth in both. He is very rarely within sight through the whole play, either rising higher than the eye of your understanding can soar, or sinking lower than it careth to stoop. But here it may perhaps be observed that I have given more frequent instances of authors who have imitated him in the sublime than in the contrary. To which I answer, first, bombast being properly a redundancy of genius, instances of this nature occur in poets whose names do more honour to our author than the writers in the doggrel, which proceeds from a cool, calm, weighty way of thinking. Instances whereof are most frequently to be found in authors of a lower class. Secondly, that the works of such authors are difficultly found at all. Thirdly, that it is a very hard task to read them, in order to extract these flowers from them. And lastly, it is very difficult to transplant them at all; they being like some flowers of a very nice nature, which will flourish in no soil but their own: for it is easy to transcribe a thought, but not the want of one. The "Earl of Essex," for instance, is a little garden of choice rarities, whence you can scarce transplant one line so as to preserve its original beauty. This must account to the reader for his missing the names of several of his acqaintance, which he had certainly found here, had I ever read their works; for which, if I have not a just esteem, I can at least say with Cicero, "Quæ non contemno, quippè quæ nunquam legerim." However, that the reader may meet with due satisfaction in this point, I have a young commentator from the university, who is reading over all the modern tragedies, at five shillings a dozen, and collecting all that they have stole from our author, which shall be shortly added as an appendix to this work.

DRAMATIS PERSONÆ.

KING ARTHUR, *a passionate sort of king, husband to* QUEEN DOL-LALLOLLA, *of whom he stands a little in fear; father to* HUN-CAMUNCA, *whom he is very fond of and in love with* GLUM-DALCA.

TOM THUMB THE GREAT, *a little hero with a great soul, something violent in his temper, which is a little abated by his love for* HUNCAMUNCA.

GHOST OF GAFFER THUMB, *a whimsical sort of ghost.*

LORD GRIZZLE, *extremely zealous for the liberty of the subject, very choleric in his temper, and in love with* HUNCAMUNCA.

MERLIN, *a conjuror, and in some sort father to* TOM THUMB.

NOODLE, DOODLE, *courtiers in place, and consequently of that party that is uppermost.*

FOODLE, *a courtier that is out of place, and consequently of that party that is undermost.*

BAILIFF, AND FOLLOWER, *of the party of the plaintiff.*

PARSON, *of the side of the church.*

QUEEN DOLLALLOLLA, *wife to* KING ARTHUR, *and mother to* HUNCAMUNCA, *a woman entirely faultless, saving that she is a little given to drink, a little too much a virago towards her husband, and in love with* TOM THUMB.

THE PRINCESS HUNCAMUNCA, *daughter to their* MAJESTIES KING ARTHUR *and* QUEEN DOLLALLOLLA, *of a very sweet, gentle, and amorous disposition, equally in love with* LORD GRIZZLE *and* TOM THUMB, *and desirous to be married to them both.*

GLUMDALCA, *of the giants, a captive queen, beloved by the king, but in love with* TOM THUMB.

CLEORA, MUSTACHA, *maids of honour in love with* NOODLE *and* DOODLE.

Courtiers, Guards, Rebels, Drums, Trumpets, Thunder and Lightning.

SCENE.—THE COURT OF KING ARTHUR, AND A PLAIN THEREABOUTS.

ACT I.

SCENE I.—*The Palace.*

DOODLE, NOODLE.

Doodle. Sure such a day* as this was never seen!
The sun himself, on this auspicious day,

---

* Corneille recommends some very remarkable day wherein to fix the action of a tragedy. This the best of our tragical writers have understood to mean a day remarkable for the serenity of the sky, or what we generally call a fine summer's day: so that, according to this their exposition, the same months are proper for tragedy which are proper for pastoral. Most of our celebrated English tragedies, as Cato, Mariamne, Tamerlane, &c., begin with their observations on the morning. Lee seems to have come the nearest to this beautiful description of our author's :—
"The morning dawns with an unwonted crimson,
The flowers all odorous seem, the garden birds
Sing louder, and the laughing sun ascends

Shines like a beau in a new birthday suit :
This down the seams embroidered, that the beams,
All nature wears one universal grin.

   Nood. This day, O Mr. Doodle, is a day,
Indeed !—a day, we never saw before.*
The mighty Thomas Thumb victorious comes ;†
Millions of giants crowd his chariot wheels,
Giants ! to whom the giants in Guildhall‡

> The gaudy earth with an unusual brightness :
> All nature smiles."—"Cæs. Borg."

Massinissa, in the new Sophonisba, is also a favourite of the sun :—

> "The sun too seems
> As conscious of my joy, with broader eye
> To look abroad the world, and all things smile
> Like Sophonisba."

Memnon, in the Persian Princess, makes the sun decline rising, that he may not peep on objects which would profane his brightness :—

> "The morning rises slow,
> And all those ruddy streaks that used to paint
> The day's approach are lost in clouds, as if
> The horrors of the night had sent 'em back,
> To warn the sun he should not leave the sea,
> To peep," &c.

* This line is highly conformable to the beautiful simplicity of the ancients. It hath been copied by almost every modern :—

> " Not to be is not to be in woe."—"State of Innocence."
> " Love is not sin but where 'tis sinful love."—"Don Sebastian."
> " Nature is nature, Lælius."—"Sophonisba."
> " Men are but men, we did not make ourselves."—" Revenge."

† Dr. B—y reads, The mighty Tall-mast Thumb. Mr. D—s, The mighty Thumbing Thumb. Mr. T—d reads, Thundering. I think Thomas more agreeable to the great simplicity so apparent in our author.

‡ That learned historian Mr. S—n, in the third number of his criticism on our author, takes great pains to explode this passage. " It is," says he, "difficult to guess what giants are here meant, unless the giant Despair in the 'Pilgrim's Progress,' or the giant Greatness in the 'Royal Villain ;' for I have heard of no other sort of giants in the reign of king Arthur." Petrus Burmannus makes three Tom Thumbs, one whereof he supposes to have been the same person whom the Greeks call Hercules ; and that by these giants are to be understood the Centaurs slain by that hero. Another Tom Thumb he contends to have been no other than the Hermes Trismegistus of the ancients. The third Tom Thumb he places under the reign of king Arthur ; to which third Tom Thumb, says he, the actions of the other two were attributed. Now, though I know that this opinion is supported by an assertion of Justus Lipsius, "Thomam illum Thumbum non alium quàm Herculem fuisse satis constat," yet shall I venture to oppose one line of Mr. Midwinter against them all :

> " In Arthur's court Tom Thumb did live."

"But then," says Dr. B—y, "if we place Tom Thumb in the court of king Arthur, it will be proper to place that court out of Britain, where no giants were ever heard of." Spenser, in his " Fairy Queen," is of another opinion, where, describing Albion, he says :—

> " Far within a savage nation dwelt
> Of hideous gants."

Are infant dwarfs.   They frown, and foam, and roar,
While Thumb, regardless of their noise, rides on.
So some cock-sparrow in a farmer's yard,
Hops at the head of an huge flock of turkeys.
Dood. When Goody Thumb first brought this Thomas forth,
The Genius of our land triumphant reign'd ;
Then, then, O Arthur ! did thy Genius reign. ·
Nood. They tell me it is whisper'd * in the books
Of all our sages, that this mighty hero,
By Merlin's art begot, hath not a bone
Within his skin, but is a lump of gristle.
Dood. Then 'tis a gristle of no mortal kind ;
Some god, my Noodle, stept into the place
Of Gaffer Thumb, and more than half begot†
This mighty Tom.
Nood. Sure he was sent express‡
From Heaven to be the pillar of our state.
Though small his body be, so very small
A chairman's leg is more than twice as large,
Yet is his soul like any mountain big ;
And as a mountain once brought forth a mouse,
So doth this mouse contain a mighty mountain.§

And in the same canto :—
> "Then Elfar, with two brethren giants had
> The one of which had two heads—
> The other three."

Risum teneatis, amici.

* "To whisper in books," says Mr. D—s, "is arrant nonsense."   I am afraid this learned man does not sufficiently understand the extensive meaning of the word whisper.   If he had rightly understood what is meant by the "senses whisp'ring the soul," in the Persian Princess, or what "whisp'ring like winds" is in Aurengzebe, or like thunder in another author, he would have understood this.   Emmeline in Dryden sees a voice, but she was born blind, which is an excuse Panthea cannot plead in Cyrus, who hears a sight :
> "Your description will surpass
> All fiction, painting, or dumb show of horror,
> That ever ears yet heard, or eyes beheld."

When Mr. D—s understands these, he will understand whispering in books.

† "Some ruffian stept into his father's place,
  And more than half begot him."—"Mary Queen of Scots."

‡ "For Ulamar seems sent express from Heaven,
  To civilize this rugged Indian clime."—"Lib. Asserted."

§ "Omne majus continet in se minus, sed minus non in se majus conti-nere potest," says Scaliger in Thumbo.   I suppose he would have cavilled at these beautiful lines in the "Earl of Essex :"
> "Thy most inveterate soul,
> That looks through the foul prison of thy body."

And at those of Dryden :
> "The palace is without too well design'd ;
> Conduct me in, for I will view thy mind."—"Aurengzebe."

Dood. Mountain indeed!   So terrible his name,
The giant nurses frighten children with it,*
And cry Tom Thumb is come, and if you are
Naughty, will surely take the child away.
   Nood. But hark ! these trumpets speak the king's approach.†
   Dood. He comes most luckily for my petition.   [*Flourish.*

SCENE II.

KING, QUEEN, GRIZZLE, NOODLE, DOODLE, FOODLE.

   King. Let nothing but a face of joy appear;‡
The man who frowns this day shall lose his head,
That he may have no face to frown withal.
Smile Dollàllolla—Ha ! what wrinkled sorrow
Hangs, sits, lies, frowns upon thy knitted brow?§
Whence flow those tears fast down thy blubber'd cheeks,
Like a swoln gutter, gushing through the streets?
   Queen. Excess of joy, my lord, I've heard folks say,||
Gives tears as certain as excess of grief.
   King. If it be so, let all men cry for joy,
Till my whole court be drowned with their tears ;¶

* Mr. Banks hath copied this almost verbatim :
   "It was enough to say, here's Essex come,
      And nurses still'd their children with the fright."—" Earl of Essex."
   † The trumpet in a tragedy is generally as much as to say : Enter king,
which makes Mr. Banks, in one of his plays, call it the trumpet's formal
sound.
   ‡ Phraortes, in the Captives, seems to have been acquainted with king
Arthur :
      " Proclaim a festival for seven days' space,
         Let the court shine in all its pomp and lustre,
         Let all our streets resound with shouts of joy ;
         Let.music's care-dispelling voice be heard ;
         The sumptuous banquet and the flowing goblet
         Shall warm the cheek and fill the heart with gladness.
         Astarbe shall sit mistress of the feast."
   § " Repentance frowns on thy contracted brow."—"Sophonisba."
      " Hung on his clouded brow, I mark'd despair."—*Ibid.*
         " A sullen gloom
         Scowls on his brow."—" Busiris."
   || Plato is of this opinion, and so is Mr. Banks :—
   " Behold these tears sprung from fresh pain and joy."—" Earl of Essex."
   ¶ These floods are very frequent in the tragic authors :—
      " Near to some murmuring brook I'll lay me down,
         Whose waters, if they should too shallow flow,
         My tears shall swell them up till I will drown."—Lee's " Soph."
   " Pouring forth tears at such a lavish rate,
      That were the world on fire they might have drown'd
      The wrath of heaven, and quench'd the mighty ruin."—" Mithridate."
One author changes the waters of grief to those of joy ;

Nay, till they overflow my utmost land,
And leave me nothing but the sea to rule.

Dood. My liege, I a petition have here got.

King. Petition me no petitions, sir, to-day :
Let other hours be set apart for business.
To-day it is our pleasure to be drunk.*
And this our queen shall be as drunk as we.

Queen. (Though I already† half-seas over am)
If the capacious goblet overflow
With arrack punch——'fore George ! I'll see it out :
Of rum and brandy I'll not taste a drop.

King. Though rack, in punch, eight shillings be a quart,
And rum and brandy be no more than six,
Rather than quarrel you shall have your will.   [*Trumpets.*
But, ha ! the warrior comes—the great Tom Thumb,
The little hero, giant-killing boy,
Preserver of my kingdom, is arrived.

> " These tears, that sprung from tides of grief,
>   Are now augmented to a flood of joy."—" Cyrus the Great."

Another :

> " Turns all the streams of heat, and makes them flow
>   In pity's channel."—" Royal Villain."

One drowns himself :

> " Pity like a torrent pours me down,
>   Now I am drowning all within a deluge."—" Anna Bullen."

Cyrus drowns the whole world :

> " Our swelling grief
>   Shall melt into a deluge, and the world
>   Shall drown in tears."—" Cyrus the Great."

* An expression vastly beneath the dignity of tragedy, says Mr. D—s, yet
we find the word he cavils at in the mouth of Mithridates less properly used,
and applied to a more terrible idea :

> " I would be drunk with death."—" Mithridates."

The author of the new Sophonisba taketh hold of this monosyllable, and
uses it pretty much to the same purpose :—

> "The Carthaginian sword with Roman blood
>   Was drunk."

I would ask Mr. D—s which gives him the best idea, a drunken king, or a
drunken sword?

Mr. Tate dresses up king Arthur's resolution in heroic :

> "Merry, my lord, o' th' captain's humour right,
>   I am resolved to be dead drunk to-night."

Lee also uses this charming word :

> " Love's the drunkenness of the mind."—" Gloriana."

† Dryden hath borrowed this, and applied it improperly :

> "I'm half-seas o'er in death."—" Cleom."

SCENE III.

TOM THUMB *to them, with* OFFICERS, PRISONERS, *and*
ATTENDANTS.

King. Oh! welcome most, most welcome to my arms.*
What gratitude can thank away the debt
Your valour lays upon me?
   Queen.   Oh! ye gods!†   [*Aside.*
   Thumb. When I'm not thank'd at all, I'm thank'd enough.‡
I've done my duty, and I've done no more.
   Queen. Was ever such a godlike creature seen?   [*Aside.*
   King. Thy modesty's a candle§ to thy merit,
It shines itself, and shows thy merit too.
But say, my boy, where didst thou leave the giants?
   Thumb. My liege, without the castle gates they stand,
The castle gates too low for their admittance.
   King. What look they like?
   Thumb. Like nothing but themselves.
   Queen. And sure thou art like nothing but thyself.|| [*Aside.*
   King. Enough! the vast idea fills my soul.
I see them—yes, I see them now before me:
The monstrous, ugly, barb'rous sons of clods.
But ha! what form majestic strikes our eyes?
So perfect, that it seems to have been drawn¶

---

   * This figure is in great use among the tragedians:
           " 'Tis therefore, therefore 'tis."—" Victim."
    " I long, repent, repent, and long again."—" Busiris."
  † A tragical exclamation.
  ‡ This line is copied verbatim in the Captives.
  § We find a candlestick for this candle in two celebrated authors:
           " Each star withdraws
     His golden head, and burns within the socket."—" Nero."
    " A soul grown old and sunk into the socket."—" Sebastian."
  || This simile occurs very frequently among the dramatic writers of both
kinds.
  ¶ Mr. Lee hath stolen this thought from our author:
        "This perfect face, drawn by the gods in council,
     Which they were long in making."—" Luc. Jun. Brut."
          " At his birth the heavenly council paused,
     And then at last cried out, This is a man!"
Dryden hath improved this hint to the utmost perfection:
        "So perfect, that the very gods who form'd you wonder'd
    At their own skill, and cried, A lucky hit
    Has mended our design! Their envy hinder'd,
    Or you had been immortal, and a pattern,
    When Heaven would work for ostentation sake,
    To copy out again."—" All for Love."
Banks prefers the works of Michael Angelo to that of the gods:
        "A pattern for the gods to make a man by,
      Or Michael Angelo to form a statue."

By all the gods in council : so fair she is,
That surely at her birth the council paused,
And then at length cry'd out, This is a woman !
 Thumb. Then were the gods mistaken—she is not
A woman, but a giantess——whom we,
With much ado, have made a shift to haul*
Within the town : for she is by a foot†
Shorter than all her subject giants were.
 Glum. We yesterday were both a queen and wife,
One hundred thousand giants own'd our sway.
Twenty whereof were married to ourself.
 Queen. Oh ! happy state of giantism where husbands
Like mushrooms grow, whilst hapless we are forced
To be content, nay, happy thought, with one.
 Glum. But then to lose them all in one black day,
That the same sun which, rising, saw me wife
To twenty giants, setting should behold
Me widow'd of them all.—— My worn-out heart,‡
That ship, leaks fast, and the great heavy lading,
My soul, will quickly sink.
   Queen.   Madam, believe
I view your sorrows with a woman's eye :
But learn to bear them with what strength you may,
To-morrow we will have our grenadiers
Drawn out before you, and you then shall choose
What husbands you think fit.
 Glum.   Madam, I am§
Your most obedient and most humble servant.
 King. Think, mighty princess, think this court your own,
Nor think the landlord me, this house my inn ;
Call for whate'er you will, you'll nothing pay.
I feel a sudden pain within my breast,‖

---

 * It is impossible, says Mr. W——, sufficiently to admire this natural
easy line.
 † This tragedy, which in most points resembles the ancients,. differs from
them in this—that it assigns the same honour to lowness of stature which
they did to height. The gods and heroes in Homer and Virgil are con-
tinually described higher by the head than their followers, the contrary of
which is observed by our author. In short, to exceed on either side is
equally admirable ; and a man of three foot is as wonderful a sight as a
man of nine.
  ‡ " My blood leaks fast, and the great heavy lading
   My soul will quickly sink."—" Mithridates."
   " My soul is like a ship."—" Injured Love."
 § This well-bred line seems to be copied in the Persian Princess :
   " To be your humblest and most faithful slave."
 ‖ This doubt of the king puts me in mind of a passage in the " Captives,"
where the noise of feet is mistaken for the rustling of leaves :—
   " Methinks I hear
  The sound of feet :
  No ; 'twas the wind that shook yon cypress boughs."

Nor know I whether it arise from love
Or only the wind-cholic.   Time must show.
O Thumb! what do we to thy valour owe!
Ask some reward, great as we can bestow.

    Thumb. I ask not kingdoms, I can conquer those;[*]
I ask not money, money I've enough;
For what I've done, and what I mean to do,
For giants slain, and giants yet unborn
Which I will slay——if this be call'd a debt,
Take my receipt in full: I ask but this,—
To sun myself in Huncamunca's eyes.[†]

    King. Prodigious bold request.
    Queen.   Be still, my soul.[‡]   [*Aside.*
    Thumb. My heart is at the threshold of your mouth,[§]
And waits its answer there.——Oh! do not frown.
I've try'd to reason's tune to tune my soul,
But love did overwind and crack the string.
Though Jove in thunder had cry'd out, YOU SHAN'T,
I should have loved her still——for oh, strange fate.
Then when I loved her least I loved her most!

    King. It is resolv'd—the princess is your own.
    Thumb. Oh! happy, happy, happy, happy Thumb.[¶]
    Queen. Consider, sir; reward your soldier's merit,
But give not Huncamunca to Tom Thumb.

    King. Tom Thumb! Odzooks! my wide-extended realm
Knows not a name so glorious as Tom Thumb.
Let Macedonia Alexander boast,
Let Rome her Cæsars and her Scipios show,
Her Messieurs France, let Holland boast Mynheers,
Ireland her O's, her Macs let Scotland boast,
Let England boast no other than Tom Thumb.

---

[*] Mr. Dryden seems to have had this passage in his eye in the first page of Love Triumphant.

[†] Don Carlos, in the Revenge, suns himself in the charms of his mistress: "While in the lustre of her charms I lay."

[‡] A tragical phrase much in use.

[§] This speech hath been taken to pieces by several tragical authors, who seem to have rifled it, and share its beauties among them:
    " My soul waits at the portal of thy breast,
      To ravish from thy lips the welcome news."—"Anna Bullen."
    " My soul stands list'ning at my ears."—"Cyrus the Great."
    " Love to his tune my jarring heart would bring,
      But reason overwinds, and cracks the string."—"D. of Guise."
      " I should have loved
Though Jove, in muttering thunder, had forbid it."—" New Sophonisba.
    " And when it (*my heart*) wild resolves to love no more,
      Then is the triumph of excessive love."—*Ibid.*

‖ Massinissa is one-fourth less happy than Tom Thumb.
    " Oh! happy, happy, happy!"—*Ibid.*

Queen. Though greater yet his boasted merit was,
He shall not have my daughter, that is pos'.
    King. Ha ! sayst thou, Dollallolla ?
Queen.   I say he shan't.
King. Then by our royal self we swear you lie.*
    Queen. Who but a dog, who but a dog†
Would use me as thou dost ? Me, who have lain
These twenty years so loving by thy side !‡
But I will be revenged.   I'll hang myself.
Then tremble all who did this match persuade,
For, riding on a cat, from high I'll fall,§
And squirt down royal vengeance on you all.
    Food. Her majesty the queen is in a passion.‖
    King. Be she, or be she not, I'll to the girl¶
And pave thy way, O Thumb.   Now by ourself,
We were indeed a pretty king of clouts
To truckle to her will—for when by force
Or art the wife her husband overreaches,
Give him the petticoat, and her the breeches.
    Thumb. Whisper, ye winds, that Huncamunca's mine !**
Echoes repeat, that Huncamunca's mine !
The dreadful bus'ness of the war is o'er,
And beauty, heav'nly beauty ! crowns my toils !
I've thrown the bloody garment now aside
And hymeneal sweets invite my bride.
So when some chimney-sweeper all the day
Hath through dark paths pursued the sooty way,
At night to wash his hands and face he flies,
And in his t'other shirt with his Brickdusta lies.

---

* " No by myself."—" Anna Bullen."
†   " Who caused
This dreadful revolution in my fate,
Ulamar.   Who but a dog —who but a dog ? "—" Liberty As."
‡   " A bride,
Who twenty years lay loving by your side."—Banks.
§ " For, borne upon a cloud, from high I'll fall,
    And rain down royal vengeance on you all."—" Alb. Queens."
‖ An information very like this we have in the tragedy of Love, where
Cyrus, having stormed in the most violent mannsr, Cyaxares observes very
calmly,   " Why, nephew Cyrus, you are moved ? "
¶   " 'Tis in your choice.
    Love me, or love me not."—" Conquest of Granada."
** There is not one beauty in this charming speech but what hath been
borrow'd by almost every tragic writer.

SCENE IV.

Grizzle (solus). Where art thou, Grizzle? * where are now thy
    glories?
Where are the drums that waken thee to honour?
Greatness is a laced coat from Monmouth Street,
Which fortune lends us for a day to wear,
To-morrow puts it on another's back.
The spiteful sun but yesterday survey'd
His rival high as Saint Paul's cupola ;
Now may he see me as Fleet Ditch laid low.

SCENE V.

QUEEN, GRIZZLE.

Queen. Teach me to scold, prodigious-minded Grizzle,†
Mountain of treason, ugly as the devil,
Teach this confounded hateful mouth of mine
To spout forth words malicious as thyself,
Words which might shame all Billingsgate to speak.
    Griz. Far be it from my pride to think my tongue
Your royal lips can in that art instruct,
Wherein you so excel.   But may I ask,
Without offence, wherefore my queen would scold?
    Queen. Wherefore? Oh! blood and thunder! han't you heard
(What ev'ry corner of the court resounds)
That little Thumb will be a great man made?
    Griz. I heard it, I confess--for who, alas!
Can‡ always stop his ears?—But would my teeth,
By grinding knives, had first been set on edge!
    Queen. Would I had heard, at the still noon of night,
The hallalloo of fire in every street!
Odsbobs! I have a mind to hang myself,
To think I should a grandmother be made
By such a rascal!—Sure the king forgets
When in a pudding, by his mother put,
The bastard, by a tinker, on a stile
Was dropp'd.—Oh, good lord Grizzle! can I bear
To see him from a pudding mount the throne?

---

* Mr. Banks has (I wish I could not say too servilely) imitated this of
Grizzle in his Earl of Essex :
            "Where art thou, Essex," &c.
    † The Countess of Nottingham, in the Earl of Essex, is apparently
acquainted with Dollallolla.
    ‡ Grizzle was not probably possessed of that glue of which Mr. Banks
speaks in his Cyrus :
            "I'll glue my ears to every word."

Or can, oh can, my Huncamunca bear
To take a pudding's offspring to her arms?

Griz. Oh, horror! horror! horror! cease, my queen.
Thy voice, like twenty screech-owls, wracks my brain.*

Queen. Then rouse thy spirit—we may yet prevent
This hated match.

Griz.   We will; nor fate itself,†
Should it conspire with Thomas Thumb, should cause it.
I'll swim through seas; I'll ride upon the clouds:
I'll dig the earth; I'll blow out every fire;
I'll rave; I'll rant; I'll rise; I'll rush; I'll roar;
Fierce as the man whom smiling‡ dolphins bore
From the prosaic to poetic shore.
I'll tear the scoundrel into twenty pieces.

Queen. Oh, no! prevent the match, but hurt him not;
For, though I would not have him have my daughter,
Yet can we kill the man that killed the giants?

Griz. I tell you, madam, it was all a trick:
He made the giants first, and then he killed them;
As fox-hunters bring foxes to the wood,
And then with hounds they drive them out again.

Queen. How! have you seen no giants? Are there not
Now in the yard ten thousand proper giants?

Griz. Indeed I cannot positively tell,§
But firmly do believe there is not one.

Queen. Hence! from my sight! thou traitor, hie away;
By all my stars! thou enviest Tom Thumb.
Go, sirrah! go, hie‖ away! hie!——thou art
A setting-dog: begone.

* "Screech-owls, dark ravens, and amphibious monsters,
     Are screaming in that voice."—"Mary Queen of Scots."
† The reader may see all the beauties of this speech in a late ode, called
the "Naval Lyrick."
‡ This epithet to a dolphin doth not give one so clear an idea as were to
be wished; a smiling fish seeming a little more difficult to be imagined than
a flying fish. Mr. Dryden is of opinion that smiling is the property of
reason, and that no irrational creature can smile:
  "Smiles not allow'd to beasts from reason move."—"State of Innocence."
§ These lines are written in the same key with those in the Earl of Essex:
     "Why, say'st thou so? I love thee well, indeed
     I do, and thou shalt find by this 'tis true."
Or with this in Cyrus:
     "The most heroic mind that ever was."
And with above half of the modern tragedies.
‖ Aristotle, in that excellent work of his, which is very justly styled his
masterpiece, earnestly recommends using the terms of art, however coarse
or even indecent they may be. Mr. Tate is of the same opinion.
  "*Bru.* Do not, like young hawks, fetch a course about.
     Your game flies fair.
  Fra. Do not fear it.
     He answers you in your hawking phrase."—"In Love."
I think these two great authorities are sufficient to justify Dollallolla in

Griz.   Madam, I go.
Tom Thumb shall feel the vengeance you have raised.
So, when two dogs are fighting in the streets,
With a third dog one of the two dogs meets,
With angry teeth he bites him to the bone,
And this dog smarts for what that dog has done.

SCENE VI.

Queen [*sola*]. And whither shall I go?—Alack a day!
I love Tom Thumb - but must not tell him so ;
For what's a woman when her virtue's gone ?
A coat without its lace ; wig out of buckle ;
A stocking with a hole in't—I can't live
Without my virtue, or without Tom Thumb.
Then let me weigh them in two equal scales ;*
In this scale put my virtue, that Tom Thumb.
Alas ! Tom Thumb is heavier than my virtue.
But hold !—perhaps I may be left a widow :
This match prevented, then Tom Thumb is mine :
In that dear hope I will forget my pain.
  So, when some wench to Tothill Bridewell's sent,
With beating hemp and flogging she's content ;
She hopes in time to ease her present pain,
At length is free, and walks the streets again.

ACT II.

SCENE I.—*The street.*

BAILIFF, FOLLOWER.

Bail. Come on, my trusty fellow, come on ;
This day discharge thy duty, and at night
A double mug of beer, and beer shall glad thee.
Stand here by me, this way must Noodle pass.
  Fol. No more, no more, O Bailiff! every word
Inspires my soul with virtue. Oh ! I long

the use of the phrase, " Hie away, hie !" when in the same line she says she
is speaking to a setting-dog.
  * We meet with such another pair of scales in Dryden's King
Arthur:
          " Arthur and Oswald, and their different fates,
          Are weighing now within the scales of heaven."
  Also in Sebastian :—
          " This hour my lot is weighing in the scales."

To meet the enemy in the street, and nab him :
To lay arresting hands upon his back,
And drag him trembling to the sponging-house.
 Bail. There when I have him, I will sponge upon him.
Oh ! glorious thought ! by the sun, moon, and stars,
I will enjoy it, though it be in thought !
Yes, yes, my follower, I will enjoy it.
 Fol. Enjoy it then some other time, for now
Our prey approaches. -
 Bail. Let us retire.

SCENE II.

Tom Thumb, Noodle, Bailiff, Follower.

 Thumb. Trust me, my Noodle, I am wondrous sick ; *
For, though I love the gentle Huncamunca,
Yet at the thought of marriage I grow pale :
For, oh !—but swear thou'lt keep it ever secret,†
I will unfold a tale will make thee stare.
 Nood. I swear by lovely Huncamunca's charms.
 Thumb. Then know—my grandmamma ‡ hath often said,
Tom Thumb, beware of marriage.
 Nood.   Sir, I blush
To think a warrior, great in arms as you,
Should be affrighted by his grandmamma.
Can an old woman's empty dreams deter
·The blooming hero from the virgin's arms ?
Think of the joy that will your soul alarm,
When in her fond embraces clasp'd you lie,
While on her panting breast, dissolved in bliss,
You pour out all Tom Thumb in every kiss. -
 Thumb. Oh ! Noodle, thou hast fired my eager soul ;
Spite of my grandmother she shall be mine ;
I'll hug, caress, I'll eat her up with love :
Whole days, and nights, and years shall be too short

---

 * Mr. Rowe is generally imagined to have taken some hints from this
scene in his character of Bajazet ; but as he, of all the tragic writers,
bears the least resemblance to our author in his diction, I am unwilling to
imagine he would condescend to copy him in this particular.
 † This method of surprising an audience, by raising their expectation to
the highest pitch, and then baulking it, hath been practised with great
success by most of our tragical authors.
 ‡ Almeyda, in Sebastian, is in the same distress :—
   " Sometimes methinks I hear the groan of ghosts,
    Thin hollow sounds and lamentable screams ;
    Then like a dying echo from afar,
    My mother's voice that cries, Wed not, Almeyda ;
    Forewarn'd, Almeyda, marriage is thy crime."

For our enjoyment ; every sun shall rise
Blushing to see us both alone together.＊
 Nood. Oh, sir ! this purpose of your soul pursue.
 Bail. Oh, sir ! I have an action against you.
 Nood. At whose suit is it ?
 Bail. At your tailor's, sir.
Your tailor put this warrant in my hands,
And I arrest you, sir, at his commands.
 Thumb. Ha ! dogs !   Arrest my friend before my face !
Think you Tom Thumb will suffer this disgrace ?
But let vain cowards threaten by their word,
Tom Thumb shall show his anger by his sword.
       [*Kills* BAILIFF *and* FOLLOWER.
 Bail. Oh, I am slain !
 Fol.   I am murdered also,
And to the shades, the dismal shades below,
My bailiff's faithful follower I go.
 Nood. Go then to hell,† like rascals as you are,
  And give our service to the bailiffs there.
 Thumb. Thus perish all the bailiffs in the land,
Till debtors at noon-day shall walk the streets,
And no one fear a bailiff or his writ.

SCENE III.—*The Princess* HUNCAMUNCA'S *Apartment.*

HUNCAMUNCA, CLEORA, MUSTACHA.

Hunc. Give me some music—see that it be sad.‡

CLEORA *sings.*

 Cupid, ease a love-sick maid,
 Bring thy quiver to her aid ;
 With equal ardour wound the swain ;
 Beauty should never sigh in vain.

＊ "As very well he may, if he hath any modesty in him," says Mr. D—s. The author of Busiris is extremely zealous to prevent the sun's blushing at any indecent object ; and therefore on all such occasions he addresses himself to the sun, and desires him to keep out of the way.
  " Rise never more, O sun ! let night prevail.
   Eternal darkness close the world's wide scene."—"Busiris."
 "Sun, hide thy face, and put the world in mourning."—*Ibid.*
 Mr. Banks makes the sun perform the office of Hymen, and therefore not likely to be disgusted at such a sight :
  " The sun sets forth like a gay brideman with you."—
            " Mary Queen of Scots."
 † Neurmahal sends the same message to heaven :
  " For I would have you, when you upwards move,
   Speak kindly of us to our friends above."—"Aurengzebe."
 We find another to hell in the Persian Princess :
  " Villain, get thee down
   To hell, and tell them that the fray's begun."
  ‡ Anthony gives the same command in the same words.

Let him feel the pleasing smart,
Drive the arrow through his heart :
When one you wound, you then destroy ;
When both you kill, you kill with joy.

Hunc. O Tom Thumb! Tom Thumb! wherefore art thou
    Tom Thumb ?*
Why hadst thou not been born of royal race?
Why had not mighty Bantam been thy father?
Or else the King of Brentford, old or new!
  Must. I am surprised that your highness can give yourself a
moment's uneasiness about that little insignificant fellow, Tom
Thumb the Great†—one properer for a plaything than a husband.
Were he my husband his horns should be as long as his body.
If you had fallen in love with a grenadier, I should not have
wondered at it. If you had fallen in love with something ; but
to fall in love with nothing!
  Hunc. Cease, my Mustacha, on thy duty cease.
The zephyr, when in flowery vales it plays,
Is not so soft, so sweet as Thummy's breath.
The dove is not so gentle to its mate.
  Must. The dove is every bit as proper for a husband.—Alas !
madam, there's not a beau about the court looks so little like a
man. He is a perfect butterfly, a thing without substance, and
almost without shadow too.
  Hunc. This rudeness is unseasonable : desist ;
Or I shall think this railing comes from love.
Tom Thumb's a creature of that charming form,
That no one can abuse, unless they love him.
  Must. Madam, the king.

SCENE IV.

KING HUNCAMUNCA.

King. Let all but Huncamunca leave the room.
              [*Exeunt* CLEORA *and* MUSTACHA.
Daughter, I have observed of late some grief
Unusual in your countenance; your eyes
That, like two open windows,‡ used to show

    * "Oh! Marius, Marius, wherefore art thou, Marius?"—
                           Otway's " Marius."
  † Nothing is more common than these seeming contradictions; such
as—
        " Haughty weakness."—" Victim."
        " Great small world."—" Noah's Flood."
  ‡ Lee hath improved this metaphor:
    " Dost thou not view joy peeping from my eyes,
      The casements open'd wide to gaze on thee?
    So Rome's glad citizens to windows rise,
      When they some young triumpher fain would see."—" Gloriana."

The lovely beauty of the rooms within,
Have now two blinds before them.   What is the cause?
Say, have you not enough of meat and drink?
We've given strict orders not to have you stinted.
    Hunc. Alas! my lord, I value not myself
That once I ate two fowls and half a pig;
Small is that praise!* but oh! a maid may want
What she can neither eat nor drink.
    King.   What's that?
    Hunc. O spare my blushes ;† but I mean a husband.
    King. If that be all, I have provided one, -
A husband great in arms, whose warlike sword
Streams with the yellow blood of slaughter'd giants,
Whose name in Terrâ Incognitâ is known,
Whose valour, wisdom, virtue, make a noise
Great as the kettledrums of twenty armies.
    Hunc. Whom does my royal father mean?
    King.   Tom Thumb. -
    Hunc. Is it possible?
    King.   Ha! the window-blinds are gone;
A country-dance of joy is in your face.‡
Your eyes spit fire, your cheeks grow red as beef.
    Hunc. Oh, there's a magic-music in that sound,
Enough to turn me into beef indeed.!
Yes, I will own, since licensed by your word,
I'll own Tom Thumb the cause of all my grief.
For him I've sigh'd, I've wept, I've gnaw'd my sheets.

    * Almahide hath the same contempt for these appetites :
      "To eat and drink can no perfection be.—" Conquest of Granada."
    The Earl of Essex is of a different opinion, and seems to place the
chief happiness of a general therein : ·
      " Were but commanders half so well rewarded,
      Then they might eat."—Banks's " Earl of Essex."
    But, if we may believe one who knows more than either, the devil himself,
we shall find eating to be an affair of more moment than is generally
imagined :
      "Gods are immortal only by their food."—
        " Lucifer, in the State of Innocence."
    † " This expression is enough of itself," says Mr. D., " utterly to destroy
the character of Huncamunca!" Yet we find a woman of no abandoned
character in Dryden adventuring farther, and thus excusing herself:
      " To speak our wishes first, forbid it pride,
      Forbid it modesty; true, they forbid it,
      But Nature does not.   When we are athirst,
      Or hungry, will imperious Nature stay,
      Nor eat, nor drink, before 'tis bid fall on?"—
                        " Cleomenes."
    Cassandra speaks before she is asked : Huncamunca afterwards. Cassandra
speaks her wishes to her lover : Huncamunca only to her father.
    ‡ " Her eyes resistless magic bear :
      Angels, I see, and gods, are dancing there."—Lee's " Sophonisba."
                                      F

King. Oh! thou shalt gnaw thy tender sheets no more.
A husband thou shalt have to mumble now.

Hunc. Oh! happy sound! henceforth let no one tell
That Huncamunca shall lead apes in hell.
Oh! I am overjoy'd!

King.　　　　　　　I see thou art.
Joy lightens in thy eyes, and thunders from thy brows;*
Transports, like lightning, dart along thy soul,
As small-shot through a hedge.

Hunc.　　　　　　　Oh! say not small.

King. This happy news shall on our tongue ride post,
Ourself we bear the happy news to Thumb.
Yet think not, daughter, that your powerful charms
Must still detain the hero from his arms;
Various his duty, various his delight;
Now in his turn to kiss, and now to fight,
And now to kiss again. So, mighty Jove,†
When with excessive thund'ring tired above,
Comes down to earth, and takes a bit—and then
Flies to his trade of thund'ring back again.

SCENE V.

GRIZZLE, HUNCAMUNCA,

Griz. Oh! Huncamunca, Huncamunca, oh!‡
Thy pouting breasts, like kettledrums of brass,
Beat everlasting loud alarms of joy;
As bright as brass they are, and oh, as hard.
Oh! Huncamunca, Huncamunca, oh!

Hunc. Ha! dost thou know me, princess as I am,
That thus of me you dare to make your game?§

---

* Mr. Dennis, in that excellent tragedy called Liberty Asserted, which is thought to have given so great a stroke to the late French king, hath frequent imitations of this beautiful speech of king Arthur:
　　"Conquest light'ning in his eyes, and thund'ring in his arm."
　　"Joy lighten'd in her eyes."　.
　　"Joys like light'ning dart along my soul."

† "Jove, with excessive thund'ring tired above,
　　Comes down for ease, enjoys a nymph, and then
　　Mounts dreadful, and to thund'ring goes again."—"Gloriana."

‡ This beautiful line, which ought, says Mr. W—, to be written in gold, is imitated in the New Sophonisba:
　　"Oh! Sophonisba; Sophonisba, oh!
　　Oh! Narva; Narva, oh!"
The author of a song called Duke upon Duke hath improved it:
　　"Alas! O Nick! O Nick, alas!"
Where, by the help of a little false spelling, you have two meanings in the repeated words,

§ Edith, in the Bloody Brother, speaks to her lover in the same familiar language:
　　"Your grace is full of game."

Griz. Oh! Huncamunca, well I know that you
A princess are, and a king's daughter, too;
But love no meanness scorns, no grandeur fears;
Love often lords into the cellar bears,
And bids the sturdy porter come up stairs.
For what's too high for love, or what's too low?
Oh! Huncamunca, Huncamunca, oh!
    Hunc. But, granting all you say of love were true,
My love, alas! is to another due.
In vain to me a suitoring you come,
For I'm already promised to Tom Thumb.
    Griz. And can my princess such a durgen wed?
One fitter for your pocket than your bed!
Advised by me, the worthless baby shun,
Or you will ne'er be brought to bed of one.
Oh, take me to thy arms, and never-flinch,
Who am a man, by Jupiter! every inch.
Then, while in joys together lost we lie,†
I'll press thy soul while gods stand wishing by.
    Hunc. If, sir, what you insinuate you prove,
All obstacles of promise you remove;
For all engagements to a man must fall,
Whene'er that man is proved no man at all.
    Griz. Oh! let him seek some dwarf, some fairy miss,
Where no joint-stool must lift him to the kiss!
But, by the stars and glory! you appear
Much fitter for a Prussian grenadier;
One globe alone on Atlas' shoulders rests,
Two globes are less than Huncamunca's breasts;
The milky way is not so white, that's flat,
And sure thy breasts are full as large as that.
    Hunc. Oh, sir, so strong your eloquence I find,
It is impossible to be unkind.
    Griz. Ah! speak that o'er again, and let the sound†
From one pole to another pole rebound;
The earth and sky each be a battledore,
And keep the sound, that shuttlecock, up an hour:
To Doctors Commons for a licence I
Swift as an arrow from a bow will fly.
    Hunc. Oh, no! lest some disaster we should meet,
'Twere better to be married at the Fleet.

* "Traverse the glitt'ring chambers of the sky,
    Borne on a cloud in view of fate I'll lie,
    And press her soul while gods stand wishing by."—"Hannibal."
† "Let the four winds from distant corners meet,
    And on their wings first bear it into France;
    Then back again to Edina's proud walls,
    Till victim to the sound th' aspiring city falls."—"Albion Queens."

F 2

Griz. Forbid it, all ye powers, a princess should.
By that vile place contaminate her blood ;
My quick return shall to my charmer prove
I travel on the post-horses of love.*

Hunc. Those post-horses to me will seem too slow
Though they should fly swift as the gods, when they
Ride on behind that post-boy, Opportunity.

SCENE VI.

TOM-THUMB, HUNCAMUNCA.

Thumb. Where is my princess? where's my Huncamunca?
Where are those eyes, those cardmatches of love,
That light up all with love my waxen soul ?†
Where is that face which artful nature made
In the same moulds where Venus' self was cast ?‡

---

* I do not remember any metaphors so frequent in the tragic poets as those borrowed from riding post.
        "The gods and opportunity ride post."—"Hannibal."
            "Let's rush together,
        For death rides post."—"Duke of Guise."
        "Destruction gallops to thy murder post."—"Gloriana."
† This image, too, very often occurs :
            "Bright as when thy eye
        First lighted up our loves."—"Aurengzebe."
    "'Tis not a crown alone lights up my name."—"Busiris."
‡ There is great dissension among the poets concerning the method of making man. One tells his mistress that the mould she was made in being lost, Heaven cannot form such another. Lucifer, in Dryden, gives a merry description of his own formation :
    "Whom heaven, neglecting, made and scarce design'd,
        But threw me in for number to the rest."—"State of Innocence."
In one place the same poet supposes man to be made of metal:
            "I was form'd
        Of that coarse metal which, when she was made,
        The gods threw by for rubbish."—"All for Love."
In another of dough:
        "When the gods moulded up the paste of man,
        Some of their clay was left upon their hands.
        And so they made Egyptians."—"Cleomenes."
In another of clay :
        "Rubbish of remaining clay."—Sebastian."
One makes the soul of wax :
        "Her waxen soul begins to melt apace."—"Anna Bullen."
Another of flint:
        "Sure our souls have somewhere been acquainted
        In former beings, or, struck out together,
        One spark to Afric flew, and one to Portugal."—"Sebastian."
    To omit the great quantities of iron, brazen, and leaden souls which are so plenty in modern authors—I cannot omit the dress of a soul as we find it in Dryden :
        "Souls shirted but with air."—"King Arthur."

Hunc. Oh! what is music to the ear that's deaf,*
Or a goose-pie to him that has no taste?
What are these praises now to me, since I
Am promised to another?
 Thumb.   Ha! promised?
 Hunc. Too sure; 'tis written in the book of fate.
 Thumb. Then I will tear away the leaf†
Wherein it's writ; or, if fate won't allow
So large a gap within its journal-book,
I'll blot it out at least.

SCENE VII.

GLUMDALCA, TOM THUMB, HUNCAMUNCA.

Glum. I need not ask if you are Huncamunca,‡
Your brandy-nose proclaims——
 Hunc.   I am a princess;
Nor need I ask who you are.
 Glum.   A giantess;
The queen of those who made and unmade queens.
 Hunc. The man whose chief ambition is to be
My sweetheart, hath destroy'd these mighty giants.
 Glum. Your sweetheart? Dost thou think the man who once
Hath worn my easy chains will e'er wear thine?
 Hunc. Well may your chains be easy, since, if fame
Says true, they have been tried on twenty husbands.
The glove or boot, so many times pull'd on,§
May well sit easy on the hand or foot.

Nor can I pass by a particular sort of soul in a particular sort of
description in the New Sophonisba.
  "Ye mysterious powers,
   Whether thro' your gloomy depths I wander,
   Or on the mountains walk, give me the calm,
   The steady smiling soul, where wisdom sheds
   Eternal sunshine, and eternal joy."
* This line Mr. Banks has plunder'd entire in his Anna Bullen.
†   "Good Heaven! the book of fate before me lay,
   But to tear out the journal of that day.
   Or, if the order of the world below
   Will not the gap of one whole day allow,
   Give me that minute when she made her vow."—
           "Conquest of Granada."
 ‡ I know some of the commentators have imagined that Mr. -Dryden, in
the altercative scene between Cleopatra and Octavia, a scene which Mr.
Addison inveighs against with great bitterness, is much beholden to our
author. How just this their observation is I will not presume to determine.
 § "A cobbling poet indeed," says Mr. D.; and yet I believe we may
find as monstrous images in the tragic authors. I'll put down one:
"Untie your folded thoughts, and let them dangle loose as a bride's hair."—
            "Injured Love."
Which line seems to have as much title to a milliner's shop as our author's
to a shoemaker's.

Glum. I glory in the number, and when I
Sit poorly down, like thee, content with one,
·Heaven change this face for one as bad as thine.

Hunc. Let me see nearer what this beauty is
That captivates the heart of men by scores.

                         [*Holds a candle to her face.*

Oh ! Heaven, thou art as ugly as the devil.

Glum. You'd give the best of shoes within your shop
To be but half so handsome.

Hunc.   Since you come
To that, I'll put my beauty to the test :*
Tom Thumb, I'm yours, if you with me will go.

Glum. Oh ! stay Tom Thumb, and you alone shall fill
That bed where twenty giants used to lie.

Thumb. In the balcóny that o'erhangs the stage,
I've seen a puss two 'prentices engage ;
One half-a-crown does in his fingers hold,
The other shows a little piece of gold ;
She the half-guinea wisely does purloin,
And leaves the larger and the baser coin.

Glum. Left, scorn'd, and loath'd for such a chit as this ;
I feel the storm that's rising in my mind,†
Tempests and whirlwinds rise, and roll, and roar.
I'm all within a hurricane, as if
The world's four winds were pent within my carcase.‡
Confusion,§ horror, murder, gripes, and death !

SCENE VIII.

KING, GLUMDALCA.

King. Sure never was so sad a king as I ! ‖
My life is worn as ragged as a coat ¶

---

   * Mr. L— takes occasion in this place to commend the great care of our
author to preserve the metre of blank verse, in which Shakespeare, Jonson,
and Fletcher, were so notoriously negligent ; and the moderns, in imitation
of our author, so laudably observant :
                        "Then does
           Your majesty believe that he can be
           A traitor ?"—" Earl of Essex."
Every page of Sophonisba gives us instances of this excellence.
   † " Love mounts and rolls about my stormy mind."—" Aurengzebe."
     " Tempests and whirlwinds thro' my bosom move."—" Cleom."
   ‡ " With such a furious tempest on his brow,
        As if the world's four winds were pent within
        His blustering carcase."—" Anna Bullen."
§ Verba Tragica.
‖ This speech has been terribly mauled by the poet.
     ¶ " My life is worn to rags,
   Not worth a prince's wearing."—" Love Triumphant."

A beggar wears ; a prince should put it off.
To love a captive and a giantess ! *
Oh love ! oh love ! how great a king art thou !
My tongue's thy trumpet, and thou trumpetest,
Unknown to me, within me.   Oh, Glumdalca ! †
Heaven thee design'd a giantess to make,
But an angelic soul was shuffled in.
I am a multitude of walking griefs,‡
And only on her lips the balm is found
To spread a plaster that might cure them all.§

   Glum. What do I hear?
   King.   What do I see ?
   Glum.   Oh !
   King.   Ah !
   Glum. Ah! wretched queen ! ‖
   King.   Oh ! wretched king !
   Glum.   Ah ! ¶
   King.   Oh !

   * "Must I beg the pity of my slave ?
        Must a king beg ? But love's a greater king,
        A tryant, nay, a devil, that possesses me.
        He tunes the organ of my voice and speaks,
          Unknown to me, within me."—" Sebastian."
 † " When thou wert form'd heaven did a man begin ;
     But a brute soul by chance was shuffled in."—" Aurengzebe."
 ‡   " I am a multitude
          Of walking griefs."—" New Sophonisba."
 §   " I will take thy scorpion blood,
        And lay it to my grief till I have ease."—" Anna Bullen."
 ‖ Our author, who everywhere shows his great penetration into human
nature, here outdoes himself : where a less judicious poet would have raised
a long scene of whining love, he, who understood the passions better, and
that so violent an affection as this must be too big for utterance, chooses
rather to send his characters off in this sullen and doleful manner, in which
admirable conduct he is imitated by the author of the justly celebrated
Eurydice.   Dr. Young seems to point at this violence of passion :
                       " Passion chokes
     Their words, and they're the statues of despair."
And Seneca tells us, " Curæ leves loquuntur, ingentes stupent."   The story
of the Egyptian king in Herodotus is too well known to need to be inserted ;
I refer the more curious reader to the excellent Montaigne, who hath written
an essay on this subject.
 ¶ " To part is death.
           'Tis death to part.
                Ah !
                    Oh ! "—" Don Carlos."

SCENE IX.

TOM THUMB, HUNCAMUNCA, PARSON.

Par. Happy's the wooing that's not long a-doing ;
For, if I guess right, Tom Thumb this night
Shall give a being to a new Tom Thumb.
Thumb. It shall be my endeavour so to do.
Hunc. Oh ! fie upon you, sir, you make me blush.
Thumb. It is the virgin's sign, and suits you well :
I know not where, nor how, nor what I am ; *
I'm so transported, I have lost myself.†
Hunc. Forbid it, all ye stars, for you're so small,
That were you lost, you'd find yourself no more.
So the unhappy sempstress once, they say,
Her needle in a pottle, lost, of hay ;
In vain she look'd, and look'd, and made her moan.
For ah, the needle was for ever gone.
Par. Long may they live, and love, and propagate,
Till the whole land be peopled with Tom Thumbs !

* " Nor know I whether
    What am I, who, or where."—" Busiris."
"I was I know not what, and am I know not how."—" Gloriana."
† To understand sufficiently the beauty of this passage, it will be neces-
sary that we comprehend every man to contain two selfs. I shall not attempt
to prove this from philosophy, which the poets make so plainly evident.
One runs away from the other :
        " Let me demand your majesty,
        Why fly you from yourself ? "—" Duke of Guise."
In a second, one self is a guardian to the other :
        "Leave me the care of me."—" Conquest of Granada."
Again :
        " Myself am to myself less near."—*Ibid.*
In the same, the first self is proud of the second :
        " I myself am proud of me."—" State of Innocence."
In a third, distrustful of him :
        " Fain I would tell, but whisper it in my ear,
        That none besides might hear, nay, not myself."—" Earl of Essex."
In a fourth, honours him :
        " I honour Rome,
        And honour too myself."—" Sophonisba."
In a fifth, at variance with him :
        " Leave me not thus at variance with myself."—" Busiris."
Again, in a sixth :
        " I find myself divided from myself."—" Medea."
        " She seemed the sad effigies of herself."—Banks.
    "Assist me, Zulema, if thou would'st be
        The friend thou seem'st, assist me against me."—" Alb. Q."
From all which it appears that there are two selfs ; and therefore Tom
Thumb's losing himself is no such solecism as it hath been represented by
men rather ambitious of criticising than qualified to criticise.

So, when the Cheshire cheese a maggot breeds,*
Another and another still succeeds :
By thousands and ten thousands they increase,
Till one continued maggot fills the rotten cheese.

SCENE X.

NOODLE, *and then* GRIZZLE.

Nood. Sure, Nature means to break her solid chain,†
Or else unfix the world, and in a rage
To hurl it from its axletree and hinges ;
All things are so confused, the king's in love,
The queen is drunk, the princess married is.
 Griz. Oh, Noodle ! Hast thou Huncamunca seen ?
 Nood. I've seen a thousand sights this day, where none
Are by the Wonderful Pig himself outdone.
The king, the queen, and all the court, are sights.
 Griz. D—n your delay, you trifler ! are you drunk, ha ?‡
I will not hear one word but Huncamunca.
 Nood. By this time she is married to Tom Thumb.
 Griz. My Huncamunca !§
 Nood. Your Huncamunca,
Tom Thumb's Huncamunca, every man's Huncamunca.
 Griz. If this be true, all womankind are curst.
 Nood. If it be not, may I be so myself.
 Griz. See where she comes ! I'll not believe a word
Against that face, upon whose ample brow‖
Sits innocence with majesty enthroned.

GRIZZLE, HUNCAMUNCA.

 Griz. Where has my Huncamunca been ? See here.
The licence in my hand !
 Hunc.   Alas ! Tom Thumb.

---

 * Mr. F. imagines this parson to have been a Welsh one, from his simile.
  Our author hath been plundered here, according to custom :
    "Great nature, break thy chain that links together
     The fabric of the world, and make a chaos
     Like that within my soul."—" Love Triumphant."
      " Startle Nature, unfix the globe,
     And hurl it from its axletree and hinges."—" Albion Queens."
     " The tott'ring earth seems sliding off its props."
  ‡ " D—n your delay, ye torturers, proceed :
    I will not hear one word but Almahide."—" Conq. of Gran.'
 § Mr. Dryden hath imitated this in All for Love.
 ‖ This Miltonic style abounds in the New Sophonisba.
    " And on her ample brow
   Sat majesty."

Griz. Why dost thou mention him ?

Hunc.   Ah, me ! Tom Thumb.

Griz. What means my lovely Huncamunca?

Hunc.   Hum ?

Griz. Oh ! speak.

Hunc.   Hum !

Griz.   Ha ! your every word is hum :
You force me still to answer you, Tom Thumb.*
Tom Thumb—I'm on the rack—I'm in a flame.
Tom Thumb, Tom Thumb, Tom Thumb—you love the name ;†
So pleasing is that sound, that, were you dumb,
You still would find a voice to cry Tom Thumb.

Hunc. Oh ! be not hasty to proclaim my doom !
My ample heart for more than one has room :
A maid like me Heaven form'd at least for two.
I married him, and now I'll marry you.‡

Griz. Ha ! dost thou own thy falsehood to my face ?
Think'st thou that I, will share thy husband's place ?
Since to that office one cannot suffice,
And since you scorn to dine one single dish on,
Go, get your husband put into commission.
Commissioners to discharge (ye gods ! it fine is)
The duty of a husband to your highness.
Yet think not long I will my rival bear,
Or unrevenged the slighted willow wear ;
The gloomy, brooding tempest, now confined
Within the hollow caverns of my mind,
In dreadful whirl shall roll along the coasts,
Shall thin the land of all the men it boasts,
And cram up ev'ry chink of hell with ghosts.§

* "Your ev'ry answer still so ends in that,
    You force me still to answer you, Morat."—" Aurengzebe.
† " Morat, Morat, Morat ! you love the name."—*Ibid.*
‡ " Here is a sentiment for the virtuous Huncamunca !" says Mr. D—s.
And yet, with the leave of this great man, the virtuous Panthea, in Cyrus,
hath a heart every whit as ample :
    "For two I must confess are gods to me,
        Which is my Abradatus first, and thee."—" Cyrus the Great."
Nor is the lady in Love Triumphant more reserved, though not so intel-
ligible :   "I am so divided,
        That I grieve most for both, and love both most."
§ A ridiculous supposition to any one who considers the great and extensive largeness of hell, says a commentator ; but not so to those who consider the great expansion of immaterial substance. Mr. Banks makes one
soul to be so expanded, that heaven could not contain it.
    " The heavens are all too narrow for her soul."—" Virtue Betrayed."
The Persian Princess hath a passage not unlike the author of this :
        " We will send such shoals of murder'd slaves,
            Shall glut hell's empty regions."
This threatens to fill hell, even though it was empty ; Lord Grizzle, only to
fill up the chinks, supposing the rest already full.

So have I seen, in some dark winter's day,*
A sudden storm rush down the sky's highway,
Sweep through the streets with terrible ding-dong,
Gush through the spouts, and wash whole clouds along.
The crowded shops the thronging vermin screen,
Together cram the dirty and the clean,
And not one shoe-boy in the street is seen.

Hunc. Oh, fatal rashness! should his fury slay
My hapless bridegroom on his wedding-day,
I, who this morn of two chose which to wed,
May go again this night alone to bed.
So have I seen some wild unsettled fool,†
Who had her choice of this and that joint-stool,
To give the preference to either loth,
And fondly coveting to sit on both,
While the two stools her sitting-part confound,
Between 'em both fall squat upon the ground.

ACT III.

SCENE I.—KING ARTHUR'S *Palace.*

Ghost‡ (solus). Hail! ye black horrors of midnight's mid-noon!

---

* Mr. Addison is generally thought to have had this simile in his eye when he wrote that beautiful one at the end of the third act of his Cato.

† This beautiful simile is founded on a proverb which does honour to the English language:
    "Between two stools the breech falls to the ground."
I am not so well pleased with any written remains of the ancients as with those little aphorisms which verbal tradition hath delivered down to us under the title of proverbs. It were to be wished that, instead of filling their pages with the fabulous theology of the pagans, our modern poets would think it worth their while to enrich their works with the proverbial sayings of their ancestors. Mr. Dryden hath chronicled one in heroic:
    "Two ifs scarce make one possibility."—"Conq. of Granada."
My Lord Bacon is of opinion that whatever is known of arts and sciences might be proved to have lurked in the Proverbs of Solomon. I am of the same opinion in relation to those above-mentioned; at least I am confident that a more perfect system of ethics, as well as economy, might be compiled out of them than is at present extant, either in the works of the ancient philosophers, or those more valuable, as more voluminous ones of the modern divines.

‡ Of all the particulars in which the modern stage falls short of the ancients, there is none so much to be lamented as the great scarcity of ghosts. Whence this proceeds I will not presume to determine. Some are of opinion that the moderns are unequal to that sublime language which a ghost ought to speak. One says, ludicrously, that ghosts are out of fashion;

Ye fairies, goblins, bats, and screech-owls, hail!
And, oh! ye mortal watchmen, whose hoarse throats
Th' immortal ghosts dread croakings counterfeit,
All hail!—Ye dancing phantoms, who, by day,
Are some condemn'd to fast, some feast in fire,
Now play in churchyards, skipping o'er the graves,
To the loud music of the silent bell,*
All hail!

SCENE II.

KING, GHOST.

King. What noise is this? What villain dares,
At this dread hour, with feet and voice profane,
Disturb our royal walls?
   Ghost.   One who defies
Thy empty power to hurt him; one who dares †
Walk in thy bedchamber.
   King.   Presumptuous slave!
Thou diest.
   Ghost.   Threaten others with that word:
I am a ghost, and am already dead.‡
   King. Ye stars! 'tis well. Were thy last hour to come,

---

another, that they are properer for comedy; forgetting, I suppose, that Aristotle hath told us that a ghost is the soul of tragedy; for so I render the ψυχή ὁ μῦθος τῆς τραγωδίας, which M. Dacier, amongst others, hath mistaken; I suppose misled by not understanding the Fabula of the Latins, which signifies a ghost as well as fable.

    "Te premet nox, fabulæque manes. '—Horace.
Of all the ghosts that have ever appeared on the stage, a very learned and judicious foreign critic gives the preference to this of our author. These are his words, speaking of this tragedy:—"Nec quidquam in illâ admirabilius quàm phasma quoddam horrendum, quod omnibus aliis spectris, quibuscum scatet Angelorum tragœdia, longè (pace D—ysii V. Doctiss. dixerim) prætulerim."

   * We have already given instances of this figure.

   † Almanzor reasons in the same manner:
                "A ghost I'll be;
    And from a ghost, you know, no place is free."—"Conq. of Gran."
   ‡ "The man who writ this wretched pun," says Mr. D., "would have picked your pocket:" which he proceeds to show not only bad in itself, but doubly so on so solemn an occasion. And yet, in that excellent play of Liberty Asserted, we find something very much resembling a pun in the mouth of a mistress, who is parting with the lover she is fond of:
      "*Ul.* Oh, mortal woe! one kiss, and then farewell.
     Irene. The gods have given to others to fare well,
       O! miserably must Irene fare."
Agamemnon, in the Victim, is full as facetious on the most solemn occasion —that of sacrificing his daughter:
      "Yes, daughter, yes; you will assist the priest;
     Yes, you must offer up your—vows for Greece."

This moment had been it ; yet by thy shroud *
I'll pull thee backward, squeeze thee to a bladder,
Till thou dost groan thy nothingness away.
Thou fly'st ! 'Tis well.   [GHOST *retires.*
I thought what was the courage of a ghost ! †
Yet, dare not, on thy life—Why say I that,
Since life thou hast not ?—Dare not walk again
Within these walls, on pain of the Red Sea.
For, if henceforth I ever find thee here,
As sure, sure as a gun, I'll have thee laid——
   Ghost. Were the Red Sea a sea of Hollands gin,
The liquor (when alive) whose very smell
I did detest, did loathe—yet, for the sake
Of Thomas Thumb, I would be laid therein.
   King. Ha ! said you ?
   Ghost.   Yes, my liege, I said Tom Thumb,
Whose father's ghost I am—once not unknown
To mighty Arthur.   But, I see, 'tis true,
The dearest friend, when dead, we all forget.
   King. 'Tis he—it is the honest Gaffer Thumb.
Oh ! let me press thee in my eager arms,
Thou best of ghosts ! thou something more than ghost ! \
   Ghost. Would I were something more, that we again
Might feel each other in the warm embrace.
But now I have th' advantage of my king,
For I feel thee, whilst thou dost not feel me.‡
   King. But say, thou dearest air,§ oh ! say what dread,
Important business sends thee back to earth ?
   Ghost. Oh ! then prepare to hear—which but to hear
Is full enough to send thy spirit hence.
Thy subjects up in arms, by Grizzle led,
Will, ere the rosy-finger'd morn shall ope
The shutters of the sky, before the gate
Of this thy royal palace, swarming spread.

---

   * " I'll pull thee backwards by thy shroud to light,
      Or else I'll squeeze thee, like a bladder, there,
        And make thee groan thyself away to air."—" Conq. of Gran.'
" Snatch me, ye gods, this moment into nothing."—" Cyrus the Great."
 † " So, art thou gone ? Thou canst no conquest boast,
   I thought what was the courage of a ghost."—"Conq. of Gran."
King Arthur seems to be as brave a fellow as Almanzor, who says most
heroically :   " In spite of ghosts I'll on."
 ‡ The ghost of Lausaria, in Cyrus, is a plain copy of this, and is there-
fore worth reading :
               "Ah, Cyrus !
   Thou may'st as well grasp water, or fleet air,
      As think of touching my immortal shade."—" Cyrus the Great."
 § " Thou better part of heavenly air."—" Conquest of Granada."

So have I seen the bees in clusters swarm,*
So have I seen the stars in frosty nights,
So have I seen the sand in windy days,
So have I seen the ghosts on Pluto's shore,
So have I seen the flowers in spring arise,
So have I seen the leaves in autumn fall,
So have I seen the fruits in summer smile,
So have I seen the snow in winter frown.

  King. D—n all thou hast seen !—dost thou, beneath the
    shape
Of Gaffer Thumb, come hither to abuse me
With similes, to keep me on the rack ?
Hence—or, by all the torments of thy hell,
I'll run thee through the body, though thou'st none.†

  Ghost. Arthur, beware ! I must this moment hence,
Not frighted by your voice, but by the cocks !
Arthur, beware, beware, beware, beware !
Strive to avert thy yet impending fate ;
For, if thou'rt kill'd to-day,
To-morrow all thy care will come too late.

SCENE III.

KING, *solus.*

  King. Oh ! stay, and leave me not uncertain thus !
And, whilst thou tellest me what's like my fate,
Oh ! teach me how I may avert it too !
Curs'd be the man who first a simile made !
Curs'd ev'ry bard who writes—So have I seen !
Those whose comparisons are just and true,
And those who liken things not like at all.
The devil is happy that the whole creation
Can furnish out no simile to his fortune.

SCENE IV.

KING, QUEEN.

  Queen. What is the cause, my Arthur, that you steal
Thus silently from Dollallolla's breast ?

* "A string of similes," says one, "proper to be hung up in the cabinet of a prince."
† This passage hath been understood several different ways by the commentators. For my part I find it difficult to understand it at all. Mr. Dryden says—
    " I've heard something how two bodies meet,
    But how two souls join I know not."
So that, till the body of a spirit be better understood, it will be difficult to understand how it is possible to run him through it.

Why dost thou leave me in the dark alone,*
When well thou know'st I am afraid of sprites?
  King. Oh, Dollallolla! do not blame my love!
I hoped the fumes of last night's punch had laid
Thy lovely eyelids fast; but, oh! I find
There is no power in drams to quiet wives;
Each morn, as the returning sun, they wake,
And shine upon their husbands.
  Queen.   Think, oh, think!
What a surprise it must be to the sun, .
Rising, to find the vanish'd world away.
What less can be the wretched wife's surprise
When, stretching out her arms to fold thee fast,
She found her useless bolster in her arms.
Think, think, on that.—Oh! think, think well on that!†
I do remember also to have read
In Dryden's Ovid's Metamorphoses,‡
That Jove in form inanimate did lie
With beauteous Danaë: and, trust me, love,
I fear'd the bolster might have been a Jove.§
  King. Come to my arms, most virtuous of thy sex!
Oh, Dollallolla! were all wives like thee,
So many husbands never had worn horns.
Should Huncamunca of thy worth partake,
Tom Thumb indeed were blest.—Oh, fatal name
For didst thou know one quarter what I know,
Then wouldst thou know—alas! what thou wouldst know!
  Queen. What can I gather hence? Why dost thou speak
Like men who carry rareeshows about?
"Now you shall see, gentlemen, what you shall see."
O, tell me more, or thou hast told too much.

SCENE V.

KING, QUEEN, NOODLE.

Nood. Long life attend your majesties serene,
Great Arthur, king, and Dollallolla, queen!
Lord Grizzle, with a bold rebellious crowd,
Advances to the palace, threat'ning loud,

  * Cydaria is of the same fearful temper with Dollalolla:
    " I never durst in darkness be alone."—" Ind. Emp."
    • " Think well of this, think that, think every way."—" Sophon."
  ‡ These quotations are more usual in the comic than in the tragic writers.
  § " This distress," says Mr. D—, " I must allow to be extremely beautiful, and tends to heighten the virtuous character of Dollallolla, who is so
exceeding delicate, that she is in the highest apprehension from the inanimate embrace of a bolster. An example worthy of imitation for all our
writers of tragedy."

Unless the princess be deliver'd straight,
And the victorious Thumb, without his pate,
They are resolv'd to batter down the gate.

SCENE VI.

KING, QUEEN, HUNCAMUNCA, NOODLE.

King. See where the princess comes ! Where is Tom Thumb ?
Hunc. Oh ! sir, about an hour and half ago
He sallied out t' encounter with the foe,
And swore, unless his fate had him misled,
From Grizzle's shoulders to cut off his head,
And serve't up with your chocolate in bed.
　King. 'Tis well, I found one devil told us both.
Come, Dollallolla, Huncamunca, come ;
Within we'll wait for the victorious Thumb :
In peace and safety we secure may stay,
While to his arm we trust the bloody fray ;
Though men and giants should conspire with gods,
He is alone equal to all these odds.*
　Queen. He is, indeed, a helmet to us all ; †
While he supports we need not fear to fall ;
His arm despatches all things to our wish,

---

　* " Credat Judæus Appella,
　　　Non ego,"
says Mr. D. " For, passing over the absurdity of being equal to odds,
can we possibly suppose a little insignificant fellow—I say again a little
insignificant fellow—able to vie with a strength which all the Samsons and
Herculeses of antiquity would be unable to encounter? ' I shall refer this
incredulous critic to Mr. Dryden's defence of his Almanzor ; and, lest that
should not satisfy him, I shall quote a few lines from the speech of a much
braver fellow than Almanzor, Mr. Johnson's Achilles :
　　" Though human race rise in embattled hosts,
　　　To force her from my arms—Oh ! son of Atreus !
　　　By that immortal pow'r, whose deathless spirit
　　　Informs this earth, I will oppose them all."—" Victim."
　† " I have heard of being supported by a staff," says Mr. D., " but never
of being supported by a helmet." I believe he never heard of sailing with
wings, which he may read in no less a poet than Mr. Dryden :
　" Unless we borrow wings and sail through air."—" Love Triumphant.
What will he say to a kneeling valley ? ·
　　　　　" I'll stand
　　　Like a safe valley, that low bends the knee
　　　To some aspiring mountain."—" Injured Love."
I am ashamed of so ignorant a carper, who doth not know ·that an epithet
in tragedy is very often no other than an expletive. Do not we read in the
New Sophonisba of " grinding chains, blue plagues, white occasions, and
blue serenity?" Nay, it is not the adjective only, but sometimes half a
sentence is put by way of expletive, as " Beauty pointed high with spirit,"
in the same play ; and " In the lap. of blessing, to be most curst," in the
Revenge.

And serves up ev'ry foe's head in a dish.
Void is the mistress of the house of care,
While the good cook presents the bill of fare ;
Whether the cod, that northern king of fish,
Or duck, or goose, or pig, adorn the dish,
No fears the number of her guests afford,
But at her hour she sees the dinner on the board.

SCENE VII.—*Plain.*

GRIZZLE, FOODLE, REBELS.

Griz. Thus far our arms with victory are crown'd ;
For, though we have not fought, yet we have found
No enemy to fight withal.*
Food.   Yet I,
Methinks, would willingly avoid this day,
This first of April to engage our foes.†
Griz. This day, of all the days of the year, I'd choose,
For on this day my grandmother was born.
Gods ! I will make Tom Thumb an April-fool ;
Will teach his wit an errand it ne'er knew,‡
And send it post to the Elysian shades.
Food. I'm glad to find our army is so stout,
Nor does it move my wonder less than joy.
Griz. What friends we have, and how we came so strong,§
I'll softly tell you as we march along.

SCENE VIII.—*Thunder and Lightning.*

TOM THUMB, GLUMDALCA, *cum suis.*

Thumb. Oh, Noodle ! hast thou seen a day like this ?
The unborn thunder rumbles o'er our heads,‖
As if the gods meant to unhinge the world,¶
And heaven and earth in wild confusion hurl ;
Yet will I boldly tread the tott'ring ball.

---

* A victory like that of Almanzor :
   " Almanzor is victorious without fight."—" Conquest of Granada."
      † " Well have we chose an happy day for fight ;
         For every man, in course of time, has found
         Some days are lucky, some unfortunate."—" King Arthur."
‡ We read of such another in Lee :
         " Teach his rude wit a flight she never made,
         And send her post to the Elysian shade."—" Gloriana."
      § These lines are copied verbatim in the Indian Emperor.
   ‖ " Unborn thunder rolling in a cloud."—" Conquest of Granada."
¶ " Were heaven and earth in wild confusion hurl'd,
   Should the rash gods unhinge the rolling world,
   Undaunted would I tread the tott'ring ball,
   Crush'd, but unconquer'd, in the dreadful fall."—" Female Warrior."

Merl. Tom Thumb!
Thumb.   What voice is this I hear?
Merl. '   Tom Thumb!
Thumb. Again it calls.
Merl.   Tom Thumb!
Glum.   It calls again.
Thumb. Appear, whoe'er thou art; I fear thee not.
Merl. Thou hast no cause to fear—I am thy friend,
Merlin by name, a conjuror by trade,
And to my art thou dost thy being owe.
Thumb. How?
Merl. Hear, then, the mystic getting of Tom Thumb.

> His father was a ploughman plain,
>   His mother milk'd the cow;
> And yet the way to get a son
>   This couple knew not how,
> Until such time the good old man
>   To learned Merlin goes,
> And there to him, in great distress,
>   In secret manner shows
> How in his heart he wish'd to have
>   A child, in time to come,
> To be his heir, though it may be
>   No bigger than his thumb:
> Of which old Merlin was foretold
>   That he his wish should have;
> And so a son of stature small
>   The charmer to him gave.*

Thou'st heard the past—look up and see the future.
    Thumb. Lost in amazement's gulf, my senses sink;†
See there, Glumdalca, see another me!‡
    Glum. O, sight of horror! see, you are devour'd
By the expanded jaws of a red cow.
    Merl. Let not these sights deter thy noble mind,
For, lo! a sight more glorious courts thy eyes.§
See from afar a theatre arise;
There ages, yet unborn, shall tribute pay

---

* See the History of Tom Thumb, p. 141.
† "Amazement swallows up my sense,
And in the impetuous whirl of circling fate
Drinks down my reason."—"Persian Princess."
‡ "I have outfaced myself.
What! am I two? Is there another me?"—"King Arthur."
§ The character of Merlin is wonderful throughout; but most so in this prophetic part. We find several of these prophecies in the tragic authors, who frequently take this opportunity to pay a compliment to their country, and sometimes to their prince. None but our author (who seems to have detested the least appearance of flattery) would have passed by such an opportunity of being a political prophet.

To the heroic actions of this day;
Then buskin tragedy at length shall choose
Thy name the best supporter of her muse.
   Thumb. Enough : let every warlike music sound.
We fall contented, if we fall renown'd.

SCENE IX.

LORD GRIZZLE, FOODLE, REBELS, *on one side;* TOM THUMB,
    GLUMDALCA, *on the other.*

   Food. At length the enemy advances nigh,
I hear them with my ear, and see them with my eye.*
   Griz. Draw all your swords : for liberty we fight,
And liberty the mustard is of life.†
   Thumb. Are you the man whom men famed Grizzle name ?
   Griz. Are you the much more famed Tom Thumb ? ‡
   Thumb. The same.
   Griz. Come on ; our worth upon ourselves we'll prove ;
For liberty I fight.
   Thumb. And I for love.

> [*A bloody engagement between the two armies; drums
>   beating, trumpets sounding, thunder, lightning,
>   They fight off and on several times. Some fall.*
> GRIZZLE *and* GLUMDALCA *remain.*

   Glum. Turn, coward, turn ; nor from a woman fly.
   Griz. Away—thou art too ignoble for my arm.
   Glum. Have at thy heart.
   Griz.   Nay, then I thrust at thine.
   Glum. You push too well ; you've run me through the body,
And I am dead.
   Griz.   Then there's an end of one.
   Thumb. When thou art dead, then there's an end of two.
Villain.§

* " I saw the villain, Myron ; with these eyes I saw him."—" Busiris."
In both which places it is intimated that it is sometimes possible to see with
other eyes than your own.
  † " This mustard," says Mr. D., " is enough to turn one's stomach. I
would be glad to know what idea the author had in his head when he wrote
it." This will be, I believe, best explained by a line of Mr. Dennis :
     " And gave him liberty, the salt of life."—" Liberty Asserted."
The understanding that can digest the one will not rise at the other.
  ‡ " *Han.* Are you the chief whom men famed Scipio call?
     Scip. Are you the much more famous Hannibal ?"—" Hannibal."
  § Dr Young seems to have copied this engagement in his Busiris :
          Myr. Villain !
          Mem. Myron !
          Myr. Rebel !
          Mem. Myron !
          Myr. Hell !
          Mem. Mandane !

Griz. Tom Thumb!
Thumb. Rebel!
Griz. Tom Thumb!
Thumb. Hell!
Griz. Huncamunca!
Thumb. Thou hast it there.
Griz. Too sure I feel it
   Thumb. To hell then, like a rebel as you are,
And give my service to the rebels there.
   Griz. Triumph not, Thumb, nor think thou shalt enjoy
Thy Huncamunca undisturb'd ; I'll send
My ghost to fetch her to the other world ;*
It shall but bait at heaven, and then return.†
But, ha ! I feel death rumbling in my brains :‡
Some kinder sprite knocks softly at my soul,§
And gently whispers it to haste away.
I come, I come, most willingly I come.
So when some city wife, for country air,
To Hampstead or to Highgate does repair,
Her to make haste her husband does implore,
And cries, " My dear, the coach is at the door : "
With equal wish, desirous to be gone,
She gets into the coach, and then she cries—" Drive on ! "
   Thumb. With those last words he vomited his soul,‖
Which, like whipt cream, the devil will swallow down.¶
Bear off the body, and cut off the head,
Which I will to the king in triumph lug.
Rebellion's dead, and now I'll go to breakfast.

   * This last speech of my Lord Grizzle hath been of great service to our
poets :
                      " I'll hold it fast
       As life, and when life's gone I'll hold this last ;
       And if thou tak'st it from me when I'm slain,
       I'll send my ghost and fetch it back again."—'' Conq. of Gran.'
   † " My soul should with such speed obey,
       It should not bait at heaven to stop its way."
Lee seems to have had this last in his eye :
       '' 'Twas not my purpose, sir, to tarry there :
       I would but go to heaven to take the air."—" Gloriana."
       " A rising vapour rumbling in my brains."—" Cleomenes."
   § " Some kind sprite knocks softly at my soul,
       To tell me fate's at hand."
Mr. Dryden seems to have had this simile in his eye, when he says :
      " My soul is packing up, and just on wing."—" Conq. of Gran."
       " And in a purple vomit pour'd his soul."—" Cleomenes."
   ¶ " The devil swallows vulgar souls
       Like whipt cream."—" Sebastian."

SCENE X.

KING, QUEEN, HUNCAMUNCA, COURTIERS.

King. Open the prisons, set the wretched free,
And bid our treasurer disburse six pounds
To pay their debts. Let no one weep to-day.
Come, Dollallolla; curse that odious name !*
It is so long, it asks an hour to speak it.
By heavens! I'll change it into Doll, or Loll,
Or any other civil monosyllable,
That will not tire my tongue. Come, sit thee down.
Here seated let us view the dancers' sports ;
Bid 'em advance. This is the wedding-day
Of Princess Huncamunca and Tom Thumb ;
Tom Thumb! who wins two victories to-day,†
And this way marches, bearing Grizzle's head.   [*A dance here.*

Nood. Oh! monstrous, dreadful, terrible—Oh! oh!
Deaf be my ears, for ever blind my eyes!
Dumb be my tongue! feet lame! all senses lost!
Howl wolves ; grunt, bears ; hiss, snakes ; shriek, all ye ghosts ! ‡

King. What does the blockhead mean ?
Nood.   I mean, my liege,
Only to grace my tale with decent horror.§
Whilst from my garret, twice two stories high,
I look'd abroad into the streets below,
I saw Tom Thumb attended by the mob ;
Twice twenty shoe-boys, twice two dozen links,
Chairmen and porters, hackney-coachmen, drabs ;
Aloft he bore the grizly head of Grizzle ;
When of a sudden through the streets there came
A cow, of larger than the usual size,
And in a moment—guess, oh! guess the rest !—
And in a moment swallow'd up Tom Thumb.

King. Shut up again the prisons, bid my treasurer
Not give three farthings out—hang all the culprits,

---

* " How I could curse my name of Ptolemy !
    It is so long, it asks an hour to write it.
    By heaven! I'll change it into Jove or Mars !
    Or any other civil monosyllable.
    That will not tire my hand."—" Cleomenes."

† Here is a visible conjunction of two days in one, by which our author
may have either intended an emblem of a wedding, or to insinuate that men
in the honeymoon are apt to imagine time shorter than it is. It brings into
my mind a passage in the comedy called the Coffee-House Politician :
        " We will celebrate this day at my house to-morrow.'

‡ These beautiful phrases are all to be found in one single speech of
King Arthur, or the British Worthy.

§ " I was but teaching him to grace his tale
        With decent horror."—" Cleomenes."

Guilty or not—no matter. Kill my cows !
Go bid the schoolmasters whip all their boys !
Let lawyers, parsons, and physicians loose,
To rob, impose on, and to kill the world.
Nood. Her majesty the queen is in a swoon.
Queen. Not so much in a swoon but I have still
Strength to reward the messenger of ill news.   [*Kills* NOODLE.
Nood. Oh ! I am slain.
Cle. My lover's kill'd, I will revenge him so. [*Kills the* QUEEN.
Hunc. My mamma kill'd ! vile murderess, beware.'
                                        [*Kills* CLEORA.
Dood. This for an old grudge to thy heart. [*Kills* HUNCAMUNCA.
Must. And this
I drive to thine, O Doodle ! for a new one.   [*Kills* DOODLE.
King. Ha ! murderess vile, take that.   [*Kills* MUST.
And take thou this.*   [*Kills himself, and falls.*
So when the child, whom nurse from danger guards,
Sends Jack for mustard with a pack of cards,
Kings, queens, and knaves, throw one another down,
Till the whole pack lies scatter'd and o'erthrown ;
So all our pack upon the floor is cast,
And all I boast is—that I fall the last.   [*Dies.*

---

* We may say with Dryden :
            "Death did at length so many slain forget,
                And left the tale, and took them by the great."
I know of no tragedy which comes nearer to this charming and bloody
catastrophe than *Cleomenes*, where the curtain covers five principal characters dead on the stage. These lines too—
            "I ask'd no questions then, of who kill'd who ?
                The bodies tell the story as they lie—"
seem to have belonged more properly to this scene of our author ; nor can
I help imagining they were originally his. The *Rival Ladies*, too, seem
beholden to this scene :
            "We're now a chain of lovers link'd in death ;
            Julia goes first, Gonsalvo hangs on her,
            And Angelina hangs upon Gonsalvo,
            As I on Angelina."
No scene, I believe, ever received greater honours than this. It was ap-
plauded by several encores, a word very unusual in tragedy. And it was
very difficult for the actors to escape without a second slaughter. This I
take to be a lively assurance of that fierce spirit of liberty which remains
among us, and which Mr. Dryden, in his essay on Dramatic Poetry, hath
observed. "Whether custom," says he, "hath so insinuated itself into our
countrymen, or nature hath so formed them to fierceness, I know not ; but
they will scarcely suffer combats and other objects of horror to be taken
from them." And indeed I am for having them encouraged in this martial
disposition ; nor do I believe our victories over the French have been owing
to anything more than to those bloody spectacles daily exhibited in our
tragedies, of which the French stage is so entirely clear,

Chrononhotonthologos:

The Most Tragical Tragedy, That Ever Was Tragediz'd by Any Company of Tragedians.

———•—•———

DRAMATIS PERSONÆ.

Chrononhotonthologos, *King of Queerummania.*
Bombardinian, *his General.*
Aldiborontiphoscophornio,
Rigdum-Funnidos, [*Courtiers.*
Captain of the Guards.
Herald.
Cook.
Doctor.
King of the Fiddlers.

King of the Antipodes.
Fadladinida, *Queen of Queerummania.*
Tatlanthe, *her favourite.*
Two Ladies of the Court.
Two Ladies of Pleasure.
Venus.
Cupid.
Guards and Attendants, &c.

SCENE.—Queerummania.

PROLOGUE.

To night our comic muse the buskin wears,
And gives herself no small romantic airs ;
Struts in heroics, and in pompous verse
Does the minutest incidents rehearse ;
In ridicule's strict retrospect displays
The poetasters of these modern days :
Who with big bellowing bombast rend our ears,
Which, stript of sound, quite void of sense appears ;
Or else their fiddle-faddle numbers flow,
Serenely dull, elaborately low.
Either extreme, when vain pretenders take,
The actor suffers for the author's sake.
The quite-tir'd audience lose whole hours ; yet pay
To go unpleas'd and unimprov'd away.
This being our scheme, we hope you will excuse
The wild excursion of the wanton muse

Who out of frolic wears a mimic mask,
And sets herself so whimsical a task :
'Tis meant to please, but if should offend,
It's very short, and soon will have an end.

SCENE.--*An Anti-Chamber in the Palace.*

Enter RIGDUM-FUNNIDOS *and* ALDIBORONTIPHOSCOPHORNIO.

Rig-Fun. Aldiborontiphoscophornio !
Where left you Chrononhotonthologos?
Aldi. Fatigu'd with the tremendous toils of war,
Within his tent, on downy couch succumbent,
Himself he unfatigues with gentle slumbers,
Lull'd by the cheerful trumpets gladsome clangour,
The noise of drums, and thunder of artillery,
He sleeps supine amidst the din of war.
And yet 'tis not definitively sleep ;
Rather a kind of doze, a waking slumber,
That sheds a stupefaction o'er his senses ;
For now he nods and snores ; anon he starts ;
Then nods and snores again.   If this be sleep,
Tell me, ye gods ! what mortal man's awake !
What says my friend to this ?
Rig.-Fun. Say ! I say he sleeps dog-sleep : What a plague
would you have me say ?
Aldi. O impious thought ! O curst insinuation !
As if great Chrononhotonthologos
To animals detestable and vile
Had aught the least similitude !
Rig. My dear friend ! you entirely misapprehend me : I
did not call the king dog by craft ; I was only going to tell you
that the soldiers have just now receiv'd their pay, and are all as
drunk as so many swabbers.
Aldi. Give orders instantly that no more money
Be issued to the troops.   Meantime, my friend,
Let the baths be filled with seas of coffee,
To stupefy their souls into sobriety.
Rig. I fancy you had better banish the sutlers, and blow the
Geneva casks to the devil.
Aldi. Thou counsel'st well, my Rigdum-Funnidos,
And reason seems to father thy advice.
But soft !—The king in pensive contemplation
Seems to resolve on some important doubt ;
His soul, too copious for his earthly fabric,
Starts forth, spontaneous, in soliloquy,
And makes his tongue the midwife of his mind.
Let us retire, lest we disturb his solitude.   [*They retire.*

Enter KING.

King. This god of sleep is watchful to torment me,
And rest is grown a stranger to my eyes :
Sport not with Chrononhotonthologos,
Thou idle slumb'rer, thou detested Somnus :
For if thou dost, by all the waking pow'rs,
I'll tear thine eyeballs from their leaden sockets,
And force thee to outstare eternity.   [*Exit in a huff.*

Re-enter RIGDUM *aud* ALDIBORONTI.

Rig. The king is in a most vile passion ! Pray who is this
Mr. Somnus he's so angry withal ?
Aldi. The son of Chaos and of Erebus.
Incestuous pair ! brother of Mors relentless,
Whose speckled robe, and wings of blackest hue,
Astonish all mankind with hideous glare ;
Himself with sable plumes, to men benevolent,
Brings downy slumbers and refreshing sleep.
Rig-Fun. This gentleman may come of a very good family,
for aught I know ; but I would not be in his place for the world.
Aldi. But, lo ! the king his footsteps this way bending,
His cogitative faculties immers'd
In cogibundity of cogitation :
Let silence close our folding-doors of speech,
Till apt attention tell our heart the purport
Of this profound profundity of thought.

Re-enter KING, NOBLES, *and* ATTENDANTS, *&c.*

King. It is resolv'd. Now, Somnus, I defy thee,
And from mankind ampute thy curs'd dominion.
These royal eyes thou never more shalt close.
Henceforth let no man sleep, on pain of death :
Instead of sleep, let pompous pageantry
Keep all mankind eternally awake.
Bid Harlequino decorate the stage
With all magnificence of decoration :
Giants and giantesses, dwarfs and pigmies,
Songs, dances, music in its amplest order,
Mimes, pantomimes, and all the magic motion
Of scene deceptiosive and sublime.   [*The flat scene draws.*
                    [*The* KING *is seated, and a grand pantomime
                        entertainment is performed, in the midst of
                        which enters a* CAPTAIN OF THE GUARD.
Capt. To arms ! to arms ! great Chrononhotonthologos !
Th' antipodean pow'rs from realms below

Have burst the solid entrails of the earth;
Gushing such cataracts of forces forth,
This world is too incopious to contain 'em :
Armies on armies, march in form stupendous ;
Not like our earthly regions, rank by rank,
But tier o'er tier, high pil'd from earth to heaven ;
A blazing bullet, bigger than the sun,
Shot from a huge and monstrous culverin,
Has laid your royal citadel in ashes.
    King. Peace, coward! were they wedg'd like golden ingots,
Or pent so close, as to admit no vacuum ;
One look from Crononhotonthologos
Shall scare them into nothing. Rigdum-Funnidos,
Bid Bombardinion draw his legions forth,
And meet us in the plains of Queerummania.
This very now ourselves shall there conjoin him ;
Meantime, bid all the priests prepare their temples
For rites of triumph : let the singing singers,
With vocal voices, most vociferous,
In sweet vociferation, outvociferize
Ev'n sound itself. So be it as we have order'd. [*Exeunt omnes.*

SCENE.—*A magnificent Apartment.*

Enter QUEEN, TATLANTHE, *and two* LADIES.

    Queen. Day's curtain drawn, the morn begins to rise,
And waking nature rubs her sleepy eyes :
The pretty little fleecy bleating flocks,
In baas harmonious warble thro' the rocks :
Night gathers up her shades in sable shrouds,
And whispering osiers tattle to the clouds.
What think you, ladies, if an hour we kill,
At basset, ombre, picquet, or quadrille?
    Tat. Your majesty was pleas'd to order tea.
    Queen. My mind is alter'd ; bring some ratifia.
                    [*They are served round with a dram.*
I have a famous fiddler sent from France.
Bid him come in. What think ye of a dance?

Enter FIDDLER.

    Fid. Thus to your majesty, says the suppliant muse,
Would you a solo or sonata choose ;
Or bold concerto or soft Sicilinia,
Alla Francese overo in Gusto Romano ?
When you command, 'tis done as soon as spoke.

Queeen. A civil fellow ! Play us the " Black Joak."

> *[Music plays.*
> [QUEEN *and* LADIES *dance the* "Black Joak."

So much for dancing ; now let's rest a while.
Bring in the tea-things. Does the kettle boil ?

Tat. The water bubbles and the tea-cups skip,
Through eager hope to kiss your royal lip. *[Tea brought in.*

Queen. Come, ladies, will you please to choose your tea ;
Or green imperial, or Pekoe Bohea ?

1st Lady. Never, no, never sure on earth was seen,
So gracious sweet and affable a queen.

2nd Lady. She is an angel.

1st Lady. She's a goddess rather.

Tat. She's angel, queen, and goddess, altogether.

Queen. Away ! you flatter me.

1st Lady. We don't indeed :
Your merit does our praise by far exceed.

Queen. You make me blush ; pray help me to a fan.

1st Lady. That blush becomes you.

Tat. Would I were a man.

Queen. I'll hear no more of these fantastic airs. *[Bell rings.*
The bell rings in. Come, ladies, let's to pray'rs.

> *[They dance off.*

SCENE.—*An Anti-Chamber.*

Enter RIGDUM-FUNNIDOS *and* ALDIBORONTIPHOSCOPHORNIO.

Rig. Egad, we're in the wrong box ! Who the devil would
have thought that Chrononhotonthologos should beat that mortal
sight of Tippodeans ? Why, there's not a mother's child of them
to be seen, egad, they footed it away as fast as their hands could
carry 'em ; but they have left their king behind 'em. We have
him safe, that's one comfort.

Aldi. Would he were still at amplest liberty.
For, oh ! my dearest Rigdum-Funnidos,
I have a riddle to unriddle to thee,
Shall make thee stare thyself into a statue.
Our queen's in love with this Antipodean.

Rigdum. The devil she is ? Well, I see mischief is going
forward with a vengeance.

Aldi. But, lo ! the conq'ror comes all crown'd with conquest !
A solemn triumph graces his return.
Let's grasp the forelock of this apt occasion,
To greet the victor, in his flow of glory.

> *[A grand triumph.]*

Enter CHRONONHOTONTHOLOGOS, GUARDS *and* ATTENDANTS,
&c., met by RIGDUM-FUNNIDOS *and* ALDIBORONTIPHOS-
COPHRONIO.

Aldi. All hail to Chrononhotonthologos !
Thrice trebly welcome to your royal subjects.
Myself, and faithful Rigdum-Funnidos,
Lost in a labyrinth of love and loyalty,
Entreat you to inspect our inmost souls,
And read in them what tongue can never utter. ·
 Chro. Aldiborontiphoscophornio,
To thee, and gentle Rigdum-Funnidos,
Our gratulations flow in streams unbounded :
Our bounty's debtor to your loyalty,
Which shall with inter'st be repaid ere long.
But where's our queen ? where's Fadladinida ?
She should be foremost in the gladsome train,
To grace our triumph ; but I see she slights me.
This haughty queen shall be no longer mine,
I'll have a sweet and gentle concubine.
 Rig. Now, my dear little Phoscophorny, for a swinging lie to
bring the queen off, and I'll run with it to her this minute, that
we may be all in a story. Say she has got the thorough-go-
nimble. [*Whispers, and steals off.*
 Aldi. Speak not, great Chrononhotonthologos,
In accents so injuriously severe
Of Fadladinida, your faithful queen :
By me she sends an embassy of love,
Sweet blandishments and kind congratulations,
But cannot, oh ! she cannot, come herself.
 King. Our rage is turn'd to fear : what ails the queen ?
 Aldi. A sudden diarrhœa's rapid force,
So stimulates the peristaltic motion,
That she by far out-does her late out-doing,
And all conclude her royal life in danger.
 King. Bid the physicians of the world assemble
In consultation, solemn and sedate :
More, to corroborate their sage resolves,
Call from their graves the learned men of old :
Galen, Hippocrates, and Paracelsus ;
Doctors, apothecaries, surgeons, chemists,
All ! all ! attend ; and see they bring their med'cines,
Whole magazines of galli-potted nostrums,
Materializ'd in pharmaceutic order. ·
The man that cures our queen shall have our empire.
[*Exeunt omnes.*

SCENE.—*A Garden.*

Enter TATLANTHE *and* QUEEN.

Queen. Heigh ho! my heart!
Tat.　　　　　　　　What ails my gracious queen?
Queen. Oh, would to Venus I had never seen!
Tat. Seen what, my royal mistress?
Queen.　　　　　　　　Too, too much!
Tat. Did it affright ycu?
Queen.　　　　　　No, 'tis nothing such.
Tat. What was it, madam?
Queen.　　　　　　Really I don't know.
Tat. It must be something!
Queen.　　　　　No!
Tat.　　　　　　　　Or nothing!
Queen.　　　　　　　　　No.
Tat. Then I conclude, of course, since it was neither,
Nothing and something jumbled well together.
Queen. Oh! my Tatlanthe, have you never seen!
Tat. Can I guess what, unless you tell, my queen?
Queen. The king I mean.
Tat.　　　　　　Just now return'd from war:
He rides like Mars in his triumphal car.
Conquest precedes with laurels in his hand;
Behind him Fame does on her tripos stand;
Her golden trump shrill thro' the air she sounds,
Which rends the earth, and then to heaven rebounds;
Trophies and spoils innumerable grace
This triumph, which all triumphs does deface:
Haste then, great queen! your hero thus to meet,
Who longs to lay his laurels at your feet.
Queen. Art mad, Tatlanthe? I meant no such thing.
Your talk's distasteful.
Tat.　　　　　　Didn't you name the king?
Queen. I did, Tatlanthe, but it was not thine;
The charming king I mean is only mine.
Tat. Who else, who else, but such a charming fair,
In Chrononhotonthologos should share?
The queen of beauty, and the god of arms,
In him and you united blend their charms.
Oh! had you seen him, how he dealt out death,
And at one stroke robb'd thousands of their breath:
While on the slaughter'd heaps himself did rise,
In pyramids of conquest to the skies.
The gods all hail'd, and fain would have him stay;
But your bright charms have call'd him thence away.

Queen. This does my utmost indignation raise :
You are too pertly lavish in his praise.
Leave me for ever !   [TATLANTH

   Tat.   Oh ! what shall I say ?
Do not, great queen, your anger thus display !
Oh, frown me dead ! let me not live to hear
My gracious queen and mistress so severe !
I've made some horrible mistake, no doubt ;
Oh ! tell me what it is !

   Queen.   No, find it out.

   Tat. No, I will never leave you ; here I'll grow
Till you some token of forgiveness show.
Oh ! all ye powers above, come down, come down !
And from her brow dispel that angry frown.

   Queen. Tatlanthe, rise, you have prevail'd at last ;
Offend no more, and I'll excuse what's past.

                   [TATLANTHE *as*

   Tat. Why, what a fool was I, not to perceive her
the topsy-turvy king—the gentleman that carries his
his heels should be !   But I must tack about, I see.

To the QUEEN.

Excuse me, gracious madam, if my heart
Bears sympathy with yours in every part ;
With you alike, I sorrow and rejoice,
Approve your passion, and commend your choice ;
The captive king.

   Queen.   That's he ! that's he ! that's he !
I'd die ten thousand deaths to set him free.
Oh ! my Tatlanthe ! have you seen his face,
His air, his shape, his mien, his ev'ry grace ?
In what a charming attitude he stands,
How prettily he foots it with his hands !
Well, to his arms, no to his legs I fly,
For I must have him, if I live or die.

SCENE.—*A Bedchamber.*

CHRONONHOTONTHOLOGOS *asleep.*

[*Rough music, viz., salt-boxes and* ?
    gridirons and tongs ; sow-gelders' ?
    rowbones and cleavers, &c. &c.

   Chro. What heav'nly sounds are these that charm
Sure 'tis the music of the tuneful spheres.

Enter CAPTAIN OF THE GUARDS.

Cap. A messenger from Gen'ral Bombardinion
Craves instant audience of your majesty.
Chro. Give him admittance.

Enter HERALD.

Her. Long life to Chrononhotonthologos !
Your faithful Gen'ral Bombardinion
Sends you his tongue, transplanted in my mouth,
To pour his soul out in your royal ears.
Chro. Then use thy master's tongue with reverence.
Nor waste it in thine own loquacity,
But briefly and at large declare thy message.
Her. Suspend awhile, great Chrononhotonthologos,
The fate of empires and the toils of war ;
And in my tent let's quaff Falernian wine
Till our souls mount and emulate the gods.
Two captive females, beauteous as the morn,
Submissive to your wishes, court your option.
Haste then, great king, to bless us with your presence.
Our scouts already watch the wish'd approach,
Which shall be welcom'd by the drums' dread rattle,
The cannons' thunder, and the trumpets' blast ;
While I, in front of mighty myrmidons,
Receive my king in all the pomp of war.
Chro. Tell him I come ; my flying steed prepare ;
Ere thou art half on horseback I'll be there.   [*Exeunt.*

SCENE.—*A Prison.*

The King of the Antipodes discover'd sleeping on a couch.
Enter QUEEN.

Queen. Is this a place, oh ! all ye gods above,
This a reception for the man I love ?
See in what sweet tranquillity he sleeps,
While Nature's self at his confinement weeps.
Rise, lovely monarch ! see your friend appear,
No Chrononhotonthologos is here ;
Command your freedom, by this sacred ring ;
Then command me. What says my charming king ?
               [*She puts the ring in his mouth, he bends the
                    sea-crab, and makes a roaring noise.*
Queen. What can this mean ! he lays his feet at mine :
Is this of love or hate, his country's sign ?

Ah! wretched queen! how hapless is thy lot,
To love a man that understands thee not!
Oh! lovely Venus, goddess all divine!
And gentle Cupid, that sweet son of thine,
Assist, assist me, with your sacred art,
And teach me to obtain this stranger's heart.

VENUS *descends in her chariot, and sings.*

AIR.

Ven. See Venus does attend thee,
       My dilding, my dolding.
Love's goddess will befriend thee,
       Lily bright and shiny.
With pity and compassion,
       My dilding, my dolding.
She sees thy tender passion,
       Lily, &c. *Da capo.*

Air changes.

To thee I yield my pow'r divine,
       Dance over the Lady Lee,
Demand whate'er thou wilt, 'tis thine,
       My gay lady.
Take this magic wand in hand,
       Dance, &c.
All the world's at thy command,
       My gay, &c. *Da capo.*

CUPID *descends and sings.*

AIR.

Are you a widow, or are you a wife?
       Gilly-flow'r, gentle rosemary.
Or are you a maiden, so fair and so bright?
       As the dew that flies over the mulberry-tree.
Queen. Would I were a widow, as I am a wife,
       Gilly-flow'r, &c.
But I'm to my sorrow, a maiden as bright,
       As the dew, &c.
Cupid. You shall be a widow before it is night,
       Gilly-flow'r, &c.
No longer a maiden so fair and so bright,
       As the dew, &c.
Two jolly young husbands your favour shall share,
       Gilly-flow'r, &c.
And twenty fine babies all lovely and fair,
       As the dew, &c.
Queen. O thanks, Mr. Cupid! for this your good news,
       Gilly-flow'r, &c.
What woman alive would such favours refuse?
       While the dew, &c.

[VENUS *and* CUPID *re-ascend; the* QUEEN *goes off,
and the King of the Antipodes follows, walking
on his hands. Scene closes.*

SCENE.—BOMBARDINION'S *Tent.*

KING *and* BOMBARDINION, *at a table, with two Ladies.*

Bomb. This honour, royal sir! so royalizes
The royalty of your most royal actions,
The dumb can only utter forth your praise ;
For we, who speak, want words to tell our meaning.
Here! fill the goblet with Falernian wine,
And, while our monarch drinks, bid the shrill trumpet
Tell all the gods, that we propine their healths.
　King. Hold, Bombardinion, I esteem it fit,
With so much wine, to eat a little bit.
　Bomb. See that the table instantly be spread,
With all that art and nature can produce.
Traverse from pole to pole ; sail round the globe,
Bring every eatable that can be eat :
The king shall eat ; tho' all mankind be starv'd.
　Cook. I am afraid his majesty will be starv'd, before I can
run round the world, for a dinner ; besides, where's the money ?
　King. Ha ! dost thou prattle, contumacious slave ?
Guards, seize the villain ? broil him, fry him, stew him ;
Ourselves shall eat him out of mere revenge.
　Cook. O pray, your majesty, spare my life ; there's some nice
cold pork in the pantry : I'll hash it for your majesty in a
minute.
　King. Be thou first hash'd in hell, audacious slave.
　　　　　　　　　　[*Kills him, and turns to* BOMBARDINION.
Hash'd pork ! shall Chrononhotonthologos
Be fed with swine's flesh. and at second-hand ?
Now, by the gods ! thou dost insult us, general !
　Bomb. The gods can witness, that I little thought
Your majesty to other flesh than this
Had aught the least propensity.　　　　[*Points to the ladies.*
　King. Is this a dinner for a hungry monarch ?
　Bomb. Monarchs, as great as Chrononhotonthologos,
Have made a very hearty meal of worse.
　King. Ha ! traitor ! dost thou brave me to my teeth ?
Take this reward, and learn to mock thy master. [*Strikes him.*
　Bomb. A blow ! shall Bombardinion take a blow?
Blush ! blush, thou sun ! start back thou rapid ocean !
Hills ! vales ! seas ! mountains ! all commixing crumble,
And into chaos pulverize the world ;
For Bombardinion has receiv'd a blow,
And Chrononhotonthologos shall die.　　　　　　[*Draws.*
　　　[*The women run off, crying, "Help ! Murder !" &c.*
　　　　　　　　　　　　　　　　　　　　　　G

King. What means the traitor?
Bomb.   Traitor in thy teeth,
Thus I defy thee!

           [They fight, he kills the King.
       Ha! what have I done?
Go, call a coach, and let a coach be call'd;
And let the man that calls it be the caller;
And, in his calling, let him nothing call,
But coach! coach! coach! Oh! for a coach, ye gods!
             [Exit raving.

Returns with a DOCTOR.

Bomb. How fares your majesty?
Doct.   My lord, he's dead.
    Bomb. Ha! dead! impossible! it cannot be!
I'd not believe it, tho' himself should swear it.
Go join his body to his soul again,
Or, by this light, thy soul shall quit thy body.
    Doct. My lord, he's far beyond the power of physic,
His soul has left his body and this world.
    Bomb. Then go to t'other world and fetch it back.
             [Kills him.
And, if I find thou triflest with me there,
I'll chase thy shade through myriads of orbs,
And drive thee far beyond the verge of Nature.
Ha!—Call'st thou, Chrononhotonthologos?
I come! your faithful Bombardinion comes!
He comes in worlds unknown to make new wars,
And gain thee empires num'rous as the stars.
             [Kills himself.

Enter QUEEN *and others.*

Aldi. O horrid! horrible, and horrid'st horror!
Our king! our general! our cook! our doctor!
All dead! stone dead! irrevocably dead!
O——h!——   *[All groan, a tragedy groan.*
    Queen. My husband dead! ye gods! what is't you mean,
To make a widow of a virgin queen?
For, to my great misfortune, he, poor king,
Has left me so; aint that a wretched thing?
    Tat. Why then, dear madam, make me no farther pother,
Were I your majesty, I'd try another.
    Queen. I think 'tis best to follow thy advice.
    Tat. I'll fit you with a husband in a trice:
Here's Rigdum-Funnidos, a proper man;
If any one can please a queen, he can.
    Rig-Fun. Ay, that I can, and please your majesty.
So, ceremonies apart, let's proceed to business.

Queen. Oh! but the mourning takes up all my care,
I'm at a loss what kind of weeds to wear.
Rig-Fun. Never talk of mourning, madam,
One ounce of mirth is worth a pound of sorrow,
Take me at once, and let us wed to-morrow.
I'll make thee a great man, my little Phoscophorny.

[*To* ALDI. *aside.*

Aldi. I scorn your bounty; I'll be king, or nothing.
Draw, miscreant! draw!
Rig.　　　　　No, sir, I'll take the law.

[*Runs behind the* QUEEN

Queen. Well, gentlemen, to make the matter easy,
I'll have you both; and that, I hope, will please ye.
And now, Tatlanthe, thou art all my care:
Where shall I find thee such another pair?
Pity that you, who've serv'd so long, so well,
Should die a virgin, and lead apes in hell.
Choose for yourself, dear girl, our empire round,
Your portion is twelve hundred thousand pound.
Aldi. Here! take these dead and bloody corps away;
Make preparation for our wedding day.
Instead of sad solemnity, and black,
Our hearts shall swim in claret, and in sack.

The next piece is taken from successive numbers of THE
ANTI-JACOBIN, *which was planned by* Canning, *and of
which the first number appeared on the 20th of November,*
1797. "*The Rovers, or the Double Arrangement,*"
was the joint work of George Canning, George Ellis,
and John Hookham Frere.

THE ROVERS;

OR, THE DOUBLE ARRANGEMENT.

DRAMATIS PERSONÆ.

PRIOR *of the* ABBEY *of* QUEDLIN-BURGH, *very corpulent and cruel.*

ROGERO, *a Prisoner in the Abbey, in love with* MATILDA POTTINGEN.

CASIMERE, *a Polish Emigrant, in Dembrowsky's Legion, married to* CECILIA, *but having several children by* MATILDA.

PUDDINGFIELD *and* BEEFINGTON, *English Noblemen exiled by the Tyranny of King John, previous to the signature of Magna Charta.*

RODERIC, *Count of Saxe Weimar, a bloody Tyrant, with red hair, and an amorous complexion.*

GASPAR, *the Minister of the Count; Author of* ROGERO'S *confinement.*

Young POTTINGEN, *brother to* MATILDA.

MATILDA POTTINGEN, *in love with* ROGERO, *and mother to* CASIMERE'S *children.*

CECILIA MÜCKENFELD, *wife to* CASIMERE.

Landlady, Waiter, Grenadiers, Troubadours, &c.

PANTALOWSKY, *and* BRITCHINDA, *children of* MATILDA, *by* CASIMERE.

JOACHIM, JABEL, *and* AMARANTHA, *children of* MATILDA, *by* ROGERO.

Children of CASIMERE *and* CECILIA, *with their respective Nurses.*

Several Children ; Fathers and Mothers unknown.

THE SCENE LIES IN THE TOWN OF WEIMAR, AND THE NEIGHBOURHOOD OF THE ABBEY OF QUEDLINBURGH.

Time, from the Twelfth to the present Century.

PROLOGUE.

(*In character.*)

TOO long the triumphs of our early times,
With civil discord, and with regal crimes,
Have stain'd these boards ; while Shakespeare's pen
    has shown
Thoughts, manners, men, to modern days unknown.
Too long have Rome and Athens been the rage ; [*Applause.*
And classic buskins soil'd a British stage,

To-night our bard, who scorns pedantic rules,
His plot has borrow'd from the German schools ;
—The German schools—where no dull maxims bind
The bold expansion of the electric mind.
Fix'd to no period, circled by no space,
He leaps the flaming bounds of time and place :
Round the dark confines of the forest raves,
With *gentle* robbers* stocks his gloomy caves ;
Tells how prime ministers† are shocking things,
And *reigning dukes* as bad as tyrant kings ;
How to *two* swains‡ *one* nymph her vows may give,
And how *two* damsels with *one* lover live !
Delicious scenes !—such scenes *our* bard displays,
Which, crown'd with German, sue for British, praise.
Slow are the steeds, that through Germania's roads
With hempen rein the slumbering post-boy goads ;
Slow is the slumbering post-boy, who proceeds
Through deep sands floundering, on those tardy steeds ;
More slow, more tedious, from his husky throat
Twangs through the twisted horn the struggling note.
These truths confess'd—Oh ! yet, ye travell'd few,
Germania's *plays* with eyes unjaundiced view !
View and approve !—though in each passage fine
The faint translation§ mock the genuine line ;
Though the nice ear the erring sight belie,
For *Ü twice dotted* is pronounced like *I;*   [*Applause.*

* See the "Robbers," a German tragedy, in which robbery is put in so fascinating a light, that the whole of a German University went upon the highway in consequence of it.

† See "Cabal and Love," a German tragedy, very severe against Prime Ministers and reigning Dukes of Brunswick. This admirable performance very judiciously reprobates the hire of German troops for the *American war* in the reign of Queen Elizabeth—a practice which would undoubtedly have been highly discreditable to that wise and patriotic princess, not to say wholly unnecessary, there being no American war at that particular time.

‡ See the "Stranger ; or, Reform'd Housekeeper," in which the former of these morals is beautifully illustrated ; and "Stella," a genteel German comedy, which ends with placing a man *bodkin* between *two wives*, like *Thames* between his *two banks*, in the "Critic." Nothing can be more edifying than these two dramas. I am shocked to hear that there are some people who think them ridiculous.

§ These are the warnings very properly given to readers, to beware how they judge of what they cannot understand. Thus, if the translation runs "lightning of my soul, fulguration of angels, sulphur of hell ;" we should recollect that this is not coarse or strange in the German language, when applied by a lover to his mistress ; but the English has nothing precisely parallel to the original Mulychause Archangelichen, which means rather "emanation of the archangelican nature"—or to Smellmynkern Vankelfer, which, if literally rendered, would signify "made of stuff of the same odour whereof the devil makes flambeaux." See Schüttenbrüch on the German Idiom.

Yet oft the scene shall Nature's fire impart,
Warm *from* the breast, and glowing *to* the heart !
Ye travell'd few, attend !   On *you* our bard
Builds his fond hope ! Do you his genius guard ! [*Applause.*
Nor let succeeding generations say—
A British audience *damn'd* a German play.
                    [*Loud and continued applauses.*
[*Flash of lightning.—The ghost of* PROLOGUE'S GRAND-
MOTHER, *by the father's side, appears to soft music, in
a white tiffany riding-hood.* PROLOGUE *kneels to
receive her blessing, which she gives in a solemn and
affecting manner, the audience clapping and crying all
the while.—Flash of lightning.—*PROLOGUE *and his*
GRANDMOTHER *sink through the trap-door.*

ACT I.—SCENE I.

*Represents a room at an Inn, at Weimar—On one side
of the stage the bar-room, with jellies, lemons in nets,
syllabubs, and part of a cold roast fowl. &c.—On the opposite side a window looking into the street, through which
persons (inhabitants of Weimar) are seen passing to and fro
in apparent agitation.—*MATILDA *appears in a great-coat
and riding habit, seated at the corner of the dinner-table,
which is covered with a clean huckaback cloth.—Plates and
napkins, with buck's-horn-handled knives and forks, are
laid as if for four persons.*

MATILDA.

Mat. Is it impossible for me to have dinner sooner ?
Land. Madam, the Brunswick post-waggon is not yet come in,
and the ordinary is never before two o'clock.
Mat. [*with a look expressive of disappointment, but im-
mediately recomposing herself*]. Well, then, I must have patience.
[*Exit Landlady.*] Oh Casimere ! How often have the thoughts
of thee served to amuse these moments of expectation ! What
a difference, alas ! Dinner—it is taken away as soon as over,
and we regret it not ! It returns again with the return of
appetite. The beef of to-morrow will succeed to the mutton of
to-day, as the mutton of to-day succeeded to the veal of yesterday. But when once the heart has been occupied by a beloved
object, in vain would we attempt to supply the chasm by
another. How easily are our desires transferred from dish to
dish ! Love only, dear, delusive, delightful love, restrains our
wandering appetites, and confines them to a particular gratifica-
tion ! . . .

Post-horn blows.—Re-enter LANDLADY.

Land. Madam, the post-waggon is come in with only a single gentlewoman.

Mat. Then show her up—and let us have dinner instantly; [*Landlady going*] and remember—[*after a moment's recollection, and with great eagerness*]—remember the toasted cheese.

[*Exit* LANDLADY.

CECILIA *enters, in a brown cloth riding-dress, as if just alighted from the post-waggon.*

Mat. Madam, you seem to have had an unpleasant journey, if I may judge from the dust on your riding-habit.

Cec. The way was dusty, madam, but the weather was delightful. It recall'd to me those blissful moments when the rays of desire first vibrated through my soul.

Mat. [*aside*]. Thank Heaven! I have at last found a heart which is in unison with my own [*to Cecilia*]. Yes, I understand you—the first pulsation of sentiment—the silver tones upon the yet unsounded harp. . . .

Cec. The dawn of life—when this blossom [*putting her hand upon her heart*] first expanded its petals to the penetrating dart of love!

Mat. Yes—the time—the golden time, when the first beams of the morning meet and embrace one another! The blooming blue upon the yet unplucked plum! . . .

Cec. Your countenance grows animated, my dear madam.

Mat. And yours too is glowing with illumination.

Cec. I had long been looking out for a congenial spirit! My heart was withered, but the beams of yours have rekindled it.

Mat. A sudden thought strikes me: let us swear an eternal friendship.

Cec. Let us agree to live together!

Mat. Willingly.   [*With rapidity and earnestness.*

Cec. Let us embrace.   [*They embrace.*

Mat. Yes; I too have loved!—you, too, like me, have been forsaken!   [*Doubtingly and as if with a desire to be informed.*

Cec. Too true!

Both. Ah, these men! these men!

LANDLADY *enters, and places a leg of mutton on the table, with sour krout and prune sauce—then a small dish of black puddings.* CECILIA *and* MATILDA *appear to take no notice of her.*

Mat. Oh, Casimere!

Cec. [*aside*]. Casimere! that name! Oh, my heart, how it is distracted with anxiety.

Mat. Heavens ! Madam, you turn pale.

Cec. Nothing—a slight megrim—with your leave, I will retire.

Mat. I will attend you.

    [*Exeunt* MATILDA *and* CECILIA. *Manent* LAND-
     LADY *and* WAITER *with the dinner on the table.*

Land. Have you carried the dinner to the prisoner in the vaults of the abbey !

Waiter. Yes. Pease-soup, as usual—with the scrag-end of a neck of mutton—the emissary of the Count was here again this morning, and offered me a large sum of money if I would consent to poison him.

Land. Which you refused ? [*With hesitation and anxiety.*

Waiter. Can you doubt it ?   [*With indignation.*

Land. [*recovering herself, and drawing up with an expression of dignity*]. The conscience of a poor man is as valuable to him as that of a prince.

Waiter. It ought to be still more so, in proportion as it is generally more pure.

Land. Thou say'st truly, Job.

Waiter [*with enthusiasm*]. He who can spurn at wealth when proffer'd as the price of crime, is greater than a prince.

Post-horn blows. Enter CASIMERE, *in a travelling dress—a light blue great-coat with large metal buttons—his hair in a long queue, but twisted at the end; a large Kevenhuller hat ; a cane in his hand.*

Cas. Here, waiter, pull of my boots, and bring me a pair of slippers [*Exit* WAITER]. And heark'ye, my lad, a bason of water [*rubbing his hands*] and a bit of soap—I have not washed since I began my journey.

Waiter [*answering from behind the door*]. Yes, sir.

Cas. Well, landlady, what company are we to have ?

Land. Only two gentlewomen, sir. They are just stepp'd into the next room—they will be back again in a minute.

Cas. Where do they come from ?

    [*All this while the* WAITER *re-enters with the
     bason and water,* CASIMERE *pulls off his boots,
     takes a napkin from the table, and washes his
     face and hands.*

Land. There is one of them, I think, comes from Nuremburgh.

Cas. [*aside*]. From Nuremburgh ; [*with eagerness*] her name ?

Land. Matilda.

Cas. [*aside*]. How does this idiot woman torment me ! What else ?

Land. I can't recollect.

Cas. Oh agony !   [*In a paroxysm of agitation.*

Waiter. See here, her name upon the travelling trunk— Matilda Pottingen.

    Cas. Ecstasy! ecstasy!   [*Embracing the* WAITER.

    Land. You seem to be acquainted with the lady—shall I call her?

    Cas. Instantly—instantly—tell her, her loved, her long lost— tell her——

    Land. Shall I tell her dinner is ready?

    Cas. Do so—and in the meanwhile I will look after my portmanteau.   [*Exeunt severally.*

*Scene changes to a subterraneous vault in the Abbey of Qued-
linburgh, with coffins, 'scutcheons, Death's heads and cross-
bones.—Toads, and other loathsome reptiles are seen travers-
ing the obscurer parts of the Stage.—*ROGERO *appears in
chains, in a suit of rusty armour, with his beard grown,
and a cap of a grotesque form upon his head.—Beside him a
crock, or pitcher, supposed to contain his daily allowance of
sustenance.—A long silence, during which the wind is heard
to whistle through the caverns.—*ROGERO *rises, and comes
slowly forward, with his arms folded.*

    Rog. Eleven years! it is now eleven years since I was first immured in this living sepulchre—the cruelty of a minister—the perfidy of a monk—yes, Matilda! for thy sake—alive amidst the dead—chained—coffined—confined—cut off from the converse of my fellow-men. Soft! what have we here? [*stumbles over a bundle of sticks*]. This cavern is so dark, that I can scarcely distinguish the objects under my feet. Oh! the register of my captivity. Let me see, how stands the account? [*takes up the sticks and turns them over with a melancholy air; then stands silent for a few moments, as if absorbed in calculation*]. Eleven years and fifteen days! Hah! the twenty-eighth of August! How does the recollection of it vibrate on my heart! It was on this day that I took my last leave of my Matilda. It was a summer evening—her melting hand seemed to dissolve in mine, as I press'd it to my bosom. Some demon whispered me that I should never see her more. I stood gazing on the hated vehicle which was conveying her away for ever. The tears were petrified under my eyelids. My heart was crystallized with agony. Anon, I looked along the road. The diligence seemed to diminish every instant. I felt my heart beat against its prison, as if anxious to leap out and overtake it. My soul whirled round as I watched the rotation of the hinder wheels. A long trail of glory followed after her, and mingled with the dust—it was the emanation of Divinity, luminous with love and beauty, like the splendour of the setting sun; but it told me that the sun of my joys was sunk for ever. Yes, here in the depths of an eternal dungeon—in the nursing cradle of hell—the suburbs of perdition

—in a nest of demons, where despair, in vain, sits brooding over the putrid eggs of hope ; where agony woos the embrace of death ; where patience, beside the bottomless pool of despondency, sits angling for impossibilities. Yet even *here*, to behold her, to embrace her—yes, Matilda, whether in this dark abode, amidst toads and spiders, or in a royal palace, amidst the more loathsome reptiles of a Court, would be indifferent to me. Angels would shower down their hymns of gratulation upon our heads—while fiends would envy the eternity of suffering love . . . . Soft, what air was that ? it seemed a sound of more than human warblings. Again [*listens attentively for some minutes*] —only the wind. It is well, however ; it reminds me of that melancholy air which has so often solaced the hours of my captivity. Let me see whether the damps of this dungeon have not yet injured my guitar. [*Takes his guitar, tunes it, and begins the following air, with a full accompaniment of violins from the orchestra.*]

[AIR, *Lanterna Magica.*]

SONG.

BY ROGERO.

I.

Whene'er with haggard eyes I view
 This dungeon that I'm rotting in,
I think of those companions true
 Who studied with me at the U—
   —niversity of Gottingen,—
   —niversity of Gottingen.
 [*Weeps, and pulls out a blue kerchief, with which he wipes his eyes ; gazing tenderly at it, he proceeds—*

II.

Sweet kerchief, check'd with heavenly blue,
 Which once my love sat knotting in !—
Alas ! Matilda *then* was true !—
 At least I thought so at the U—
   —niversity of Gottingen—
   —niversity of Gottingen.
    [*At the repetition of this line*, ROGERO *clanks his chains in cadence.*

III.

Barbs ! barbs ! alas ! how swift you flew,
 Her neat post-waggon trotting in !
Ye bore Matilda from my view ;
 Forlorn I languish'd at the U—
   —niversity of Gottingen—
   —niversity of Gottingen.

IV.

This faded form ! this pallid hue !
This blood my veins is clotting in,
My years are many—they were few
When first I entered at the U—
  —niversity of Gottingon—
  —niversity of Gottingen.

V.

There first for thee my passion grew,
Sweet ! sweet Matilda Pottingen !
Thou wast the daughter of my tu—
—tor, Law Professor at the U—
  —niversity of Gottingen—
  —niversity of Gottingen.

VI.

Sun, moon, and thou, vain world, adieu,
That kings and priests are plotting in :
Here doom'd to starve on water gru—
—el, never shall I see the U—
  —niversity of Gottingen—
  —niversity of Gottingen.

[*During the last stanza,* ROGERO *dashes his head repeatedly against the walls of his prison ; and, finally, so hard as to produce a visible contusion. He then throws himself on the floor in an agony. The curtain drops—the music still continuing to play till it is wholly fallen.*

We have received, in the course of the last week, several long, and to say the truth, dull letters, from unknown hands, reflecting, in very severe terms, on Mr. Higgins, for having, as it is affirmed, attempted to pass upon the world, as a faithful sample of the productions of the German Theatre, a performance no way resembling any of those pieces, which have of late excited, and which bid fair to engross the admiration of the British public.

As we cannot but consider ourselves as the guardians of Mr. Higgins's literary reputation, in respect to every work of his which is conveyed to the world through the medium of our paper (though, what we think of the danger of his principles, we have already sufficiently explained for ourselves, and have, we trust, succeeded in putting our readers upon their guard against them)—we hold ourselves bound not only to justify the fidelity of the imitation, but (contrary to our original intention)-to give a further specimen of it in our present number, in order to bring the question more fairly to issue between our author and his calumniators.

In the first place, we are to observe that Mr. Higgins professes to have taken his notion of German plays wholly from the translations which have appeared in our language. If *they* are totally dissimilar from the originals, Mr. H. may undoubtedly have been led into error; but the fault is in the translators, not in him. That he does not differ widely from the models which he proposed to himself, we have it in our power to prove satisfactorily; and might have done so in our last number, by subjoining to each particular passage of his play, the scene in some one or other of the German plays, which he had in view when he wrote it. These parallel passages were faithfully pointed out to us by Mr. H. with that candour which marks his character; and if they were suppressed by us (as in truth they were), on our heads be the blame, whatever it may be. Little, indeed, did we think of the imputation which the omission would bring upon Mr. H., as, in fact, our principal reason for it was the apprehension that, from the extreme closeness of the imitation in most instances, he would lose in praise for invention more than he would gain in credit for fidelity.

The meeting between Matilda and Cecilia, for example, in the first-act of the " Rovers," and their sudden intimacy, has been censured as unnatural. Be it so. It is taken *almost word for word* from " Stella," a German (or professedly a German) piece now much in vogue; from which also the catastrophe of Mr. Higgins's play is in part borrowed, so far as relates to the agreement to which the ladies come, as the reader will see by-and-by, to share Casimere between them.

The dinner scene is copied partly from the published translation of the " Stranger," and partly from the first scene of "Stella." The song of Rogero, with which the first act concludes, is admitted on all hands to be in the very first taste; and if no German original is to be found for it, so much the worse for the credit of German literature.

An objection has been made by one anonymous letter-writer, to the names of Puddingfield and Beefington, as little likely to have been assigned to English characters by any author of taste or discernment. In answer to this objection, we have, in the first place, to admit that a small, and we hope not an unwarrantable alteration has been made by us since the MS. has been in our hands. These names stood originally Puddincrantz and Beefinstern, which sounded to our ears as being liable, especially the latter, to a ridiculous inflection—a difficulty that could only be removed by furnishing them with English terminations. With regard to the more substantial syllables of the names, our author proceeded in all probability on the authority of Goldoni, who, though not a German, is an Italian writer of considerable reputation; and who, having heard that the English were distinguished for their love of liberty and beef, has judiciously compounded the two words *Runnymede* and *beef*, and thereby produced an English nobleman, whom he styles *Lord Runny-beef.*

To dwell no longer on particular passages—the best way perhaps of explaining the whole scope and view of Mr. H.'s imitation, will be to transcribe the short sketch of the plot, which that gentleman transmitted to us, together with his drama ; and which it is perhaps the more necessary to give at length, as the limits of our paper not allowing of the publication of the whole piece, some general knowledge of its main design may be acceptable to our readers, in order to enable them to judge of the several extracts which we lay before them.

PLOT.

Rogero, son of the late Minister of the Count of Saxe Weimar, having, while he was at college, fallen desperately in love with Matilda Pottingen, daughter of his tutor, Doctor Engelbertus Pottingen, Professor of Civil Law ; and Matilda evidently returning his passion, the doctor, to prevent ill consequences, sends his daughter on a visit to her aunt in Wetteravia, where she becomes acquainted with Casimere, a Polish officer, who happens to be quartered near her aunt's, and has several children by him.

Roderic, Count of Saxe Weimar, a prince of tyrannical and licentious disposition, has for his Prime Minister and favourite, Gaspar, a crafty villain, who had risen to his post by first ruining, and then putting to death, Rogero's father. Gaspar, apprehensive of the power and popularity which the young Rogero may enjoy at his return to Court, seizes the occasion of his intrigue with Matilda (of which he is apprised officially by Doctor Pottingen) to procure from his master an order for the recall of Rogero from college, and for committing him to the care of the prior of the Abbey of Quedlinburgh, a priest, rapacious, savage, and sensual, and devoted to Gaspar's interests—sending at the same time private orders to the prior to confine him in a dungeon.

Here Rogero languishes many years. His daily sustenance is administered to him through a grated opening at the top of a cavern, by the landlady of the Golden Eagle at Weimar, with whom Gaspar contracts, in the Prince's name, for his support; intending, and more than once endeavouring, to corrupt the waiter to mingle poison with the food, in order that he may get rid of Rogero for ever.

In the meantime Casimere, having been called away from the neighbourhood of Matilda's residence to other quarters, becomes enamoured of, and marries Cecilia, by whom he has a family ; and whom he likewise deserts after a few years' cohabitation, on pretence of business which calls him to Kamtschatka.

Doctor Pottingen, now grown old and infirm, and feeling the want of his daughter's society, sends young Pottingen in search of her, with strict injunctions not to return without her ; and to bring with her either her present lover Casimere, or, should that not be possible, Rogero himself, if he can find him ; the doctor having set his heart upon seeing his children comfortably settled before his death.   Matilda, about the same period, quits her aunt's in search of Casimere ; and Cecilia having been advertised (by an anonymous letter) of the falsehood of his Kamtschatka journey, sets out in the post-waggon on a similar pursuit.

It is at this point of time the play opens—with the accidental meeting of Cecilia and Matilda at the inn at Weimar.   Casimere arrives there soon after, and falls in first with Matilda, and then with Cecilia.   Successive *éclaircissements* take place, and an arrangement is finally made, by which the two ladies are to live jointly with Casimere.

Young Pottingen, wearied with a few weeks' search, during which he has not been able to find either of the objects of it, resolves to stop at Weimar, and wait events there.   It so happens, that he takes up his lodging in the same house with Puddincrantz and Beefinstern, two English noblemen, whom the tyranny of King John has obliged to fly from their country ; and who, after wandering about the Continent for some time, have fixed their residence at Weimar.

The news of the signature of Magna Charta arriving, determines Puddincrantz and Beefinstern to return to England. Young Pottingen opens his case to them, and entreats them to stay to assist him in the object of his search.   This they refuse ; but coming to the inn where they are to set off for Hamburgh, they meet Casimere, from whom they have both received many civilities in Poland.

Casimere, by this time tired of his " Double Arrangement," and having learned from the waiter that Rogero is confined in the vaults of the neighbouring Abbey *for love*, resolves to attempt his rescue, and to make over Matilda to him as the price of his deliverance.   He communicates his scheme to Puddingfield and Beefington, who agree to assist him ; as also does young Pottingen.   The waiter of the inn proving to be a *Knight Templar* in disguise, is appointed leader of the expedition.   A band of troubadours, who happen to be returning from the Crusades, and a company of Austrian and Prussian Grenadiers returning from the Seven Years' War, are engaged as troops.

The attack on the Abbey is made with success.   The Count of Weimar and Gaspar, who are feasting with the prior, are seized and beheaded in the refectory.   The prior is thrown into the dungeon, from which Rogero is rescued.   Matilda and Cecilia rush in.   The former recognizes Rogero, and agrees to live with him. The children are produced on all sides; and young Pottingen is commissioned to write to his father, the doctor, to detail the joyful events which have taken place, and to invite him to Weimar, to partake of the general felicity.

ACT II.

SCENE.—*A Room in an ordinary Lodging-house at Weimar.*— PUDDINGFIELD *and* BEEFINGTON *discovered, sitting at a small deal table, and playing at All-fours.*—*Young* POT-TINGEN, *at another table in the corner of the room, with a pipe in his mouth, and a Saxon mug of a singular shape beside him, which he repeatedly applies to his lips, turning back his head, and casting his eyes towards the firmament. At the last trial he holds the mug for some moments in a directly inverted position; then replaces it on the table, with an air of dejection, and gradually sinks into a profound slumber. The pipe falls from his hand, and is broken.*

Beef. I beg.
Pudd. [*deals three cards to* BEEFINGTON]. Are you satisfied?
Beef. Enough. What have you?
Pudd. High—low—and the game.
Beef. Ah! 'tis my deal [*deals—turns up a knave*]. One for his heels!   [*Triumphantly.*
Pudd. Is king highest?
Beef. No [*sternly*]. The game is mine. The knave gives it me.
  Pudd. Are knaves so prosperous?
Ay, marry are they in this world. They have the game in their hands. Your kings are but *noddies* * to them.
Pudd. Ha! ha! ha!—still the same proud spirit, Beefington, which procured thee thine exile from England.
Beef. England! my native land!—when shall I revisit thee?
    [*During this time* PUDDINGFIELD *deals, and begins to arrange his hand.*
Beef. [*continues*]. Phoo—hang all-fours; what are they to a mind ill at ease? Can they cure the heart-ache? Can they sooth banishment? Can they lighten ignominy? Can all-fours do this? Oh! my Puddingfield, thy limber and lightsome spirit

---

* This is an excellent joke in German; the point and spirit of which is but ill-rendered in a translation. A Noddy, the reader will observe, has two significations—the one a "knave at all-fours;" the other a "fool or booby." See the translation by Mr. Render of "Count Benyowsky; or, the Conspiracy of Kamtschatka," a German tragi-comi-comi-tragedy: where the play opens with a scene of a game at chess (from which the whole of this scene is copied), and a joke of the same point and merriment about pawns—*i.e.*, boors being *a match* for kings.

bounds up against affliction—with the elasticity of a well-bent bow ; but mine—O ! mine—

> [*Falls into an agony, and sinks back in his chair.* YOUNG POTTINGEN *awakened by the noise, rises, and advances with a grave demeanour towards* BEEFINGTON *and* PUDDINGFIELD. *The former begins to recover.*

Y. Pot. What is the matter, comrades ?*—you seem agitated. Have you lost or won ?

Beef. Lost. I have lost my country.

Y. Pot. And I my sister. I came hither in search of her.

Beef. O England !

Y. Pot. O Matilda !

Beef. Exiled by the tyranny of an usurper, I seek the means of revenge, and of restoration to my country.

Y. Pot. Oppressed by the tyranny of an abbot, persecuted by the jealousy of a count, the betrothed husband of my sister languishes in a loathsome captivity. Her lover is fled no one knows whither—and I, her brother, am torn from my paternal roof, and from my studies in chirurgery, to seek him and her, I know not where—to rescue Rogero, I know not how. Comrades, your counsel—my search fruitless—my money gone—my baggage stolen ! What am I to do ? In yonder abbey—in these dark, dank vaults, there, my friends—there lies Rogero—there Matilda's heart——

SCENE II.

Enter WAITER.

Waiter. Sir, here is a person who desires to speak with you.

Beef. [*goes to the door, and returns with a letter, which he opens—on perusing it his countenance becomes illuminated, and expands prodigiously*]. Hah, my friend, what joy !

> [*Turning to* PUDDINGFIELD.

Pudd. What ? tell me—let your Puddingfield partake it.

Beef. See here—   [*Produces a printed paper.*

Pudd. What ?   [*With impatience.*

Beef. [*in a significant tone*]. A newspaper !

Pudd. Hah, what sayst thou ! A newspaper !

Beef. Yes, Puddingfield, and see here [*shows it partially*], from England.

Pudd. [*with extreme earnestness*]. Its name !

Beef. The " Daily Advertiser "—

Pudd. Oh, ecstasy !

Beef. [*with a dignified severity*]. Puddingfield, calm yourself—repress those transports—remember that you are a man.

---

* This word in the original is strictly " fellow-lodgers "—" co-occupants of the same room, in a house let out at a small rent by the week." There is no single word in English which expresses so complicated a relation, except, perhaps, the cant term of " chum," formerly in use at our universities.

Pudd. [*after a pause with suppressed emotion*]. Well, I will be—I am calm—yet tell me, Beefington, does it contain any news?

Beef. Glorious news, my dear Puddingfield—the Barons are victorious—King John has been defeated—Magna Charta, that venerable, immemorial inheritance of Britons, was signed last Friday was three weeks, the third of July Old Style.

Pudd. I can scarce believe my ears—but let me satisfy my eyes—show me the paragraph.

Beef. Here it is, just above the advertisements.

Pudd. [*reads*]. " The great demand for Packwood's razor straps "——

Beef. 'Pshaw! what, ever blundering—you drive me from my patience—see here, at the head of the column.

Pudd. [*reads*]. " A hireling print, devoted to the Court,
    Has dared to question our veracity
    Respecting the events of yesterday ;
    But by to-day's accounts, our information
    Appears to have been perfectly correct.
    The charter of our liberties received
    The royal signature at five o'clock,
    When messengers were instantly dispatch'd
    To Cardinal Pandulfo ; and their majesties,
    After partaking of a cold collation,
    Return'd to Windsor."—I am satisfied.

Beef. Yet here again—there are some further particulars [*turns to another part of the paper*], " Extract of a letter from Egham—My dear friend, we are all here in high spirits—the interesting event which took place this morning at Runnymede, in the neighbourhood of this town "——

Pudd. Hah! Runnymede, enough—no more—my doubts are vanished—then are we free indeed!

Beef. I have, besides, a letter in my pocket from our friend, the immortal Bacon, who has been appointed Chancellor. Our outlawry is reversed! What says my friend—shall we return by the next packet?

Pudd. Instantly, instantly !

Both. Liberty! Adelaide !—Revenge !

[*Exeunt. Young* POTTINGEN *following, and waving his hat, but obviously without much consciousness of the meaning of what has passed.*

Scene changes to the outside of the Abbey. A summer's evening —moonlight. Companies of Austrian and Prussian Grenadiers march across the stage, confusedly, as if returning from the Seven Years' War. Shouts, and martial music. The Abbey gates are opened. The monks are seen passing in procession, with the Prior at their head. The choir is heard chanting vespers. After which a pause. Then a bell is heard, as if ringing for supper. Soon after, a noise of singing and jollity.

*Enter from the Abbey, pushed out of the gates by the Porter, a
    Troubadour, with a bundle under his cloak, and a Lady
    under his arm.   Troubadour seems much in liquor, but
    caresses the female minstrel.*

Fem. Min. Trust me, Gieronymo, thou seemest melancholy.
What hast thou got under thy cloak?
Trou. 'Pshaw, women will be inquiring.   Melancholy! not I.
I will sing thee a song, and the subject of it shall be thy ques-
tion—"What have I got under my cloak?" It is a riddle,
Margaret—I learnt it of an almanac-maker at Gotha—if thou
guessest it after the first stanza, thou shalt have never a drop for
thy pains.   Hear me—and, d'ye mark! twirl thy thingumbob
while I sing.
Fem. Min. 'Tis a pretty tune, and hums dolefully.
              [*Plays on the balalaika.* * Troubadour sings.*

> I bear a secret comfort here,
> [*putting his hand on the bundle, but without showing it.*
>   A joy I'll ne'er impart;
>   It is not wine, it is not beer,
>   But it consoles my heart.

Fem. Min. [*interrupting him*]. I'll be hang'd if you don't mean
the bottle of cherry-brandy that you stole out of the vaults in the
Abbey cellar.
Trou. I mean!—Peace, wench, thou disturbest the current of
my feelings.
              [*Fem. Min. attempts to lay hold of the bottle.   Trou-
                  badour pushes her aside, and continues singing
                  without interruption.*

> This cherry-bounce, this lov'd noyau,
>   My drink for ever be;   ·   -
> But, sweet my love, thy wish forego,
>   I'll give no drop to thee!

(*Both together.*)

Trou.	{This }	cherry bounce	{this }	lov'd noyau,
F. M.	{That }		{that }	
Trou.	{My }	drink for ever be;		
F. M.	{Thy }			
Trou.	} But, sweet my love,	{thy wish forego!		
F. M.	}	{one drop bestow.		
Trou.	{I }	keep it all for	{me!	
F. M.	{Nor }		{thee!	

              [*Exeunt struggling for the bottle, but without anger
                  or animosity, the Fem. Min. appearing, by degrees,
                  to obtain a superiority in the contest.*

---

* The balalaika is a Russian instrument, resembling the guitar.—See the
play of "Count Benyowsky," rendered into English.

Act the Third contains the *eclaircissements* and final arrangement between Casimere, Matilda, and Cecilia : which so
nearly resemble the concluding act of " Stella," that we forbear
to lay it before our readers.

ACT IV.

SCENE—*The Inn door—Diligence drawn up.* CASIMERE *appears
superintending the package of his portmanteaus, and giving
directions to the Porters.*

Enter BEEFINGTON *and* PUDDINGFIELD.

Pudd. Well, Coachey, have you got two inside places ?
Coach. Yes, your honour.
Pudd. [*seems to be struck with* CASIMERE'S *appearance. He
surveys him earnestly, without paying any attention to the
coachman, then doubtingly pronounces*] Casimere !
Cas. [*turning round rapidly, recognises* PUDDINGFIELD, *and
embraces him*]. My Puddingfield !
Pudd. My Casimere !
Cas. What, Beefington too ! [*discovering him*]. Then is my joy
complete.
Beef. Our fellow-traveller, as it seems.
Cas. Yes, Beefington—but wherefore to Hamburgh ?
Beef. Oh, Casimere*—to fly—to fly—to return—England—
our country—Magna Charta—it is liberated—a new era—House
of Commons—Crown and Anchor—Opposition——
Cas. What a contrast ! you are flying to liberty and your
home—I, driven from my home by tyranny—am exposed to
domestic slavery in a foreign country.
Beef. How domestic slavery ?
Cas. Too true—two wives [*slowly, and with a dejected air—
then after a pause*]—you knew my Cecilia ?
Pudd. Yes, five years ago.
Cas. Soon after that period I went upon a visit to a lady in
Wetteravia—my Matilda was under her protection—alighting at
a peasant's cabin, I saw her on a charitable visit, spreading
bread-and-butter for the children, in a light-blue riding habit.
The simplicity of her appearance—the fineness of the weather—
all conspired to interest me—my heart moved to hers—as if by

---

* See "Count Benyowsky ; or, the Conspiracy of Kamschatka," where
Crustiew, an old gentleman of much sagacity, talks the following nonsense :
  Crustiew [*with youthful energy and an air of secrecy and confidence*].
" To fly, to fly, to the Isles of Marian—the island of Tinian—a terrestrial
paradise. Free—free—a mild climate—a new created sun—wholesome
fruits—harmless inhabitants—and Liberty—tranquillity."

a magnetic sympathy—we wept, embraced, and went home together—she became the mother of my Pantalowsky. But five years of enjoyment have not stifled the reproaches of my conscience—her Rogero is languishing in captivity—if I could restore her to *him!*

Beef. Let us rescue him.

Cas. Will without power * is like children playing at soldiers.

Beef. Courage without power† is like a consumptive running footman.

Cas. Courage without power is a contradiction.‡　Ten brave men might set all Quedlinburgh at defiance.

Beef. Ten brave men—but where are they to be found?

Cas. I will tell you—marked you the waiter?

Beef. The waiter?　　　　　　　　　　　　[*Doubtingly.*

Cas. [*in a confidential tone*]. No waiter, but a Knight Templar. Returning from the crusade, he found his Order dissolved, and his person proscribed. He dissembled his rank, and embraced the profession of a waiter. I have made sure of him already. There are, besides, an Austrian and a Prussian grenadier. I have made them abjure their national enmity, and they have sworn to fight henceforth in the cause of freedom. These, with Young Pottingen, the waiter, and ourselves, make seven—the troubadour, with his two attendant minstrels, will complete the ten.

Beef. Now then for the execution.　　　[*With enthusiasm.*

Pudd. Yes, my boys—for the execution.

　　　　　　　　　　　　　[*Clapping them on the back.*

Waiter. But hist! we are observed.

Trou. Let us by a song conceal our purposes.

RECITATIVE ACCOMPANIED.§

Cas.	Hist! hist! nor let the airs that blow
	From Night's cold lungs, our purpose know!
Pudd.	Let Silence, mother of the dumb,
Beef.	Press on each lip her palsied thumb!
Wait.	Let privacy, allied to sin,
	That loves to haunt the tranquil inn—
Gren. }	And Conscience start, when she shall view,
Trou. }	The mighty deed we mean to do!

GENERAL CHORUS—*Con spirito.*

Then friendship swear, ye faithful bands,
Swear to save a shackled hero!

* See "Count Benyowsky," as before.　　† See "Count Benyowsky."
‡ See "Count Benyowsky" again; from which play this and the preceding references are taken word for word. We acquit the Germans of such reprobate silly stuff. It must be the translator's.
§ We believe this song to be copied, with a small variation in metre and meaning, from a song in "Count Benyowsky; or, the Conspiracy of Kamtschatka,"—where the conspirators join in a chorus, *for fear of being overheard.*

See where yon Abbey frowning stands !
Rescue, rescue, brave Rogero !   .

Cas.   Thrall'd in a Monkish tyrant's fetters,
Shall great Rogero hopeless lie?

Y. Pot. In my pocket I have letters,
Saying, "help me, or I die !"

Allegro Allegretto.

Cas. Beef. Pudd. Gren. Trou. } Let us fly, let us fly,
Waiter, and Pot. with enthusiasm } Let us help, ere he die!

[*Exeunt omnes, waving their hats.*

SCENE.—*The Abbey gate, with ditches, drawbridges, and spikes.
Time—about an hour before sunrise. The conspirators
appear as if in ambuscade, whispering, and consulting
together, in expectation of the signal for attack. The*
WAITER *is habited as a Knight Templar, in the dress of his
Order, with the cross on his breast, and the scallop on his
shoulder;* PUDDINGFIELD *and* BEEFINGTON *armed with
blunderbusses and pocket pistols; the Grenadiers in their
proper uniforms. The Troubadour, with his attendant
Minstrels, bring up the rear—martial music—the conspirators come forward, and present themselves before the
gate of the Abbey.—Alarum—firing of pistols—the Convent
appear in arms upon the walls—the drawbridge is let down
—a body of choristers and lay-brothers attempt a sally, but
are beaten back, and the verger killed. The besieged attempt
to raise the drawbridge—*PUDDINGFIELD *and* BEEFINGTON
*press forward with alacrity, throw themselves upon the
drawbridge, and by the exertion of their weight, preserve it
in a state of depression—the other besiegers join them, and
attempt to force the entrance, but without effect.* PUDDING-
FIELD *makes the signal for the battering ram. Enter*
QUINTUS CURTIUS *and* MARCUS CURIUS DENTATUS, *in
their proper military habits, preceded by the Roman Eagle
—the rest of their legion are employed in bringing forward
a battering ram, which plays for a few minutes to slow
time, till the entrance is forced. After a short resistance,
the besiegers rush in with shouts of victory.*   ¦

*Scene changes to the interior of the Abbey. The inhabitants of
the Convent are seen flying in all directions.*

The COUNT OF WEIMAR *and* PRIOR, *who had been feasting in
the refectory, are brought in manacled. The* COUNT *appears
transported with rage, and gnaws his chains. The* PRIOR
remains insensible, as if stupefied with grief. BEEFINGTON
takes the keys of the dungeon, which are hanging at the
PRIOR'S *girdle, and makes a sign for them both to be led
away into confinement.—Exeunt* PRIOR *and* COUNT *properly guarded. The rest of the conspirators disperse in
search of the dungeon where* ROGERO *is confined.*   . ⁻

Bombastes Furioso.

FIRST PERFORMED AT THE THEATRE ROYAL HAYMARKET,
AUGUST 7, 1810.

—————

DRAMATIS PERSONÆ.

ARTAXOMINOUS, *King of Utopia.*
FUSBOS, *Minister of State.*
GENERAL BOMBASTES.
Attendants or Courtiers.

Army—a long Drummer, a short Fifer, and two (sometimes three) Soldiers of different dimensions.
DISTAFFINA.

SCENE I.—*Interior of the Palace.*

The KING *in his chair of state.—A table set out with punch-bowl, glasses, pipes, &c.—*ATTENDANTS *on each side.*

TRIO.—" *Tekeli.*"

1st Atten.	What will your majesty please to wear?
	Or blue, green, red, black, white, or brown?
2nd Atten.	D'ye choose to look at the bill of fare? [*Showing long bill.*
King.	Get out of my sight, or I'll knock you down.
2nd Atten.	Here is soup, fish, or goose, or duck, or fowl, or pigeons,
	pig, or hare!
1st Atten.	Or blue, or green, or red, or black, or white, or brown,
	What will your Majesty, &c.
King.	Get out of my sight, &c.

[*Exeunt* ATTENDANTS.

Enter FUSBOS, *and kneels to the* KING.

Fusbos. Hail, Artaxominous! yclep'd the Great!
I come, an humble pillar of thy state,
Pregnant with news—but ere that news I tell,'
First let me hope your Majesty is well.
   King. Rise, learned Fusbos! rise, my friend, and know
We are but middling—that is, *so so!*
   Fusbos. Only *so so!* Oh, monstrous, doleful thing!
Is it the mulligrubs affects the king?

Or, dropping poisons in the cup of joy,
Do the blue devils your repose annoy ?

King. Nor mullïgrubs nor devils blue are here,
But yet we feel ourselves a little queer.

Fusbos. Yes, I perceive it in that vacant eye,
The vest unbutton'd, and the wig awry ;
So sickly cats neglect their fur-attire,
And sit and mope beside the kitchen fire.

King. Last night, when undisturb'd by state affairs,
Moist'ning our clay, and puffing off our cares,
Oft the replenish'd goblet did we drain,
And drank and smok'd, and smok'd and drank again !
Such was the case, our very actions such,
Until at length we got a drop too much.

Fusbos. So when some donkey on the Blackheath Road,
Falls, overpower'd, beneath his sandy load ;
The driver's curse unheeded swells the air,
Since none can carry more than they can bear.

King. The sapient Doctor Muggins came in haste,
Who suits his physic to his patient's taste ;
He, knowing well on what our heart is set,
Hath just prescrib'd, " To take a morning whet ; "
The very sight each sick'ning pain subdues.
Then sit, my Fusbos, sit and tell thy news.

Fusbos [sits]. Gen'ral Bombastes, whose resistless force
Alone exceeds by far a brewer's horse,
Returns victorious, bringing mines of wealth !

King. Does he, by jingo ? then we'll drink his health !
                                               [*Drum and Fife.*

Fusbos. But hark ! with loud acclaim, the fife and drum
Announce your army near ; behold, they come !

Enter BOMBASTES, *attended by one* DRUMMER, *one* FIFER,
and two SOLDIERS, *all very materially differing in
size.—They march round the stage and back.*

Bombas. Meet me this ev'ning at the Barley Mow ;
I'll bring your pay—you see I'm busy now :
Begone, brave army, and don't kick up a row. [*Exeunt* SOLDIERS.
[*To the* KING]. Thrash'd are your foes—this watch and silken
                string,
Worn by their chief, I as a trophy bring ;
I knock'd him down, then snatch'd it from his fob ;
" Watch, watch," he cried, when I had done the job.
" My watch is gone," says he—says I, " Just so ;
Stop where you are—watches were made to go."

King. For which we make you Duke of Strombelo.
              [BOMBASTES *kneels ; the* KING *dubs him with a pipe,
                and then presents the bowl.*

From our own bowl here drink, my soldier true,
And if you'd like to take a whiff or two,
He whose brave arm hath made our foes to crouch,
Shall have a pipe from this our royal pouch.
    Bombas. [*rises*]. Honours so great have all my toils repaid
My liege, and Fusbos, here's " Success to trade."
    Fusbos. Well said, Bombastes ! Since thy mighty blows
Have given a quietus to our foes,
Now shall our farmers gather in their crops,
And busy tradesmen mind their crowded shops
The deadly havoc of war's hatchet cease ;
Now shall we smoke the calumet of peace,
    King. I shall smoke short-cut, you smoke what you please
    Bombas. Whate'er your Majesty shall deign to name,
Short cut or long to me is all the same.

Bombas. and *Fusbos.*	In short, so long, as we your favours claim, Short cut or long, to us is all the same.

    King. Thanks, gen'rous friends ! now list whilst I impart
How firm you're lock'd and bolted in my heart ;
So long as this here pouch a pipe contains,
Or a full glass in that there bowl remains,
To you an equal portion shall belong ;
This do I swear, and now—let's have a song.
    Fusbos. My liege shall be obeyed.
                        [*Advances and attempts to sing.*
    Bombas.   Fusbos, give place,
You know you haven't got a singing face ;
Here nature, smiling, gave the winning grace.

SONG.—" *Hope told a flatt'ring Tale.*"

Hope told a flattering tale,
  Much longer than my arm,
That love and pots of ale
  In peace would keep me warm :
The flatt'rer is not gone,
She visits number one :
In love I'm monstrous deep.
Love ! odsbobs, destroys my sleep,
Hope told a flattering tale,
  Lest love should soon grow cool ;
A tub thrown to a whale,
  To make the fish a fool :
Should Distaffina frown,
  Then love's gone out of town ;
And when love's dream is o'er,
  Then we wake and dream no more.

                                    [*Exit.*
[*The* KING *evinces strong emotions during the song, and
  at the conclusion starts up.*

Fusbos. What ails my liege ? ah ! why that look so sad ?
King [*coming forward*]. I am in love ! I scorch, I freeze, I'm
   mad !
Oh, tell me, Fusbos, first and best of friends,
You, who have wisdom at your fingers' ends,
Shall it be so, or shall it not be so ?
Shall I my Griskinissa's charms forego,
Compel her to give up the regal chair,
And place the rosy Distaffina there ?
In such a case, what course can I pursue ?
I love my queen, and Distaffina too.
   Fusbos. And would a king his general supplant ?
I can't advise, upon my soul I can't.
   King. So when two feasts, whereat there's nought to pay,
Fall unpropitious on the self-same day,
The anxious Cit each invitation views,
And ponders which to take or which refuse :
From this or that to keep away is loth,
And sighs to think he cannot dine at both.   [*Exit.*
   Fusbos. So when some school-boy, on a rainy day,
Finds all his playmates will no longer stay,
He takes the hint himself—and walks away.   [*Exit.*

Scene II.—*An Avenue of Trees.*

Enter the King.

King. I'll seek the maid I love, though in my way
A dozen gen'rals stood in fierce array !
Such rosy beauties nature meant for kings ; ·
Subjects have treat enough to see such things.

Scene III.—*Inside of a Cottage.*

Enter Distaffina.

Distaf. This morn, as sleeping in my bed I lay,
I dreamt (and morning dreams come true they say),
I dreamt a cunning man my fortune told,
And soon the pots and pans were turned to gold !
Then I resolv'd to cut a mighty dash ;
But, lo ! ere I could turn them into cash,
Another cunning man my heart betray'd,
Stole all away, and left my debts unpaid.

Enter the King.

And pray, sir, who are you, I'd wish to know ?
   King. Perfection's self, oh, smooth that angry brow !

For love of thee, I've wander'd thro' the town,
And here have come to offer half a crown.
  Distaf. Fellow! your paltry offer I despise;
The great Bombastes' love alone I prize.
  King. He's but a general—damsel, I'm a king;
  Distaf. Oh, sir, that makes it quite another thing.
  King. And think not, maiden, I could e'er design
A sum so trifling for such charms as thine.
No! the half crown that ting'd thy cheeks with red,
And bade fierce anger o'er thy beauties spread;
Was meant that thou should'st share my throne and bed.
  Distaf. [*aside*]. My dream is out, and I shall soon behold
The pots and pans all turn to shining gold.
  King [*puts his hat down to kneel on*]. Here, on my knees
      (those knees which ne'er till now
To man or maid in suppliance bent) I vow
Still to remain, till you my hopes fulfil,
Fixt as the Monument on Fish Street Hill.
  Distaf. [*kneels*]. And thus I swear, as I bestow my hand,
As long as e'er the Monument shall stand,
So long I'm yours——
  King.   Are then my wishes crown'd?
  Distaf. La, sir! I'd not say no for twenty pound;
Let silly maids for love their favours yield,
Rich ones for me—a king against the field.

SONG.—"*Paddy's Wedding.*"

Queen Dido at
Her palace gate
Sat darning of her stocking O;
She sung and drew
The worsted through,
Whilst her foot was the cradle rocking O;
(For a babe she had
By a soldier lad,
Though hist'ry passes it over O);
"You tell-tale brat,
I've been a flat,
Your daddy has proved a rover O.
What a fool was I
To be cozen'd by
A fellow without a penny O;
When rich ones came,
And ask'd the same,
For I'd offers from never so many O;
But I'll darn my hose,
Look out for beaux,
And quickly get a new lover O;
Then come, lads, come,
Love beats the drum,
And a fig for Æneas the rover O."

King. So Orpheus sang of old, or poets lie,
And as the brutes were charmed, e'en so am I.
Rosy-cheek'd maid, henceforth my only queen,
Full soon shalt thou in royal robes be seen ;
And through my realm I'll issue this decree,
None shall appear of taller growth than thee :
Painters no other face portray—each sign
O'er alehouse hung shall change its head for thine.
Poets shall cancel their unpublish'd lays,
And none presume to write but in thy praise.
    Distaf. [*fetches a bottle and glass*]. And may I then, without
      offending, crave
My love to taste of this, the best I have?
    King. Were it the vilest liquor upon earth,
Thy touch would render it of matchless worth ;
Dear shall the gift be held that comes from you ;
Best proof of love [*drinks*], 'tis full-proof Hodges' too ;
Through all my veins I feel a genial glow,
It fires my soul——
    Bombastes [*within*]. Ho, Distaffina, ho !
    King. Heard you that voice ?
    Distaf.   O yes, 'tis what's his name,
The General ; send him packing as he came.
    King. And is it he ? and doth he hither come?
Ah me ! my guilty conscience strikes me dumb :
Where shall I go ? say, whither shall I fly?
Hide me, oh hide me from his injur'd eye !
    Distaf. Why, sure you're not alarm'd at such a thing?
He's but a general, and you're a king.
              [KING *conceals himself in a closet in flat.*

Enter BOMBASTES.

    Bombas. Lov'd Distaffina ! now by my scars I vow,
Scars got—I haven't time to tell you how ;
By all the risks my fearless heart hath run,
Risks of all shapes from bludgeon, sword, and gun,
Steel traps, the patrole, bailiff shrewd, and dun ;
By the great bunch of laurel on my brow,
Ne'er did thy charms exceed their present glow !
Oh ! let me greet thee with a loving kiss——   [*Sees the hat.*
Why, what the devil !—say, whose hat is this ?
    Distaf. Why, help your silly brains, that's not a hat.
    Bombas. No hat?
    Distaf.   Suppose it is, why, what of that ?
A hat can do no harm without a head !
    Bombas. Whoe'er it fits, this hour I doom him dead ;

Alive from hence the caitiff shall not stir——[*Discovers the* KING.
Your most obedient, humble servant, sir.
   King. Oh, general, oh !
   Bombas.   My much-loved master, oh'!
What means all this?
   King.   Indeed I hardly know——
   Distaf. You hardly know ?—a very pretty joke,
If kingly promises so soon are broke !
Arn't I to be a queen, and dress so fine?
   King. I do repent me of the foul design :
To thee, my brave Bombastes, I restore
Pure Distaffina, and will never more
Through lane or street with lawless passion rove,
But give to Griskinissa all my love.
   Bombas. No, no, I'll love no more ; let him who can
Fancy the maid who fancies ev'ry man.
In some lone place I'll find a gloomy cave,
There my own hands shall dig a spacious grave.
Then all unseen I'll lay me down and die,
Since woman's constancy is—all my eye.

TRIO.—"*O Lady Fair !*"

Distaf.	O, cruel man ! where are you going?
	Sad are my wants, my rent is owing.
Bombas.	I go, I go, all comfort scorning ;
	Some death I'll die before the morning.
Distaf.	Heigho, heigho ! sad is that warning—
	Oh, do not die before the morning !
King.	I'll follow him, all danger scorning ;
	He shall not die before the morning.
Bombas.	I go, I go, &c.
Distaf.	Heigho, heigho, &c.
King.	I'll follow him, &c.

[*They hold him by the coat-tails, but he gradually tugs
them off.*

SCENE IV.—*A Wood.*

Enter FUSBOS.

   Fusbos. This day is big with fate : just as I set
My foot across the threshold, lo ! I met
A man whose squint terrific struck my view ;
Another came, and lo ! he squinted too ;
And ere I'd reach'd the corner of the street,
Some ten short paces, 'twas my lot to meet

A third who squinted more—a fourth, and he
Squinted more vilely than the other three.
Such omens met the eye when Cæsar fell,
But cautioned him in vain ; and who can tell
Whether those awful notices of fate
Are meant for kings or ministers of state ;
For rich or poor, old, young, or short or tall,
The wrestler Love trips up the heels of all.

SONG.—"*My Lodging is on the Cold Ground.*"

My lodging is in Leather Lane,
   A parlour that's next to the sky ;
'Tis exposed to the wind and the rain,
   But the wind and the rain I defy :
Such love warms the coldest of spots,
   As I feel for Scrubinda the fair ;
Oh, she lives by the scouring of pots,
   In Dyot Street, Bloomsbury Square.

Oh, were I a quart, pint, or gill,
   To be scrubb'd by her delicate hands,
Let others possess what they will
   Of learning, and houses, and lands ;
My parlour that's next to the sky
   I'd quit, her blest mansion to share ;
So happy to live and to die
   In Dyot Street, Bloomsbury Square.

And oh, would this damsel be mine,
   No other provision I'd seek ;
On a look I could breakfast and dine,
   And feast on a smile for a week.
But ah ! should she false-hearted prove,
   Suspended, I'll dangle in air ;
A victim to delicate love,
   In Dyot Street, Bloomsbury Square.

                                         [*Exit.*

Enter BOMBASTES, *preceded by a Fifer, playing* " *Michael
              Wiggins.*"

Bombas. Gentle musician, let thy dulcet strain
Proceed—play " Michael Wiggins " once again [*he does so*].
Music's the food of love ; give o'er, give o'er,
For I must batten on that food no more.   [*Exit* FIFER.
My happiness is chang'd to doleful dumps,
Whilst, merry Michael, all thy cards were trumps.
So, should some youth by fortune's blest decrees,
Possess at least a pound of Cheshire cheese,
And bent some favour'd party to regale,
Lay in a kilderkin, or so, of ale ;

Lo, angry fate ! In one unlucky hour
Some hungry rats may all the cheese devour,
And the loud thunder turn the liquor sour [*forms his sash into
a noose*].
Alas ! alack ! alack ! and well-a-day,
That ever man should make himself away !
That ever man for woman false should die,
As many have, and so, and so [*prepares to hang himself, tries
the sensation, but disapproves of the result*] won't I !
No, I'll go mad ! 'gainst all I'll vent my rage,
And with this wicked wanton world a woeful war I'll wage !
      [*Hangs his boots to the arm of a tree, and, taking a scrap
        of paper, with a pencil writes the following couplet,
        which he attaches to them, repeating the words :—*
" Who dares this pair of boots displace,
  Must meet Bombastes face to face."
Thus do I challenge all the human race.
        [*Draws his sword, and retires up the stage, and off,*

Enter the KING.

King. Scorning my proffer'd hand, he frowning fled,
Curs'd the fair maid, and shook his angry head [*perceives the
boots and label*].
" Who dares this pair of boots displace,
  Must meet Bombastes face to face."
Ha ! dost thou dare me, vile obnoxious elf ?
I'll make thy threats as bootless as thyself :
Where'er thou art, with speed prepare to go
Where I shall send thee—to the shades below [*knocks down the
boots*].
    Bombas. [*coming forward*]. So have I heard on Afric's burn-
ing shore,
A hungry lion give a grievous roar ;
The grievous roar echo'd along the shore.
    King. So have I heard on Afric's burning shore
Another lion give a grievous roar,
And the first lion thought the last a bore.
    Bombas. Am I then mocked ? Now by my fame I swear
You soon shall have it—There !   [*They fight.*
    King.   Where ?
    Bombas.   There and there !
    King. I have it sure enough—Oh ! I am slain !
I'd give a pot of beer to live again [*falls on his back*] ;
Yet ere I die I something have to say :
My once-lov'd gen'ral, pri'thee come this way !
Oh ! oh ! my Bom——   [*Dies.*

Bombas.   —Bastes he would have said ;
But ere the word was out, his breath was fled.
Well, peace be with him, his untimely doom
Shall thus be mark'd upon his costly tomb :— ·
" Fate cropt him short—for be it understood.
  He would have liv'd much longer—if he could."

[*Retires again up the stage.*

Enter FUSBOS.

Fusbos. This was the way they came, and much I fear
There's mischief in the wind.   What have we here?
King Artaxominous bereft of life !
Here'll be a pretty tale to tell his wife.
  Bombas. A pretty tale, but not for thee to tell,
For thou shalt quickly follow him to hell ;
There say I sent thee, and I hope he's well.
  Fusbos. No, thou thyself shalt thy own message bear ;
Short is the journey, thou wilt soon be there.

[*They fight*—BOMBASTES *is wounded.*

  Bombas. Oh, Fusbos, Fusbos ! I am diddled quite,
Dark clouds come o'er my eyes—farewell, good night !
Good night I my mighty soul's inclined to roam,
So make my compliments to all at home.

[*Lies down by the* KING.

  Fusbos. And o'er thy grave a monument shall rise,
Where heroes yet unborn shall feast their eyes ;
And this short epitaph that speaks thy fame,
Shall also there immortalize my name :—
" Here lies Bombastes, stout of heart and limb,
  Who conquered all but Fusbos—Fusbos him."

Enter DISTAFFINA.

Distaf. Ah, wretched maid !   Oh, miserable fate !
I've just arrived in time to be too late ;
What now shall hapless Distaffina do ?
Curse on all morning dreams, they come so true !
  Fusbos. Go, beauty go, thou source of woe to man,
And get another lover where you can :
The crown now sits on Griskinissa's head,
To her I'll go——
  Distaf.   But are you sure they're dead ?
  Fusbos. Yes, dead as herrings—herrings that are red.

FINALE.

Distaf.	Briny tears I'll shed,	
King.	I for joy shall cry, too;	[*Rising.*
Fusbos.	Zounds ! the King's alive !	
Bombas.	Yes, and so am I, too !	[*Rising.*
Distaf.	It was better far,	
King.	Thus to check all sorrow ;	
Fusbos.	But, if some folks please,	
Bombas.	We'll die again to-morrow !	

Distaf.	Tu ral, lu ral, la,
King.	Tu ral, lu ral, laddi ;
Fusbos.	Tu ral, lu ral, la,
Bombas.	Tu ral, lu ral, laddi !

They take hands and dance round, repeating Chorus.

Rejected Addresses.

PREFACE.

ON the 14th of August, 1812, the following advertisement appeared in most of the daily papers :

"Rebuilding of Drury Lane Theatre.

"The Committee are desirous of promoting a free and fair competition for an Address to be spoken upon the opening of the Theatre, which will take place on the 10th of October next. They have therefore thought fit to announce to the public, that they will be glad to receive any such compositions, addressed to their Secretary, at the Treasury Office, in Drury Lane, on or before the 10th of September, sealed up, with a distinguishing word, number, or motto, on the cover, corresponding with the inscription on a separate sealed paper containing the name of the author, which will not be opened, unless containing the name of the successful candidate."

Upon the propriety of this plan, men's minds were, as they usually are upon matters of moment, much divided. Some thought it a fair promise of the future intention of the Committee to abolish that phalanx of authors who usurp the stage, to the exclusion of a large assortment of dramatic talent blushing unseen in the background ; while others contended, that the scheme would prevent men of real eminence from descending into an amphitheatre in which all Grub Street (that is to say, all London and Westminster) would be arrayed against them. The event has proved both parties to be in a degree right, and in a degree wrong. One hundred and twelve Addresses have been sent in, each sealed and signed, and mottoed, "as per order," some written by men of great, some by men of little, and some by men of no talent.

Many of the public prints have censured the taste of the Committee, in thus contracting for Addresses as they would for nails—by the gross; but it is surprising that none should have censured their *temerity*. One hundred and eleven of the Addresses must, of course, be unsuccessful : to each of the authors, thus infallibly classed with the *genus irritabile,* it would be very hard to deny six staunch friends, who consider his the best of all possible Addresses, and whose tongues will be as ready to laud him as to hiss his adversary. These, with the potent aid of the bard himself, make seven foes per Address, and thus will be created seven hundred and seventy-seven implacable auditors, prepared to condemn the strains of Apollo himself; a band of adversaries which no prudent manager would think of exasperating.

But leaving the Committee to encounter the responsibility they have incurred, the public have at least to thank them for ascertaining and establishing one point, which might otherwise have admitted of controversy. When it is considered that many amateur writers have been discouraged from becoming competitors, and that few, if any, of the professional authors can afford to write for nothing, and of course have not been candidates for the honorary prize at Drury Lane, we may confidently pronounce, that, as far as regards *number,* the present is undoubtedly the Augustan age of English poetry. Whether or not this distinction will be extended to the *quality* of its productions, must be decided at the tribunal of posterity, though the natural anxiety of our authors on this score ought to be considerably diminished, when they reflect how few will, in all probability, be had up for judgment.

It is not necessary for the Editor to mention the manner in which he became possessed of this "fair sample of the present state of poetry in Great Britain." It was his first intention to publish the whole ; but a little reflection convinced him that, by so doing, he might depress the good, without elevating the bad. He has therefore culled what had the appearance of flowers, from what possessed the reality of weeds, and is extremely sorry that, in so doing, he has diminished his collection to twenty-one. Those which he has rejected may possibly make their appearance in a separate volume, or they may be admitted as volunteers in the files of some of the newspapers ; or, at all events, they are sure of being received among the awkward squad of the Magazines. In general, they bear a close resemblance to each other : thirty of them contain extravagant compliments to the immortal Wellington, and the indefatigable Whitbread ; and, as the last-mentioned gentleman is said to dislike praise in the exact proportion in which he deserves it, these laudatory writers have probably been only building a wall, against which they might run their own heads.

The Editor here begs leave to advance a few words in behalf of that useful and much-abused bird, the Phœnix, and in so doing he is biassed by no partiality, as he assures the reader he not only never saw one, but (*mirabile dictu !*) never caged one in a simile in the whole course of his life. Not less than sixty-nine of the competitors have invoked the aid of this native of Arabia ; but as from their manner of using him, after they had caught him, he does not by any means appear to have been a native of Arabia *Felix*, the Editor has left the proprietors to treat with Mr. Polito, and refused to receive this *rara avis*, or black swan, into the present collection. One exception occurs, in which the admirable treatment of this feathered incombustible entitles the author to great praise. That Address has been preserved, and in the ensuing pages takes the lead, to which its dignity entitles it.

Perhaps the reason why several of the subjoined productions of the MUSÆ LONDINENSES have failed of selection, may be discovered in their being penned in a metre unusual upon occasions of this sort, and in their not being written with that attention to stage effect, the want of which, like want of manners in the concerns of life, is more prejudicial than a deficiency of talent. There is an art in writing for the Theatre, technically called *touch and go,* which is indispensable when we consider the small quantum of patience which so motley an assemblage as a London audience can be expected to afford. All the contributors have been very exact in sending their initials and mottoes. Those belonging to the present collection have been carefully preserved, and each has been affixed to its respective poem. The letters that accompanied the Addresses having been honourably destroyed unopened, it is impossible to state the real authors with any certainty, but the ingenious reader, after comparing the initials with the motto, and both with the poem, may form his own conclusions.

The Editor does not anticipate any disapprobation from thus giving publicity to a small portion of the REJECTED ADDRESSES; for, unless he is widely mistaken in assigning the respective authors, the fame of each individual is established on much too firm a basis to be shaken by so trifling and evanescent a publication as the present :

> neque ego illi detrahere ausim
> Hærentem capiti multâ cum laude coronam.

Of the numerous pieces already sent to the Committee for performance, he has only availed himself of three vocal Travesties, which he has selected, not for their merit, but simply for their brevity. Above one hundred spectacles, melodramas, operas, and pantomimes have been transmitted, besides the two first acts of one legitimate comedy. Some of these evince considerable smartness of manual dialogue, and several brilliant repartees of chairs, tables, and other inanimate wits ; but the authors seem to have forgotten that in the new Drury Lane the audience can hear as well as see. Of late our theatres have been so constructed that John Bull has been compelled to have very long ears, or none at all; to keep them dangling about his skull like discarded servants, while his eyes were gazing at piebalds and elephants, or else to stretch them out to an asinine length to catch the congenial sound of braying trumpets. An auricular revolution is, we trust, about to take place ; and, as many people have been much puzzled to define the meaning of the new era, of which we have heard so much, we venture to pronounce, that as far as regards Drury Lane Theatre, the new era means the reign of ears. If the past affords any pledge for the future, we may confidently expect from the Committee of that House, everything that can be accomplished by the union of taste and assiduity.

LOYAL EFFUSION.

By W. T. F.

Quicquid dicunt, laudo : id rursum si negant
Laudo id quoque.—TERENCE.

HAIL, glorious edifice, stupendous work !
God bless the Regent and the Duke of York !
    Ye Muses ! by whose aid I cried down Fox,
Grant me in Drury Lane a private box,
Where I may loll, cry bravo, and profess
The boundless powers of England's glorious press ;
While Afric's sons exclaim, from shore to shore,
"Quashee ma boo !" the slave-trade is no more.
    In fair Arabia (happy once, now stony,
Since ruined by that arch apostate, Boney),
A phœnix late was caught : the Arab host
Long ponder'd, part would boil it, part would roast :
But while they ponder, up the pot-lid flies,
Fledged, beak'd, and claw'd, alive, they see him rise
To heaven, and caw defiance in the skies.
So Drury, first in roasting flames consumed,
Then by old renters to hot water doom'd,
By Wyatt's trowel patted, plump and sleek,
Soars without wings, and caws without a beak.
Gallia's stern despot shall in vain advance
From Paris, the metropolis of France ;
By this day month the monster shall not gain
A foot of land in Portugal or Spain.
See Wellington in Salamanca's field
Forces his favourite general to yield,

Breaks thro' his lines, and leaves his boasted Marmont
Expiring on the plain without his arm on :
Madrid he enters at the cannon's mouth,
And then the villages still further south.
Base Buonaparté, fill'd with deadly ire,
Sets, one by one, our playhouses on fire ;
Some years ago he pounced with deadly glee on
The Opera House, then burnt down the Pantheon ;
Nay, still unsated, in a coat of flames,
Next at Millbank he crossed the river Thames :
Thy hatch, O halfpenny ! pass'd in a trice,
Boil'd some black pitch, and burnt down Astley's twice ;
Then buzzing on thro' ether with a vile hum,
Turn'd to the left hand, fronting the asylum,
And burnt the Royal Circus in a hurry,—
('Twas call'd the Circus then, but now the Surrey).
   Who burnt (confound his soul !) the houses twain
Of Covent Garden and of Drury Lane ?
Who, while the British squadron lay off Cork
(God bless the Regent and the Duke of York),
With a foul earthquake ravaged the Caraccas,
And raised the price of dry goods and tobaccos ?
Who makes the quartern loaf and Luddites rise ?
Who fills the butchers' shops with large blue flies ?
Who thought in flames St. James's Court to pinch ?
Who burnt the wardrobe of poor Lady Finch ?
Why he, who, forging for this isle a yoke,
Reminds me of a line I lately spoke,
" The tree of freedom is the British oak."
   Bless every man possessed of aught to give ;
Long may Long Tilney Wellesley Long Pole live ;
God bless the army, bless their coats of scarlet,
God bless the navy, bless the Princess Charlotte,
God bless the guards, though worsted Gallia scoff,
And bless their pigtails, tho' they're now cut off ;
And oh, in Downing Street should Old Nick revel,
England's prime minister, then bless the Devil !

THE BABY'S DEBUT.

By W. W.

Thy lisping prattle and thy mincing gait,
All thy false mimic fooleries I hate,
For thou art Folly's counterfeit, and she
Who is right foolish hath the better plea;
.Nature's true Idiot I prefer to thee.—CUMBERLAND.

[*Spoken in the character of* NANCY LAKE, *a girl eight years of
age, who is drawn upon the stage in a child's chaise, by*
SAMUEL HUGHES, *her uncle's porter.*]

My brother Jack was nine in May,
And I was eight on New-year's-day;
   So in Kate Wilson's shop
Papa (he's my papa and Jack's)
Bought me, last week, a doll of wax,
   And brother Jack a top.

Jack's in the pouts, and this it is,
He thinks mine came to more than his,
   So to my drawer he goes,
Takes out the doll, and, oh, my stars!
He pokes her head between the bars,
   And melts off half her nose!

Quite cross, a bit of string I beg,
And tie it to his peg-top's peg,
   And bang, with might and main,
Its head against the parlour door:
Off flies the head, and hits the floor,
   And breaks a window-pane.

This made him cry with rage and spite:
Well, let him cry, it serves him right.
   A pretty thing, forsooth!
If he's to melt, all scalding hot,
Half my doll's nose, and I am not
   To draw his peg-top's tooth!

Aunt Hannah heard the window break,
And cried, " O naughty Nancy Lake,
   Thus to distress your aunt:
No Drury Lane for you to-day!"
And while papa said, " Pooh, she may!"
   Mamma said, " No, she shan't!"

Well, after many a sad reproach,
They got into a hackney coach,
   And trotted down the street.
I saw them go : one horse was blind,
The tails of both hung down behind,
   Their shoes were on their feet.

The chaise in which poor brother Bill
Used to be drawn to Pentonville,
   Stood in the lumber-room :
I wiped the dust from off the top,
While Molly mopp'd it with a mop,
   And brush'd it with a broom.

My uncle's porter, Samuel Hughes,
Came in at six to black the shoes
   (I always talk to Sam) :
So what does he, but takes, and drags
Me in the chaise along the flags,
   And leaves me where I am.

My father's walls are made of brick,
But not so tall, and not so thick,
   As these ; and, goodness me !
My father's beams are made of wood,
But never, never half so good,
   As these that now I see.

What a large floor ! 'tis like a town !
The carpet, when they lay it down,
   Won't hide it, I'll be bound.
And there's a row of lamps ! my eye !
How they do blaze ! I wonder why
   They keep them on the ground.

At first I caught hold of the wing,
And kept away ; but Mr. Thing-
   umbob, the prompter man,
Gave with his hand my chaise a shove,
And said, " Go on, my pretty love,
   Speak to 'em, little Nan.

" You've only got to curtsey, whisp-
er, hold your chin up, laugh and lisp,
   And then you're sure to take :
I've known the day when brats not quite
Thirteen got fifty pounds a night ;
   Then why not Nancy Lake ? "

But while I'm speaking, where's papa?
And where's my aunt? and where's mamma?
    Where's Jack?   Oh, there they sit !
They smile, they nod, I'll go my ways,
And order round poor Billy's chaise,
    To join them in the pit.

And now, good gentlefolks, I go
To join mamma, and see the show ;
    So, bidding you adieu,
I curtsey, like a pretty miss,
And if you'll blow to me a kiss,
    I'll blow a kiss to you.

                    [*Blows kiss, and exit.*

AN ADDRESS WITHOUT A PHŒNIX.

By S. T. P.

This was look'd for at your hand, and this was baulk'd.—
                    WHAT YOU WILL.

WHAT stately vision mocks my waking sense ?
Hence, dear delusion, sweet enchantment, hence!
Ha ! is it real?—can my doubts be vain ?
It is, it is, and Drury lives again !
Around each grateful veteran attends,
Eager to rush and gratulate his friends,
Friends whose kind looks, retraced with proud delight,
Endear the past, and make the future bright.
Yes, generous patrons, your returning smile
Blesses our toils, and consecrates our pile.

    When last we met, Fate's unrelenting hand
Already grasp'd the devastating brand ;
Slow crept the silent flame, ensnared its prize,
Then burst resistless to the astonish'd skies.
The glowing walls, disrobed of scenic pride,
In trembling conflict stemm'd the burning tide,
Till crackling, blazing, rocking to its fall,
Down rush'd the thundering roof, and buried all !

    Where late the sister Muses sweetly sung,
And raptur'd thousands on their music hung,
Where Wit and Wisdom shone by Beauty graced,
Sate lonely Silence, empress of the waste ;
And still had reign'd—but he whose voice can raise
More magic wonders than Amphion's lays,
Bade jarring bands with friendly zeal engage,
To rear the prostrate glories of the stage.

Up leap'd the Muses at the potent spell,
And Drury's genius saw his temple swell,
Worthy, we hope, the British Drama's cause,
Worthy of British arts, and your applause.

Guided by you, our earnest aims presume
To renovate the Drama with the dome ;
The scenes of Shakespeare and our bards of old,
With due observance splendidly unfold,
Yet raise and foster with parental hand
The living talent of our native land.
O ! may we still, to sense and nature true,
Delight the many, nor offend the few.
Tho' varying tastes our changeful drama claim,
Still be its moral tendency the same,
To win by precept, by example warn,
To brand the front of vice with pointed scorn,
And Virtue's smiling brows with votive wreaths adorn.

CUI BONO?

By Lord B.

I.

SATED with home, of wife, of children tired,
The restless soul is driven abroad to roam ;
Sated abroad, all seen, yet nought admired,
The restless soul is driven to ramble home ;
Sated with both, beneath new Drury's dome
The fiend Ennui awhile consents to pine,
There growls, and curses, like a deadly gnome,
Scorning to view fantastic columbine,
Viewing with scorn and hate the nonsense of the Nine.

II.

Ye reckless dupes, who hither wend your way,
To gaze on puppets in a painted dome,
Pursuing pastimes glittering to betray,
Like falling stars in life's eternal gloom,
What seek ye here? Joy's evanescent bloom?
Woe's me ! the brightest wreaths she ever gave
Are but as flowers that decorate a tomb.
Man's heart the mournful urn o'er which they wave,
Is sacred to despair, its pedestal the grave.

III.

Has life so little store of real woes,
That here ye wend to taste fictitious grief?
Or is it that from truth such anguish flows,

Ye court the lying drama for relief?
Long shall ye find the pang, the respite brief,
Or if one tolerable page appears
In folly's volume, 'tis the actor's leaf,
Who dries his own by drawing others' tears,
And, raising present mirth, makes glad his future years.

IV.

Albeit how like young Betty doth he flee!
Light as the mote that danceth in the beam,
He liveth only in man's present e'e,
His life a flash, his memory a dream,
Oblivious down he drops in Lethe's stream;
Yet what are they, the learned and the great?
Awhile of longer wonderment the theme!
Who shall presume to prophesy their date,
Where nought is certain, save the uncertainty of fate?

V.

This goodly pile, upheav'd by Wyatt's toil,
Perchance than Holland's edifice more fleet,
Again red Lemnos' artisan may spoil;
The fire alarm, and midnight drum may beat,
And all be strew'd ysmoking at your feet.
Start ye? Perchance Death's angel may be sent
Ere from the flaming temple ye retreat,
And ye who met on revel idlesse bent
May find in pleasure's fane your grave and monument.

VI.

Your debts mount high—ye plunge in deeper waste,
The tradesman calls—no warning voice ye hear;
The plaintiff sues—to public shows ye haste;
The bailiff threats—ye feel no idle fear.
Who can arrest your prodigal career?
Who can keep down the levity of youth?
What sound can startle age's stubborn ear?
Who can redeem from wretchedness and ruth
Men true to falshood's voice, false to the voice of truth?

VII.

To thee, blest saint! who doff'd thy skin to make
The Smithfield rabble leap from theirs with joy,
We dedicate the pile—arise! awake!—
Knock down the Muses, wit and sense destroy,
Clear our new stage from reason's dull alloy,

Charm hobbling age, and tickle capering youth
With cleaver, marrow-bone, and Tunbridge toy ;
While, vibrating in unbelieving tooth,
Harps twang in Drury's walls, and make her boards a booth.

VIII.

For what is Hamlet, but a hare in March?
And what is Brutus, but a croaking owl?
And what is Rolla? Cupid steep'd in starch,
Orlando's helmet in Augustine's cowl.
Shakespeare, how true thine adage, "fair is foul;"
To him whose soul is with fruition fraught
The song of Braham is an Irish howl,
Thinking is but an idle waste of thought,
And nought is everything, and everything is nought.

IX.

Sons of Parnassus? whom I view above,
Not laurel-crown'd but clad in rusty black,
Not spurring Pegasus through Tempé's grove,
But pacing Grub Street on a jaded hack,
What reams of foolscap, while your brains ye rack,
Ye mar to make again ! for sure, ere long,
Condemn'd to tread the bard's time-sanctioned track,
Ye all shall join the bailiff-haunted throng,
And reproduce in rags the rags ye blot in song.

X.

So fares the follower in the Muses' train,
He toils to starve, and only lives in death ;
We slight him till our patronage is vain,
Then round his skeleton a garland wreathe,
And o'er his bones an empty requiem breathe—
Oh ! with what tragic horror would he start
(Could he be conjured from the grave beneath),
To find the stage again a Thespian cart,
And elephants and colts down trampling Shakespeare's art

XI.

Hence, pedant Nature ! with thy Grecian rules !
Centaurs (not fabulous) those rules efface ;
Back, sister Muses, to your native schools ;
Here booted grooms usurp Apollo's place,
Hoofs shame the boards that Garrick used to grace,
The play of limbs succeeds the play of wit ;
Man yields the drama to the Houynim race,
His prompter spurs, his licencer the bit,
The stage a stable-yard, a jockey-club the pit.

·XII.

Is it for these ye rear this proud abode?
Is it for these your superstition seeks
To build a temple worthy of a god,
To laud a monkey, or to worship leeks?
Then be the stage, to recompense your freaks,
A motley chaos, jumbling age and ranks,
Where Punch, the lignum vitæ Roscius, squeaks,
And Wisdom weeps, and Folly plays his pranks,
And moody Madness laughs, and hugs the chain he clanks.

To the Secretary of the Managing Committee of Drury Lane
Playhouse.

SIR,

To the gewgaw fetters of rhyme (invented by the monks to enslave the people) I have a rooted objection. I have therefore written an address for your theatre in plain, homespun, yeoman's prose; in the doing whereof I hope I am swayed by nothing but an independent wish to open the eyes of this gulled people, to prevent a repetition of the dramatic bamboozling they have hitherto laboured under. If you like what I have done, and mean to make use of it, I don't want any such aristocratic reward as a piece of plate with two griffins sprawling upon it, or a dog and a jackass fighting for a ha'p'worth of gilt gingerbread, or any such Bartholomew Fair nonsense. All I ask is, that the door-keepers of your playhouse may take all the sets of my Register, now on hand, and force everybody who enters your door to buy one, giving afterwards a debtor and creditor account of what they have received, post-paid, and in due course remitting me the money and unsold Registers, carriage-paid.

I am, &c.,
W. C.

IN THE CHARACTER OF A HAMPSHIRE FARMER.

Rabidâ qui concitus irâ
Implevit pariter ternis latratibus auras
Et sparsit virides spumis albentibus agros.—OVID.

MOST THINKING PEOPLE,

When persons address an audience from the stage, it is usual, either in words or gesture, to say, "Ladies and Gentlemen, your servant," If I were base enough, mean enough, paltry enough, and brute beast enough, to follow that fashion, I should tell two lies in a breath. In the first place, you are not ladies and gentlemen, but I hope something better—that is to say, honest men and women ; and in the next place, if you were ever so much ladies, and ever so much gentlemen, I am not, nor ever will be, your humble servant. You see me here, most thinking people, by mere chance. I have not been within the doors of a playhouse before for these ten years, nor till that abominable custom of taking money at the doors is discontinued, will I ever sanction a theatre with my presence. The stage-door is the only gate of freedom in the whole edifice, and through that I made my way from Bagshaw's in Brydges Street, to accost you. Look about you. Are you not all comfortable? Nay, never slink, mun ; speak out, if you are dissatisfied, and tell me so before I leave town. You are now (thanks to Mr. Whitbread) got into a large, comfortable house. Not into a gimcrack palace ; not into a Solomon's temple; not into a frost-work of Brobdingnag filagree ; but into a plain, honest, homely. industrious, wholesome, brown, brick playhouse. You have been struggling for independence and elbow-room these three years ; and who gave it you? Who helped you out of Lilliput? Who routed you from a rat-hole, five inches by four, to perch you in a palace? Again and again I answer, Mr. Whitbread. You might have sweltered in that place with the Greek name till Doomsday, and neither Lord Castlereagh, Mr. Canning, no, nor the Marquis Wellesley, would have turned a trowel to help you out! Remember that. Never forget that. Read it to your children, and to your children's children ! And now, most thinking people, cast your eyes over my head to what the builder (I beg his pardon, the architect) calls the proscenium. No motto, no slang, no Popish Latin to keep the people in the dark. No *Veluti in speculum.* Nothing in the dead languages, properly so called, for they ought to die, ay, and be damned to boot ! The Covent Garden manager tried that, and a pretty business he made of it ! When a man says *Veluti in speculum,* he is called a man of letters. Very well, and is not a man who cries O.P. a man of letters too? You ran your O.P. against his *Veluti in speculum,* and pray which beat? I prophesied that, though I never told anybody. I take it for granted, that every intelligent man, woman, and child, to whom I address myself, has stood severally and respectively in Little Russell Street, and cast their, his, her, and its eyes on the outside of this building before they paid their money to view the inside. Look at the brick-work, English audience ! Look at the brick-work ! All plain and smooth like a quaker's meeting. None of your Egyptian pyramids, to entomb subscribers' capitals. No overgrown colonnades of stone, like an alderman's gouty legs in white cotton stockings, fit only to use as rammers for paving

Tottenham Court Road. This house is neither after the model of a temple in Athens, no, nor a temple in Moorfields, but it is built to act English plays in, and provided you have good scenery, dresses, and decorations, I dare say you wouldn't break your hearts if the outside were as plain as the pikestaff I used to carry when I was a sergeant. *Apropos*, as the French valets say, who cut their masters' throats—*apropos*, a word about dresses. You must, many of you, have seen what I have read a description of—Kemble and Mrs. Siddons in " Macbeth," with more gold and silver plastered on their doublets than would have kept an honest family in butchers' meat and flannel from year's end to year's end ! I am informed (now mind, I do not vouch for the fact), but I am informed that all such extravagant idleness is to be done away with here. Lady Macbeth is to have a plain quilted petticoat, a cotton gown, and a mob cap (as the court parasites call it ; it will be well for them if, one of these days, they don't wear a mob cap—I mean a white cap, with a mob to look at them), and Macbeth is to appear in an honest yeoman's drab coat, and a pair of black calamanco breeches. Not *Sal*amanca ; no, nor Talavera neither, my most noble Marquis, but plain, honest, black calamanco, stuff breeches. This is right ; this is as it should be. Most thinking people, I have heard you much abused. There is not a compound in the language but is strung fifty in a rope, like onions, by the *Morning Post*, and hurled in your teeth. You are called the mob, and when they have made you out to be the mob, you are called the scum of the people, and the dregs of the people. I should like to know how you can be both. Take a basin of broth—not cheap soup, Mr. Wilberforce, not soup for the poor at a penny a quart, as your mixture of horses' legs, brick-dust, and old shoes was denominated, but plain, wholesome, patriotic beef or mutton broth ; take this, examine it, and you will find— mind, I don't vouch for the fact, but I am told you will find the dregs at the bottom, and the scum at the top. I will endeavour to explain this to you : England is a large earthenware pipkin. John Bull is the beef thrown into it. Taxes are the hot water he boils in. Rotten boroughs are the fuel that blazes under this same pipkin. Parliament is the ladle that stirs the hodge-podge, and sometimes—but hold, I don't wish to pay Mr. Newman a second visit. I leave you better off than you have been this many a day. You have a good house over your head ; you have beat the French in Spain ; the harvest has turned out well ; the comet keeps its distance ; and red slippers are hawked about in Constantinople for next to nothing, and for all this, again and again I tell you, you are indebted to Mr. Whitbread !

THE LIVING LUSTRES.

BY T. M.

Jam te juvaverit
Viros relinquere,
Doctæque conjugis
Sinu quiescere.—SIR T. MORE.

I.

O WHY should our dull retrospective Addresses
   Fall damp as wet blankets on Drury Lane fire?
Away with blue devils, away with distresses,
   And give the gay spirit to sparkling desire!

II.

Let artists decide on the beauties of Drury,
   The richest to me is when woman is there:
The question of houses I leave to the jury;
   The fairest to me is the house of the fair.

III.

When woman's soft smile all our senses bewilders,
   And gilds while it carves her dear form on the heart,
What need has New Drury of carvers and gilders,
   With Nature so bounteous, why call upon Art?

IV.

How well would our actors attend to their duties,
   Our house save in oil, and our authors in wit,
In lieu of yon lamps, if a row of young beauties
   Glanced light from their eyes between us and the pit.

V.

The apples that grew on the fruit-tree of knowledge
   By woman were pluck'd, and she still wears the prize,
To tempt us in Theatre, Senate, or College;
   I mean the love-apples that bloom in the eyes.

VI.

There too is the lash which, all statutes controlling,
   Still governs the slaves that are made by the fair,
For man is the pupil, who, while her eye's rolling,
   Is lifted to rapture or sunk in despair.

VII.

'Bloom, Theatre, bloom, in the roseate blushes
  Of beauty illumed by a love-breathing smile ;
And flourish, ye pillars, as green as the rushes
  That pillow the nymphs of the Emerald Isle.

VIII.

For dear is the Emerald Isle of the Ocean,
  Whose daughters are fair as the foam of the wave,
Whose sons, unaccustomed to rebel commotion,
  Tho' joyous are sober, tho' peaceful are brave.

IX.

The shamrock their olive, sworn foe to a quarrel,
  Protects from the thunder and lightning of rows ;
Their sprig of shillelagh is nothing but laurel,
  Which flourishes rapidly over their brows.

X.

Oh ! soon shall they burst the tyrannical shackles,
  Which each panting bosom indignantly names,
Until not one goose at the capital cackles,
  Against the grand question of Catholic claims.

XI.

And then shall each Paddy, who once on the Liffy
  Perchance held the helm of some mack'rel hoy,
Hold the helm of the state, and dispense in a jiffy
  More fishes than ever he caught when a boy.

XII.

And those who now quit their hods, shovels, and barrows,
  In crowds to the bar of some ale-house to flock,
When bred to *our* bar shall be Gibbs's and Garrows,
  Assume the silk gown and discard the smock-frock.

XIII.

For Erin surpasses the daughters of Neptune,
  As Dian outshines each encircling star,
And the spheres of the Heavens could never have kept tune
  Till set to the music of Erin-go-bra !

THE REBUILDING.

BY R. S.

—per audaces nova dithyrambos
Verba devolvit, numerisque fertur
Lege solutis.—HORAT.

Spoken by a GLENDOVEER.

I am a blessed Glendoveer;
'Tis mine to speak, and yours to hear.

MIDNIGHT, yet not a nose
From Tower Hill to Piccadilly snored!
Midnight, yet not a nose
From Indra drew the essence of repose!
See with what crimson fury,
By Indra fann'd, the god of fire ascends the walls of
Drury;
The tops of houses, blue with lead,
Bend beneath the landlord's tread.

Master and 'prentice, serving man and lord,
Nailer and tailor,
Grazier and brazier,
Thro' streets and alleys pour'd,
All, all abroad to gaze,
And wonder at the blaze.
Thick calf, fat foot, and slim knee,
Mounted on roof and chimney,
The mighty roast, the mighty stew
To see;
As if the dismal view
Were but to them a Brentford jubilee.

Vainly, all radiant Surya, sire of Phaeton,
(By the Greeks called Apollo)
Hollow
Sounds from thy harp proceed;
Combustible as reed,
The tongue of Vulcan licks thy wooden legs:
From Drury's top, dissever'd from thy pegs,
Thou tumblest,
Humblest,
Where late thy bright effulgence shone on high:
While, by thy somerset excited, fly
Ten million,
Billion
Sparks from the pit, to gem the sable sky.

Now come the men of fire to quench the fires,
To Russell Street see Globe and Atlas run,
Hope gallops first, and second Sun ;
On flying heel,
See Hand-in-Hand
O'ertake the band ;
View with what glowing wheel
He nicks
Phœnix ;
While Albion scampers from Bridge Street, Blackfriars,
Drury Lane ! Drury Lane !
Drury Lane ! Drury Lane !
They shout and they bellow again and again.
All, all in vain !
Water turns steam ;
Each blazing beam
Hisses defiance to the eddying spout,
It seems but too plain that nothing can put it out !
Drury Lane ! Drury Lane !
See, Drury Lane expires !

Pent in by smoke-dried beams, twelve moons or more,
Shorn of his ray,
Surya in durance lay :
The workmen heard him shout,
But thought it would not pay
To dig him out.
When lo ! terrific Yamen, lord of hell,
Solemn as lead,
Judge of the dead,
Sworn foe to witticism,
By men called criticism,
Came passing by that way :
"Rise !" cried the fiend, "behold a sight of gladness !
Behold the rival theatre,
I've set O.P. at her,
Who, like a bull-dog bold,
Growls and fastens on his hold ;
The many-headed rabble roar in madness :
Thy rival staggers ; come and spy her
Deep in the mud as thou art in the mire."

So saying, in his arms he caught the beaming one,
And crossing Russell Street,
He placed him on his feet,
'Neath Covent Garden dome.   Sudden a sound
As of the bricklayers of Babel rose :
Horns, rattles, drums, tin trumpets, sheets of copper,

Punches and slaps, thwacks of all sorts and sizes,
From the knobb'd bludgeon to the taper switch,
Ran echoing round the walls ; paper placards
Blotted the lamps, boots brown with mud the benches :
A sea of heads roll'd roaring in the pit ;
On paper wings O.P.'s
Reclin'd in lettered ease ;
While shout and scoff,
" Ya ! ya ! off ! off ! "
Like thunderbolt on Surya's ear-drum fell,
And seem'd to paint
The savage oddities of Saint
Bartholomew in hell.

Tears dimm'd the god of light ;
" Bear me back, Yamen, from this hideous sight,
Bear me back, Yamen, I grow sick,
Oh ! bury me again in brick ;
Shall I on New Drury tremble,
To be O.P.'d like Kemble ?
No,
Better remain by rubbish guarded,
Than thus hubbubish groan placarded ;
Bear me back, Yamen, bear me quick,
And bury me again in brick."
Obedient Yamen
Answer'd, Amen,
And did
As he was bid.

There lay the buried god, and Time
Seem'd to decree eternity of lime ;
But pity, like a dewdrop, gently prest
Almighty Veeshnoo's adamantine breast :
He, the preserver, ardent still
To do whate'er he says he will,
From South-hill urg'd his way,
To raise the drooping lord of day.
All earthly spells the busy one o'erpower'd ;
He treats with men of all conditions,
Poets and players, tradesmen, and musicians ;
Nay, even ventures
To attack the renters,
Old and new :
A list he gets
Of claims and debts,
And deems nought done while aught remains to do
Yamen beheld and wither'd at the sight ;

Long had he aim'd the sunbeam to control,
    For light was hateful to his soul :
"Go on," cried the hellish one, yellow with spite,
"Go on," cried the hellish one yellow with spleen,
"Thy toils of the morning, like Ithaca's queen,
    I'll toil to undo every night."

        Ye sons of song, rejoice !
Veeshnoo has still'd the jarring elements,
        The spheres hymn music ;
        Again the god of day
        Peeps forth with trembling ray,
And pours at intervals a strain divine.
"I have an iron yet in the fire," cried Yamen ;
    "The vollied flame rides in my breath,
        My blast is elemental death ;
This hand shall tear their paper bonds to pieces ;
Ingross your deeds, assignments, leases,
        My breath shall every line erase,
        Soon as I blow the blaze."

The lawyers are met at the Crown and Anchor,
And Yamen's visage grows blanker and blanker,
The lawyers are met at the Anchor and Crown,
And Yamen's cheek is a russety brown,
    Veeshnoo, now thy work proceeds ;
        The solicitor reads,
        And, merit of merit !
        Red wax and green ferret,
    Are fix'd at the foot of the deeds !

        Yamen beheld and shiver'd ;
        His finger and thumb were cramp'd ;
        His ear by the flea in't was bitten,
When he saw by the lawyer's clerk written,
        "Sealed and delivered,"
        Being first duly stamped.

"Now for my turn," the demon cries, and blows
A blast of sulphur from his mouth and nose ;
    Ah ! bootless aim ! the critic fiend,
    Sagacious Yamen, judge of hell,
        Is judged in his turn ;
        Parchment won't burn !
His schemes of vengeance are dissolv'd in air,
        Parchment won't tear !

    Is it not written in the Himakoot book
    (That mighty Baly from Kehama took),

" Who blows on pounce
Must the Swerga renounce ? "
It is ! it is ! Yamen, thine hour is nigh ;
Like as an eagle claws an asp,
Veeshnoo has caught him in his mighty grasp,
And hurl'd him in spite of his shrieks and his squalls,
Whizzing aloft like the Temple fountain,
Three times as high as Meru mountain,
Which is
Ninety-nine times as high as St. Paul's.
Descending, he twisted like Levy the Jew,
Who a durable grave meant
To dig in the pavement
Of Monument Yard ;
To earth by the laws of attraction he flew,
And he fell, and he fell,
To the regions of hell ;
Nine centuries bounced he from cavern to rock,
And his head, as he tumbled, went nickety-nock,
Like a pebble in Carisbrooke well.

Now Veeshnoo turn'd round to a capering varlet,
Array'd in blue and white and scarlet,
And cried, " Oh ! brown of slipper as of hat !
Lend me, harlequin, thy bat ! "
He seiz'd the wooden sword, and smote the earth,
When lo ! upstarting into birth,
A fabric, gorgeous to behold,
Outshone in elegance the old,
And Veeshnoo saw, and cried, " Hail, playhouse mine ! "
Then, bending his head, to Surya he said,
" Go, mount yon edifice,
And show thy steady face
In renovated pride,
More bright, more glorious than before ! "
But ah ! coy Surya still felt a twinge,
Still smarted from his former singe,
And to Veeshnoo replied,
In a tone rather gruff,
" No, thank you ! one tumble's enough ! "

DRURY'S DIRGE.

By Laura Matilda.

You praise our sires: but though they wrote with force,
Their rhymes were vicious, and their diction coarse:
We want their strength, agreed ; but we atone
For that and more, by sweetness all our own.—GIFFORD.

I.

BALMY Zephyrs lightly flitting,
   Shade me with your azure wing ;
On Parnassus' summit sitting,
   Aid me, Clio, while I sing.

II.

Softly slept the dome of Drury,
   O'er the empyreal crest,
When Alecto's sister-fury,
   Softly slumb'ring sunk to rest.

III.

Lo ! from Lemnos limping lamely,
   Lags the lowly Lord of Fire,
Cytherea yielding tamely,
   To the Cyclops dark and dire.

IV.

Clouds of amber, dreams of gladness,
   Dulcet joys and sports of youth,
Soon must yield to haughty sadness,
   Mercy holds the veil to Truth.

V.

See Erostratus the second,
   Fires again Diana's fane ;
By the Fates from Orcus beckon'd,
   Clouds envelop Drury Lane.

VI.

Lurid smoke and frank suspicion,
   Hand in hand reluctant dance ;
While the god fulfils his mission,
   Chivalry, resign thy lance.

VII.

Hark ! the engines blandly thunder,
  Fleecy clouds dishevell'd lie,
And the firemen, mute with wonder,
  On the son of Saturn cry.

VIII.

See the bird of Ammon sailing,
  Perches on the engine's peak,
And the Eagle firemen hailing,
  Soothes them with its bickering beak.

IX.

Juno saw, and mad with malice,
  Lost the prize that Paris gave ;
Jealousy's ensanguin'd chalice,
  Mantling pours the orient wave.

X.

Pan beheld Patroclus dying,
  Nox to Niobe was turn'd ;
From Busiris Bacchus flying,
  Saw his Semele inurn'd.

XI.

Thus fell Drury's lofty glory,
  Levell'd with the shuddering stones,
Mars with tresses black and gory,
  Drinks the dew of pearly groans.

XII.

Hark ! what soft Eolian numbers,
  Gem the blushes of the morn ;
Break, Amphion, break your slumbers,
  Nature's ringlets deck the thorn.

XIII.

Ha ! I hear the strain erratic,
  Dimly glance from pole to pole,
Raptures sweet and dreams ecstatic
  Fire my everlasting soul.

XIV.

Where is Cupid's crimson motion ?
  Billowy ecstasy of woe,
Bear me straight, meandering ocean,
  Where the stagnant torrents flow.

XV.

Blood in every vein is gushing,
    Vixen vengeance lulls my heart,
See, the Gorgon gang is rushing !
    Never, never let us part.

A TALE OF DRURY LANE.

By W. S.

Thus he went on, stringing one extravagance upon another, in the style his books of chivalry had taught him, and imitating as near as he could their very phrase.—DON QUIXOTE.

To be spoken by MR. KEMBLE *in a Suit of the Black Prince's Armour, borrowed from the Tower.*

SURVEY this shield all bossy bright ;
These cuisses twain behold ;
Look on my form in armour dight
Of steel inlaid with gold.
My knees are stiff in iron buckles,
Stiff spikes of steel protect my knuckles.
These once belong'd to sable prince,
Who never did in battle wince ;
With valour tart as pungent quince,
    He slew the vaunting Gaul :
Rest there awhile, my bearded lance,
While from green curtain I advance
To yon footlights, no trivial dance,
And tell the town what sad mischance
    Did Drury Lane befall.

The Night.

On fair Augusta's towers and trees
Flitted the silent midnight breeze,
Curling the foliage as it past,
Which from the moon-tipp'd plumage cast
A spangled light like dancing spray.
Then reassumed its still array :
Whenas night's lamp unclouded hung,
And down its full effulgence flung,
It shed such soft and balmy power,
That cot and castle, hall and bower,
And spire and dome, and turret height,
Appear'd to slumber in the light.

From Henry's chapel, Rufus' hall,
To Savoy, Temple, and St. Paul,
From Knightsbridge, Pancras, Camden Town,
To Redriff, Shadwell, Horsleydown,
No voice was heard, no eye unclosed,
But all in deepest sleep reposed.
They might have thought, who gazed around
Amid a silence so profound,
    It made the senses thrill,
That 'twas no place inhabited,
But some vast city of the dead,
    All was so hush'd and still.

The Burning.

As Chaos which, by heavenly doom,
Had slept in everlasting gloom,
Started with terror and surprise,
When light first flash'd upon her eyes;
So London's sons in night-cap woke,
    In bed-gown woke her dames,
For shouts were heard 'mid fire and smoke,
And twice ten hundred voices spoke,
    "The Playhouse is in flames."
And lo! where Catherine Street extends,
A fiery tale its lustre lends
    To every window-pane;
Blushes each spout in Martlet Court,
And Barbican, moth-eaten fort,
And Covent Garden kennels sport,
    A bright ensanguin'd drain;
Meux's new brewhouse shows the light,
Rowland Hill's chapel, and the height
    Where patent shot they sell:
The Tennis Court, so fair and tall,
Partakes the ray, with Surgeons' Hall,
The ticket porter's house of call,
Old Bedlam, close by London Wall,
Wright's shrimp and oyster shop withal,
    And Richardson's Hotel.

Nor these alone, but far and wide
Across the Thames's gleaming tide,
To distant fields the blaze was borne,
And daisy white and hoary thorn
In borrow'd lustre seem'd to sham
The rose or red sweet Wil-li-am.

To those who on the hills around
  Beheld the flames from Drury's mound,
As from a lofty altar rise ;
  It seem'd that nations did conspire,
  To offer to the god of fire
Some vast stupendous sacrifice !
The summon'd firemen woke at call,
And hied them to their stations all.
Starting from short and broken snooze,
Each sought his pond'rous hobnail'd shoes,
But first his worsted hosen plied,
Plush breeches next in crimson dyed,
  His nether bulk embraced ;
Then jacket thick of red or blue,
Whose massy shoulder gave to view
The badge of each respective crew,
  In tin or copper traced.
The engines thunder'd thro' the street,
Fire-hook, pipe, bucket, all complete,
And torches glared, and clattering feet
  Along the pavement paced.

And one, the leader of the band,
From Charing Cross along the Strand,
Like stag by beagles hunted hard,
Ran till he stopp'd at Vin'gar Yard.
The burning badge his shoulder bore,
The belt and oilskin hat he wore,
The cane he had his men to bang,
Show'd foreman of the British gang.
His name was Higginbottom ; now
'Tis meet that I should tell you how
  The others came in view :
The Hand-in-Hand the race begun,
Then came the Phœnix and the Sun,
Th' Exchange, where old insurers run,
  The Eagle, where the new ;
With these came Rumford, Bumford, Cole,
Robins from Hockley-in-the-Hole,
Lawson and Dawson, cheek by jowl,
  Crump from St. Giles's Pound :
Whitford and Mitford join'd the train,
Huggins and Muggins from Chick Lane,
And Clutterbuck, who got a sprain
  Before the plug was found.
Hobson and Jobson did not sleep,
But ah ! no trophy could they reap,
For both were in the Donjon Keep
  Of Bridewell's gloomy mound !

E'en Higginbottom now was posed,
For sadder scene was ne'er disclosed ;
Without, within, in hideous show,
Devouring flames resistless glow,
And blazing rafters downward go,
And never halloo " heads below ! "
    Nor notice give at all :
The firemen, terrified, are slow
To bid the pumping torrent flow,
    For fear the roof should fall.
Back, Robins, back ! Crump, stand aloof !
Whitford, keep near the walls !
Huggins, regard your own behoof,
For lo ! the blazing rocking roof
Down, down in thunder falls !

An awful pause succeeds the stroke,
And o'er the ruins volumed smoke,
Rolling around its pitchy shroud,
Conceal'd them from th' astonish'd crowd.
At length the mist awhile was clear'd,
When lo ! amid the wreck uprear'd,
Gradual a moving head appear'd,
    And Eagle firemen knew :
'Twas Joseph Muggins, name revered,
    The foreman of their crew.
Loud shouted all in signs of woe,
" A Muggins to the rescue, ho ! "
    And pour'd the hissing tide :
Meanwhile the Muggins fought amain,
And strove and struggled all in vain,
For rallying but to fall again,
    He totter'd, sunk, and died !

Did none attempt, before he fell,
To succour one they loved so well ?
Yes, Higginbottom did aspire
(His fireman's soul was all on fire)
    His brother chief to save ;
But ah ! his reckless generous ire
    Served but to share his grave !
'Mid blazing beams and scalding streams,
Thro' fire and smoke he dauntless broke,
    Where Muggins broke before.
But sulphury stench and boiling drench,
Destroying sight, o'erwhelm'd him quite,
    He sunk to rise no more.

Still o'er his head, while fate he braved,
His whizzing water-pipe he waved ;
"Whitford and Mitford, ply your pumps,
You, Clutterbuck, come, stir your stumps,
Why are you in such doleful dumps ?
A fireman and afraid of bumps !
What are they fear'd on ? fools ! 'od rot 'em ! "
Were the last words of Higginbottom.

The Revival.

Peace to his soul ! new prospects bloom,
And toil rebuilds what fires consume !
Eat we and drink we, be our ditty,
" Joy to the managing committee."
Eat we and drink we, join to rum
Roast beef and pudding of the plum ;
Forth from thy nook, John Horner, come,
With bread of ginger brown thy thumb,
        For this is Drury's gay day :
·Roll, roll thy hoop, and twirl thy tops,
And buy, to glad thy smiling chops,
Crisp parliament with lollipops,
        And fingers of the lady.

Didst mark, how toil'd the busy train
From morn to eve, till Drury Lane
Leap'd like a roebuck from the plain ?
Ropes rose and sunk, and rose again,
        And nimble workmen trod ;
To realize bold Wyatt's plan
Rush'd many a howling Irishman,
Loud clatter'd many a porter can,   .
And many a ragamuffin clan,
        With trowel and with hod.

Drury revives ! her rounded pate
Is blue, is heavenly blue with slate ;
She " wings the midway air " elate,
        As magpie, crow, or chough ;
White paint her modish visage smears,
Yellow and pointed are her ears,
No pendant portico appears
Dangling beneath, for Whitbread's shears
        Have cut the bauble off.

Yes, she exalts her stately head,
And, but that solid bulk outspread,

Opposed you on your onward tread,
And posts and pillars warranted
That all was true that Wyatt said,
You might have deem'd her walls so thick,
Were not composed of stone or brick,
But all a phantom, all a trick,
Of brain disturb'd and fancy-sick,
So high she soars, so vast, so quick.

JOHNSON'S GHOST.

Ghost of DR. JOHNSON *rises from trap-door P.S. and Ghost of* BOSWELL *from trap-door O.P. The latter bows respectfully to the House, and obsequiously to the Doctor's Ghost, and retires.*

Doctor's Ghost loquitur.

THAT which was organized by the moral ability of one, has been executed by the physical efforts of many, and Drury Lane Theatre is now complete. Of that part behind the curtain, which has not yet been destined to glow beneath the brush of the varnisher, or vibrate to the hammer of the carpenter, little is thought by the public, and little need be said by the committee. Truth, however, is not to be sacrificed for the accommodation of either, and he who should pronounce that our edifice has received its final embellishment, would be disseminating falsehood without incurring favour, and risking the disgrace of detection without participating the advantage of success.

Professions lavishly effused and parsimoniously verified are alike inconsistent with the precepts of innate rectitude and the practice of external policy : let it not then be conjectured, that because we are unassuming, we are imbecile ; that forbearance is any indication of despondency, or humility of demerit. He that is the most assured of success will make the fewest appeals to favour, and where nothing is claimed that is undue, nothing that is due will be withheld. A swelling opening is too often succeeded by an insignificant conclusion. Parturient mountains have ere now produced muscipular abortions, and the auditor who compares incipient grandeur with final vulgarity, is reminded of the pious hawkers of Constantinople, who solemnly perambulate her streets, exclaiming, " In the name of the Prophet—figs ! "

Of many who think themselves wise, and of some who are thought wise by others, the exertions are directed to the revival of mouldering and obscure dramas ; to endeavours to exalt that which is now rare only because it was always worthless, and whose deterioration, while it condemned it to living obscurity, by a strange obliquity of moral perception constitutes its title to posthumous renown.   To embody the flying colours of folly, to arrest evanescence, to give to bubbles the globular consistency as well as form, to exhibit on the stage the piebald denizen of the stable, and the half-reasoning parent of combs, to display the brisk locomotion of Columbine, or the tortuous attitudinizing of Punch ; these are the occupations of others, whose ambition, limited to the applause of unintellectual fatuity, is too innocuous for the application of satire, and too humble for the incitement of jealousy.

Our refectory will be found to contain every species of fruit, from the cooling nectarine and luscious peach, to the puny pippin and the noxious nut.   There indolence may repose, and inebriety revel ; and the spruce apprentice, rushing in at second account, may there chatter with impunity, debarred by a barrier of brick and mortar from marring that scenic interest in others, which nature and education have disqualified him from comprehending himself.

Permanent stage-doors we have none.   That which is permanent cannot be removed, for if removed it soon ceases to be permanent.   What stationary absurdity can vie with that ligneous barricado, which, decorated with frappant and tintinabulant appendages, now serves, as the entrance of the lowly cottage, and now as the exit of a lady's bed-chamber ; at one time insinuating plastic Harlequin into a butcher's shop, and at another, yawning as the flood-gate to precipitate the Cyprians of St. Giles's into the embraces of Macheath.   To elude this glaring absurdity, to give to each respective mansion the door which the carpenter would doubtless have given, we vary our portal with the varying scene, passing from deal to mahogany, and from mahogany to oak, as the opposite claims of cottage, palace, or castle may appear to require.

Amid the general hum of gratulation which flatters us in front, it is fit that some regard should be paid to the murmurs of despondence that assail us in the rear.   They, as I have elsewhere expressed it, " who live to please," should not have their own pleasures entirely overlooked.   The children of Thespis are general in their censures of the architect in having placed the locality of exit at such a distance from the oily irradiators which now dazzle the eyes of him who addresses you.   I am, cries the Queen of Terrors, robbed of my fair proportions.   When the king-killing Thane hints to the breathless auditory the murders he means to perpetrate in the castle of Macduff " ere his purpose cool," so vast is the interval he has to travel before he can escape from the stage, that his purpose has even time to freeze.   Your condition, cries the Muse of Smiles, is hard, but it is cygnet's down in comparison with mine.   The peerless peer of capers and congees has laid it down as a rule, that the best good thing uttered by the morning visitor should conduct him rapidly to the doorway, last impressions vieing in durability with first. But when on this boarded elongation it falls to my lot to say a good thing, to ejaculate " keep moving," or to chaunt " hic hoc horum genetivo," many are the moments that must elapse ere I can hide myself from public vision in the recesses of O.P. or P.S.

To objections like these, captiously urged and querulously maintained, it is time that equity should conclusively reply. Deviation from scenic propriety has only to vituperate itself for the consequences it generates. Let the actor consider the line of exit as that line beyond which he should not soar in quest of spurious applause : let him reflect that in proportion as he advances to the lamps, he recedes from nature ; that the truncheon of Hotspur acquires no additional charm from encountering the cheek of beauty in the stage-box, and that the bravura of Mandane may produce effect, although the throat of her who warbles it should not overhang the orchestra. The Jove of the modern critical Olympus, Lord Mayor of the theatric sky, has, *ex cathedrâ*, asserted that a natural actor looks upon the audience part of the theatre as the third side of the chamber he inhabits. Surely of the third wall thus fancifully erected, our actors should by ridicule or reason be withheld from knocking their heads against the stucco.

Time forcibly reminds me that all things which have a limit must be brought to a conclusion. Let me, ere that conclusion arrives, recall to your recollection that the pillars which rise on either side of me, blooming in varied antiquity, like two massy evergreens, had yet slumbered in their native quarry, but for the ardent exertions of the individual who called them into life : to his never-slumbering talents you are indebted for whatever pleasure this haunt of the Muses is calculated to afford. If, in defiance of chaotic malevolence, the destroyer of the temple of Diana yet survives in the name of Erostratus, surely we may confidently predict, that the rebuilder of the temple of Apollo will stand recorded to distant posterity in that of—SAMUEL WHITBREAD.

THE BEAUTIFUL INCENDIARY.

By the Hon. W. S.

Formosam resonare doces Amaryllida silvas.—Virgil.

Scene draws, and discovers a Lady asleep on a couch.
Enter Philander.

PHILANDER.

I.

Sobriety, cease to be sober,
    Cease, Labour, to dig and to delve,
And hail to this tenth of October,
    One thousand eight hundred and twelve.
Hah ! whom do my peepers remark ?
    'Tis Hebe with Jupiter's jug ;
Oh no, 'tis the pride of the Park,
    Fair Lady Elizabeth Mugg.

II.

Why, beautiful nymph, do you close
    The curtain that fringes your eye ?
Why veil in the clouds of repose
    The sun that should brighten our sky ?
Perhaps jealous Venus has oil'd
    Thy hair with some opiate drug,
Not choosing her charms should be foil'd
    By Lady Elizabeth Mugg.

III.

But ah ! why awaken the blaze
    The bright burning-glasses contain,
Whose lens with concentrated rays
    Proved fatal to old Drury Lane.
'Twas all accidental they cry,—
    Away with the flimsy humbug !
'Twas fired by a flash from the eye
    Of Lady Elizabeth Mugg.

IV.

Thy glance can in us raise a flame,
    Then why should old Drury be free ?
Our doom and its doom are the same,
    Both subject to beauty's decree.

No candles the workmen consum'd,
　　When deep in the ruins they dug,
Thy flash still their progress illum'd,
　　Sweet Lady Elizabeth Mugg.

V.

Thy face a rich fireplace displays ;
　　The mantel-piece marble—thy brows ;
Thine eyes are the bright beaming blaze,
　　Thy bib which no trespass allows,
The fender's tall barrier marks ;
　　Thy tippet's the fire-quelling rug,
Which serves to extinguish the sparks
　　Of Lady Elizabeth Mugg.

VI.

The Countess a lily appears,
　　Whose tresses the dewdrops emboss ;
The Marchioness blooming in years,
　　A rosebud envelop'd in moss ;
But thou art the sweet passion-flower,
　　For who would not slavery hug,
To pass but one exquisite hour
　　In the arms of Elizabeth Mugg ?

VII.

When at Court, or some dowager's rout,
　　Her diamond aigrette meets our view,
She looks like a glow-worm dress'd out,
　　Or tulips bespangled with dew.
Her two lips denied to man's suit,
　　Are shared with her favourite Pug ;
What lord would not change with the brute,
　　To live with Elizabeth Mugg ?

VIII.

Could the stage be a large *vis-à-vis*,
　　Reserv'd for the polish'd and great,
Where each happy lover might see
　　The nymph he adores *tête-à-tête ;*
No longer I'd gaze on the ground,
　　And the load of despondency lug,
For I'd book myself all the year round,
　　To ride with the sweet Lady Mugg.

IX.   ·

Yes, she in herself is a host,
   And if she were here all alone,
Our house might nocturnally boast
   A bumper of fashion and ton.
Again should it burst in a blaze,
   In vain would they ply Congreve's plug,
For nought could extinguish the rays
   From the glance of divine Lady Mugg.

X.

O could I as Harlequin frisk,
   And thou be my Columbine fair,
My wand should with one magic whisk
   Transport us to Hanover Square ;
St. George should lend us his shrine,
   The parson his shoulders might shrug,
But a licence should force him to join
   My hand in the hand of my Mugg.

XI.

Court-plaister the weapons should tip,
   By Cupid shot down from above,
Which cut into spots for thy lip,
   Should still barb the arrows of love.
The god who from others flies quick,
   With us should be slow as a slug,
As close as a leech he should stick
   To me and Elizabeth Mugg.

XII.   ·

For Time would, like us, 'stead of sand,
   Put filings of steel in his glass,
To dry up the blots of his hand,
   And spangle life's page as they pass.
Since all flesh is grass ere 'tis hay,
   O may I in clover live snug,
And when old Time mows me away,
   Be stack'd with defunct Lady Mugg.

FIRE AND ALE.

By M. G. L.

Omnia transformat sese in miracula rerum.—VIRGIL.

MY palate is parch'd with Pierian thirst,
 Away to Parnassus I'm beckon'd ;
List, warriors and dames, while my lay is rehears'd,
I sing of the singe of Miss Drury the first,
 And the birth of Miss Drury the second.

The Fire King one day rather amorous felt ;
 He mounted his hot copper filly ;
His breeches and boots were of tin, and the belt
Was made of cast iron, for fear it should melt
 With the heat of the copper colt's belly.

Sure never was skin half so scalding as his !
 When an infant, 'twas equally horrid,
For the water when he was baptized gave a fizz,
And bubbled and simmer'd and started off, whizz !
 As soon as it sprinkled his forehead.

Oh ! then there was glitter and fire in each eye,
 For two living coals were the symbols ;
His teeth were calcined, and his tongue was so dry,
It rattled against them as though you should try
 To play the piano in thimbles.

From his nostrils a lava sulphureous flows,
 Which scorches wherever it lingers,
A snivelling fellow he's call'd by his foes,
For he can't raise his paw up to blow his red nose,
 For fear it should blister his fingers.

His wig is of flames curling over his head,
 Well powder'd with white smoking ashes ;
He drinks gunpowder tea, melted sugar of lead,
Cream of tartar, and dines on hot spice gingerbread,
 Which black from the oven he gnashes.

Each fire nymph his kiss from her countenance shields,
 'Twould soon set her cheekbone a-frying :
He spit in the tenter-ground near Spitalfields,
And the hole that it burnt and the chalk that it yields
 Make a capital limekiln for drying.

When he open'd his mouth out there issued a blast,
　　(*Nota bene*, I do not mean swearing,)
But the noise that it made and the heat that it cast,
I've heard it from those who have seen it, surpass'd
　　A shot manufactory flaring.

He blaz'd and he blaz'd as he gallop'd to snatch
　　His bride, little dreaming of danger ;
His whip was a torch, and his spur was a match,
And over the horse's left eye was a patch,
　　To keep it from burning the manger.

And who is the housemaid he means to enthral
　　In his cinder-producing alliance ?
'Tis Drury Lane Playhouse, so wide, and so tall,
Who, like other combustible ladies, must fall,
　　If she cannot set sparks at defiance.

On his warming-pan knee-pan he clattering roll'd,
　　And the housemaid his hand would have taken,
But his hand, like his passion, was too hot to hold,
And she soon let it go, but her new ring of gold
　　All melted, like butter or bacon !

Oh ! then she look'd sour, and indeed well she might,
　　For Vinegar Yard was before her,
But, spite of her shrieks, the ignipotent knight,
Enrobing the maid in a flame of gas-light,.
　　To the skies in a sky-rocket bore her.

Look ! look ! 'tis the Ale King, so stately and starch,
　　Whose votaries scorn to be sober ;
He pops from his vat, like a cedar or larch ;
Brown stout is his doublet, he hops in his march,
　　And froths at the mouth in October.

His spear is a spigot, his shield is a bung ;
　　He taps where the housemaid no more is,
When lo ! at his magical bidding, upsprung
A second Miss Drury, tall, tidy, and young,
　　And sported *in loco sororis.*

Back, lurid in air, for a second regale,
　　The Cinder King, hot with desire,
To Brydges Street hied ; but the Monarch of Ale,
With uplifted spigot and faucet, and pail,
　　Thus chided the Monarch of Fire ;

"Vile tyrant, beware of the ferment I brew,
　　I rule the roast here, dash the wig o' me !
If, spite of your marriage with Old Drury, you
Come here with your tinderbox, courting the New,
　　I'll have you indicted for bigamy !"

PLAYHOUSE MUSINGS.

By S. T. C.

Ille velut fidis arcana sodalibus olim
Credebat libris ; neque si male cesserat, usquam
Decurrens alio, neque si bene.—HORAT.

MY pensive public, wherefore look you sad?
I had a grandmother, she kept a donkey
To carry to the mart her crockery ware,
And when that donkey look'd me in the face,
His face was sad ! and you are sad, my public !

Joy should be yours : this tenth day of October
Again assembles us in Drury Lane.
Long wept my eye to see the timber planks
That hid our ruins; many a day I cried,
"Ah me ! I fear they never will rebuild it !"
Till on one eve, one joyful Monday eve,
As along Charles Street I prepared to walk,
Just at the corner, by the pastry-cook's,
I heard a trowel tick against a brick.
I look'd me up, and straight a parapet
Uprose at least seven inches o'er the planks.
"Joy to thee, Drury !" to myself I said :
"He of Blackfriars Road who hymn'd thy downfall
In loud hosannahs, and who prophesied
That flames, like those from prostrate Solyma,
Would scorch the hand that ventured to rebuild thee,
Has proved a lying prophet." From that hour,
As leisure offer'd, close to Mr. Spring's
Box-office door, I've stood and eyed the builders.
They had a plan to render less their labours ;
Workmen in elder times would mount a ladder
With hodded heads, but these stretch'd forth a pole
From the wall's pinnacle, they placed a pulley
Athwart the pole, a rope athwart the pulley ;
To this a basket dangled ; mortar and bricks
Thus freighted, swung securely to the top,
And in the empty basket workmen twain
Precipitate, unhurt, accosted earth.

Oh ! 'twas a goodly sound to hear the people
Who watch'd the work, express their various thoughts !
While some believ'd it never would be finish'd,
Some on the contrary believ'd it would.

I've heard our front that faces Drury Lane
Much criticis'd; they say 'tis vulgar brick-work,
A mimic manufactory of floor-cloth.
One of the morning papers wish'd that front
Cemented like the front in Brydges Street ;
As it now looks they call it Wyatt's Mermaid,
A handsome woman with a fish's tail.

White is the steeple of St. Bride's in Fleet Street,
The Albion (as its name denotes) is white ;
Morgan and Saunders' shop for chairs and tables
Gleams like a snowball in the setting sun ;
White is Whitehall.   But not St. Bride's in Fleet Street,
The spotless Albion, Morgan, no, nor Saunders,
Nor white Whitehall is white as Drury's face.

Oh, Mr. Whitbread ! fie upon you, sir !
I think you should have built a colonnade ;
When tender Beauty, looking for her coach,
Protrudes her gloveless hand, perceives the shower,
And draws the tippet closer round her throat.
Perchance her coach stands half a dozen off,
And, ere she mounts the step, the oozing mud
Soaks thro' her pale kid slipper.   On the morrow
She coughs at breakfast, and her gruff papa
Cries, " There you go ! this comes of playhouses ! "
To build no portico is penny wise :
Heaven grant it prove not in the end pound foolish !

Hail to thee, Drury ! Queen of Theatres !
What is the Regency in Tottenham Street,
The Royal Amphitheatre of Arts,
Astley's Olympic, or the Sans Pareil,
Compar'd with thee ? Yet when I view thee push'd
Back from the narrow street that christen'd thee,
I know not why they call thee Drury Lane.

Amid the freaks that modern fashion sanctions,
It grieves me much to see live animals
Brought on the stage. Grimaldi has his rabbit,
Laurent his cat, and Bradbury his pig ;
Fie on such tricks ! Johnson, the machinist
Of former Drury, imitated life
Quite to the life. The elephant in Blue Beard,

Stuff'd by his hand, wound round his lithe proboscis,
As spruce as he who roar'd in Padmanaba.
Nought born on earth should die.   On hackney stands
I reverence the coachman who cries " Gee,"
And spares the lash.   When I behold a spider
Prey on a fly, a magpie on a worm,
Or view a butcher with horn-handle knife
Slaughter a tender lamb as dead as mutton,
Indeed, indeed, I'm very, very sick !   [*Exit hastily.*

DRURY LANE HUSTINGS.

A NEW HALFPENNY BALLAD.

BY A PIC-NIC POET.

This is the very age of promise. To promise is most courtly and fashion-able.   Performance is a kind of will or testament, which argues a great sickness in his judgment that makes it.—TIMON OF ATHENS.

To be sung by MR. JOHNSTONE *in the character of*
LOONEY M'TWOLTER.

I.

" MR. JACK, your address," says the prompter to me,
So I gave him my card—" No, that a'nt it," says he,
" 'Tis your public address."   " Oh !" says I, " never fear,
If address you are bother'd for, only look here."
                              [*Puts on hat affectedly.*
                              Tol de rol lol, &c.

II.

With Drurys for sartain we'll never have done,
We've built up another, and yet there's but one ;
The old one was best, yet I'd say, if I durst,
The new one is better—the last is the first.
                              Tol de rol, &c.

III.

These pillars are called by a Frenchified word,
A something that's jumbled of antique and verd,
The boxes may show us some verdant antiques,
Some bold harridans who beplaster their cheeks.
                              Tol de rol, &c.

IV.

Only look how high Tragedy, Comedy, stick,
Lest their rivals, the horses, should give them a kick !
If you will not descend when our authors beseech ye,
You'll stop there for life, for I'm sure they can't reach ye.
Tol de rol, &c.

V.

Each one shilling god within reach of a nod is,
And plain are the charms of each gallery goddess,
You, brandy-faced Moll, don't be looking askew,
When I talked of a goddess I didn't mean you.
Tol de rol, &c

VI.

Our stage is so prettily fashion'd for viewing,
The whole house can see what the whole house is doing.
'Tis just like the hustings, we kick up a bother,
But saying is one thing and doing's another.
Tol de rol, &c.

VII.

We've many new houses, and some of them rum ones,
But the newest of all is the new House of Commons,
'Tis a rickety sort of a bantling I'm told,
It will die of old age when it's seven years old.
Tol de rol, &c.

VIII.

As I don't know on whom the election will fall,
I move in return for returning them all ;
But for fear Mr. Speaker my meaning should miss,
The house that I wish 'em to sit in is this.
Tol de rol, &c.

IX.

Let us cheer our great Commoner, but for whose aid
We all should have gone with short commons to bed,
And since he has saved all the fat from the fire,
I move that the House be call'd Whitbread's Entire.
Tol de rol, &c.

ARCHITECTURAL ATOMS.

TRANSLATED BY DR. B.

Lege, Dick, Lege!—JOSEPH ANDREWS.

To be recited by the Translator's Son.

AWAY, fond dupes ! who smit with sacred lore,
Mosaic dreams in Genesis explore,
Dote with Copernicus, or darkling stray
With Newton, Ptolemy, or Tycho Brahe :
To you I sing not, for I sing of truth,
Primæval systems, and creation's youth ;
Such as of old, with magic wisdom fraught,
Inspired Lucretius to the Latians taught.

I sing how casual bricks, in airy climb,
Encounter'd casual horse-hair, casual lime ;
How rafters borne through wondering clouds elate,
Kiss'd in their slope blue elemental slate,
Clasp'd solid beams in chance-directed fury,
And gave to birth our renovated Drury.
Thee, son of Jove, whose sceptre was confessed,
Where fair Œolia springs from Tethys' breast :
Thence on Olympus 'mid Celestials placed,
God of the winds, and Ether's boundless waste,
Thee I invoke ! Oh, *puff* my bold design,
Prompt the bright thought, and swell the harmonious line;
Uphold my pinions, and my verse inspire
With Winsor's patent gas, or wind of fire,
In whose pure blaze thy embryo form enroll'd,
The dark enlightens, and enchafes the cold.

But while I court thy gifts, be mine to shun
The deprecated prize Ulysses won ;
Who sailing homeward from thy breezy shore,
The prison'd winds in skins of parchment bore :—
Speeds the fleet bark, till o'er the billowy green
The azure heights of Ithaca are seen ;
But while with favouring gales her way she wins,
His curious comrades ope the mystic skins :
When lo ! the rescued winds, with boisterous sweep,
Roar to the clouds, and lash the rocking deep;
Heaves the smote vessel in the howling blast,
Splits the stretch'd sail, and cracks the tottering mast.

Launch'd on a plank, the buoyant hero rides
Where ebon Afric stems the sable tides,
While his duck'd comrades o'er the ocean fly,
And sleep not in the whole skins they untie.

So when to raise the wind some lawyer tries,
Mysterious skins of parchment meet our eyes.
On speed the smiling suit, " Pleas of our Lord
The King " shine jetty on the wide record :
Nods the prunella'd bar, attornies smile,
And siren jurors flatter to beguile ;
Till stript—nonsuited—he is doom'd to toss
In legal shipwreck, and redeemless loss ;
Lucky, if, like Ulysses, he can keep
His head above the waters of the deep.

Æolian monarch ! Emperor of Puffs !
We modern sailors dread not thy rebuffs ;
See to thy golden shore promiscuous come
Quacks for the lame, the blind, the deaf, the dumb ;
Fools are their bankers—a prolific line,
And every mortal malady's a mine.
Each sly Sangrado, with his poisonous pill,
Flies to the printer's devil with his bill,
Whose Midas touch can gild his asses' ears,
And load a knave with folly's rich arrears.
And lo ! a second miracle is thine,
For sloe-juiced water stands transform'd to wine.
Where Day and Martin's patent blacking roll'd,
Burst from the vase Pactolian streams of gold ;
Laugh the sly wizards glorying in their stealth,
Quit the black art, and loll in lazy wealth.
See Britain's Algerines, the Lottery fry,
Win annual tribute by the annual lie.
Aided by thee—but whither do I stray ?
Court, city, borough, own thy sovereign sway :
An age of puffs the age of gold succeeds,
And windy bubbles are the spawn it breeds.

If such thy power, O hear the Muse's prayer !
Swell thy loud lungs, and wave thy wings of air ;
Spread, viewless giant, all thy arms of mist
Like windmill sails to bring the poet grist ;
As erst thy roaring son with eddying gale
Whirl'd Orithyia from her native vale—
So, while Lucretian wonders I rehearse,
Augusta's sons shall patronize my verse.

I sing of Atoms, whose creative brain,
With eddying impulse, built new Drury Lane;
Not to the labours of subservient man,
To no young Wyatt appertains the plan;
We mortals stalk, like horses in a mill,
· Impassive media of Atomic will;
Ye stare! then truth's broad talisman discern—
'Tis Demonstration speaks.—Attend and learn!

From floating elements in chaos hurl'd,
Self-form'd of atoms, sprang the infant world.
No great First Cause inspired the happy plot,
But all was matter, and no matter what.
Atoms, attracted by some law occult,
Settling in spheres, the globe was the result;
Pure child of Chance, which still directs the ball,
As rotatory atoms rise or fall.
In ether launch'd, the peopled bubble floats,
A mass of particles and confluent motes,
So nicely pois'd, that if one atom flings
Its weight away, aloft the planet springs,
And wings its course thro' realms of boundless space,
Outstripping comets in eccentric race.
Add but one atom more, it sinks outright
Down to the realms of Tartarus and night.
What waters melt or scorching fires consume,
In different forms their being reassume;
Hence can no change arise, except in name,
For weight and substance ever are the same.

Thus with the flames that from old Drury rise,
Its elements primæval sought the skies,
There, pendulous to wait the happy hour,
When new attractions should restore their power.
So in this procreant theatre elate,
Echoes unborn their future life await;
Here embryo sounds in ether lie conceal'd,
Like words in northern atmosphere congeal'd.
Here many a fœtus laugh and half encore
Clings to the roof, or creeps along the floor.
By puffs concipient some in ether flit,
And soar in bravos from the thundering pit;
Some forth on ticket nights from tradesmen break,
To mar the actor they design to make;
While some this mortal life abortive miss,
Crush'd by a groan, or strangled by a hiss.
So, when "dog's-meat" re-echoes through the streets,
Rush sympathetic dogs from their retreats,

Beam with bright blaze their supplicating eyes,
Sink their hind-legs, ascend their joyful cries;
Each, wild with hope, and maddening to prevail,
Points the pleased ear, and wags the expectant tail.

Ye fallen bricks ! in Drury's fire calcined,
Since doom'd to slumber, couch'd upon the wind,
Sweet was the hour, when tempted by your freaks,
Congenial trowels smooth'd your yellow cheeks.
Float dulcet serenades upon the ear,
Bends every atom from its ruddy sphere,
Twinkles each eye, and, peeping from its veil,
Marks in the adverse crowd its destined male.
The oblong beauties clap their hands of grit,
And brick-dust titterings on the breezes flit;
Then down they rush in amatory race,
Their dusty bridegrooms eager to embrace.
Some choose old lovers, some decide for new,
But each, when fix'd, is to her station true.
Thus various bricks are made as tastes invite,
The red, the grey, the dingy, or the white.

Perhaps some half-baked rover, frank and free,
To alien beauty bends the lawless knee,
But of unhallow'd fascinations sick,
Soon quits his Cyprian for his married brick;
The Dido atom calls and scolds in vain,
No crisp Æneas soothes the widow's pain.

So in Cheapside, what time Aurora peeps,
A mingled noise of dustmen, milk, and sweeps,
Falls on the housemaid's ear; amaz'd she stands,
Then opes the door with cinder-sabled hands,
And "matches" calls. The dustman, bubbled flat,
Thinks 'tis for him, and doffs his fan-tail'd hat;
The milkman, whom her second cries assail,
With sudden sink, unyokes the clinking pail;
Now louder grown, by turns she screams and weeps; ·
Alas ! her screaming only brings the sweeps.
Sweeps but put out—she wants to raise a flame,
And calls for matches, but 'tis still the same.
Atoms and housemaids ! mark the moral true,
If once ye go astray, no *match* for you !

As atoms in one mass united mix,
So bricks attraction feel for kindred bricks;
Some in the cellar view, perchance, on high,
Fair chimney chums on beds of mortar lie;

Enamour'd of the sympathetic clod,
Leaps the red bridegroom to the labourer's hod,
And up the ladder bears the workman, taught
To think he bears the bricks —mistaken thought !
A proof behold—if near the top they find
The nymphs or broken corner'd, or unkind,
Back to the bottom leaping with a bound,
They bear their bleeding carriers to the ground.

So legends tell, along the lofty hill
Paced the twin heroes, gallant Jack and Jill ;
On trudged the Gemini to reach the rail
That shields the well's top from the expectant pail,
When ah ! Jack falls ; and, rolling in the rear,
Jill feels the attraction of his kindred sphere ;
Head over heels begins his toppling track,
Throws sympathetic somersets with Jack,
And at the mountain's base, bobbs plump against him,
  whack !

Ye living atoms, who unconscious sit,
Jumbled by chance in gallery, box, and pit,
For you no Peter opes the fabled door,
No churlish Charon plies the shadowy oar ;—
Breathe but a space, and Boreas' casual sweep
Shall bear your scatter'd corses o'er the deep,
To gorge the greedy elements, and mix
With water, marl, and clay, and stones and sticks ;
While, charged with fancied souls, sticks, stones and clay,
Shall take your seats, and hiss or clap the play.

O happy age ! when convert Christians read
No sacred writings but the Pagan creed ;
O happy age ! when spurning Newton's dreams,
Our poet's sons recite Lucretian themes,
Abjure the idle systems of their youth,
And turn again to atoms and to truth.
O happier still ! when England's dauntless dames,
Awed by no chaste alarms, no latent shames,
The bard's fourth book unblushingly peruse,
And learn the rampant lessons of the stews !

All hail, Lucretius, renovated sage !
Unfold the modest mystics of thy page ;
Return no more to thy sepulchral shelf,
But live, kind bard,—that I may live myself !

THEATRICAL ALARM BELL.

By the Editor of the M. P.

Bounce, Jupiter, bounce !—O'Hara.

LADIES AND GENTLEMEN,

As it is now the universally-admitted, and indeed pretty-generally-suspected aim of Mr. Whitbread and the infamous, bloodthirsty, and, in fact, illiberal faction to which he belongs, to burn to the ground this free and happy Protestant city, and establish himself in St. James's Palace, his fellow committee-men have thought it their duty to watch the principles of a theatre built under his auspices. The information they have received from undoubted authority, particularly from an old fruit-woman who had turned king's evidence, and whose name for obvious reasons we forbear to mention, though we have had it some weeks in our possession, has induced them to introduce various reforms : not such reforms as the vile faction clamour for, meaning thereby revolution, but such reforms as are necessary to preserve the glorious constitution of the only free, happy, and prosperous country now left upon the face of the earth. From the valuable and authentic source above alluded to, we have learnt that a sanguinary plot has been formed by some united Irishmen, combined with a gang of Luddites, and a special committee sent over by the Pope at the instigation of the beastly Corsican fiend, for destroying all the loyal part of the audience on the anniversary of that deeply-to-be-abhorred and highly-to-be-blamed stratagem, the gunpowder plot, which falls this year on Thursday, the 5th of November. The whole is under the direction of a delegated committee of O.P.'s, whose treasonable exploits at Covent Garden you all recollect, and all of whom would have been hung from the chandeliers at that time but for the mistaken lenity of government. At a given signal a well-known O.P. was to cry out from the gallery, "Nosey ! Music !" whereupon all the O.P.'s were to produce from their inside pockets a long pair of shears, edged with felt to prevent their making any noise, manufactured expressly by a wretch at Birmingham, one of Mr. Brougham's evidences, and now in custody. With these they were to cut off the heads of all the loyal N.P.'s in the house, without distinction of sex or age. At the signal, similarly given, of " Throw him over," which it now appears always alluded to the overthrow of our never-sufficiently-enough-to-be-deeply-and-universally-to-be-venerated constitution, all the heads of the N.P.'s were to be thrown at the fiddlers, to prevent their appearing in evidence, or perhaps as a false and illiberal insinuation that they have no heads of their own. All that we know of the further designs of these incendiaries is, that they are by-a-great-deal-too-much too-horrible-to-be-mentioned.

The manager has acted with his usual promptitude on this trying occasion. He has contracted for 300 tons of gunpowder, which are at this moment placed in a small barrel under the pit, and a descendant of Guy Faux, assisted by Colonel Congreve, has undertaken to blow up the house, when necessary, in so novel and ingenious a manner, that every O.P. shall be annihilated, while not a whisker of the N.P.'s shall be singed. This strikingly displays the advantages of loyalty and attachment to government. Several other hints have been taken from the theatrical regulations of the not-a-bit-the-less-on-that-account-to-be-universally-execrated monster Bonaparte. A park of artillery, provided with chain-shot, is to be stationed on the stage, and play upon the audience in case of any indication of misplaced applause or popular discontent (which accounts for the large space between the curtain and the lamps) ; and the public will participate our satisfaction in learning that the indecorous custom of standing up with the hat on is to be abolished, as the Bow Street officers are provided with daggers, and have orders to stab all such persons to the heart, and send their bodies to Surgeons' Hall ; gentlemen who cough are only to be slightly wounded. Fruit-women bawling "Bill of the Play" are to be forthwith shot, for which purpose soldiers will be stationed in the slips, and ball-cartridge is to be served out with the lemonade. If any of the spectators happen to sneeze or spit they are to be transported for life, and any person who is so tall as to prevent another seeing, is to be dragged out and sent on board the tender, or, by an instrument taken out of the pocket of Procrustes, to be forthwith cut shorter, either at the head or foot, according as his own convenience may dictate.

Thus, ladies and gentlemen, have the committee, through my medium, set forth the not-in-a-hurry-to-be-paralleled plan they have adopted for preserving order and decorum within the walls of their magnificent edifice. Nor have they, while attentive to their own concerns, by any means overlooked those of the cities of London and Westminster. Finding, on enumeration, that they have with a with-two-hands-and-one-tongue-to-be-applauded liberality, contracted for more gunpowder than they want, they have parted with the surplus to the mattock-carrying and hustings-hammering high bailiff of Westminster, who has, with his own shovel, dug a large hole in the front of the parish church of St. Paul, Covent Garden, that, upon the least symptom of ill-breeding in the mob at the general election, the whole of the market may be blown into the air. This, ladies and gentlemen, may at first make provisions *rise*, but we pledge the credit of our theatre that they will soon *fall* again, and people be supplied as usual with vegetables in the in-general-strewed-with-cabbage-stalks-but-on-Saturday-night-lighted-up-with-lamps market of Covent Garden.

I should expatiate more largely on the other advantages of the glorious constitution of these by-the-whole-of-Europe-envied realms, but I am called away to take an account of the ladies, and other artificial flowers, at a fashionable rout, of which a full and particular account will hereafter appear. For the present, my fashionable intelligence is scanty, on account of the opening of Drury Lane; and the ladies and gentlemen who honour me with their attention, will not be surprised if they find nothing under my usual head!

THE THEATRE.

By the Rev. G. C.

Nil intentatum nostri liquêre poetæ,
Nec minimum meruère decus, vestigia Græca
Ausi deserere, et celebrare domestica facta.—HORAT.

A PREFACE OF APOLOGIES.

IF the following poem should be fortunate enough to be selected for the opening Address, a few words of explanation may be deemed necessary, on my part, to avert invidious misrepresentation. The animadversion I have thought it right to make on the noise created by tuning the orchestra, will, I hope, give no lasting remorse to any of the gentlemen employed in the band. It is to be desired that they would keep their instruments ready tuned, and strike off at once. This would be an accommodation to many well-meaning persons who frequent the theatre, who not being blest with the ear of St. Cecilia, mistake the tuning for the overture, and think the latter concluded before it is begun.

> "one fiddle will
> Give, half-ashamed, a tiny flourish still—"

was originally written "one hautboy will," but having providentially been informed, when this poem was upon the point of being sent off, that there is but one hautboy in the band, I averted the storm of popular and managerial indignation from the head of its blower; as it now stands, "one fiddle" among many, the faulty individual will, I hope, escape detection. The story of the flying playbill is calculated to expose a practice, much too common, of pinning playbills to the cushions, insecurely, and frequently, I fear, not pinning them at all. If these lines save one playbill only from the fate I have recorded,

I shall not deem my labour ill employed. The concluding episode of Patrick Jennings, glances at the boorish fashion of wearing the hat in the one-shilling gallery. Had Jennings thrust his between his feet at the commencement of the play, he might have leaned forward with impunity, and the catastrophe I relate would not have occurred. The line of handkerchiefs formed to enable him to recover his loss, is purposely so crossed in texture and materials, as to mislead the reader in respect of the real owner of any one of them. For, in the satirical view of life and manners, which I occasionally present, my clerical profession has taught me how extremely improper it would be by any allusion, however slight, to give any uneasiness, however trivial, to any individual, however foolish or wicked.

G. C.

THE THEATRE.

Interior of a theatre described.—Pit gradually fills.—The check-taker.—Pit full.—The orchestra tuned.—One fiddle rather dilatory.—Is reproved—and repents.—Evolutions of a playbill.—Its final settlement on the spikes.—The gods taken to task—and why.—Motley group of playgoers.—Holywell Street, St. Pancras.—Emanuel Jennings binds his son apprentice.—Not in London—and why.—Episode of the hat.

'TIS sweet to view, from half-past five to six,
Our long wax-candles, with short cotton wicks,
Touch'd by the lamplighter's Promethean art,
Start into light and make the lighter start ;
To see red Phœbus through the gallery pane
Tinge with his beam the beams of Drury Lane,
While gradual parties fill our widen'd pit,
And gape, and gaze, and wonder, ere they sit.

At first, while vacant seats give choice and ease,
Distant or near, they settle where they please ;
But when the multitude contracts the span,
And seats are rare, they settle where they can.

Now the full benches, to late comers, doom
No room for standing, miscall'd *standing-room.*

Hark ! the check-taker moody silence breaks,
And bawling " Pit full," gives the check he takes ;
Yet onward still, the gathering numbers cram,
Contending crowders shout the frequent damn,
And all is bustle, squeeze, row, jabbering, jam.

See to their desks Apollo's sons repair ;
Swift rides the rosin o'er the horse's hair ;

In unison their various tones to tune
Murmurs the hautboy, growls the hoarse bassoon ;
In soft vibration sighs the whispering lute,
Tang goes the harpsichord, too-too the flute,
Brays the loud trumpet, squeaks the fiddle sharp,
Winds the French-horn, and twangs the tingling harp ;
Till, like great Jove, the leader, figuring in,
Attunes to order the chaotic din.
Now all seems hush'd—but no, one fiddle will
Give, half-ashamed, a tiny flourish still ;
Foil'd in his crash, the leader of the clan
Reproves with frowns the dilatory man ;
Then on his candlestick thrice taps his bow,
Nods a new signal, and away they go.
Perchance, while pit and gallery cry, " Hats off,"
And awed Consumption checks his chided cough,
Some giggling daughter of the Queen of Love
Drops, reft of pin, her playbill from above ;
Like Icarus, while laughing galleries clap,
Soars, ducks, and dives in air the printed scrap ;
But, wiser far than he, combustion fears,
And, as it flies, eludes the chandeliers ;
Till sinking gradual, with repeated twirl,
It settles, curling, on a fiddler's curl ;
Who from his powder'd pate the intruder strikes,
And, for mere malice, sticks it on the spikes.

Say, why these Babel strains from Babel tongues ?
Who's that calls " Silence " with such leathern lungs ?
He who, in quest of quiet, " silence " hoots,
Is apt to make the hubbub he imputes.

What various swains our motley walls contain !
Fashion from Moorfields, honour from Chick Lane ;
Bankers from Paper Buildings here resort,
Bankrupts from Golden Square and Riches Court ;
From the Haymarket canting rogues in grain,
Culls from the Poultry, sots from Water Lane ;
The lottery cormorant, the auction shark,
The full-price master, and the half-price clerk ;
Boys who long linger at the gallery door,
With pence twice five, they want but twopence more,
Till some Samaritan the twopence spares,
And sends them jumping up the gallery stairs.

Critics we boast who ne'er their malice baulk,
But talk their minds, we wish they'd mind their talk ;
Big-worded bullies, who by quarrels live,
Who give the lie, and tell the lie they give ;

Jews from St. Mary Axe, for jobs so wary,
That for old clothes they'd even axe St. Mary;
And bucks with pockets empty as their pate,
Lax in their gaiters, laxer in their gait,
Who oft, when we our house lock up, carouse
With tippling tipstaves in a lock-up house.

Yet here, as elsewhere, chance can joy bestow,
Where scowling fortune seem'd to threaten woe.

John Richard William Alexander Dwyer
Was footman to Justinian Stubbs, Esquire;
But when John Dwyer listed in the Blues,
Emanuel Jennings polish'd Stubbs's shoes.
Emanuel Jennings brought his youngest boy
Up as a corn-cutter, a safe employ;
In Holywell Street, St. Pancras, he was bred
(At number twenty-seven, it is said),
Facing the pump, and near the Granby's Head:
He would have bound him to some shop in town,
But with a premium he could not come down;
Pat was the urchin's name, a red-hair'd youth,
Fonder of purl and skittle-grounds than truth.

Silence, ye gods! to keep your tongues in awe,
The Muse shall tell an accident she saw.

Pat Jennings in the upper gallery sat,
But, leaning forward, Jennings lost his hat;
Down from the gallery the beaver flew,
And spurn'd the one to settle in the two.
How shall he act? Pay at the gallery door
Two shillings for what cost, when new, but four?
Or till half-price, to save his shilling, wait,
And gain his hat again at half-past eight?
Now, while his fears anticipate a thief,
John Mullins whispers, "Take my handkerchief."
"Thank you," cries Pat, "but one won't make a line;"
"Take mine," cried Wilson, and cried Stokes, "take mine.'
A motley cable soon Pat Jennings ties,
Where Spitalfields with real India vies.
Like Iris' bow, down darts the painted hue,
Starr'd, striped, and spotted, yellow, red, and blue,
Old calico, torn silk, and muslin new.
George Green below, with palpitating hand,
Loops the last 'kerchief to the beaver's band.
Up soars the prize; the youth, with joy unfeign'd,
Regain'd the felt, and felt what he regain'd,
While to the applauding galleries grateful Pat
Made a low bow, and touch'd the ransom'd hat.

To the Managing Committee of the New Drury Lane
Theatre.

GENTLEMEN,

Happening to be wool-gathering at the foot of Mount Parnassus, I was suddenly seized with a violent travestie in the head. The first symptoms I felt were several triple rhymes floating about my brain, accompanied by a singing in my throat, which quickly communicated itself to the ears of everybody about me, and made me a burthen to my friends, and a torment to Doctor Apollo, three of whose favourite servants, that is to say, Macbeth, his butcher, Mrs. Haller, his cook, and George Barnwell, his book-keeper, I waylaid in one of my fits of insanity, and mauled after a very frightful fashion. In this woeful crisis I accidentally heard of your invaluable New Patent Hissing Pit, which cures every disorder incident to Grub Street. I send you enclosed a more detailed specimen of my case; if you could mould it into the shape of an Address to be said or sung on the first night of your performance, I have no doubt that I should feel the immediate effects of your invaluable New Patent Hissing Pit, of which they tell me one hiss is a dose.

I am, &c.

MOMUS MEDLAR.

CASE No. I.

MACBETH.

Enter MACBETH *in a red nightcap.* PAGE *following*
with a torch.

GO, boy, and thy good mistress tell
(She knows that my purpose is cruel),
I'd thank her to tingle her bell,
As soon as she's heated my gruel.
Go, get thee to bed and repose,
To sit up so late is a scandal ;
But ere you have ta'en off your clothes,
Be sure that you put out that candle.
        Ri fol de rol tol de rol lol.

My stars, in the air here's a knife !
I'm sure it cannot be a hum ;
I'll catch at the handle, add's life,
And then I shall not cut my thumb.

I've got him !—no, at him again,
Come, come, I'm not fond of these jokes :
This must be some blade of the brain :
Those witches are given to hoax.

I've one in my pocket, I know,
My wife left on purpose behind her,
She bought this of Teddy-high-ho,
The poor Caledonian grinder.
I see thee again ! o'er thy middle
Large drops of red blood now are spill'd,
Just as much as to say diddle diddle,
Good Duncan pray come and be kill'd.

It leads to his chamber, I swear ;
I tremble and quake every joint ;
No dog at the scent of a hare
Ever yet made a cleverer point.
Ah, no ! 'twas a dagger of straw—
Give me blinkers to save me from starting ;
The knife that I thought that I saw,
Was nought but my eye, Betty Martin.

Now o'er this terrestrial hive
A life paralytic is spread,
For while the one half is alive,
The other is sleepy and dead.
King Duncan in grand majesty
Has got my state bed for a snooze,
I've lent him my slippers, so I
May certainly stand in his shoes.

Blow softly, ye murmuring gales,
Ye feet rouse no echo in walking,
For though a dead man tells no tales,
Dead walls are much given to talking.
This knife shall be in at the death,
I'll stick him, then off safely get.
Cries the world, this could not be Macbeth,
For he'd ne'er stick at anything yet.

Hark, hark, 'tis the signal by goles,
It sounds like a funeral knell :
O hear it not, Duncan, it tolls
To call thee to heaven or hell.
Or if you to heaven won't fly,
But rather prefer Pluto's ether,
Only wait a few years till I die,
And we'll go to the devil together,

Ri fol de rol, &c.

CASE No. II.

THE STRANGER.

WHO has e'er been at Drury must needs know the Stranger,
A wailing old Methodist, gloomy and wan,
A husband suspicious, his wife acted Ranger,
She took to her heels, and left poor Hypochon.
Her martial gallant swore that truth was a libel,
That marriage was thraldom, elopement no sin ;
Quoth she, " I remember the words of my Bible,
My spouse is a Stranger, and I'll take him in."
    With my sentimentalibus lachrymæ roar'em,
    And pathos and bathos delightful to see ;
    And chop and change ribs a-la-mode Germanorum,
    And high diddle ho diddle, pop tweedle dee.

To keep up her dignity, no longer rich enough,
Where was her plate ? why 'twas laid on the shelf.
Her land fuller's earth, and her great riches kitchen stuff,
Dressing the dinner instead of herself.
No longer permitted in diamonds to sparkle,
Now plain Mrs. Haller, of servants the dread,
With a heart full of grief and a pan full of charcoal,
She lighted the company up to their bed.

Incensed at her flight, her poor hubby in dudgeon
Roam'd after his rib in a gig and a pout,
Till, tired with his journey, the peevish curmudgeon,
Sat down and blubber'd just like a church spout.
One day on a bench as dejected and sad he laid,
Hearing a squash, he cried, " Hullo, what's that ? "
'Twas a child of the Count's, in whose service lived Adelaide,
Soused in the river and squalled like a cat.

Having drawn his young excellence up to the bank, it
Appear'd that himself was all dripping, I swear,
No wonder he soon became dry as a blanket,
Exposed as he was to the Count's *son* and *heir*.
" Dear sir," quoth the Count, " in reward of your valour,
To show that my gratitude is not mere talk,
You shall eat a beefsteak which my cook, Mrs. Haller,
Cut from the rump with her own knife and fork."

Behold, now the Count gave the Stranger a dinner,
With gunpowder tea, which you know brings a ball,
And, thin as he was, that he might not grow thinner,
He made of the Stranger no stranger at all ;

At dinner fair Adelaide brought up a chicken,
A bird that she never had met with before,
But, seeing him, scream'd, and was carried off, kicking,
And he bang'd his nob 'gainst the opposite door.

To finish my tale without roundaboutation,
Young master and missee besieged their papa,
They sung a quartetto in grand blubberation ;
The Stranger cried " Oh ! " Mrs. Haller cried " Ah ! "
Though pathos and sentiment largely are dealt in,
I have no good moral to give in exchange,
For though she as a cook might be given to melting,
The Stranger's behaviour was certainly strange,
   With his sentimentalibus lachrymæ roar'em,
   And pathos and bathos delightful to see,
   And chop and change ribs a-la-mode Germanorum,
   And high diddle ho diddle, pop tweedle dee.

CASE No. III.

GEORGE BARNWELL.

GEORGE BARNWELL stood at the shop door,
A customer hoping to find, sir ;
His apron was hanging before,
But the tail of his coat was behind, sir.
A lady so painted and smart,
Cried, " Sir, I've exhausted my stock o' late,
I've got nothing left but a groat,
Could you give me four penn'orth of chocolate ?
   Rum ti, &c.

Her face was rouged up to the eyes,
Which made her look prouder and prouder,
His hair stood on end with surpise,
And hers with pomatum and powder.
The business was soon understood ;
The lady, who wish'd to be more rich,
Cries, " Sweet sir, my name is Milwood,
And I lodge at the Gunner's, in Shoreditch."
   Rum ti, &c.

Now nightly he stole out, good lack,
And into her lodging would pop, sir,
And often forgot to come back,
Leaving master to shut up the shop, sir,

Her beauty his wits did bereave;
Determin'd to be quite the crack O,
He lounged at the Adam and Eve,
And call'd for his gin and tobacco.
　　　　Rum ti, &c.

And now (for the truth must be told)
Though none of a 'prentice should speak ill,
He stole from the till all the gold,
And ate the lump sugar and treacle.
In vain did his master exclaim,
" Dear George, don't engage with that Dragon,
She'll lead you to sorrow and shame,
And leave you the devil a rag on
　　　　Your Rum ti," &c.

In vain he entreats and implores
The weak and incurable ninny,
So kicks him at last out of doors,
And Georgy soon spends his last guinea.
His uncle, whose generous purse
Had often relieved him, as I know,
Now finding him grow worse and worse,
Refused to come down with the rhino.
　　　　Rum ti, &c.

Cried Milwood, whose cruel heart's core,
Was so flinty that nothing could shock it,
" If ye mean to come here any more,
Pray come with more cash in your pocket.
Make nunky surrender his dibs,
Rub his pate with a pair of lead towels,
Or stick a knife into his ribs,
I'll warrant he'll then show some bowels."
　　　　Rum ti, &c.

A pistol he got from his love,
'Twas loaded with powder and bullet,
He trudged off to Camberwell Grove,
But wanted the courage to pull it.
" There's nunky as fat as a hog,
While I am as lean as a lizard ;
Here's at you ! you stingy old dog ! "
And he whips a long knife in his gizzard.
　　　　Rum ti, &c.

All you who attend to my song,
A terrible end of the farce shall see,
If you join the inquisitive throng
That followed poor George to the Marshalsea.

" If Milwood were here, dash my wigs ! "
Quoth he, " I would pummel and lam her well !
Had I stuck to my prunes and my figs,
I ne'er had stuck nunky at Camberwell."
    Rum ti, &c.

Their bodies were never cut down,
For granny relates with amazement,
A witch bore 'em over the town
And hung them on Thorowgood's casement.
The neighbours, I've heard the folks say,
The miracle noisily brag on,
And the shop is to this very day,
The sign of the George and the Dragon.
    Rum ti, &c.

PUNCH'S APOTHEOSIS.

By T. H.

Rhymes the rudders are of verses,
With which, like ships, they steer their courses.—
                HUDIBRAS.

Scene draws, and discovers PUNCH *on a throne surrounded by* LEAR, LADY MACBETH, MACBETH, OTHELLO, GEORGE BARNWELL, HAMLET, GHOST, MACHEATH, JULIET, FRIAR, APOTHECARY, ROMEO, *and* FALSTAFF.—PUNCH *descends, and addresses them in the following*

RECITATIVE.

As manager of horses Mr. Merryman is,
So I with you am master of the ceremonies,—
These grand rejoicings, let me see, how name ye 'em ?
Oh, in Greek lingo 'tis E—pi—thalamium.
October's tenth it is, toss up each hat to-day,
And celebrate with shouts our opening Saturday.
On this great night 'tis settled by our manager,
That we, to please great Johnny Bull, should plan a jeer,
Dance a bang-up theatrical cotillon,
And put on tuneful Pegasus a pillion ;
That every soul, whether or not a cough he has,
May kick like Harlequin, and sing like Orpheus.
So come, ye pupils of Sir John Gallini,
Spin up a teetotum like Angiollini ;
That John and Mrs. Bull from ale and teahouses,
May shout huzza for Punch's Apotheosis !
                [They dance and sing.

.   AIR—"*Sure such a day.*"—TOM THUMB.

Lear. Dance, Regan, dance with Cordelia and Goneril,
'Down the middle, up again, poussette, and cross ;
Stop Cordelia, do not tread upon her heel,
Regan feeds on coltsfoot, and kicks like a horse.
·See, she twists her mutton fists like Molyneux or Beelzebub,
And t'other's clack, who pats her back, is louder far than Hell's
        hubbub.
They tweak my nose, and round it goes, I fear they'll break the
        ridge of it,
Or leave it all just like Vauxhall, with only half the bridge of it.
    Omnes. Round let us bound, for this is Punch's holiday,
Glory to tomfoolery. Huzza ! huzza !
    Lady Macbeth. I kill'd the King, my husband is a heavy dunce,
He left the grooms unmassacred, then massacred the stud,
One loves long gloves, for mittens, like King's evidence,
Let truth with the fingers out, and won't hide blood.
    Macbeth. When spooneys on two knees implore the aid of
        sorcery.
To suit their wicked purposes they quickly put the laws awry,
With Adam I in wife may vie, for none could tell the use of her,
Except to cheapen golden pippins hawk'd about by Lucifer.
    Omnes. Round let us bound, for this is Punch's holiday,
Glory to tomfoolery. Huzza ! huzza !
    Othello. Wife, come to life, forgive what your black lover did,
Spit the feathers from your mouth and munch roast beef ;
Iago he may go and be toss'd in the coverlid,
That smother'd you because you pawn'd my handkerchief.
    Geo. Barnwell. Why, neger, so eager about your rib immacu-
        late?
Milwood shows for hanging us they've got an ugly knack o' late ;
If on beauty stead of duty but one peeper bent he sees,
Satan waits with Dolly baits to hook in us apprentices.
    Omnes. Round let us bound, for this is Punch's holiday,
Glory to tomfoolery. Huzza ! huzza !
    Hamlet. I'm Hamlet in camlet, my ap and perihelia,
The moon can fix which lunatics makes sharp or flat.
I stuck by ill-luck, enamour'd of Ophelia,
Old Polony like a sausage, and exclaim'd, "Rat ! Rat !"
    Ghost. Let Gertrude sup the poisoned cup, no more I'll be an
        actor in
Such sorry food, but drink home-brew'd of Whitbread's manu-
        facturing.
    Macheath. I'll Polly it, and folly it, and dance it quite the
        dandy O,
But as for tunes I have but one, and that is "Drops of Brandy O."

Omnes. Round let us bound, for this is Punch's holiday,
Glory to tomfoolery.   Huzza ! huzza !
   Juliet. I'm Juliet Capulet, who took a dose of hellebore,
A Hell-of-a-bore I found it to put on a pall.
   Friar. And I am the friar who so corpulent a belly bore.
   Apothecary. And that is why poor skinny I have none at all.
   Romeo. I'm the resurrection man of buried bodies amorous.
   Falstaff. I'm fagg'd to death, and out of breath, and am for
      quiet clamorous,
For though my paunch is round and staunch, I ne'er begin to
      fill it ere I
Feel that I have no stomach left for entertainment military.
   Omnes. Round let us bound, for this is Punch's holiday,
Glory to tomfoolery;   Huzza ! huzza !

[Exeunt dancing.

Odes and Addresses to Great People.

(1825.)

———•+•———

ODE TO MR. GRAHAM.

THE AËRONAUT.

Up with me !—up with me into the sky !—
.WORDSWORTH—ON A LARK !

I.

DEAR Graham, whilst the busy crowd,
The vain, the wealthy, and the proud,
  Their meaner flights pursue,
Let us cast off the foolish ties
That bind us to the earth, and rise
  And take a bird's-eye view !

II.

A few more whiffs of my cigar
And then, in Fancy's airy car,
  Have with thee for the skies :
How oft this fragrant smoke upcurl'd
Hath borne me from this little world,
  And all that in it lies !

III.

Away !—away !—the bubble fills—
Farewell to earth and all its hills !—
  We seem to cut the wind !—
So high we mount, so swift we go,
The chimney-tops are far below,
  The Eagle's left behind !

IV.

Ah me! my brain begins to swim!—
The world is growing rather dim;
    The steeples and the trees—
My wife is getting very small!
I cannot see my babe at all!—
    The Dollond, if you please!—

V.

Do, Graham, let me have a quiz,
Lord! what a Lilliput it is,
    That little world of Mogg's!—
Are those the London Docks?—that channel,
The mighty Thames?—a proper kennel
    For that small Isle of Dogs!

VI.

What is that seeming tea-urn there!
That fairy dome, St. Paul's!—I swear,
    Wren must have been a wren!—
And that small stripe?—it cannot be
The City Road!—Good lack? to see
    The little ways of men!

VII.

Little, indeed!—my eyeballs ache
To find a turnpike. I must take
    Their tolls upon my trust!—
And where is mortal labour gone?
Look, Graham, for a little stone
    MacAdamized to dust!

VIII.

Look at the horses!—less than flies!—
Oh, what a waste it was of sighs
    To wish to be a Mayor!
What is the honour?—none at all,
One's honour must be very small
    For such a civic chair!

IX.

And there's Guildhall!—'tis far aloof—
Methinks, I fancy thro' the roof
    Its little guardian Gogs,
Like penny dolls—a tiny show!—
Well,—I must say they're ruled below
    By very little logs!

X.

Oh! Graham, how the upper air
Alters the standards of compare ;
   One of our silken flags
Would cover London all about—
Nay, then—let's even empty out
   Another brace of bags !

XI.

Now for a glass of bright champagne
Above the clouds !—Come, let us drain
   A bumper as we go !
But hold !—for God's sake do not cant
The cork away—unless you want
   To brain your friends below.

XII.

Think ! what a mob of little men
Are crawling just within our ken,
   Like mites upon a cheese !
Pshaw !—how the foolish sight rebukes
Ambitious thoughts !—can there be *Dukes*
   Of *Gloster* such as these !

XIII.

Oh ! what is glory?—what is fame ?
Hark to the little mob's acclaim,
   'Tis nothing but a hum !
A few near gnats would trump as loud
As all the shouting of a crowd
   That has so far to come !

XIV.

Well—they are wise that choose the near,
A few small buzzards in the ear,
   To organs ages hence !—
Ah me, how distance touches all ;
It makes the true look rather small,
   But murders poor pretence.

XV.

" The world recedes !—it disappears !
Heav'n open on my eyes—my ears
   With buzzing noises ring ! "
A fig for Southey's Laureate lore !—
What's Rogers here ?—who cares for Moore
   That hears the angels sing !

K

XVI.

A fig for earth, and all its minions !—
We are above the world's opinions,
    Graham ! we'll have our own !—
Look what a vantage height we've got !—
Now——*do* you think Sir Walter Scott
    Is such a Great Unknown ?

XVII.

Speak up !—or hath he hid his name
To crawl thro' " subways " into fame,
    Like Williams of Cornhill ?—
Speak up, my lad !—when men run small
We'll show what's little in them all,
    Receive it how they will !

XVIII.

Think now of Irving !—shall he preach
The princes down—shall he impeach
    The potent and the rich,
Merely on ethic stilts,—and I
Not moralize at two miles high
    The true didactic pitch !

XIX.

Come :—what d'ye think of Jeffrey, sir ?
Is Gifford such a Gulliver
    In Lilliput's Review,
That like Colossus he should stride
Certain small brazen inches wide
    For poets to pass through ?

XX.

Look down ! the world is but a spot.
Now say—Is Blackwood's *low* or not,
    For all the Scottish tone ?
It shall not weigh us here—not where
The sandy burden's lost in air—
    Our lading—where is't flown !

XXI.

Now,—like you Croly's verse indeed—
In heaven—where one cannot read
    The " Warren " on a wall ?
What think you here of that man's fame ?
'Tho' Jerdan magnified his name,
    To me 'tis very small !

XXII.

And, truly, is there such a spell
In those three letters, L. E. L.,
  To witch a world with song ?
On clouds the Byron did not sit,
Yet dared on Shakespeare's head to spit,
  And say the world was wrong !

XXIII.

And shall not we ? Let's think aloud !
Thus being couch'd upon a cloud,
  Graham, we'll have our eyes !
We felt the great when we were less,
But we'll retort on littleness
  Now we are in the skies.

XXIV.

O Graham, Graham, how I blame
The bastard blush,—the petty shame,
  That used to fret me quite,—
The little sores I cover'd then,
No sores on earth, nor sorrows when
  The world is out of sight !

XXV.

My name is Tims. I am the man
That North's unseen diminish'd clan
  So scurvily abused !
I am the very P. A. Z.
The London's Lion s small pin's head
  So often hath refused !

XXVI.

Campbell—(you cannot see him here)—
Hath scorn'd my *lays :*—do his appear
  Such great eggs from the sky ?
And Longman, and his lengthy Co,
Long, only, in a little Row,
  Have thrust my poems by !

XXVII.

What else ?—I'm poor, and much beset
With petty duns—that is—in debt
  Some grains of golden dust !
But only worth, above, is worth.
What's all the credit of the earth ?
  An inch of cloth on trust !

K 2

XXVIII.

What's Rothschild here, that wealthy man !
Nay, worlds of wealth ?—Oh, if you can
   Spy out,—the *Golden Ball !*
Sure as we rose, all money sank :
What's gold or silver now?—the Bank
   Is gone—the 'Change and all !

XXIX.

What's all the ground-rent of the globe ?—
Oh, Graham, it would worry Job
   To hear its landlords prate !
But after this survey, I think
I'll ne'er be bullied more, nor shrink
   From men of large estate !

XXX.

And less, still less, will I submit
To poor mean acres' worth of wit—
   I that have Heaven's span—
I that like Shakespeare's self may dream
Beyond the very clouds, and seem
   An Universal Man !

XXXI.

Oh, Graham, mark those gorgeous crowds !
Like birds of paradise the clouds
   Are winging on the wind !
But what is grander than their range ?
More lovely than their sunset change ?—
   The free creative mind !

XXXII.

Well ! the Adults' School's in the air !
The greatest men are lesson'd there
   As well as the lessee !
Oh could earth's Ellistons thus small
Behold the greatest stage of all,
   How humbled they would be !

XXXIII.

" Oh would some god the giftie gie 'em,
To see themselves as others see 'em,"
   'Twould much abate their fuss !
If they could think that from the skies
They are as little in our eyes
   As they can think of us !

XXXIV.

Of us ! are *we* gone out of sight ?
Lessen'd ! diminish'd ! vanish'd quite !
  Lost to the tiny town !
Beyond the Eagle's ken—the grope
Of Dollond's longest telescope !
  Graham ! we're going down !

XXXV.

Ah me ! I've touch'd a string that opes
The airy valve !—the gas elopes—
  Down goes our bright balloon !—
Farewell the skies ! the clouds ! I smell
The lower world !   Graham, farewell,
  Man of the silken moon !

XXXVI.

The earth is close ! the City nears—
Like a burnt paper it appears,
  Studded with tiny sparks !
Methinks I hear the distant rout
Of coaches rumbling all about—
  We're close above the Parks !

XXXVII.

I hear the watchmen on their beats,
Hawking the hour about the streets.
  Lord ! what a cruel jar
It is upon the earth to light !
Well—there's the finish of our flight !
  I've smoked my last cigar !

ODE TO MR. M'ADAM.

Let us take to the road !—BEGGAR'S OPERA.

I.

M'ADAM, hail !
Hail, Roadian ! hail, Colossus ! who dost stand
Striding ten thousand turnpikes on the land !
  Oh, universal Leveller ! all hail !
To thee, a good, yet stony-hearted man,
  The kindest one, and yet the flintiest going—
To thee—how much for thy commodious plan,
  Lanark Reformer of the Ruts, is Owing !

The Bristol mail
Gliding o'er ways, hitherto deem'd invincible,
  When carrying patriots now shall never fail
Those of the most "*unshaken* public principle."
    Hail to thee, Scott of Scots !
  Thou northern light, amid those heavy men !
Foe to Stonehenge, yet friend to all beside,
Thou scatter'st flints and favours far and wide,
      From palaces to cots ;
      Dispenser of coagulated good !
      Distributor of granite and of food !
Long may thy fame its even path march on,
      E'en when thy sons are dead !
Best benefactor ! though thou giv'st a stone
      To those who ask for bread !

II.

Thy first great trial in this mighty town
Was, if I rightly recollect, upon
    That gentle hill which goeth
Down from "the County" to the Palace gate,
    And, like a river, thanks to thee, now floweth
Past the Old Horticultural Society,—
The chemist Cobb's, the house of Howell and James,
Where ladies play high shawl and satin games—
      A little *Hell* of lace !
And past the Athénæum, made of late,
      Severs a sweet variety
Of milliners and booksellers who grace
      Waterloo Place,
Making division, the Muse fears and guesses,
'Twixt Mr. Rivington's and Mr. Hessey's.
Thou stood'st thy trial, Mac ! and shav'd the road
From Barber Beaumont's to the King's abode
So well, that paviours threw their rammers by,
Let down their tuck'd shirt-sleeves, and with a sigh
Prepar'd themselves, poor souls, to chip or die !

III.

Next, from the palace to the prison, thou
    Didst go, the highway's watchman, to thy beat,—
    Preventing though the *rattling* in the street,
      Yet kicking up a row,
Upon the stones—ah ! truly watchman-like,
Encouraging thy victims all to strike,
    To further thy own purpose, Adam, daily ;—

Thou hast smooth'd, alas, the path to the Old Bailey !
   And to the stony bowers
Of Newgate, to encourage the approach,
   By caravan or coach,—
Hast strew'd the way with flints as soft as flowers.

IV.

   Who shall dispute thy name !
Insculpt in stone in every street,
   We soon shall greet
Thy trodden down, yet all-unconquer'd fame !
Where'er we take, even at this time, our way,
Nought see we, but mankind in open air,
Hammering thy fame, as Chantrey would not dare ;
   And with a patient care,
Chipping thy immortality all day !
Demosthenes, of old,—that rare old man,—
Prophetically, *follow'd*, Mac ! thy plan :—
   For he, we know
   (History says so),
Put *pebbles* in his mouth when he would speak
   The *smoothest* Greek !

V.

It is "impossible, and cannot be,"
   But that thy genius hath,
   Beside the turnpike, many another path
Trod, to arrive at popularity.
O'er Pegasus, perchance, thou hast thrown a thigh,
Nor ridden a roadster only ;—mighty Mac !
And 'faith I'd swear, when on that winged hack,
Thou hast observ'd the highways in the sky !
Is the path up Parnassus rough and steep,
   And "hard to climb," as Dr. B. would say ?
Dost think it best for sons of song to keep
   The noiseless *tenor* of their way ? (see Gray).
What line of road *should* poets take to bring
   Themselves unto those waters, lov'd the first !—
Those waters which can wet a man to sing !
   Which, like thy fame, "from *granite* basins burst,
   Leap into life, and, sparkling, woo the thirst ?"

VI.

That thou'rt a proser, even thy birthplace might
Vouchsafe ;—and Mr. Cadell *may*, God wot,
Have paid thee many a pound for many a blot,—

Cadell's a wayward wight !
Although no Walter, still thou art a Scot,
And I can throw, I think, a little light
Upon some works thou hast written for the town,—
And publish'd, like a Lilliput Unknown !
  " Highways and Byeways " is thy book, no doubt
          (One whole edition's out),
            And next, for it is fair
              That Fame,
Seeing her children, should confess she had 'em ;—
" Some *Passages* from the life of Adam Blair "—
      (Blair is a Scottish name),
What are they, but thy own good roads, M'Adam ?

VII.

          O ! indefatigable labourer
In the paths of men ! when thou shalt die, 'twill be
A mark of thy surpassing industry,
    That of the monument, which men shall rear
Over thy most inestimable bone,
Thou didst thy very self lay the first stone !
Of a right ancient line thou comest,—through
Each crook and turn we trace the unbroken clue,
Until we see thy sire before our eyes,
Rolling his gravel walks in Paradise !
But he, our great Mac Parent, err'd, and ne'er
          Have our walks since been fair !
Yet Time, who, like the merchant, lives on 'Change,
For ever varying, through his varying range,
    · Time maketh all things even !
In this strange world, turning beneath high heaven !
  He hath redeem'd the Adams, and contriv'd—
      (How are Time's wonders hiv'd !)
  In pity to mankind, and to befriend 'em—
      (Time is above all praise)
That he, who first did make our evil ways,
Reborn in Scotland, should be first to mend 'em !

ODE TO THE GREAT UNKNOWN.

O breathe not his name!—MOORE.

I.

THOU Great Unknown!
I do not mean Eternity nor Death,
    That vast incog!
For I suppose thou hast a living breath,
Howbeit we know not from whose lung 'tis blown,
    Thou man of fog!
Parent of many children—child of none!
    Nobody's son!
Nobody's daughter—but a parent still!
Still but an ostrich parent of a batch
Of orphan eggs,—left to the world to hatch.
    Superlative Nil!
A vox and nothing more,—yet not Vauxhall;
A head in papers, yet without a curl!
    Not the Invisible Girl!
No hand—but a hand-writing on a wall—
    A popular nonentity,
Still call'd the same,—without identity!
    A lark, heard out of sight,—
A nothing shin'd upon,—invisibly bright,
    " Dark with excess of light!"
Constable's literary John-a-nokes—
The real Scottish wizard—to no which,
      Nobody—in a niche;
      Every one's hoax!
      Maybe Sir Walter Scott—
        Perhaps not!
Why dost thou so conceal and puzzle curious folks?

II.

Thou—whom the second-sighted never saw,
The Master Fiction of fictitious history!
    Chief Nong tong paw!
No mister in the world—and yet all mystery!
The " tricksy spirit" of a Scotch Cock Lane—
A *novel* Junius puzzling the world's brain—
A man of magic—yet no talisman!
A man of clair obscure—not him o' the moon!
    A star—at noon.
A non-descriptus in a caravan.
A private—of no corps—a northern light

In a dark lantern,—Bogie in a crape—
　　A figure—but no shape ;
　　A vizor—and no knight ;
The real abstract hero of the age ;
The staple Stranger of the stage ;
A Some One made in every man's presumption,
Frankenstein's monster—but instinct with gumption ;
Another strange state captive in the north,
　　Constable-guarded in an iron mask—
　　　　Still let me ask,
　　Hast thou no silver platter,
No door-plate, or no card—or some such matter,
To scrawl a name upon, and then cast forth ?

III.

Thou Scottish Barmecide, feeding the hunger
Of Curiosity with airy gammon ?
　　Thou mystery-monger,
Dealing it out like middle cut of salmon,
That people buy and can't make head or tail of it
(Howbeit that puzzle never hurts the sale of it) ;
Thou chief of authors mystic and abstractical,
That lay their proper bodies on the shelf—
Keeping thyself so truly to thyself,
　　Thou Zimmerman made practical !
Thou secret fountain of a Scottish style,
　　　　That, like the Nile,
Hideth its source wherever it is bred,
　　But still keeps disemboguing
　　(Not disembroguing)
Thro' such broad sandy mouths without a head !
Thou disembodied author—not yet dead,—
The whole world's literary Absentee !
　　Ah ! wherefore hast thou fled,
Thou learned Nemo—wise to a degree,
　　Anonymous LL.D. !

IV.

　　Thou nameless captain of the nameless gang
That do—and inquests cannot say who did it !
　　Wert thou at Mrs. Donatty's death-pang ?
Hast thou made gravy of Wear's watch—or hid it ?
Hast thou a Blue Beard chamber ? Heaven forbid it !
　　I should be very loth to see thee hang !
I hope thou hast an alibi well plann'd,
An innocent, altho' an ink-black hand.

Tho' thou hast newly turn'd thy private bolt on
　　The curiosity of all invaders—
I hope thou art merely closeted with Colton,
Who knows a little of the *Holy Land*,
　　Writing thy next new novel—The Crusaders !

V.

　　Perhaps thou wert even born
To be unknown.　Perhaps hung, some foggy morn,
At Captain Coram's charitable wicket,
　　　Penn'd to a ticket
That Fate had made illegible, foreseeing
The future great unmentionable being.
　　Perhaps thou hast ridden
A scholar poor on St. Augustine's back,
Like Chatterton, and found a dusty pack
　Of Rowley novels in an old chest hidden ;
A little hoard of clever simulation,
　That took the town—and Constable has bidden
Some hundred pounds for a continuation—
To keep and clothe thee in genteel starvation.

VI.

I liked thy Waverley—first of thy breeding ;
　I like its modest "sixty years ago,"
As if it was not meant for ages' reading.
　　I don't like Ivanhoe,
Tho' Dymoke does—it makes him think of clattering
　In iron overalls before the king,
Secure from battering, to ladies flattering,
　Tuning his challenge to the gauntlets' ring—
Oh better far than all that anvil clang
　It was to hear thee touch the famous string
Of Robin Hood's tough bow and make it twang,
　Rousing him up, all verdant, with his clan,
　　Like Sagittarian Pan !

VII.

I like Guy Mannering—but not that sham son
Of Brown.　I like that literary Sampson,
Nine-tenths a Dyer, with a smack of Porson.
I like Dirk Hatteraick, that rough sea Orson
　　That slew the Gauger ;
And Dandie Dinmont, like old Ursa Major ;
And Merrilies, young Bertram's old defender,
　　That Scottish Witch of Endor,
That doom'd thy fame.　She was the Witch, I take it,
To tell a great man's fortune—or to make it !

VIII.

I like thy Antiquary.   With his fit on,
  He makes me think of Mr. Britton,
Who has—or had—within his garden wall,
A *miniature Stone Henge,* so very small
      The sparrows find it difficult to sit on;
And Dousterswivel, like Poyais' M'Gregor ;
And Edie Ochiltree, that old *Blue Beggar,*
        Painted so cleverly,
I think thou surely knowest Mrs. Beverly !
I like thy Barber—him that fir'd the *Beacon—*
But that's a tender subject now to speak on !

IX.

I like long-arm'd Rob Roy.   His very charms
Fashion'd him for renown !   In sad sincerity,
    The man that robs or writes must have long arms,
If he's to hand his deeds down to posterity !
Witness Miss Biffin's posthumous prosperity !
Her poor brown crumpled mummy (nothing more)
        Bearing the name she bore,
A thing Time's tooth is tempted to destroy !
But Roys can never die—why else, in verity,
Is Paris echoing with " Vive le *Roy !*"
    Ay, Rob shall live again, and deathless Di
Vernon, of course, shall often live again—
Whilst there's a stone in Newgate, or a chain,
        Who can pass by
Nor feel the Thief's in prison and at hand ?
There be Old Bailey Jarveys on the stand !

X.

I like thy Landlord's Tales !—I like that Idol
Of love and Lammermoor—the blue-eyed maid
That led to church the mounted cavalcade,
    And then pull'd up with such a bloody bridal !
Throwing equestrian Hymen on his haunches—
I like the family—not silver, branches
        That hold the tapers
    To light the serious legend of Montrose.
I like M'Aulay's second-sighted vapours,
As if he could not walk or talk alone,
Without the devil—or the Great Unknown—
    Dalgetty is the dearest of Ducrows !

XI.

I like St. Leonard's Lily—drench'd with dew !
I like thy Vision of the Covenanters,
That bloody-minded Graham shot and slew.
    I like the battle lost and won,
    The hurly-burly's bravely done,
The warlike gallops and the warlike *canters* !
I like that girded chieftain of the ranters,
Ready to preach down heathens, or to grapple,
    With one eye on his sword,
    And one upon the Word—
How *he* would cram the Caledonian Chapel !
I like stern Claverhouse, though he doth dapple
    His raven steed with blood of many a corse—
I like dear Mrs. Headrigg, that unravels
    Her texts of Scripture on a trotting horse—
She is so like Rae Wilson when he travels !

XII.

I like thy Kenilworth—but I'm not going
    To take a Retrospective Re-Review
Of all thy dainty novels—merely showing
    The old familiar faces of a few,
    The question to renew,
How thou canst leave such deeds without a name,
Forego the unclaim'd dividends of fame,
Forego the smiles of literary houris—
Mid Lothian's trump, and Fife's shrill note of praise,
    And all the Carse of Gowrie's,
When thou might'st have thy statue in Cromarty—
Or see thy image on Italian trays,
Betwixt Queen Caroline and Buonaparté,
    Be painted by the Titian of R.A.'s,
Or vie in signboards with the Royal Guelph !
    Perhaps have thy bust set cheek by jowl with Homer's,
Perhaps send out plaster proxies of thyself
    To other Englands with Australian roamers—
        Mayhap, in literary Owhyhee
        Displace the native wooden gods, or be
The China-Lar of a Canadian shelf !

XIII.

    It is not modesty that bids thee hide—
She never wastes her blushes out of sight :
        It is not to invite
The world's decision, for thy fame is tried,—

And thy fair deeds are scatter'd far and wide,
Even royal heads are with thy readers reckon'd,—
 From men in trencher caps to trencher scholars
   In crimson collars,
And learned serjeants in the forty-second !
Whither by land or sea art thou not beckon'd ?
Mayhap exported from the Frith of Forth,
Defying distance and its dim control ;
 Perhaps read about Stromness, and reckon'd worth
A brace of Miltons for capacious soul—
 Perhaps studied in the whalers, further north,
And set above ten Shakespeares near the pole !

XIV.

Oh, when thou writest by Aladdin's lamp,
With such a giant genius at command,
  For ever at thy stamp,
To fill thy treasury from Fairy Land,
When haply thou might'st ask the pearly hand
Of some great British Vizier's eldest daughter,
  Tho' princes sought her,
And lead her in procession hymeneal,
Oh, why dost thou remain a Beau Ideal!
Why stay, a ghost, on the Lethean wharf,
Envelop'd in Scotch mist and gloomy fogs ?
Why, but because thou art some puny dwarf,
Some hopeless imp, like Riquet with the Tuft,
Fearing, for all thy wit, to be rebuff'd,
Or bullied by our great reviewing Gogs ?

XV.

 What in this masquing age
Maketh Unknowns so many and so shy ?
 What but the critic's page ?
One hath a cast, he hides from the world's eye,
Another hath a wen—he won't show where ;
  A third has sandy hair,
A hunch upon his back, or legs awry,
Things for a vile reviewer to espy !
Another hath a mangel-wurzel nose—
  Finally, this is dimpled,
 Like a pale crumpet face, or that is pimpled;
Things for a monthly critic to expose—
Nay, what is thy own case—that being small,
Thou choosest to be nobody at all !

XVI.

Well, thou art prudent, with such puny bones –
   E'en like Elshender, the mysterious elf,
   That shadowy revelation of thyself—
To build thee a small hut of haunted stones—
For certainly the first pernicious man
That ever saw thee, would quickly draw thee
In some vile literary caravan—
     Shown for a shilling
     Would be thy killing.
Think of Crachami's miserable span !
No tinier frame the tiny spark could dwell in
    Than there it fell in—
But when she felt herself a show, she tried
To shrink from the world's eye, poor dwarf ! and died !

XVII.

   O since it was thy fortune to be born
A dwarf on some Scotch *Inch*, and then to flinch
From all the Gog-like jostle of great men.
    Still with thy small crow pen
Amuse and charm thy lonely hours forlorn—
Still Scottish story daintily adorn,
  Be still a shade—and when this age is fled,
When we poor sons and daughters of reality
  Are in our graves forgotten and quite dead,
And Time destroys our mottoes of morality,
The lithographic hand of Old Mortality
Shall still restore thy emblem on the stone,
    A featureless death's head,
And rob Oblivion ev'n of the Unknown ! –

TO SYLVANUS URBAN, ESQUIRE,

EDITOR OF THE GENTLEMAN'S MAGAZINE.

> Dost thou not suspect my years ?—
>   Much Ado About Nothing.

I.

Oh ! Mr. Urban ! never must *thou* lurch
  A sober age made serious drunk by thee ;
Hop in thy pleasant way from church to church,
  And nurse thy little bald Biography.

II.

Oh, my Sylvanus ! what a heart is thine !
    And what a page attends thee ! Long may I
Hang in demure confusion o'er each line
    That asks thy little questions with a sigh !

III.

Old tottering years have nodded to their falls,
    Like pensioners that creep about and die ;
But thou, Old Parr of periodicals,
    Livest in monthly immortality !

IV.

How sweet !--as Byron of *his* infant said,—
    " Knowledge of objects " in thine eye to trace ;
To see the mild no-meanings of thy head,
    Taking a quiet nap upon thy face !

V.

How dear through thy Obituary to roam,
    And not a name of any name to catch !
To meet thy Criticism walking home
    Averse from rows, and never calling " Watch !

VI.

Rich is thy page in soporific things,—
    Composing compositions,—lulling men,—
Faded old posies of unburied rings,—
    Confessions dozing from an opiate pen :—

VII.

Lives of Right Reverends that have never liv'd,—
    Deaths of good people that have really died,—
Parishioners,—hatch'd, husbanded, and wiv'd,—
    Bankrupts and Abbots breaking side by side !

VIII.

The sacred query,—the remote response,—
    The march of serious mind, extremely slow,—
The graver's cut at some right aged sconce,
    Famous for nothing many years ago !

IX.

B. asks of C. if Milton e'er did write
    " Comus," obscured beneath some Ludlow lid ;—
And C., next month, an answer doth indite,
    Informing B. that Mr. Milton did !

X.

X. sends the portrait of a genuine flea,
   Caught upon Martin Luther years agone ;
And Mr. Parkes, of Shrewsbury, draws a bee,
   Long dead, that gather'd honey for King John.

XI.

There is no end of thee,—there is no end,
   Sylvanus, of thy A, B, C, D-merits !
Thou dost, with alphabets, old walls attend,
   And poke the letters into holes, like ferrets.

XII.

Go on, Sylvanus !—Bear a wary eye,
   The churches cannot yet be quite run out !
Some parishes must yet have been pass'd by,—
   There's Bullock-Smithy has a church no doubt !

XIII.

Go on—and close the eyes of distant ages !
   Nourish the names of the undoubted dead !
So epicures shall pick thy lobster-pages,
   Heavy and lively, though but seldom *red*.

XIV.

Go on ! and thrive ! Demurest of odd fellows !
   Bottling up dulness in an ancient binn !
Still live ! still prose !—continue still to tell us
   Old truths ! no strangers, though we take them in !

AN ADDRESS TO THE STEAM WASHING
COMPANY.

Archer. How many are there, Scrub?
Scrub. Five-and-forty, Sir.—BEAUX STRATAGEM.

For shame—let the linen alone !—M. W. OF WINDSOR.

MR. SCRUB—Mr. Slop—or whoever you be !
The Cock of Steam Laundries,—the head Patentee
Of Associate Cleansers,—chief founder and prime
Of the firm for the wholesale distilling of grime—
Co-partners and dealers, in linen's propriety—
That make washing public—and wash in society—

O lend me your ear! if that ear can forego,
For a moment, the music that bubbles below,—
From your new Surrey Geisers* all foaming and hot,—
That soft "*simmer's* sang" so endear'd to the Scot—
If your hands may stand still, or your steam without danger—
If your suds will not cool, and a mere simple stranger,
Both to you and to washing, may put in a rub—
O wipe out your Amazon arms from the tub—
And lend me your ear,—Let me modestly plead
For a race that your labours may soon supersede—
For a race that, now washing no living affords—
Like Grimaldi must leave their aquatic old boards,
Not with pence in their pockets to keep them at ease,
Not with bread in the funds—or investments of cheese—
But to droop like sad willows that liv'd by a stream,
Which the sun has suck'd up into vapour and steam.
Ah, look at the laundress, before you begrudge
Her hard daily bread to that laudable drudge ;
When chanticleer singeth his earliest matins,
She slips her amphibious feet in her pattens,
And beginneth her toil while the morn is still grey,
As if she was washing the night into day—
Not with sleeker or rosier fingers Aurora
Beginneth to scatter the dewdrops before her ;
Not Venus that rose from the billow so early,
Look'd down on the foam with a forehead more *pearly*†—
Her head is involv'd in an aërial mist,
And a bright-beaded bracelet encircles her wrist ;
Her visage glows warm with the ardour of duty ;
She's Industry's moral— she's all moral beauty !
Growing brighter and brighter at every rub—
Would any man ruin her?   No, Mr. Scrub !
No man that is manly would work her mishap—
No man that is manly would covet her cap—
Nor her apron—her hose—nor her gown made of stuff—
Nor her gin, nor her tea, nor her wet pinch of snuff !
Alas ! so *she* thought, but that slippery hope
Has betrayed her, as tho' she had trod on her soap !
And she—whose support, like the fishes that fly,
Was to have her fins wet, must now drop from her sky ;
She whose living it was, and a part of her fare,
To be damp'd once a day, like the great white sea bear,
With her hands like a sponge, and her head like a mop—
Quite a living absorbent that revell'd in slop—
She that paddled in water, must walk upon sand,
And sigh for her deeps like a turtle on land !

* Geisers, the boiling springs in Iceland.
† Query, *purly* ?—Printer's Devil.

Lo, then, the poor laundress, all wretched she stands,
Instead of a counterpane, wringing her hands !
All haggard and pinch'd, going down in life's vale,
With no faggot for burning, like Allan-a-dale !
No smoke from her flue—and no steam from her pane,
Where once she watch'd heaven, fearing God and the rain—
Or gaz'd o'er her bleach-field so fairly engross'd,
Till the lines wander'd idle from pillar to post !
Ah, where are the playful young pinners—ah, where
The harlequin quilts that cut capers in air—
The brisk waltzing stockings—the white and the black,
That danc'd on the tight-rope, or swung on the slack—
The light sylph-like garments, so tenderly pinn'd,
That blew into shape, and embodied the wind !
There was white on the grass—there was white on the spray—
Her garden—it look'd like a garden of May !
But now all is dark—not a shirt's on a shrub—
You've ruin'd her prospects in life, Mr. Scrub !
You've ruin'd her custom—now families drop her—
From her silver reduc'd—nay, reduc'd from her *copper !*
The last of her washing is done at her eye,
One poor little 'kerchief that never gets dry !
From mere lack of linen she can't lay a cloth,
And boils neither barley nor alkaline broth ;
But her children come round her as victuals grow scant,
And recall, with foul faces, the source of their want—
When she thinks of their poor little mouths to be fed,
And then thinks of her trade that is utterly dead,
And even its pearlashes laid in the grave—
Whilst her tub is a dry rotting, stave after stave,
And the greatest of coopers, ev'n he that they dub
Sir Astley, can't bind up her heart or her tub,—
Need you wonder she curses your bones, Mr. Scrub !
Need you wonder, when steam has depriv'd her of bread,
If she prays that the evil may visit *your* head—
Nay, scald all the heads of your Washing Committee—
If she wishes you all the soot blacks of the city—
In short, not to mention all plagues without number,
If she wishes you all in the *Wash* at the Humber !

Ah, perhaps, in some moment of drowth and despair,
When her linen got scarce, and her washing grew rare—
When the sum of her suds might be summ'd in a bowl,
And the rusty cold iron quite enter'd her soul—
When, perhaps, the last glance of her wandering eye
Had caught the " Cock Laundresses' Coach " going by,
Or her lines that hung idle, to waste the fine weather,
And she thought of her wrongs and her rights both together,

In a lather of passion that froth'd as it rose,
Too angry for grammar, too lofty for prose,
On her sheet—if a sheet were still left her—to write,
Some remonstrance like this then, perchance, saw the light—

LETTER OF REMONSTRANCE

FROM BRIDGET JONES,

TO THE NOBLEMEN AND GENTLEMEN FORMING THE WASHING COMMITTEE.

IT's a shame, so it is,—men can't Let alone
Jobs as is Woman's right to do—and go about there Own—
Theirs Reforms enuff Alreddy without your new schools
For washing to sit Up,—and push the Old Tubs from their
     stools !
But your just like the Raddicals,—for upsetting of the Sudds
When the world wagged well enuff—and Wommen washed
     your old dirty duds,
I'm Certain sure Enuff your Ann Sisters had no stream Ingins,
     that's Flat,—
But I Warrant your Four Fathers went as tidy and gentlemanny
     for all that—
I suppose your the Family as lived in the Great Kittle
I see on Clapham Commun, some times a very considerable
     period back when I were little,
And they Said it went with Steem,—But that was a joke !
For I never see none come of it,—that's out of it—but only
     sum Smoak—
And for All your Power of Horses about your Ingins you never
     had but Two
In my time to draw you About to Fairs—and curse you, you
     know that's true !
And for All your fine Perspectuses,—howsomever you bewhich
     'em,
Theirs as Pretty ones off Primcrows Hill, as ever a one at
     Mitchum,
Thof I cant sea What Prospectives and washing has with one
     another to Do—
It aant as if a Bird'seye Hankicher can take a Bird'shigh view !
But Thats your look out—I've not much to do with that—But
     pleas God to hold up fine,
Id show you caps and pinners and small things as lillywhit as
     Ever crosst the Line
Without going any Father off then Little Parodies Place,
And Thats more than you Can—and Ill say it behind your
     face—

But when Folks talks of washing, it ant for you too Speak,—
As kept Dockter Pattyson out of his Shirt for a Weak!
Thinks I, when I heard it—Well thear's a Pretty go!
That comes o' not marking of things, or washing out the marks,
    and Huddling 'em up so!
Till Their friends comes and owns them, like drownded corpeses
    in a Vault,
But may Hap you havint Larn'd to spel—and that ant your
    Fault.
Only you ought to leafe the Linnens to them as has larn'd,—
For if it warnt for Washing,—and whare Bills is concarnd
What's the Yuse, of all the world, for a Wommans Edica-
    tion,
And Their Being maid Schollards of Sundays—fit for any
    Cityation.

Well, what I says is This—when every Kittle has its spout,
Theirs no nead for Companys to puff steam about!
To be sure its very Well, when Their ant enuff Wind -
For blowing up Boats with,—but not to hurt human kind
Like that Pearkins with his Blunderbush, that's loaded with
    hot water,
Thof a Sheriff might know Better, than make things for
    slaughter,
As if War warnt Cruel enuff—wherever it befalls,
Without shooting poor sogers, with sich scalding hot washing
    balls,—
But thats not so Bad as a Sett of Bear Faced Scrubbs
As joins their Sopes together, and sits up Stream rubbing
    Clubs,
For washing Dirt Cheap,—and eating other Peple's grubs!
Which is all verry Fine for you and your Patent Tea,
But I wonders How Poor Wommen is to get Their Bo-He!
They must drink Hunt wash (the only wash God nose there
    will be!)
And their Little drop of Somethings as they takes for their
    Goods,
When you and your Steam has ruined (G—d forgive mee!)
    their lively Hoods,
Poor Women as was born to Washing in their youth!
And now must go and Larn other Buisnesses Four Sooth!
But if so be They leave their Lines what are they to go at—
They won't do for Angell's—nor any Trade like That,
Nor we cant Sow Babby Work,—for that's all Bespoke,—
For the Queakers in Bridle! and a vast of the confind Folk
Do their own of Themselves—even the bettermost of em—
    aye, and even them of middling degrees—
Why God help you Babby Linen ant Bread and Cheese!

Nor we can't go a hammering the roads into Dust,
But we must all go and be Bankers,—and that's what we
    must !
God nose you oght to have more Concern for our Sects,
When you nose you have suck'd us and hanged round our
    Mutherly necks,
And remembers what you Owes to Wommen Besides wash-
    ing—
You ant, curse you, like Men to go a slushing and sloshing
In mob caps, and pattins, adoing of Females Labers
And prettily jear'd At you great Horse God Meril things, ant
    you now by you next door neighbours—
Lawk I thinks I see you with your Sleaves tuckt up
No more like Washing than is drownding of a Pupp—
And for all Your Fine Water Works going round and round
They'll scruntch your Bones some day—I'll be bound
And no more nor be a gudgement,—for it cant come to good
To sit up agin Providince, which your a doing,—nor not fit It
    should,
For man warnt maid for Wommens starvation,
Nor to do away Laundrisses as is Links of Creation—
And cant be dun without in any Country But a Hottinpot
    Nation.
Ah, I wish our Minister would take one of your Tubbs
And preach a Sermon in it, and give you some good rubs—
But I warrants you reads (for you cant spel we nose) nayther
    Bybills or Good Tracks,
Or youd know better than Taking the Close off one's Backs—
And let your neighbours oxin and Asses alone,—
And every Thing thats hern,—and give every one their Hone !

    Well, its God for us All, and every Washer Wommen for
        herself,
And so you might, without shoving any on us off the shelf,
But if you warnt Noddis youd Let wommen abe
And pull off Your Pattins,—and leave the washing to we
That nose what's what—Or mark what I say,
Youl make a fine Kittle of fish of Your Close some Day—
When the Aulder men wants Their Bibs and their ant nun
    at all,
And Crist mass cum—and never a Cloth to lay in Gild Hall,
Or send a damp shirt to his Woship the Mare
Till hes rumatiz Poor Man, and cant set uprite in his Chare—
Besides Miss-Matching Larned Ladys Hose, as is sent for
    you not to wash (for you dont wash) but to stew
And make Peples Stockins yeller as oght to be Blew
With a vast more like That,—and all along of Steam
Which warnt meand by Nater for any sich skeam—

But thats your Losses and youl have to make It Good,
And I cant say I'm Sorry afore God if you shoud,
For men mought Get their Bread a great many ways
Without taking ourn,—aye, and Moor to your Prays
If You Was even to Turn Dust Men a dry sifting Dirt,
But you oughtint to Hurt Them as never Did You no Hurt!

Yourn with Anymocity,

BRIDGET JONES.

ODE TO R. W. ELLISTON, ESQUIRE,

THE GREAT LESSEE!

Rover. Do you know, you villain, that I am this moment the greatest man living?—WILD OATS.

I.

OH! Great Lessee! Great Manager! Great Man!
Oh, Lord High Elliston! Immortal Pan
Of all the pipes that play in Drury Lane!
Macready's master! Westminster's high *Dane!*
As Galway Martin, in the House's walls,
Hamlet and Doctor Ireland justly calls!
Friend to the sweet and ever-smiling Spring!
Magician of the lamp and prompter's ring!
Drury's Aladdin! Whipper-in of Actors,
Kicker of rebel-preface-malefactors!
Glass-blowers' corrector! King of the cheque-taker!
At once Great Leamington and Winston-Maker!
Dramatic Bolter of plain Bunns and cakes!
In silken *hose* the most reform'd of *Rakes!*
Oh, Lord High Elliston! lend me an ear!
(Poole is away, and Williams shall keep clear)
While I, in little slips of prose, not verse,
Thy splendid course, as pattern-work, rehearse!

II.

Bright was thy youth—thy manhood brighter still—
The greatest Romeo upon Holborn Hill—
Lightest comedian of the pleasant day,
When Jordan threw her sunshine o'er a play!
But these, though happy, were but subject times,
And no man cares for bottom-steps that climbs—
Far from my wish it is to stifle down
The hours that saw thee snatch the Surrey crown!

Tho' now thy hand a mightier sceptre wields,
Fair was thy reign in sweet St. George's Fields.
Dibdin was *Premier*—and a golden *age*
For a short time enrich'd the subject stage.
Thou hadst, than other Kings, more peace-and-plenty ;
Ours but one Bench could boast, but thou hadst twenty ;
But the times changed—and Booth-acting no more
Drew Rulers' shillings to the gallery door.
Thou didst, with bag and baggage, wander thence,
Repentant, like thy neighbour Magdalens !

III.

Next, the Olympic Games were tried, each feat
Practis'd, the most bewitching in Wych Street.
Charles had his royal ribaldry restor'd,
And in a downright neighbourhood drank and whor'd ;
Rochester there in dirty ways again
Revell'd—and liv'd once more in Drury Lane :
But thou, R. W. ! kept thy moral ways,
Pit-lecturing 'twixt the farces and the plays,
A lamplight Irving to the butcher boys
That soil'd the benches and that made a noise :—
" YOU,—in the back !—can scarcely hear a line !
Down from those benches—butchers—they are MINE ! "

IV.

Lastly—and thou wert built for it by nature !—
Crown'd was thy head in Drury Lane The*a*tre !
Gentle George Robins saw that it was good,
And renters cluck'd around thee in a brood.
King thou wert made of Drury and of Kean !
Of many a lady and of many a Quean !
With Poole and Larpent was thy reign begun—
But now thou turnest from the Dead and Dun,
Hook's in thine eye, to write thy plays, no doubt,
And Colman lives to cut the damnlet's out !
Oh, worthy of the house ! the King's commission !
Isn't thy condition " a most bless'd condition ? "
Thou reignest over Winston, Kean, and all
The very lofty and the very small—
Showest the plumbless Bunn the way to kick—
Keepest a Williams for thy veriest stick—
Seest a Vestris in her sweetest moments,
Without the danger of newspaper comments —
Tellest Macready, as none dared before,
Thine open mind from the half-open door !—

(Alas ! I fear he has left Melpomene's crown,
To be a Boniface in Buxton town !)—
Thou hold'st the watch, as half-price people know,
And callest to them, to a moment, "Go !"
Teachest the sapient Sapio how to sing—
Hangest a cat most oddly by the wing—
Hast known the length of a Cubitt-foot—and kiss'd
The pearly whiteness of a Stephens' wrist—
Kissing and pitying—tender and humane !
" By heaven she loves me ! Oh, it is too plain !"
A sigh like this thy trembling passion slips,
Dimpling the warm Madeira at thy lips !

V.

Go on, Lessec ! Go on, and prosper well !
Fear not, though forty glass-blowers should rebel—
Show them how thou hast long befriended them,
And teach Dubois *their* treason to condemn !
Go on ! addressing pits in prose and worse !
Be long, be slow, be anything but terse—
Kiss to the gallery the hand that's glov'd—
Make Bunn the Great, and Winston the Belov'd,
Go on—and but in this reverse the thing,
Walk backward with wax lights before the King—
Go on ! Spring ever in thine eye ! Go on !
Hope's favourite child ! ethereal Elliston !

ODE TO RICHARD MARTIN, ESQUIRE,

M.P. FOR GALWAY.

I.

How many sing of wars,
Of Greek and Trojan jars—
The butcheries of men !
The Muse hath a "Perpetual Ruby Pen !"
Dabbling with heroes and the blood they spill ;
But no one sings the man
That, like a pelican,
Nourishes Pity with his tender *Bill !*

II.

Thou Wilberforce of hacks !
Of whites as well as blacks,

Piebald and dapple gray,
Chestnut and bay—
No poet's eulogy thy name adorns !
But oxen, from the fens,
Sheep—in their pens,
Praise thee, and red cows with their winding horns !
Thou art sung on brutal pipes !
Drovers may curse thee,
Knackers asperse thee,
And sly M.P.'s bestow their cruel wipes ;
But the old horse neighs thee,
And zebras praise thee,
Asses, I mean—that have as many stripes !

III.

Hast thou not taught the drover to forbear,
In Smithfield's muddy, murderous, vile environ,—
Staying his lifted bludgeon in the air !
Bullocks don't wear
Oxide of iron !
The cruel Jarvy thou hast summon'd oft,
Enforcing mercy on the coarse Yahoo,
That thought his horse the *courser* of the two—
Whilst Swift smiled down aloft !—
O worthy pair ! for this, when ye inhabit
Bodies of birds—(if so the spirit shifts
From flesh to feather)—when the clown uplifts
His hand against the sparrow's nest, to *grab* it,—
He shall not harm the MARTINS and the *Swifts* !

IV.

Ah ! when Dean Swift was *quick*, how he enhanc'd
The horse !—and humbled biped man like Plato !
But now he's dead, the charger is mischanc'd—
Gone backward in the world—and not advanc'd,—
Remember Cato !
Swift was the horse's champion—not the King's,
Whom Southey sings,
Mounted on Pegasus—would he were thrown !
He'll wear that ancient hackney to the bone,
Like a mere clothes-horse airing royal things !
Ah well-a-day ! the ancients did not use
Their steeds so cruelly !—let it debar men
From wanton rowelling and whip's abuse—
Look at the ancients' *Muse* !
Look at their *Carmen* !

V.

O, Martin! how thine eye—
That one would think had put aside its lashes,—
    That can't bear gashes
Thro' any horse's side, must ache to spy
That horrid window fronting Fetter Lane,—
For there's a nag the crows have pick'd for victual,
Or some man painted in a bloody vein—
    Gods! is there no *Horse-spital!*
That such raw shows must sicken the humane!
        Sure Mr. Whittle
        Loves thee but little,
To let that poor horse linger in his *pane!*

VI.

O build a Brookes's Theatre for horses!
O wipe away the national reproach—
    And find a decent Vulture for their corses!
        And in thy funeral track
Four sorry steeds shall follow in each coach!
    Steeds that confess "the luxury of *wo!*"
True mourning steeds, in no extempore black,
        And many a wretched hack
Shall sorrow for thee,—sore with kick and blow
And bloody gash—it is the Indian knack—
(Save that the savage is his own tormentor)—
Banting shall weep too in his sable scarf—
The biped woe the quadruped shall enter,
    And Man and Horse go half and half,
As if their griefs met in a common *Centaur!*

ODE TO W. KITCHENER, M.D.

*Author of the Cook's Oracle—Observations on Vocal Music—the Art of
Invigorating and Prolonging Life—Practical Observations on Telescopes,
Opera Glasses, and Spectacles—the Housekeeper's Ledger—and the Pleasure
of Making a Will.*

I rule the roast, as Milton says!—CALEB QUOTEM.

I.

HAIL! multifarious man!
Thou Wondrous, Admirable Kitchen Crichton!
    Born to enlighten

The laws of optics, peptics, music, cooking—
Master of the piano—and the pan—
As busy with the kitchen as the skies !
   Now looking
At some rich stew thro' Galileo's eyes,
Or boiling eggs—timed to a metronome—
   As much at home
In spectacles as in mere isinglass—
In the art of frying brown—as a digression
On music and poetical expression,—
Whereas, how few of all our cooks, alas !
Could tell Calliope from "Calliopee!"
   How few there be
Could leave the lowest for the highest stories,
   (Observatories,)
And turn, like thee, Diana's calculator,
However *cook's* synonymous with *Kater !* *
   Alas ! still let me say,
   How few could lay
The carving-knife beside the tuning-fork,
Like the proverbial *Jack* ready for any work !

II.

Oh, to behold thy features in thy book !
Thy proper head and shoulders in a plate,
   How it would look !
With one rais'd eye watching the dial's date,
And one upon the roast, gently cast down—
   Thy chops—done nicely brown—
The garnish'd brow—with "a few leaves of bay "—
   The hair—"done Wiggy's way !"
And still one studious finger near thy brains,
   As if thou wert just come
   From editing some
New soup—or hashing Dibdin's cold remains !
Or, Orpheus-like—fresh from thy dying strains
Of music—Epping luxuries of sound,
   As Milton says, "in many a bout
   Of linked sweetness long drawn out,"
Whilst all thy tame stuff'd leopards listen'd round !

III.

Oh, rather thy whole proper length reveal,
Standing like Fortune,—on the jack—thy wheel.

  * Captain Kater, the Moon's Surveyor.

(Thou art, like Fortune, full of chops and changes,
Thou hast a fillet too before thine eye!)
Scanning our kitchen, and our vocal ranges,
As tho' it were the same to sing or fry—
Nay, so it is—hear how Miss Paton's throat
        Makes "fritters" of a note!
And is not reading near akin to feeding,
   Or why should Oxford sausages be fit
       Receptacles for wit?
   Or why should Cambridge put its little, smart,
       Minc'd brains into a tart?
Nay, then, thou wert but wise to frame receipts,
       Book-treats,
Equally to instruct the cook and cram her—
   Receipts to be devour'd, as well as read,
       The culinary art in gingerbread—
       The Kitchen's *Eaten* Grammar!

IV.

Oh, very pleasant is thy motley page—
   Ay, very pleasant in its chatty vein—
   So—in a kitchen—would have talk'd Montaigne,
That merry Gascon—humorist, and sage!
Let slender minds with single themes engage,
   Like Mr. Bowles with his eternal Pope,—
Or Lovelass upon Wills,—thou goest on
Plaiting ten topics, like Tate Wilkinson!
   Thy brain is like a rich kaleidoscope,
Stuff'd with a brilliant medley of odd bits,
   And ever shifting on from change to change,
Saucepans—old songs—pills—spectacles—and spits!
   Thy range is wider than a Rumford range!
Thy grasp a miracle!—till I recall
Th' indubitable cause of thy variety—
Thou art, of course, th' epitome of all
That spying—frying—singing—mix'd Society
Of Scientific Friends, who used to meet
Welsh Rabbits—and thyself—in Warren Street!

V.

Oh, hast thou still those conversazioni,
Where learned visitors discoursed—and fed?
       There came Belzoni,
Fresh from the ashes of Egyptian dead—
   And gentle Poki—and that royal pair,
       Of whom thou didst declare—

" Thanks to the greatest *Cooke* we ever read—
They were—what *Sandwiches* should be—half *bred!* "
There fam'd M'Adam from his manual toil
Relax'd—and freely own'd he took thy hints
　　　On " making *broth* with *flints* "—
There Parry came, and show'd the polar oil
For melted butter—Coombe with his medullary
　　　Notions about the *scullery*,
And Mr. Poole, too partial to a broil—
There witty Rogers came, that punning elf !
　　　Who used to swear thy book
　　　　Would really look
A *Delphic* " Oracle," if laid on *Delf*—
There, once a month, came Campbell and discuss'd
His own—and thy own—" *Magazine* of *Taste* "—
　　　There Wilberforce the Just
Came, in his old black suit, till once he trac'd
　Thy sly advice to *poachers* of black folks,
　　　That " do not break their *yolks*,"—
Which huff'd him home, in grave disgust and haste !

VI.

There came John Clare, the poet, nor forbore
Thy *patties*—thou wert hand-and-glove with Moore,
Who call'd thee *Kitchen Addison*—for why ?
Thou givest rules for health and peptic pills,
Forms for made dishes, and receipts for wills,
" *Teaching us how to live and how to die!* "
There came thy cousin-cook, good Mrs. Fry—
There Trench, the Thames projector, first brought on
　　　His sine *Quay* non,—
There Martin would drop in on Monday eves,
Or Fridays, from the pens, and raise his breath
　　　'Gainst cattle days and death,—
Answer'd by Mellish, feeder of fat beeves,
　Who swore that Frenchmen never could be eager
　　　For fighting on soup meagre—
" And yet (as thou wouldst add) the French have seen
　　A Marshal *Tureen!* "

VII.

Great was thy evening cluster !—often grac'd
With Dollond—Burgess—and Sir Humphry Davy !
'Twas there M'Dermot first inclin'd to taste,—
There Colburn learn'd the art of making paste
For puffs—and Accum analysed a gravy.

Colman, the cutter of Colman Street, 'tis said
Came there, and Parkins with his Ex-wise-head,
(His claim to letters)—Kater, too, the Moon's
Crony,—and Graham, lofty on balloons,
There Croly stalk'd with holy humour heated,
(Who wrote a light-horse play, which Yates completed),
    And Lady Morgan, that grinding organ,
And Brasbridge telling anecdotes of spoons,
Madame Valbrèque thrice honour'd thee, and came
With great Rossini, his own bow and fiddle,—
And even Irving spar'd a night from fame,
And talk'd—till thou didst stop him in the middle,
    To serve round *Tewah-diddle !* *

VIII.

Then all the guests rose up, and sighed good-bye !
So let them :—thou thyself art still a *Host !*
    Dibdin—Cornaro—Newton—Mrs. Fry !
    Mrs. Glasse—Mr. Spec !—Lovelass—and Weber,
    Mathews in Quotem—Moore's fire-worshipping
        Gheber—
Thrice-worthy worthy ! seem by thee engross'd !
Howbeit the peptic cook still rules the roast,
Potent to hush all ventriloquial snarling,—
And ease the bosom pangs of indigestion !
    Thou art, sans question,
The Corporation's love—its Doctor *Darling !*
Look at the civic palate—nay, the bed
  Which set dear Mrs. Opie on supplying
    " Illustrations of *Lying !* "
Ninety square feet of down from heel to head
    It measured, and I dread
Was haunted by a terrible night *Mare,*
A monstrous burthen on the corporation !—
Look at the bill of fare, for one day's share,
Sea-turtles by the score—oxen by droves,
Geese, turkeys, by the flock—fishes and loaves
  Countless, as when the Lilliputian nation
Was making up the huge man-mountain's ration !

IX.

Oh ! worthy Doctor ! surely thou hast driven
The squatting demon from great Garratt's breast—
    (His honour seems to rest !—)
And what is thy reward ?—Hath London given

* The Doctor's composition for a *nightcap.*

Thee public thanks for thy important service?
        Alas ! not even
The tokens it bestow'd on Howe and Jervis !—
Yet could I speak as orators should speak
Before the worshipful the Common Council
(Utter my bold bad grammar and pronounce ill),
Thou shouldst not miss thy freedom, for a week,
Richly engross'd on vellum :—Reason urges
That he who rules our cookery—that he
Who edits soups and gravies, ought to be
A *Citizen*, where sauce can make a *Burgess* !

THE END.

PRINTED BY BALLANTYNE, HANSON AND CO.
LONDON AND EDINBURGH